The Bighead

Edward Lee

The Bighead

Edward Lee

OVERLOOK CONNECTION PRESS
INFINITY
1999

—Never have I been so ashamed of myself for laughing so hard at something so utterly depraved!

—JOHN MASON SKIPP, co-author of *Light at the End, The Bridge,* and *Animals.*

A demented Henry Miller of horror. Sexually revolting, outrageous, disgusting, THE BIGHEAD is the sickest piece of fiction I've ever read!

—DOUGLAS CLEGG, author of *Goat Dance, Children's Hour,* and *The Halloween Man.*

The grossest book I've ever read, an all-you-can-stomach fictive fanfare of nonstop perversity, pulp horror themes yanked inside-out with a vengeance, forabsolutely shocking entertainment. THE BIGHEAD would make the *Marquie de Sade* wince!

—T. WINTER-DAMON, author of *Rex Miller: The Complete Revelations*, and over 250 stories.

Novels by Edward Lee

Ghouls
Coven
Incubi
Succubi
Creekers
The Chosen
Sacrifice (as Richard Kinion)
The Bighead (Necro version)
Shifters (w/John Pelan)
Portrait of the Psychopath as a Young Woman
(w/Elizabeth Steffen)
Operator B
The Stickmen

THE BIGHEAD

By Lee Seymour © 1999

Published by
OVERLOOK CONNECTION PRESS
PO BOX 526
WOODSTOCK, GA 30188

Phone: 770-926-1762
Fax: 770-516-1469
E-Mail: OverlookCN@aol.com
URL: http://www.OverlookConnection.com/ocpmain.htm

Call, write, or e-mail for a complete catalog list of OCP books.
Visit our web page on Edward Lee titles at
http://www.overlookconnection.com/oclee.htm

Cover and Interior Art by Erik Wilson © 1999
© 1999 Overlook Connection Press

First Trade Paperback Edition ISBN: 1-892950-13-8

All rights reserved. This book is a work of fiction. No part of this book may be reproduced or transmitted in any form or by any means, electronic, mechanical, or otherwise, without the written permission of the Publisher.

The Overlook Connection Press would like to thank Lee Seymour in his faith and belief in getting this project done during a busy time in his career. You came through Lee and the next one's on me ! We would also like to thank Erik Wilson who took this project and ran with it. Erik, you've outdone yourself in enthusiasm and art my friend. In fact, drinks on the house for both author and artist! You guys are the best. Thank you!

This edition is for Geoff Cooper and Ryan Harding.

Though in debt to many, the author would like to particularly thank Dave Barnett (for the first endeavor) and Dave Hinchberger (for the second). Believe it or not, both are very cool guys in spite of their publishing this book! Additional thanks to Erik Wilson for the tremendous artwork.

AUTHOR'S NOTE

Technically, I suppose, this edition of *The Bighead* would less be deemed a second printing and more be cited as the author's "preferred text." In May, 1997, Dave Barnett and Necro Publications printed the first edition of this novel, and he did a wonderful job for which I will always be grateful. However, Dave wanted me to change an aspect of the last twenty pages, because he didn't care for the conceptual angle. I made these changes without hesitation, but I really can't elaborate much on their nature because if I did, I'd spoil this edition of the book for you. At any rate, the Necro version of this book sold out fast and caused a bit of a stir in the limited-edition horror market. This version, which Dave Hinchberger has been kind enough to have published, is the *original* version. It's the same book as the Necro edition, except for changes in the final twenty pages. I hope you like it!

Edward Lee
Seattle, Washington
January, 1999

Prologue

She stove the baby's head in with a cast-iron skillet. The head burst like a pale, ripe fruit.

They'd heard her sobs, of course—but at least they'd stayed out of the room while she'd done it.

The wood-plank door creaked. One of the men looked in. "You done it yet?"

"Yes!" she shrieked.

There could be no comfort here, no consolation. The man's eyes looked blank in their hardness. "It hadda be done, ya know that, don't'cha?"

She sat with her head between her knees. "Yes," she croaked. "I know..."

Only an hour before...

She set the swaddled bundle on the heavy table. Of course, they'd want to see the baby's body—they'd insist. *They'll be back soon,* she realized, gazing affrighted at the mantle clock. A broth of chicken stock simmered on the stove.

They'll never know, they'll never know.

But now the man's eyes thinned in query. "Did you…," he began. He scratched stiff whiskers on his face. "I'se mean, was it awake when ya—"

"No," she croaked again. She pointed to the wood stove.

"Uh-yuh."

Now more men peered into the room, long-faced, eyes chiseled in determination yet somehow feeling for her. But then those same eyes strayed past her, to the table—

The tender gore on the table.

"We know it weren't easy, but it hadda be done," he said. "You done right—we all did. But now…it's gotta be buried. One'a us'll do it."

"No!" her voice cracked. She stood up, shaking, then picked up the dead baby, careful to not let the spillage fall to the floor.

"I'll bury it," she said.

She walked forward, her arms full. The men, in total silence, made way for her.

Geraldine, oh, Geraldine, she thought. *It's over now.* A small wooden packing crate sufficed for a coffin. Nightsounds abounded; the moonlight teemed through glowering trees.

Yes. Thank God it's over now.

She dug as deep as her weary muscles would allow, then buried the dead child.

Heat lightning flashed silently, from miles off. She sighed, wiping sweat and tears off her face.

Yes, it was over now. This was the end.

But all she could think about, all she could remember, was the beginning. Nine months ago—

—when that *thing* had come.

1 2 3 4 5 6 7 8 9 0
ONE
ERIK
1999

ONE

(I)

The Bighead licked his chops and tasted the dandy things: blood and fat, pussystink, the salt-slime of his own semen that he'd just slurped out'a the dead girl's bellybutton. His bone had split her pussy right open; weren't no fun humpin' redneck pussy when yer rod were going in an' out of a busted cervix an' posterior wall. No sir. Girls 'round these parts, purdy as they was an' few of 'em as he'd seed, they was just never big enough. No one were big enough fer The Bighead.

They called him The Bighead, on account of the congenital hydrocephaly, not that The Bighead hisself would ever know what fuckin' congenital hydrocephaly was, nor, a'corse, would he know what a cervix 'er posterior wall was. His head were about the size and shape of a watermelon, big an' bald, with big lopsided ears like squashed potato buns. Rumor was Bighead's mama had up and died right off when she'd dropped him, and further rumor attested that The Bighead's crooked awl-sharp teeth had et hisself the rest of the way out when the goin's got tough. Bighead believed it. 'Corse, they coulda called him Bighead fer another reason too, that reason bein' the 14-inch pecker 'tween his legs. Fourteen inchers, no lie, and wider than a reglar fella's forearm. Rumor had it he'd been hard whiles bein' born. Yessir, poppin' a big stiffer 'fore he'd even et his way outa his mama's cunt.

Bighead believed it.

He squeezed out the last'a his cocksnot, hauled up his overalls, and finished ettin' the dead gal's brain. Human brains, by the way, tasted kinda like warm salty scrambled eggs, fer those'a ya who didn't know. The Bighead liked 'em just fine, he did, and he liked the liver too. Good eats they was. He also liked chewin' on a little tittie-meat whiles he was lopin' around the woods, the way a reglar fella chawed backer.

But it weren't just poon that Bighead was searchin' fer. He hadn't had much, n'fact, just a stray here'n there back when he'n his grandpap had lived all those years back in The Lower Woods. *The Lower Woods,* Grandpap had called 'em. *Livin' back here, Bighead, in The Lower Woods, we ain'ts gotta worry 'bout The World Outside.*

The World Outside?

The Bighead had always wondered 'bout that, 'bout what it was, 'cos he never knowed. He always wanted ta, though, but Grandpap told him The World Outside were just an evil place fulla bad folks, an' they was far better off here. But now Grandpap was dead...

And The Bighead figgurt it were high time he gotta move on, got out'a the darkness'a The Lower Woods and inta this Outside World. See, after Grandpap had up'n died, Bighead got this itchin' in his soul, an' he couldn't quite figger it, he couldn't. It were almost like he was bein' summoned by this here Outside World, same way trout were summoned up the lake durin' breedin' time, same way a starling were summoned by the call of another starling, like that. So it seemed ta Bighead, though he weren't too smart in a lotta ways, that it was The World Outside that were *callin'* ta him, that were *summonin'* him.

Yes indeedy, *somethin'* were callin' The Bighead, fer shore. Maybe it were the voice'a God, or the whisper of his predesterination. He didn't rightly know.

But The Bighead knowed this:

Whatever it was, he were shorely gonna find out.

(II)

The note he'd left, its half-thought, hapless scrawl, lingered in her mind. *Dear Charity: Sorry things didn't work out last night. Hope you have a nice trip. Nate.* What did that mean? Sorry things didn't work out? But—

Things never work out, Charity thought. It mystified her. She and Nate, for instance. He was nice, smart, had tenure in the English Department. He was attractive, too. They'd had a nice dinner at Peking Gourmet, good conversation. She'd told him all about her upcoming trip to her aunt's, and he'd seemed genuinely interested in all she had to say. Then they got back to her place and—

It all fell to pieces. It always did...

Was it her fault that she felt nothing during love-making? But the men must sense her unfeeling too, their primitive egos ruptured. Then they were gone, and not once did they ever come back, or even call. At least Nate had been thoughtful enough to leave a note. But he'd never ask her out again, either—Charity knew this. He'd never look at her again in the same way.

Her despair steeled her. After all these years, she was used to it. Now, of course, was not the time to be stewing over her ceaseless romantic failures.

The trip, she forced herself to think. *Aunt Annie.* It had been years since Charity had heard from her aunt, and decades since she'd seen her. A long story, and Charity knew most of it had to do with guilt. Her aunt had raised her until she'd turned eight (Charity's father had been killed in a mine cave-in, and her mother committed suicide shortly thereafter), and was the only mother Charity had ever really had. But this was back in Luntville, not College Park, Maryland, which was just a hair away from Washington D.C. The sticks, the boonies, a tiny wedge between the Allegheny Mountains and the Appalachians. Aunt Annie's boarding house had slowly but surely plummeted; with no money coming in, her aunt had been declared by the state as an "unfit domestic guardian." Hence, Charity had been spirited away by the state, placed in an out-of-state orphanage (no room in her own state), and that was the end of the story. Or, in a sense, the beginning.

Twenty-two years later, she found she still remembered a lot about "home." The rural hills, a world apart from where she lived now. Aunt Annie had called last week, had enticed Charity to "come back home."

And home wasn't here, was it? Home was where she'd been born…

Why not? she'd thought.

It would be good to get away from here for awhile, and God knew she had enough vacation time piled up. Just hearing Annie's voice, she had to admit, seemed a beckoning, an invitation to fly away back to her roots. The strip malls and smog and noisy rush hour walking along University Boulevard, and everything else, only goaded her further. *I'm going to go back to Luntville,* she decided the same night. *I'm going to go back to the place where I came from, to visit the woman who tried her best to raise me.*

Reasserting this now, wiped her mind clean of her other problems, her other failures. It made her feel freshened. Backwoods notwithstanding, there certainly were a lot of things that could be said of the area from whence she came. Simple folk, simple ideologies, the antithesis of this rat race she consigned herself to. It would do her good to go back.

And though she didn't have a car, she did have a driver. Charity had placed an ad in the area newspapers, among them *The Washington Post.* One of the *Post's* writers had called her immediately, a Jerrica Perry, stating that she was looking to make a short trip to the same area. And *she* had a car, and would be happy to take Charity along in exchange for a contribution to expenses. It was all set. She'd be leaving in the morning.

And she'd be leaving more than College Park, Maryland, wouldn't she? She'd be leaving all the blights of her life, all the disappointments and regrets.

Not that she actually *was* a failure. She'd risen above incredible odds, hadn't she? The orphanage, the loneliness, the nights she lay awake wondering why she didn't fit in? She'd trudged ahead, worked hard to get her G.E.D. and the admin job at the college, and harder still with her night classes. It would take time, but she knew, especially with a 3.4 GPA, she'd eventually get her degree in Accounting. She'd make it.

But for now…

The idea captured her.

Tomorrow, Charity Wells thought, gazing out her apartment window, *I'm going home.*

(III)

The article should be the only thing on her mind. $1500 the paper was paying her, and another thousand once she'd turned the pieces in. That was good money for a specialty assignment, and her base salary wasn't too shabby either. "Keep your mind on your business, Jerrica," she muttered aloud.

The row she'd had with Darren—Jesus! He just wouldn't let go. "You really do have a problem, Jerr," he'd said the night he'd walked in. Jerrica had been in bed with not one but two men at the time. "*This* is what you want?" he'd asked, unabashed by what he was witnessing. The two men had pulled their clothes on in record time, had left. But Darren remained. "*This* gives you fulfillment? Picking up stray men in a bar, and—and having—*threesomes?*"

"Fuck off!" she'd shouted, but that wasn't really what she'd wanted to say. What else *could* she say, though? It was—well—it was embarrassing, being caught like this.

"And what the hell are you doing in my apartment anyway!" she shouted further, drawing besmirched sheets to her bosom.

"You gave me a key, remember?"

"Well..."

There was really little else she could say. What? I can't help it? I can't help myself? I'm sorry? With Darren, that might work, but she just couldn't say it.

I'm sorry, she thought.

"You need help, Jerr," he'd proclaimed. "I mean, do you even *know* those guys?" He'd frowned then. "Don't answer. All I'm saying is I still think we have a pretty good thing going, and you're going to destroy it all. Why?"

Why? How could Jerrica reply? Especially now, with semen in her hair and her vagina so sore she'd probably have trouble walking?

"Get out!" was what she said, because it was the only thing she could think to say that wouldn't completely decimate her pride. "Just get out!"

He'd moved away, so slowly it seemed forlorn. Darren loved her, she could tell, and no other man in her life ever really had. Nevertheless, he didn't storm out, as most men would.

"I love you, Jerrica," he'd whispered, only half his face peering past the bedroom door. "We can work this out if you want to."

It took everything, then, every bad spirit in her soul to answer.

"Get out."

So he did.

What's wrong with me? she asked herself in the mirror. She was twenty-eight but she still looked a decade younger. Flowing, silken blond hair, all the right curves in all the right places, a firm, high bosom. Darren was a good man. What was she looking for?

She shrugged in the mirror, beads of shower water still glinting on her tanned skin.

I need help, she agreed with Darren. She knew she did. But what? She saw a counselor twice a month for $75 an hour. What? She was supposed to go to Sex Addicts Anonymous? No way she'd subject herself to that freak show again. Beating cocaine addiction had been tough enough, but *sex* addiction? *I just have to sort things out myself,* she deluded herself.

I've got an assignment. I'm going to the Appalachian Mountains tomorrow. I'm going to have a good time, and I'm not going to worry about Darren or men, or myself or anything else, she determined.

Jerrica Perry slipped on her robe. She sighed, even wiped a tear away.

Then she began to pack her bags.

(IV)

But, lordy! today musta been The Bighead's day 'cos no sooner had he stomped a mile after that last splittail (see, that's what Grandpap had always called gals, splittails, on account'a you look at 'em bass-akwards an' their tails 'er kinda split), he spotted hisself another one, a cute little brownie-head pixie squatin' to pee by a stump just off the this fairly big road he come across. She was barefoot an' bright-eyed, wearin' just the purdiest tight little scrap of a dress Bighead ever did seed, (a fuchsia shade, not that Bighead were well-read enough ta know what tha fuck fuchsia was) and this dress he just up an' ripped right off her purdy back 'fore she were even finished with her pee. She didn't scream much, no sir, on account of it were differcult ta scream when yer throat was tored out. See, Bighead didn't bother layin' no pipe 'cos he seed her pussy whiles she was peein', and it was plain as barn paint she didn't have no slot on her that could take The Bighead's thang. So's he just kilt her, just like that, and had hisself a quick jack on her titties. Second nut of the day always felt the best, just like Grandpap always tolt him. The Bighead about grunted like a Berkshire hog humpin' a sheep. Got hisself off a *nice* nut, yes sir, whiles the gal gargled her own blood in pretty red bubbles. Went down on her too, whiles she were still dyin', just to have hisself a lick of her girlystuff. Seemed a waste not to. She tasted fierce: pussystink, fresh pee, and, a'corse, sheer fuckin' terror. It all kinda mixed together down there for a tasty lick, and Bighead liked that. His big lopsided red eyes slitted in satis-er-faction. Then he were done an' he moseyed off inta the brambles, away from The Low Woods, and—

Out toward the World Outside.

Bighead figgurt it wouldn't take him too's long ta git there.

1 2 3 4 5 6 7 8 9 0
TWO
ERIK
1999

TWO

(I)

Joyclyn, look!

I know. He's waking up!

Giggles seemed to chitter, a suffusion unreal as the grains in the air. The priest moaned into his pillow.

This is going to be so much fun...

The pallor of dawn licked his brow with pasty sweat; he felt emslimed, his face gnawed on by misgivings, his eyes pressed in to the bursting point by small phantasmal thumbs. Exhausted from the vigors of nightmare, he looked up to the foot of his spartan rectory bed.

God, I beg of thee, he thought, *I'm so scared! Protect me!*

Perhaps God did, then, because the fear, which made the priest feel as though he were drowning in a hot tarn, subsided.

But the vision...

Christ...

The aftervision didn't subside just quite yet.

The two nuns stood looking down, chuckling munchkin-like. In a patina of dim morning light, they grinned. Their eyes were dull as death, their mouths like thin slashes in gray meat. Then they lifted their black clerical skirts—

God in Heaven...

—and began to urinate.

Right there on the rectory carpet, in hot, steady steams, their fingers forked against their pubic mounds, baring tender, tiny urethras…

Their high, witchy chuckles faded, as so did their images, as the priest came fully awake.

Fuck, the priest thought. *Fuckin'-A…*

But there was something else, only for a split-second.

An image lingering in the space of a blink.

A black maw stretched wide as a garbage-can lid, full of teeth sharp as ice-picks…

(II)

"Well, it's nice to meet you," Charity said once she'd loaded her bags into the tiny trunk and got in.

"Nice to meet you too," the blond woman said. For some reason, Charity couldn't remember her name. Jennifer? Jessica?

"And I like your car," Charity added, for lack of anything else. It was a bright-red Miata, a two-seat convertible. It was nice. Expensive too, probably. *One day I'll own a car like this,* Charity swore to herself. *Once I get my degree…*

"It was great that you put that ad in," the blond woman said. "It was perfect. I mean, how many people need to take trips to the sticks?" Then she paused, her face tensed. "I'm sorry. You're from around there, right? I didn't mean to say that your home is the sticks. It's just a figure of speech."

"Don't worry about it," Charity said. The little car bolted off onto the beltway, and at once her long, curly dark hair lifted in the breeze. "It *is* the sticks. Simple people, simple ways. Actually, it has its advantages."

"Tell me about it!" The blond woman erupted, then honked at a black Fiero that cut her off on the exit. "I'll bet they don't have people who drive like that!"

Charity smiled. *High-strung,* she realized very quickly. *And… Jerrica! That's her name! Jerrica Perry.* "So… I don't quite remember. You're a writer?"

"I'm a journalist for the *Washington Post,*" Jerrica corrected behind the padded steering wheel. "Local Section. Been there four years."

"Wow. A newspaper writer."

"It's no big deal. But every now and then one of the senior editors'll assign you a good, high-paying piece. That's what happened to me. They gave me a three-part article on Rural Appalachia. Good money, too."

Charity wondered how much. Good money to Jerrica was probably outstanding money to Charity.

"So what's this about your aunt?" Jerrica asked, heading up the beltway toward the Richmond exit.

"Well, she kind of raised me, up until I was eight. Then..." Why should she be embarrassed about the truth? "Her boarding house ran out of money, and I got put in an orphanage."

"Jesus, that's tough."

"It wasn't too bad," Charity lied. Actually it had been *quite* tough. She felt like a misfit to the world. But why go over all that with a woman she'd just met today? She'd turned out all right.

"I got out at eighteen, got two jobs, got my G.E.D. Now I'm working at the University, and I'm taking night classes, because they pay half of the tuition. I want to be an accountant."

"Sounds good. Good money." Everything, for whatever reason, with Jerrica, was money.

"Anyway," Charity went on, "my aunt invited me up, and since I don't have a car yet, I put the ad in the papers."

Jerrica lit a cigarette, its plume of smoke sailing away. "And your aunt, you say she runs a boarding house?"

"That's right. It went under for a while, but then she got it back on track."

"You think she'll give us a good rate?"

"Oh, I think so. I don't think she'll charge us at all."

"That sounds *real* good. The paper's paying for me, but the more I save, the more I can spend on other things."

Charity couldn't imagine what Jerrica expected to spend on "other things," not in Luntville, not in Russell County. But something distracted her just then, a golden glint.

A ring.

Charity couldn't help but notice the diamond ring on Jerrica's finger as she steered up the long exit to I-95.

"That's beautiful," she said. "You're engaged?"

Jerrica seemed to suck her cigarette hard at the question. "Sort of," she answered. "I mean, I don't really know now."

Charity felt captured, but she knew it was really envy. It wasn't just Nate and all the other men—it was more conglomerated than that. She wanted someone to love her, and—

Nobody even calls me back after a first date...

It's a beautiful ring," she said. "I hope he's a nice man."

"He is," Jerrica said, though it seemed like she'd said it too quickly. "But... I guess the engagement is off."

"What went wrong?" Charity dared to ask.

Jerrica didn't flinch at the personal question. If there was one thing Charity could tell about Jerrica, it was that she *liked* personal questions. "Don't really know. Me, probably. Maybe I'm just not ready for that scene. I *want* to be, but... It's hard to explain. And you're right, Darren is a good guy. He works for a big genetic company, makes good money. And—well, there's nothing bad I can say about him. It's all me, I guess."

Charity wilted a bit. *All me.* How much of her own failures in love had been—*All me?* How could she ever really know?

Jerrica prattled on, "I'm hoping this trip will give me time to get my head together. You know, working in D.C., for the *Post,* it can weigh you down. Maybe that's my problem: I'm too caught up in work that I can't see the rest of my life."

Charity fully understood, but there was something...

What was it?

She'd sensed it many times in the past, with many different people. Sometimes she thought she could merely *feel* what was on other people's minds. So that's why she said what she said next.

"But you love him, don't you?"

Jerrica flicked her half-smoked cigarette out the side. The beltway blurred past. "Am I that easy to read?"

"Well, yes, I think so."

Another pause, another cigarette. "You're right. I do love him. I just don't know if I even know what love is. And a lot of times I don't think I'm worthy of being loved."

"What a horrible thing to say!" Charity objected. But, actually, how many times had she felt that way herself? Sure, she'd sensed Jerrica's feelings, but that was all. She didn't know the entire story, and it wasn't right for her to make judgments. Instead, she elected to say, "Well, once this trip is over, maybe things will work out."

Jerrica's face seemed to harden behind the wheel. She hadn't once really looked at Charity, not full in the face, and maybe there was a reason for that. Charity felt more emotion wafting off the blond's head. Guilt. Shame. Disgrace. And more guilt.

Let it go, she thought.

"We'll see," Jerrica somewhat agreed. "But, for now, I'm not even going to worry about it. I'm headin' down the highway, to write my story and see the country."

"That's good."

"But-what about you? I didn't even ask. Are you married, engaged, have a boyfriend?"

"No to all three," Charity glumly replied. "I don't understand it, but—" It was there that she chose to cut it off. The last thing Jerrica needed to hear was here own romantic quandaries. What could she say? I go out with lots of men, I even sleep with them—but they never call me back? "I guess I just haven't met the right guy yet," she slipped in instead.

"Shit." Jerrica, for the first time now, looked over at Charity, and cast a big, bright smile. "Maybe there isn't any such thing as the right man. But do you think I give a shit?"

They both laughed, then, as their hair flurried over the car's open top.

If anything, it looked like a beautiful day.

(III)

"What a fucked up day," Balls said.

"Looks all right ta me," Dicky Caudill replied at the wheel. They was Dicky's wheels, and *nice* ones at that: a jet-black, 10-coat-lacquered '69 El Camino, with a tricked cam and a souped 427. Rock-crusher trans, a Hurst shifter, Edelbrock manifold, oh, yeah, an' open Thorley headers an' chambered exhaust too. Took Dicky *years* to get it fixed back up nice, an' lookin' at it now, you think it'd just been droved off the showroom floor. Had a long bench seat with shiny 'polstery, not buckets, which were fine 'cos—well, sometimes they had passengers. And the Camino was fast, see, did a quarter mile in low thirteens, and those 450-plus-horses pumpin' outa that big block gave 'er a top end'a one-fifty easy. They'd out-runned plenty'a police cars in their time, and once even a State Police Pursuit Car out on the Route. Blowed his fuckin' doors *right* off!

"Yeah, well. Hail. Ever-day's a fucked-up day ya ask me."

"Whuh—why's that Balls?"

"I likes the nights." Balls took a sip'a shine, then, an' gazed out the passenger winder, as if reflectin' peaceful things. It was late afternoon now, an' they was just on their ways back from run up'n the north ridge just over the line past Big Stone Gap. "Ya knows, Dicky," he stated, "the way I'se see it, we ain't got it too bad. Yessir, we gots ourselfs a pretty dandy life."

Dicky down-shifted the Hurst 'round the next bend'a Tick Neck Road, headin' up fer Eads Hills. "I say, you're right 'bout that Balls, quite right," surprised that his best ruckin' pal'd make a observation'a gratitude. "Could be a lot worse, ya know, an' we'se got a lot ta be grateful fer, what with so many folks starvin' in the world an' dyin' of genercide, an' all them poor folks livin' in ghettos an all."

"Aw, *fuck* them, Dicky," Balls winced. "Hail. That ain't's what I'm talkin' about. I'se could give a booger 'bout a bunch'a buck porch monkeys in welfare ghettos, er folks starvin' an' dyin' in wars an' all that. Let 'em starve, let 'em die, I say. They ain't no good fer the proper world noways. What I'se talkin' 'bout is *our* lives, and the ways things are fer *us*."

Dicky didn't quite foller now. Well, maybe he sorta did, 'cos Lord knew Tritt Balls Conner had some pretty fierce ideas 'bout things. "Oh, yeah, I'se guess you mean that we'se gots a lot ta be grateful fer, 'bout this fine life God has given us."

"Aw, no, Dicky," Balls winced again. "That ain't what I'se talkin' 'bout neither. What God ever do fer us anyways?"

"Well—" Dicky paused to thumb a booger. "He's gave us this fine life, didn't He?"

"Aw, He ain't given us nothin' worth more'n' two squirts'a piss out a dead dog's dick, Dicky! Shee-it, you don't know nothin'. You don't hear a word I'se say."

Dicky's brow ticked a bit, in confusion, as he took a slight swig off his own jar. "Then—then...what'cha mean, Balls?"

"What I'se mean, Dicky-Boy, is we'se got ourselfs a fine an' dandy life—not on account'a God but on account'a *us.* Hail. Ever-thing we'se got, we'se made on our own."

"Uh...oh. Yeah," Dicky agreed and clammed up. He didn't wanna get Balls goin' on one'a his rants, 'cos he'd heard 'em too many times. So's Dicky just sat back an' drove and kept quiet. Tritt "Balls" Conner and Dicky Caudill were local boys, both growed up just outside'a Luntville, nears Whiskey Bottom'n Cotswold. They'd met back in seventh grade at Clintwood Middle School, the grade they both dropped out'a. Mid-twennies they both was now, Dicky bein' kinda short an' fat with a buzzcut, and Tritt Balls bein' a right tall an' big-framed, long-hairt, with a hard, mean face an' chopburns an' always wearin' a John Deere hat evens though he ain't worked on his daddy's farm in years. Dicky knowed Balls wore the hat on account he had a bald spot that he were real senser-tive about, so's Dicky never mentioned it. And the reason they needed fast wheels, see, was 'cos it gave 'em a fast getaway when they was out on a run. Neither of 'em hadda real job, didn't need one. What they did 'nstead was run hooch for Clyde Nale, who had hisself a bunch'a stills up'n the woods just outside'a Kimberlin. It was a right big set-up ol' Clyde Nale had, an' he needed runners with balls, so's that's why Balls an' Dicky got the highest payin' runs on account they had about the fastest set'a wheels in the county and they knowed all the back roads so's the state cops and those ATF chumps hardly ever got a line on 'em, an' Balls Conner, well he had the balls not ta take no shit off them hillbillies over the line, which were why he was called Balls in the first place. What they did, see, was four or five times a week, they drove over a two-hunnert-gallon load'a moonshine 'cross the Kentucky line ta distribiters in Harlan. Clyde Nale, he played it smart; Russell County was "wet" so's that's why he brewed his hooch here—less cops—and then paid Dicky an' Balls ta run over the line ta Harlan, where they sold it to the "dry" counties over that ways. And since this was a long an' risky run, Nale paid 'em a thousand per month, which Balls an' Dicky split. They was hard workin' young men, was what they was in other words.

But like the sayin' went: all work an' no play make Balls an' Dicky a fairly dull pair'a boys. So's 'tween runs they had thereselfs *all kinda* play, doin' what they referred ta as "tear-assin'." Rapin' gals, runnin' folks off the road, hidin' out behind the roadside bars an' jackin' fellas in the noggins so's ta take their scratch. An' well—

Killin' folks too, on occasion.

Dead crackers tell no tales, were what Balls said that first time. It was just after a run to Harlan, an' on theirs way back they spotted the *purdiest* li'l gal you ever did seed, a blondie wearin' tight shorts'n almost nothin' up top, hitchin' along Furnace Branch Road round about midnight. A hill gal she was, and whens they pulled over ta offer her a ride, why she just up an' smiled the whitest, purdiest smile an' says "Shore, boys, Thank ya much." So's she slid right in next ta Balls on the bench seat, an' Dicky pulls off the shoulder figgurin' they was gonna give her a ride home, when he hears *SMACK! SMACK! SMACK!* and he looks over aghasted ta see that Balls had 'mediately cracked her upside the head with his homemade jack. "What'cha go an do that fer!" Dicky wailed. "Pulls up the next dirt road ya see," was all Balls had answered, an' when Dicky did...well ain't too purdy recitin' what happened then, so's let's just say that Tritt "Balls" Conner had hisself one hell of a romp. He laid dick twice on that gal, he did, 'fore she even come to, right there off the side'a the road. Yessir, she were a fine lookin' thing but probably weren't but fourteen 'er so, an' once she come to right in the middle'a Balls' second nut, she started screamin' like ta wake all the dead outa Beall Cemetery, but all Balls did was laugh out loud like the devil hisself, continuin' ta hump her poor young pussy right inta the ground. Dicky hisself stood aside ta watch, an', well, seein' this cute li'l gal with her clothes ripped off her, an' her li'l cupcakelike tittes bobbin' an' all that—it put a stiffer on Dicky a might quick, so's he's couldn't help but pull that bad boy out and have hisself a good wank in the weeds. But just 'cos he had a wank didn't mean that he 'proved'a what Balls'd done. Come on! Snatchin' a local gal right off the road? Beatin' her in the head and humpin' her poon 'gainst her will? That were rape was what that were, an' if this here gal could 'dentify 'em, why, Dicky and Balls'd be pullin' 'bout fifteen years apiece in the county detent, gettin' cornholed by big an' mostly black fellas evernight, an' havin' ta suck peter 'less they wanted ta wind up with their guts on the floor from a some con's prison shiv. So's after Dicky were finished shakin' the last'a his snot out his dick, he objectered, "Hey, Balls! What's're we gonna do now?"

"I don't knows 'bout you, Dicky, but I'll tells ya what *I'm* gonna do now. Hail. I'se gonna cornhole me this bitch." And just like that he up'n flips this poor screamin' gal over, takes a big hock 'tween her cheeks, an' starts ta lay a butt-fuckin' on her somethin' fierce, alls the while blood leakin' out her pussy like a busted pipe.

"That ain't whats I mean, Balls!" Dicky fairly cried out. "I mean what if she up'n tells the cops what we looks like?"

"Shut up whiles I have me my nut," Balls grunted aside, still humpin' away. By now the gal's screamin' fit had wound down an' she were passin' out again after pukin' once. Balls stepped up his humpin', murmurin', "Yeah, oh daddy yeah! This is some cracker butt, I'll'se tell ya! I'se gonna squirt me a load'a the dicksnot right'n the middle'a her shit!" An', so, that's just what Tritt "Balls" Conner done just then, and when he were finished he pulled out an' wiped his dirty bone off on her purdy blond hair an' then hocked a lunger on her head.

"Jesus Chrast, Balls!' Dicky contin-yer'd ta object. "She's gonna up an' tell the poe-leece what we'se look like!"

"How's that, Dicky?" Balls inquired with that evil, cut grin'a his, an' then he sat right smack down onta the middle'a her back, pulled back on her head until—

crack!

—her neck up'n broke.

"She ain't gonna tells no one nothin', 'cos dead crackers tell no tales," Balls said, sniffin' the air. "Hail. Don't'cha just hate the way yer dick stinks after a cornholin'?"

Anyways, that were the first killin' they done, an' after that there was many more. A hitchhiker here, a broke down motorist there, gals, fellas, it didn't make much matter ta Balls. Shee-it, coupla times they'd pulled over to some fella broke down and Balls'd pop him—BAM! Just like that!—in the head with that big rusty pistol his daddy'd left him. Then another time they'se was drivin' down Davidsonville Road an' they seed this old lady wheelin' out ta the end'a her drive ta git her mail, an' they'se just pulled over lickety-split an' Balls plucked her outa that chair an' throwed her in the back. Put a fierce conrholin' on her too—didn't bother with her poon on account it was old an' shriveled an' a might ugly—once Dicky pulled off on one'a the old loggin' roads 'fore the Boone Federal Game Reserve. "How's that fer a butt-dickin' grandmammy?" Balls gusted laughter. "Bet'cha ain't had it like that in fifty years!" Then Balls took a pause, starin' down, an' Dicky seed it too, this strange kinda bag hangin' off the side'a the ol' lady's belly. "Wells don't that beat all!" Balls exclaimed.

"Whuh-what it is, Balls?" Dicky inquired.

"It's a colosteramy bag! I know 'cos my Uncle Nat had one. See, the docs give ya one'a these when ya cain't shit out yer a-hole no more. They'se repipe yer guts to yer side an' make a hole there an' then they'se hook this plastic bag ta the hole so's whenever ya et, yer shit comes out'n the bag."

"Aw, shee-it, Balls," Dicky moaned, closing his eyes. "Ya mean that's what that there bag is fulla?"

"Shore is, Dicky, but we'se ain't got no use fer the bag." An' with that, Balls ripped that disgustin' brown-filt bag right offa that poor ol' lady's side, an' then ya know what he did?

Balls dropped his pants again.

"What'cha—" Dicky gulped. "What'cha droppin' trow fer, Balls?"

"Shee-it, Dicky. A nut's a nut, ain't it? Hail. I'se hard agin, so I'se gonna fuck me this ol' lady's colosteramy hole!"

Dicky, see, though he liked ta watch a good rompin', he didn't have no desire ta watch this. An' when Balls were finished humpin' that hole, he cracked the poor ol' lady's head open with his homemade jack till her brains were layin' all over the dirt, an' then he grabbed that brown plastic bag an' squirted its stinky contents right onta the brains. Just fer kicks.

So's anyway, that's the kinda fella Tritt "Balls" Conner were, an' this is the type'a shennan-er-gans they did fer fun 'tween their hooch runs fer Clyde Nale. And—

"Well bless my soul!" Balls about shouted out just then in the passenger seat.

Aw, no, Dicky thought, 'cos he saw it too.

Standin' there in the fine bright light'a day, there she was, a sweet-lookin' li'l brunette with long slim legs an' cutoff shorts an' what looked ta be a fine set'a milkers strainin' against her halter top. An' she were standin' there on the shoulder'a Tick Neck Road, smilin' just pretty as you please, an' stickin' her thumb out.

"Hail," Balls remarked. "Pull this jalopy over, Dicky. We'se gonna give this gal a ride."

(IV)

Jerrica didn't quite know what to make of her passenger. Charity was very nice, a very pretty woman, and she seemed very introspective and intelligent. But—

Hmm, Jerrica thought at the Miata's wheel.

There was something almost mysterious about her, resting anxiously behind the shy and introverted veneer. *She's thirty but she's not married, doesn't even have a boyfriend.* This, of course, Jerrica Perry could scarcely conceive. Was she gay? Was she catholic or something?

"So, what exactly is it that you do?" Jerrica asked next. Interstate 199 had nearly run its course for them, the 23 exit should be coming along in just another twenty miles or so. "You work at University of Maryland?"

"I'm just an administration clerk," Charity revealed, her sable curls roving in the breeze. "But I'm taking classes too."

"Where did you go to high school? I went to Seaton."

"I didn't go to high school, I had to get a job once I got out of the orphanage."

Orphanage. Shit, Jerrica, you sure know how to ask the wrong question! But at least she'd broken the proverbial ice. "I guess that was pretty hard, huh?"

"I made out better than most," Charity admitted. "But the way the system works—well, it's almost impossible to graduate from high school under those circumstances. It's a different world. And once you turn eighteen, they kick you out, give you a hundred dollars, and say good luck. I worked three crummy jobs to make ends meet, took my G.E.D. through the state. But what happens to a lot of these kids, they put them out on the street, nowhere to go, next thing they know they're being stabled by a pimp and they're hooked on drugs. I was really fortunate."

Jerrica tried to think of something appropriate to say, but all her mind came up with were sociology stats she'd read in her own newspaper. "Yeah, I was reading, right now this country's got 800,000 orphans but only one-third of them even get a G.E.D. and get jobs. The rest either disappear or work the streets."

"Right, and that's the sad part. My aunt raised me, but the state took custody because she didn't make enough money. I would've been better off staying with her, though, I'm certain of it."

"I guess you miss your aunt, not seeing her for so long."

"Yeah, well, kind of. It's been twenty years, and after that much time, a person becomes only a vague memory. I mean, I still remember her—believe it or not, I still remember so much about home—but it's so distant it doesn't seem real. That's why I'm a little bit nervous. I'm not sure what it's going to be like seeing her again, and seeing Luntville."

"Well, you're certainly entitled to be nervous," Jerrica offered, but she could imagine how phony that sounded. What did she know about the real world? Raised in Potomac by millionaire parents, private schools her whole life, a brand-new Z28 for her sixteenth birthday. *I don't know shit,* she admitted.

"So what were you saying?" Charity asked next. "About this guy Darren?"

Wow. Not it was Jerrica's turn. All at once, though, and considering Charity's own confession, she felt remarkably open. "A real fox, thirty, good job—he works for a bio-engineering firm in Bethesda. A prime catch, for sure. And, well, he was *dynamite* in bed."

Charity blushed slightly and obviously quickened to recover. "But didn't you say that *you* were the one who broke off the engagement?"

Jerrica's mind raced to figure it out. "I don't know, it's hard to say. I—I threw him out."

"Why?"

More faltering. *Be honest!* she demanded of herself. And what did it matter? Charity was someone she'd just met and would probably never see again after this trip. Jerrica lit another Salem, set her teeth and blinked. "He caught me."

"*Caught* you?"

"He caught me with two other guys. I was cheating on him."

Charity's face seemed to tint in confusion. "But I thought you just said he was—"

"Yeah, I know, I said he was dynamite in bed. It's true. But...I guess I have a problem. I mean, I loved the guy, I *still* do. But I cheated on him right and left, and I've cheated on every boyfriend I've ever had. It was never about love, it was never about Darren not giving me what I needed. It was... something else. I don't know. Maybe I'm a sex addict or something."

"Maybe you should see a counselor," Charity suggested.

Ordinarily, Jerrica would've fumed. But, for some reason, Charity saying it was different. "Darren suggested the same thing, he wanted me to go to Sex Addicts Anonymous or some shit, and I just couldn't see myself sitting in the middle of *that.* And I'd been to some counselors for a while in the past, but I never got anything out of it." Her thoughts backtracked then. *Wait a minute... Is that what I am? A sex addict?* It sounded so cliched, just another excuse of the modern age to pursue indulgence and recklessness. Nothing was weakness anymore; it was all a "disease"; alcoholism, drug addiction, gambling, for Christ's sake, eating too much. And sex too. Shit, in this day and age, even shoplifting was a disease. Jerrica couldn't believe that, not even considering her own indiscretions.

And there'd been many.

She'd kept a tally, hadn't she? Over five hundred since she'd lost her virginity at sixteen. *Five hundred.* And she was only twenty-eight. Obliquely, then, she tried to explain. "I don't know what comes over me. When I'm with a man, it's like I become a different person. I need... I need the sensation, the stimulation. At least I guess that's what it is." She'd read something once, in *Cosmo,* about how some people were "sensualists." They craved the feelings administered by others. More excuses to exploit the human self. Jerrica didn't believe it for a minute. But then...

She didn't know what she believed.

And only then did she realize what she was saying in the first place. *My God,* her thoughts croaked. Charity was, essentially, a stranger, and here Jerrica was telling her things of her utmost personal life. Well, maybe that was okay. A person needed to talk about things, to people who were safe. And that's what Charity was: Safe.

But enough was enough; Jerrica's mind raced like a rat in a maze, scurried for exit. She lit another Salem and changed the subject. "So how about some more about you? You've already told me you're not married and don't have a boyfriend."

Charity at once looked down at her lap. Not embarrassment, but puzzlement. Like Jerrica, Charity Walsh felt puzzled, not by the world and the people in it, but by her own self. "I don't understand it," she said. "I've dated a lot of men—I *like* men—but...but, never in my life have I had more than one date with the same guy. I just don't get it. I just can't figure out what it is I'm doing wrong."

"Hey, don't blame yourself because things don't turn out," Jerrica assured. "Christ, I like men too, but I'll be the first to tell you that they're all assholes. But, I mean—I mean, did you..."

"Did I have sex with them on those first dates?" Charity blushed again. "Yes. Every time. But it just didn't...work."

Didn't work. Even Jerrica, in her wild complexity, couldn't quite get a handle on that. *Maybe she's a lousy lay,* she considered. *Maybe she doesn't know how to give head...* But these things, of course, she could never give voice to.

"Something just doesn't work, just doesn't *happen*, you know?" Charity went sheepishly on. "I don't know what it is."

This statement could be deciphered in innumerable ways. Did Charity mean orgasm? Did she mean chemistry? "Look," she offered without speculating further. "I think what it all boils down to is finding the right guy. Maybe that's our problem. We just haven't found the right guy."

Charity's thin shoulders rose and fell.

Yeah, maybe that was it.

They veered off onto Route 23, the little red car whisking along the open country road, long fields passing them by. Right now they were dividing the Allegheny and Appalachian Mountains; the world had changed over indeed, prolapsing from a domain of skyscrapers and smog to one of forestlines and scarecrows. For Jerrica it was strange but refreshing nonetheless. She couldn't wait to write her article on Appalachian rural culture. This trip enthused her, but there was one thing ticking at the back of her mind...

How long can I go without—

She didn't dare even finish the query.

"It's so good to be back," Charity said.

"What?"

"I wasn't sure how I'd feel, but now that we're getting back into the old hill country, I can see I made the right choice to come back. The people here are simple, and so is the life. But it's so much more honest and real than where we come from."

Jerrica thought about this, flicking yet another butt out the side. The engine purred, the car's frame sucking down onto the blacktop through each winding turn. To either side came a blurred spread of beautiful sweeping green—the forests. And the air smelled so clean Jerrica thought she was getting high.

And Charity was the perfect riding mate. She knew the area, plus her aunt had the boarding house—they'd be all set up. She followed Charity's coming directions, and within an hour, they passed a corroded green roadsign which read LUNTVILLE.

Luntville. Jerrica had known all along that that was where they were going. But the name sent a tick in her head just then. Something she'd read. "Hey, didn't I read something in the papers a long time ago, about some convent or monastery near Luntville?"

"It was an abbey, I think," Charity corrected. "But I really don't know anything about it. You can ask my aunt, though."

That's right, it wasn't the papers she read it in, it was her Nexus notes. There was some controversy, if Jerrica remembered correctly. Something about a hospice, dying priests. *Hmmm.* But before she could think any more on it, Charity declared, her finger pointing, "Turn here!"

Jerrica veered off. *Yeah, yeah,* Jerrica thought. Christ, they'd been on the road over ten hours. Were they ever going to get there?

"We're here!" Charity said, her roundish face bright with exhilaration.

Jerrica slowed past the wood-post sign, then turned and idled up a long gravel road. At the end, an opening bloomed. And in the middle of the opening sat a beautiful stained-wood country inn, with a long wraparound porch, cedar shingles, and big bay windows, all nestled nicely in a plush, wooded dell. A high wood sign announced: ANNIE'S BOARDING HOUSE. $20 PER NIGHT. VACANCIES.

"This is it?" Jerrica asked. Her bright blond hair, finally, lowered against the breeze.

"This," Charity said, "is it."

1 2 3 4 5 6 7 8 9 0
THREE
ERIK
1999

THREE

(I)

"Aunt...*Annie!*" Charity exclaimed. She threw her arms up. The woman who'd come out onto the porch looked about sixty. Snow-white hair, attractive in spite of her age, a warm smile set into subtly weathered facial features. She was wearing a threadbare white summer dress and, quite proverbially, black workboots. Cool blue eyes seemed to fasten on them as they got out of the Miata.

The woman burst immediately into tears right there on the old porch.

Charity stood in time-jag. The world stopped. Everything she was looking at seemed to freeze, and suddenly she was looking at herself more than anything else. No, she hadn't known at all how she felt about coming back, nor had she known how she'd feel about seeing Annie. Luntville, her aunt, this house—they were all the broken shards of her life, best left behind with everything else, the deeper things: her father's death, her mother's mental problems and eventual suicide, parents she'd never known, shadows. But now, as she stood amid this freeze frame of recollection, she knew at once that she'd done the right thing. The only thing, actually.

Coming back to Luntville would give Charity the chance to reconfront herself, refit the pieces of herself that had never quite found the right gap. There were a lot of pieces.

Charity, in sudden tears herself now, hugged her aunt on the front steps.

"My gracious, Charity," Aunt Annie wept. "Seein' you…is a gift from God."

"But you girls must be *so* tired," Aunt Annie speculated, inviting them into the front parlor. "Such a long drive."

"It wasn't that bad," Jerrica said. "About ten hours."

"Oh, I'm sorry," Charity apologized, neglecting to introduce her travel-mate. "This is my friend, Jerrica Perry. She works for the big newspaper in Washington."

"Very pleased ta meet you," Annie said, offering her small, white hand. "A newsperson, is that it?"

"Not really," Jerrica admitted. "I write for the Local section of the *Post.* I'm on the staff but I only get particular assignments. And that's why this whole thing is so great, Charity and I driving up together."

Aunt Annie paused, trying not to show her befuddlement. "I'm not quite sure what ya mean."

Christ, Jerrica thought. *I guess Charity didn't even mention me.* "Charity and I met in the classifieds. We both put in ads for a drive to the area. My newspaper contracted me to write a series of articles about rural areas in proximity to Washington, D.C. The first set will be about this area right here, between the Allegheny and Appalachian Mountains."

"It sounds like a wonderful opportunity fer a pretty young girl such as yerself, in your profession, I mean."

Jerrica stalled minutely. She wasn't quite sure what that meant. Ordinarily she would've been offended; she didn't like her gender mentioned with regards to career. But then she took into consideration: *She's from a different world, a different society…* "Yes, it is," she responded, and actually it was. She'd been working for the paper since just after graduating Maryland, and this was the first quality field assignment she'd been given. She tried to liven up the conversation. "It's an opportunity, all right, and the best part is—my boss is paying my whole way!"

Aunt Annie's head went slightly atilt. "Well, ya needn't worry about room and board." Then she patted Charity on the shoulder. "I wouldn't dream of charging a friend of my little girl's."

"I appreciate your generosity," Jerrica replied, but she couldn't help but be stricken by the quick look on Charity's face. *This is a domestic Chinese fire drill,* she thought. *I better not even ask...*

"It's wonderful about all the signs," Charity said then, finally relaxing back into the big cushions of the couch. "We saw them all along the interstates. 'Annie's Boarding House,' every twenty or thirty miles. They must've cost a fortune."

"Well, they did," Annie admitted, "and that's just more of what we have to talk about."

But before Annie could continue, Charity cut in once more. "And the house itself—it looks terrific. It looks almost brand new."

"Not 'xactly brand new," Annie discretely chuckled. "But I did put a lot inta refurbishments. The McKully brothers—do you remember them? They did a wonderful job fixin' up the place, and they did it for a song, considering the economy. And as for the road-signs—they cost a lot, but they bring in the business, 'specially in the fall and spring."

Charity leaned eagerly forward in the couch. "But, Aunt Annie, how could you afford it?"

Again, Annie's poise seemed discrete, reluctant. "I came into a little money. Everyone did on the north ridge. I'll—I'll tell you all about it later."

"That's *wonderful!*" Charity celebrated.

But Jerrica got the vibe: Annie didn't want to talk about it, for whatever reason, not now, at any rate. Hence, she added quickly enough, "But Charity's right, Ms. Walsh. The boarding house really looks nice."

"Oh, you silly thing," Annie chuckled. "Please, call me Annie. Oh—let me get the tea!"

Aunt Annie rose from the couch, quick and nimble for a woman of her age, and disappeared through dark-scarlet curtains. "Your aunt really is cool," Jerrica took the opportunity to cite.

"She is." Charity gazed into a long pause. "She's the most wonderful person. I don't understand how I could've forgotten."

"Well, when you're apart from someone for so long, they kind of fade from your memory."

"I know," Charity admitted. "But Annie's different. Lots of people are from around these parts. She's..."

"Exclusive," Jerrica offered.

Charity's face beamed. "That's it! That's the perfect word!"

"What's the perfect word?" Aunt Annie inquired, arriving with a beautiful silver service of steaming tea cups.

"Oh, nothing, Aunt Annie," Charity said. "Just girls talking."

Annie smiled. "Really? Well, you might not believe this, but I used to be a girl myself. And I know how girls talk. 'N fact, that's why I saw fit ta put Jerrica's room right next ta yours, Charity. 'Cos there's a connectin' door, which yawl kin leave open to talk yer girl talk."

Jerrica, aside, assessed this. *There's a loaded comment...*

"Thank you, Aunt Annie, that was very thoughtful." Then Charity's voice turned dreamy. "It's just so great to be back."

"And it's great to have *you* back. I always thought that ya never should've left, but then..."

"Aunt Annie, don't," Charity rushed in, leaning forward again. "It wasn't your fault."

Annie sat back stolid in her seat. Then a pause unreeled.

"Do you mind if I smoke?" Jerrica asked, to break the odd ice. She'd already noticed the turtle-shell upturned on the hardwood table.

"Oh, please do," Annie invited. Jerrica relievingly lit a Salem, took a deep drag, and then watched with something like astonishment as Annie withdrew a long meerschaum pipe and loaded it with tobacco. The stereotypes dazzled her: *Christ,* Jerrica thought. *This place is so hick. I'm surprised she didn't pull out a* corncob *pipe!*

Jerrica then took a moment to look closely at Annie's face. Yes, it was weathered yet genteel, crinkled yet pretty. Her blue eyes clear as a teenager's. She seemed to have a terrific figure for a woman her age. *I hope I'm so lucky.*

Then her gaze flicked to Charity. Different hair, different shape of face, but still pretty in some odd, backwoods way. However, the silence was piling up. Jerrica knew she needed to cut it. "Oh, that's what I wanted to ask you about. It's in my Lexus notes. Tell me about the abbey."

At once, Annie looked afrighted, pipesmoke sifting from her tiny white bowl. "The abbey? Oh, my goodness," she eventually recovered. "That old place has been closed for decades."

"I remember you mentioning something about an abbey," Charity said, "in one of your letters."

Annie sighed. "Oh, of course, but there wasn't much to tell. It was after—well—after the state took ya. Wroxeter, they called it. Way on back in the woods past Croll's fields. It's nothing. The Catholics had some of their nuns running it for a time, as a rest center for priests."

"You mean a *hospice*," Jerrica remembered from her Nexus search all too quickly. "For dying priests?" The abbey was obviously a sore point; it ruffled Charity's aunt so quickly, Jerrica would've been a fool not to notice. Nevertheless, according to her research, Wroxeter Abbey had been reopened by the diocese as a care ward for priests. But what was the controversy?

"There were problems there," Annie finally admitted. "But that's all in the past." The shift in topics, then, was so quick, Jerrica knew she'd run afoul with her comment. "I'm sure you girls will like your rooms," Annie said next. "Charity, of course, has her old room. And you, Jerrica, right next door, you have Governor Thomas' suite. They named the road after him, you know."

"Governor Thomas?" Jerrica queried over her Salem.

"He was governor a hundred years ago, and, well, he was, you know, he was a fella who liked to get together with other fellas." Aunt Annie smiled. "Back then, of course, being that way—gay's what I guess ya call it—wasn't something you told folks about. He had a wife, for show. But every Thursday night he'd bring his boy-lover to the house... Oh, I'm sorry, I didn't even consider." Aunt Annie's clear blue eyes focused with concern on Jerrica. "Maybe staying in such a room, with such goings on, might be offensive to ya."

Jerrica nearly laughed. "Not at all, Annie," Jerrica said, "I'd be honored to stay in Governor Thomas' room."

"Good, good," Annie said. "Fine. 'Cos it's a nice room, it is. Perfect view into the woods. Goop!"

Jerrica and Charity nearly jumped out of their seats at the exclamation. *Goop?* Jerrica wondered. *What is that?*

At once, though, a tall man in overalls appeared at the parlor curtains. Jerrica nearly stared at him. *Another cliche, another stereotype.* Overalls, workboots, there were even a few strands of straw in his disheveled, shoulder-length hair. In fact, his hair length was the only thing that didn't meet the cliches. His physique, though—*Christ!* Jerrica thought. All hard muscles on a large, tapered frame.

"This here's Goop Gooder, and this is Jerrica Perry and this over here's my wonderful niece Charity, who I've told ya 'bout many'a time," Annie said briskly, an edge of sternness to her drawl. "So don't you mind 'em. You just leave 'em alone."

"Yes ma'am," Goop said.

"Jerrica, why don't ya give Goop yer keys so Goop can git your bags out the trunk'a your car?"

"Sure," Jerrica said. She passed the keys. She smiled. "Hi, Goop." *Goop? You gotta be kidding me! That's a name?* "Nice to meet you."

Goop's shucksy face blushed. "Aw, aw, hi—I'se pleased ta meet'cha too, Miss Jerrica, and you'd too, Miss Char—"

"Goop!" Annie yelled. "Just get the dagged bags and take 'em up to their rooms!"

Goop shrugged, without losing his grin, and ambled out for the front door, his big workboots scuffing the hardwood floor.

"I know you're a city gal," Annie aimed at Jerrica, "and you might not think it's too nice for me to be talkin' ta Goop that way. But what'cha gotta understand is that Goop's about the finest handyman in these parts, but he's also quite slow in the head, and he can get a bit riled over pretty women."

"I understand," Jerrica said. More backwoods convention, still more cliche. *Slow in the head? Well, he looked fairly well packed in the pants,* she boldly thought, unable to not notice the considerable endowment in Goop Goodman's lower regions... It was something she always noted of men, something she, even if unconsciously, couldn't help but flick her eyes on. This Goop's crotch looked like he'd put the entirety of the *Post's* sports section in his shorts.

"Come on up, girls," Annie bid. "She pushed through the parlor curtain, her arm around Charity's shoulder, and led them toward a winding staircase. "Let me show yawl to your rooms."

Charity's arm, in turn, slipped around Annie's slim back. "Are there many guests right now?" she asked.

"Well, hon, no, none right now, but I do gotta reservation comin' tomorrah." And at that instant, Annie paused on the stairs and looked over her shoulder at Jerrica.

"It's a priest, as a matter of fact," Annie said. "Stayin' here a week or so."

"A priest?" Jerrica asked.

"That's right, hon. A Catholic priest...comin' all the way from Richmond."

Why on earth? Jerrica frowned. *A priest? Coming to this place? Why?* But Jerrica didn't even need to ask.

Annie continued up the steps, finishing her revelation. "He's comin' here to reopen Wroxeter Abbey."

(II)

Had Alexander ever even heard of it?

Shit, the priest thought. *Wroxeter Abbey?*

"That's right, Tom, we're sending you to Wroxeter. Assessment and evaluation, you might call it." Monsignor Halford's high, cushioned chair creaked minutely when he'd leaned back, his fingers steepled in his lap. Halford was Chancellor of the Richmond Diocesan Pastoral Center. "In fact, we've already made arrangements for your accommodations. You'll be staying at a nearby boarding house, since the abbey itself isn't habitable as yet. It'll be a nice project for you to take over. And, you'll be happy to know, the diocese doesn't consider this TDY, so you'll maintain your benefice pay status."

Oh, that's just fuckin' great, Alexander considered now, Richmond long behind him. Like the extra hundred bucks a month on benefice should appease him. Alexander didn't give a shit about money; his spirit had long since outgrown that. *Benefice, my ass,* he thought now. *The diocese is greasing me, that's what they're doing. They'll never give me my own goddamn parish, and they don't have the balls to tell me to my face. So they send me on these little trips instead.* At least Halford had let him take the old parish Mercedes, so the gruelling drive wouldn't be all that intolerable.

The reasons were legion, and none too surprising. Bureaucracy, like God, worked in intricate ways. He'd seen its many webs throughout his life: on the battlefield in South East Asia, on the college campus, in taverns and strip joints, and now, if not more so, in the Church. Alexander had been a priest for twelve years; they were no closer to giving him his own parish now than the day he'd graduated from the seminary. *You're a firebrand, Tom,* Monsignor Halford had told him a hundred times. *You're like a high-powered engine that burns a little too hot.*

All right. Maybe it was true. Forty-five now, and fifty seemed dreadfully close. But he'd been an unlikely candidate for the clergy since day one. At twenty, he'd been an Army Ranger, 5th Special Operations Group. He'd sat in the bush behind Claymores, reading Thomas Merton and St. Ignatius between firefights. He'd killed dozens of men, and even a woman once—it was almost too proverbial—a *pregnant* woman. She'd been ten yards away from tossing a two-kilo satchel charge into a field hospital full of wounded. What appalled Alexander most was not the war itself but the notion in general. *There's no reason for this,* he concluded each time he dropped Charlie in the peep-sight of his M16. Not in The Nam, not anywhere. It was the only thing he'd learned during his twelve-month combat tour, and perhaps the only *real* thing he'd ever learn in his life. C-rats, trenchfoot, crotch-rot; dysentery; chiggers the size of hazelnuts under his skin, mosquito bites more like dog bites—none of that bothered him. It was just the notion. There was simply no reason for people to kill each other.

He'd slummed for a year after his hitch, working civvie jobs and doing the things that twenty-one-year-olds do, and quite a few of those things involved women. But the civilian world only reinforced what he'd learned in the field. Too much of life revolved solely around itself, everyone looking out for number one. Alexander didn't want to be like that, and he knew there was a way out:

God.

The G.I. Bill took him through Catholic U. and a 3.9 grade-point average with a double major, philosophy and psych. Then, two more years divided between pissant jobs and volunteer work, mostly AIDS hospices. You knew you cared about people when you cleaned the shit out of their pants for free. But…

Would the Church take a former soldier, a killer?

Admission to the seminary didn't come easy. Talk about ball-breakers. It had been Halford himself who'd done the preliminary interviewing for Christ The King Seminary, upstate. "Why do you want to be a priest, Tom?"

"So I can tell people how much I love Jesus. So I can draw them closer to Him," came Alexander's simple yet honest answer.

"Not good enough," Halford said. "Stock answer."

"I want to do things for the world instead of for me,"

"Still not good enough."

But then Alexander had slapped several dissertations onto the priest's desk. Abstracts he'd written on his own: the modern applications of the works of Ignatius, Aquinas, Kierkegaard, Christian philosophies made functional in the 90's. Alexander had graduated from the seminary first in his class at the age of thirty-two.

But it didn't take him long to realize they'd never give him his own parish. *You're too valuable as a psychologist, Tom,* had been Halford's favorite excuse for years. Valuable? Sometimes a priest would quit, and it was Alexander's job to reel them back. He generally succeeded but always wondered if it was the right thing. Why goad a man to do what he doesn't want to do anymore? The rest of the time he sat in the little office behind the Richmond Main Rectory, trying to put broken men back together. Priests never came to him on their own, they were *ordered* to psychotherapy by either the diocese or the court. He got a lot of drunks and a lot of alleged pedophiles.

Antabuse for the drunks, behavioralist thrashings for the pedos. "You're a goddamn *priest,* you asshole!" he'd rail at them. "Priests don't feel up kids! And I don't want to hear a bunch of liberal horse-shit about bad childhoods and hormonal imbalances. You're a *priest,* and you have *responsibilities!* People *trust* you because of that candyass collar around your neck, and you have an *obligation* to them. If you screw around with anymore kids, you're gonna go to fuckin' jail, then you're *really* gonna know what sexual abuse is. Is that what you want, tough guy? You want to be the cellblock bitch? You got any idea what cons do to pedophiles in the joint? They'll make you boy-pussy, chief. They'll turn you to a punk in less time than it takes you to say three Hail Marys, and they'll be trading you back and forth every night for cigarettes. But that'll be the least of your worries, hoss, because if you do it again, I'm gonna kick your ass so bad your own mama won't recognize you."

He put them on Depo-Prevera and left them to wonder. Needless to say, there were many complaints about Alexander's methodologies. But the diocese never stepped on his tail because his success rate was so high. Any priest gone bad was an embarrassment, and the Church didn't like embarrassments. *Here's the problem. Fix it.* They didn't care how.

But what of Alexander's own problems? Celibate since twenty-eight, not once had he even considered breaking his vows. *Hell, I don't even jerk off.* He smoked and drank in moderation, and—well—he had a propensity for foul language, not a priestly trait. Once he'd called Monsignor Tipton an asshole at an ordination reception during an argument over whether or not girls should be allowed to acolyte. Halford had nearly shit his cassock. "Damn it, Tom! That man's going to be a cardinal someday, and you just called him an asshole!"

Alexander shrugged. "He *is* an asshole."

"That's beside the point! He could request a reprimand! You want that on your Church record? He could have you reassigned to a mission in Africa, for God's sake."

"Let him," Alexander said. "I'll kick his bootie with my tooty fruity."

"He deserves respect!"

"He deserves my foot up his ass."

"You're impossible, Tom!" Halford continued with his tirade. "You're so indecorous, so...profane. You cuss worse than a longshoreman. There's absolutely no excuse for a priest to use that kind of language."

"What language would you prefer? French? German? How about Lower Latin or Sanskrit? Anyway you look at it, Tipton's an antediluvian asshole with medieval ideas that are contrary to the needs of the worshippers. It's guys like him that keep the Church in a constant state of regression, and I told him so. I call them like I see them. Tipton's a shmuck. A shit-head. A pantywaist Church-bureaucratic dick-lick who's in the bizz only for his own self-aggrandizement, and if the Pope ever makes him a cardinal, I'll bend over and blow chunky on his raiments."

"God Almighty, Tom," Halford groaned.

Such, then, was Alexander's clerical plight. If he couldn't be a priest in any real way, he wouldn't want to be one at all. And if the diocese wanted to keep him swept under a benefice rug because he had a foul mouth, then so be it. At least they couldn't fire him. *Though art a priest forever,* they'd promised at his own ordination. *They're stuck with me, and I like that. Besides, I'm probably the best diocesan psychologist in the country, and they know it.*

It was almost amusing. Any priest wanted his own parish, and Alexander knew he'd never—ever in a million years—get his. And why?

He laughed out loud behind the wheel. *Because I cuss!*

So let the cards fall where they may. It was fate, wasn't it? It was Calvian predestination, which Alexander didn't even believe in.

If God doesn't want me to have my own parish, he reckoned, *then I guess He's got a good reason, and I ain't gonna argue with Him.*

And in the meantime:

There was always Wroxeter Abbey. He'd be up there at least a month, to assess the cost of reopening, to recalculate maintenance expenditures, and to supervise preliminary refurbishments. Well, it would be good to get away for awhile. Richmond was beautiful in the fall, winter, and spring, but, conversely, a drab, hot, ugly city in the summer.

Yeah, it'll be nice to get out into the great outdoors.

Deep in Virginia hill country now, Alexander took the old Mercedes around the next bend, to the exit off of 23.

He'd be there in less than an hour.

(III)

The girl screamed as The Bighead et out her clitoris and surroundin' folds'a girlskin. Lotta blood down there already— from the corin' he'd just given her—and Bighead liked the taste'a blood, yessir, 'specially when it were mixed with the taste'a girlmeat. He'd popped her open fierce when he'd first slid his bone in, busted her up bad, but The Bighead were gettin' used ta that now. Had yet ta find a woman with big enough a poon ta take all's his dickmeat.

Too bad.

She were purdy, she was. A right purdy li'l thing he'd found by the big creek leadin' out'a the Lower Woods. She were bendin' over quite nice, pluckin' cattails off their stems, probably ta make cattail pancakes like the way Grandpappy showed him once. They were a might good.

She had barely no hair at all down their on her girlcut, as Grandpappy like ta call it, an' she hadda right nice smell ta her. Musky an' sharp, but not all stinky like most the gals Bighead had come acrost'a late. Had li'l tufts'a hair unner her arms too, which Bighead bit right out an' swallered once her was done bustin' his nut inta her bloody hole. She's also had cute li'l feet on her, tiny li'l things, so's Bighead brushed the dirt off the bottom of 'em, then et the skin off her toes, kinda like fer a tidbit.

Then he whacked open her noggin with a log an' et her brain.

Real salty-like, this one were, much more so than that last splittail. Meatier. Burstin' with flavor…

Gawd damn, but weren't it good ta et a raw brain busted fresh out the skull!

A'corse, 'fore he et her brain, he gave her butthole a good suckin' outs too. Bighead, he liked the taste'a buttcrack, he did. It were unyoo-sher-all, a word his grandpappy tolt him. Liked ta suck the hot poop right out'a that tight li'l hole, and it were always easier when they was dead. This gal here, this li'l blondie—well, Bighead could just tell what she'd et yesterday. Fresh corn an' ham hock an' steamed collard greens. Coupla fresh water clams in there too, he's could tell 'cos clams were always kinda chewy and'd stick 'tween his back teeth. Ta The Bighead, food always were best comin' out'a gal's butt. Ta be sure! Try it sometime!

Then he sat on a stump, lookin up at the bright blue sky, lookin' at the birds frolickin' in the trees, an' such other visions'a beauty. But humpin' that blondie—just thinkin' back on it, mind ya—well, it made The Bighead hard as Grandpappy's cherrywood walkin' stick. So's Bighead whupped it out'a his overalls an' jacked hisself a second nut right then'n there, he did. *Good* nut, it was, *real* good, like ta make his knees knock! He comed in his hand an' slurped it up right quick, 'cos, see, Bighead didn't like ta waste nothin', not even his own peckersnot.

'Sides, it tasted good.

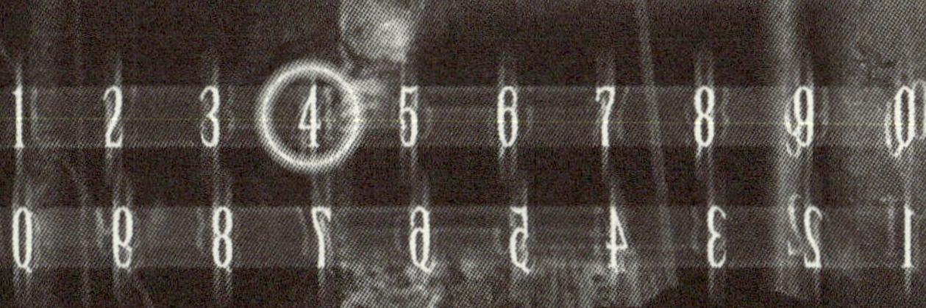

FOUR

FOUR

(I)

"My God!" Jerrica exclaimed, gazing out over the weathered wood veranda. "Look at all the flowers!"

"I know," Charity said. She was remembering more and more, just in the few hours she'd been here. Aunt Annie was a bonafide green thumb. The back yard, right up the treeline, was a carpet of flowers. Flanks of mallows and bluecurls. Dense beds of day lilies and chickory and blazing-purple bellflowers. A veritable explosion of colors and scents.

Jerrica, unimpeded in only panties and bra, seemed seized in awe. More to herself than to Charity, she murmured, "I don't think I've ever seen anything so beautiful in my life."

Charity distractedly agreed. What distracted her was Jerrica's state of dress, or lack thereof. Only moments ago, she'd boldly waltzed through the connecting door into Charity's bedroom. "I'm such a ditz!" she announced. "I was just about to take a shower when I realized I forgot my deodorant! Do you have any I can borrow?"

"Uh, sure," Charity said, and quickly rummaged through her suitcase for her can of Dry Care spray. The sudden vision shook her: Jerrica's physique covered so scantily. White-lace panties and bra, nearly see-through. Charity tried to act normal but it was hard. Jerrica stood casually in her underthings, long sleek legs rising to give shape to a physique of well-defined, feminine curves. And she was so *tan,* every inch of exposed skin a shiny, deep nut-brown, which offered a sharp contrast to the linen-white orbs of her breasts. Dark-pink nipples easily showed through the lace, and so did the puffing tuft of dark, blond hair at her pubis. And the white-blond hair on her head only furthered the contrast; like glossing silk, the color of bleached straw, it hung straight to her shoulders. *She's beautiful,* Charity thought. Certainly it wasn't any erotic appreciation by which she appraised Jerrica Perry. It was, instead, a diversion of observations: envy and objective surveyance. Maybe some jealousy too. *I'd give anything to look like her,* Charity pined to herself.

"You...wow. You have a nice tan," was the only thing Charity could summon to say.

"Thanks," Jerrica offered. "It ain't the sun, believe me. I go to a tanning salon in Bowie three times a week, year round. But...Christ, Charity." Jerrica, then, casually as everything else about her, touched Charity's shoulder, pushing aside very slightly the bra strap showing beneath her summer dress. "You look like you haven't been in the sun in years."

"I—well, I haven't, really."

"That's what we can do while we're here!" Jerrica excitedly exclaimed, her eyes brightening. "Tomorrow we can go out back and do some sunbathing."

The idea seemed alien to Charity, and she remained thoroughly distracted by Jerrica's close-to-naked body. "Uh, well, okay. That would be nice." Charity, sheepishly then, handed Jerrica the deodorant.

"Oh, wow! Check this out!" Jerrica was exclaiming again. That's when she'd noticed the open french doors to Charity's veranda. She marched out and gazed in astonishment over the heavy wood rail.

Charity followed her. "Aunt Annie loves flowers. That's why the back yard's full of them. It's funny, how well I remember it all."

Jerrica's sheerly brassiered breasts compressed as she leaned on the rail, peering out. "The only flowers I see in the city are fake." As she leaned further, though, Charity couldn't keep her eyes off the perfectly formed rump. More envy, more jealousy. Seeing her companion like this only made Charity feel more inept and dissociated. *Maybe if I had a body like hers,* she surmised, *men would call me back...*

"She's always loved flowers," she roused from her secret muse. Suddenly, and quite unexpectedly, she felt misted with sweat. "When I was little, before the state took me, I'd wander around the garden for hours, every day during the summer."

"I don't blame y—" Jerrica began, then halted. She pointed over the rail. "Hey, isn't that Goop?"

Charity hadn't noticed. But, yes, back by the compost shed, there he stood, a huge flesh-sculpture in overalls. Goop Gooder, her aunt's handyman. He was staring up at the veranda. "That's him all right. And it looks like you've got a secret admirer."

The moment Goop saw that they'd noticed him, he jerked around, went back to reeling up watering hoses.

"He's kind of, well—" Jerrica paused. "He's cute."

Goop Gooder! Charity couldn't believe it. *He's a hick!* But, again, she couldn't prevent her eyes from side-glancing up the sleek slope of Jerrica's legs and back.

"Hi, Goop!" Jerrica fairly shouted, and waved. Her barely covered breasts swayed—*more* jealousy on Charity's part—and her smile beamed down.

"Uh-uh-uh, hi there, Ms., uh, Jerrica," he blathered and went back to his work.

"That guy's a trip," Jerrica said to Charity. "He's such a cliche."

Wait till you've been in town for a week, Charity thought.

"Well, anyway, thanks for loaning me your deodorant. I'll bring it right back."

"Talk to you later," Charity offered.

And then, for the last time, Charity's eyes fell on Jerrica as she walked out and closed the connecting door between their two rooms.

Charity didn't falter. She rushed to the mirror, skimmed off her clothes. What glinted back at her was a body she hated. Her breasts were beginning to sag, her navel sunk, and her nipples were ovaled, so much unlike the pert, full, and perfectly round nipples of her riding companion. *And I'm fat,* she condemned herself, though she really wasn't. She had a distinctive *poshness* under her skin, not fat at all, and well-formed feminine curves too. But it was the sheer indefectibility of Jerrica Perry that made her self-conscious. She couldn't stop seeing it: that tight abdomen; the sleek, muscled legs; a tight, full buttocks. *I should take better care of myself,* Charity knew.

Her skin shone milk white, all over. Her pubic patch remained untrimmed. She hadn't nearly the muscle tone of her friend, nor the beaming vitality. And her hair, which she also positively hated, hung about her head in unruly, chocolate curls. Being naturally curly, thanks to magazines such as *Cosmopolitan, Vogue* and *Elle,* seemed like more of a curse…

No wonder men never want to go out with me more than once, she considered her curse. Charity was a beautiful woman, but she'd never realize that thanks to the brain-washing designs of a cosmetic society.

Her hand, then, very discretely, brushed upward against the gentle furrow of her sex. A dull spark shot off, and for a single second, her breasts felt tingly and full. But then it all collapsed.

Just like it always did.

She showered quickly in cool water, dressed even more quickly. Yes, it was wonderful to be back, but what did that show her?

More failure. More disappointment and unfulfillment.

Back on the veranda, she tried to erase her self-condemnations. She gazed out onto the explosive beds of flowers, inhaling their meld of scents. Coming home was just what she needed, but, now, it seemed, it didn't matter where she went. She would always feel second-rate, inferior.

An ugly duckling…

A sound swished at her ears. She gazed harder. *What is that?* she wondered. She was sure she'd heard a sound.

Then—

Aunt Annie, she saw.

Along the narrow aisle through the flowers, her aunt walked, her arms cradled with flowers.

Where is she going? Charity wondered.

There would be, of course, no answer. Eventually her aunt disappeared into the curtain of the woodline, and disappeared.

(II)

Gawd! Goop Gooder thought. Dirt scuffed off in his hands as he reeled in more hose, the sun on his back. His simple mind felt light and airy with wonders; he'd just seen the blond city woman, and with only her underwear on!

Done reeling in the hose, Goop scurried back into the house, carrying a bucket for some unknown reason. At the very least, he knew he was a handyman, and he figured that being seen with a bucket might make sense to an onlooker. Ms. Annie, though, had already left, with fresh-picked flowers, on her walk to the woods. It was something she did most every day.

And with Miss Annie out of the house, Goop didn't have to worry about getting caught, did he?

He'd found it years ago, the loose panel in the back of his closet. He closed his bedroom door, set down the bucket. He couldn't help it—he had to rub his crotch, and when he did so he felt that undeniable ooze of pre-ejaculatory fluid run up his pipe, because just seeing Miss Jerrica like that, all soft and tan in those pretty girl undies of hers, that had him hard in his pants in no time. He set back the sheetrock panel, then entered the oblong, black entry behind. A tiny pen light showed his way, through a modest labyrinth, and soon he'd arrived at the proper dot. See, Goop had long ago drilled the tiniest holes through the walls of most every room. The first hole he came to showed only Miss Charity, Annie's beloved niece, sitting amope in a different dress than the one she'd come in. Miss Charity was a fair-looking woman, for sure, but when Goop put his open eye to the next hole, all he could think was:

Gawd!

It was that city blond, Miss Jerrica, just stepping out of the shower. All big tits and tan legs and a big blond bush on her. She began drying off with a towel, kind of slowly, kind of like she was savoring the feel of that towel against her skin...

Aw, God...

Goop, of course, expected her to put on her clothes, and that would be the end of it. Instead, though, what she did was this:

She laid down on the bed.

What the—

There was this look on her face. Pretty as her face was, the look made Goop Gooder a bit sad, for it was a look of unhappiness, even desperation. But all things considering, Goop didn't pay it much mind when he saw what she did next.

Lying right there flat out on the bed, she spread her legs.

And fine legs they were, no doubt, long and lean and tan like those California girls Goop had seen in the girlie mags. And the plot on her…

She had a plot that popped a stiffer on Goop right quick. It was kind of a dark blond, and Goop ain't never seen a bush on a girl that wasn't black. But this Miss Jerrica, she ran her hand through it just then, and her legs stiffened, and her ass, well, it flexed up. And—

Good Gawd!

Her other hand slid up that trim belly of hers, and gave one of her hooters a tight squeeze.

She was just so beautiful, Goop couldn't stop himself. He liked her so much, and she must like him too, otherwise why would she have said hi to him when she was standing on Miss Charity's balcony?

Yeah, maybe she likes me…

Goop unzipped and had his dog in his hand in about a second. He was hanging hard, he was, and he got to pulling his pud right quick. It felt so much better, doing himself while watching a pretty woman lie naked on a bed. But then she began to do more, like she got to really touching herself, and sinking her fingers deep into her slot, and her pretty ass was squirming all over. Goop loved those white tits on her, and that deep white patch of skin just above her plot. The rest of her was so brown, like the toast Aunt Annie made in her oven…

Aw, Gawd, aw, Gawd—

Goop's balls pulled up as he was watching Miss Jerrica, and he shot a spunker right onto the inside wall. It drooled down like a long white worm, but, of course, it wasn't the first time. Goop had jacked off spying female guests many a time. Only thing was—

This was different.

It wasn't simply that he liked looking at this blond city woman. He could tell by the way she'd looked at him and by the way she'd said "hi" earlier.

Gawds Almighty, he thought, stuffing his deflated penis back into his pants. *I think I loves her...*

(III)

"Hold 'er down, Dicky, come ons!" Tritt "Balls" Conner exclaimed. "Hail! Ya *gots* ta hold her down harder'n that!"

They'd just got off a hooch run from Big Stone Gap just 'cross the state line, droppin' a coupla hunnert gallons fer Clyde Nale, when they sawwed this creeker chick lyin' passed out by one'a the fermentin' tanks. "Takes that alky bitch outa here, ya want," said the Kentucky cracker who runned the joint. "Blammed alkerholic she is, hangin' round here ever-day givin' my boys blowjobs fer hooch. We'se all sick"a her, we is. So's you take her outa here if ya want, fuck her, kill her, bury her, what ever ya wants. We'se don't wants ta see her no more."

Which sounded fine ta Balls, so he an' Dicky, they throwed her passed-out dead-drunk skinny ass in the back'a the El Camino, covered her up with the tarp and tooks off. Hour later they was back 'cross the line and she *still* ain't woked up, so drunk she was! Dicky parked the 'Mino up one'a the byroads off the Route and they'se hauled her out. Balls didn't waste no time gettin' the stinky clothes off her, and she were a sight, she were. All skinny and may-sher-ated on account'a bein' a corn junkie, ribs an' hipbones stickin' out, ratty dirty head'a hair on her, titties all little an' shriveled. Had long stretchmaarks, too, on her skinny belly, which meaned she'd had kids, an' they was probably retarts 'cos she no doubt dranked like a fish whiles she were preggered, but who know fer shore? Had big long dirty toenails, too, an' a yap full'a rotten teeth that was almost black and caked with crap in 'tween 'em. Weren't no prize, this gal. Nevertheless, Balls dropped trow, hocked a spitter inner dirty mufff, and gots right ta work. "Chrast, she a *bony* bitch, Dicky," Tritt Balls observed once he got ta humpin' her passed out girlmeat. "Fuckin' hipbones like ta stab me in the belly!"

Dicky had his dick out, givin' hisself a wank, but he just weren't into it. Wouldn't git hard, it wouldn't. "Shee-it, Balls, let's just leave and git outa here. This rummy ain't worth havin' a nut in."

Balls, still humpin' away, looked up a might disapprovin'ly. "Lets me tell ya somethin' Dicky. Hail," he berated. "If it's a hole, it's worth havin' a nut in, 'cos that's what holes're fer... Shee-it! She a *stanky* bitch, too! Ripe!"

Tritt's ass rose an' fell a country mile a minute, whiles Dicky just up'n shook his head, puttin' his pecker back. Weren't a whole hell of a lot'a fun roustin' a bitch when she were all passed out and smellin' worse'n a pig's butt. But Balls, he knew, were different. Shee-it, he humped *fellas* on occasion, when there weren't no gals around, and a coupla times he'd even humped hisself some sheep. "Hail, Dicky," he'd excused. "'S'all pink on the inside, ain't it?"

Just then, though, this rummy creeker gal perked up and started screamin', she did, once she were conscious enough ta realize what were bein' done ta her. "Hold 'er down, Dicky! Hold 'er down," Balls had then started exclaimin'. "She's fightin' a might fierce!"

Dicky feebly attempted ta do so, pinnin' her arms ta the dirt, but it weren't ta much use. "You dirty crackers!" she wailed, and then—ya know what she did then? She hocked a stinky spitter right in Tritt Balls' face.

Well, anyone who knowed Tritt Balls Conner could tell ya. One thing ya never do is call him a cracker, and another thing you never do is hock in his face. "Dicky!" he fairly yelled. "Git the ballpeen out the truck."

Aw, shee-it, Dickey complained in his thoughts. Balls were havin' another swivet, he were. That rummy gal got him *all* fired up mad. *Problee be outs here all night, so's he kin fuck with her...* Dicky retrieved the aforementioned hammer an' gave it ta Balls, who 'mediately brought it down hard—SMACK-SMACK!—on her skinny, stickin'-out collarbones ands then—SMACK-SMACK!—on her hips, so's she couldn't move withouts causin' a greeverous 'mount'a pain. Naw, she couldn't move much now at all—Balls' job with the ballpeen had taken the fight outa her a right fast, it did—but she could still scream ta holy heck, so's Balls, then, he stucks the hammer handle inner yap and pulled it back, stretchin' her mouth open wide, and puttin' a end ta her noise. Then he leaned down real close like, coughin' up a good many chest oysters and took ta hockin' 'em right inner open yap. Shee-it, Balls about *filled* her mouth up with his spit'n phlegm, and it were a might gross ta watch. Then he pulled out that hammer handle and palmed up on her chin, shuttin' her yap 'fore she's could hock it out. "Swaller, bitch," Balls commanded, increasin' the pressure 'gainst her chin. "Swaller all them there loogies 'less ys wanna broke neck. You needs ta be taught ta never—an' I means NEVER—hock a spitter in Tritt Balls' face!"

Eventually, the poor gal obliged, swallerin' that big snotty, lumpy mouthful'a hock. Then she bursted a fresh scream from her broken bones scrapin' as Balls flipped her over an' got ta conrholin' her real hard'n fast. "Hail, Dicky," he pointed out. "Ain't no shit up her butt, like none at all! A'corse, I'se guess that makes sense on account she probably ain't et no food in months. Just livin' on corn liquor an' all that Kentucky cracker peckersnot she suck out fer free hooch, huh!"

Balls worked her butt but good, humpin' it twennie minutes at least. Then he grunted out an' had his nut right up her dry backside, he did. "Hail Dicky, that was *shore* a fine nut. Shore ya don't wanna piece?"

"Naw, I'll'se pass, Balls."

Balls pulled out, wiped his dick off inner ratty hair. By now, a'corse, there weren't much fire left inner at all. She just lay there on her skinny belly, moanin' an' groanin', with blood smeared alls over her skinny buttcheeks. *Lotta* blood, it were, shellackin' her like a ten-coat lacquer job. Yeah, ol' Balls shore had tored her ass up. In fact, when Dicky looked close he swored he could see half the inside'a her asshole hangin' out that there busted hole, likes a bunch'a ground pork slicin's sittin' right there 'tween her cheeks.

"Come ons," Balls saaid. "Let's git outa here."

"But, Balls!" Dickey interjectered. "Ain't we'se gonna kill her? I'se mean, we *gots* ta kill her, don't we'se? The cops might find her, ands she could give 'em our descrip-sher-uns."

Balls sniffed his fingers after stuffin' his pecker back'n his drawers. "Shee-it, Dicky. Ain't not cops 'round here. Ain't no ones gonna find this rummy cracker whore this far back'n the woods."

"But—but—" Dicky didn't understand. "Don't'cha wanna kill 'er?"

"Naw, Dicky Boy. She cain't move a lick after that ballpeenin'. Best ta just leave her, ya know?" Balls brushed his long hair out his eyes, readjustered his John Deere hat, an' laughed high an' hard. "Best ta leave the possums somethin' ta et. They'll et her up good, those possums will, an' I'se say let 'em et her up *alive.*"

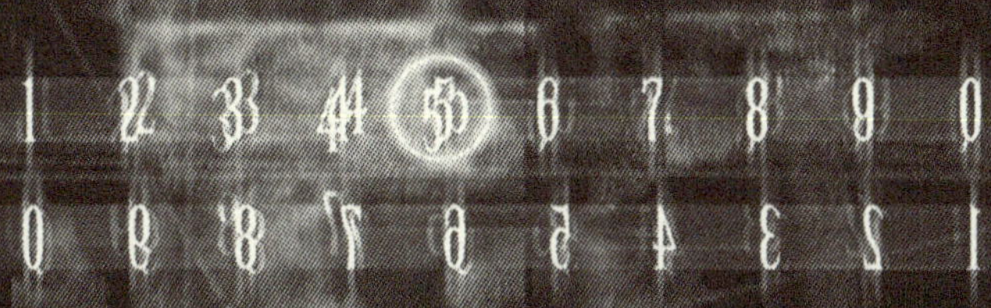
1 2 3 4 5 6 7 8 9 0
0 9 8 7 6 5 4 3 2 1
FIVE
ERIK
1999

FIVE

(I)

"That was a fantastic meal your aunt made for us," Jerrica commented, jingling her car keys. "Christ, I haven't had a home-cooked meal in—well, I can't even remember. Since I got hired by the *Post,* I've been living on coffee and chili dogs from the corner stand on 15th Street."

Charity's aunt had prepared dinner, and Jerrica was right, it was very good. Country fried steak, local butter beans, homemade sourdough rolls. Charity hadn't eaten much herself, though, her appetite stymied. Somehow, the presence of Jerrica's slim, vital physique made Charity self-conscious. *Chili dogs, huh? I wish I could eat chili dogs and have your figure.* Even Jerrica's scant attire—cutoff jeans and a parrot-green halter—made Charity feel frumpish in her plain blouse and billowy blue skirt, an old maid before her time. It was a peculiar clash of notions: that she could like Jerrica so much yet be so secretly jealous.

After dinner, they'd decided to go for a drive; Jerrica wanted to see the town, in order to begin some basic notes for her article. "Are you sure you don't mind showing me around?" Jerrica asked. "I mean, if you're too tired, that's okay; we can go tomorrow."

"I'm fine," Charity said, opening the passenger door. "It's funny—we've been on the move since six this morning, but I'm not tired at all."

"Me either. I'm really excited about being here." But just as Jerrica would start the car, a voice called out behind them.

"Oh, girls!"

They both looked over their shoulder. It was Aunt Annie standing behind the porch screen.

"It's getting dark, so mind the roads. And watch for the 'shiners."

"Don't worry, Aunt Annie," Charity called back, repressing a smile. "We'll be real careful."

Jerrica turned the small red car around the circled drive. She seemed perplexed, pushing locks of blond hair back. "'Shiners?" she asked.

"Moonshiners," Charity added the proper prefix.

Jerrica gazed agape. "You've got to be *kidding* me! You mean like white lightning, bootleg whiskey, stuff like that?"

"Sure," Charity replied. "Around here they just call it 'corn,' as in corn liquor. You saw all those cornfields on the drive up—well, they don't sell it to Green Giant, I can tell you that. Moonshining is big business in these parts, it's the only steady work for a good chunk of the population. Keep in mind, in Russell County, the unemployment rate is over fifty percent. Almost everybody's poor, so there's an instant market for 150-proof liquor that only costs ten dollars a gallon. But the 'shiners make even more money selling the stuff on the other side of the state line. There are a lot of counties in Kentucky that are dry."

"What do you mean, dry?"

Charity gave a shrug. "Alcoholic beverages are illegal, so there's a huge demand."

"Wow," Jerrica remarked, pulling off onto the Route. Gravel dust skittered behind them. "I had no idea stuff like that still went on. I thought it was just a southern platitude."

"Around here," Charity offered, "platitudes are a way of life. The 'shiners have to use the backroads to keep the police off their backs; that's what my aunt meant. They drive like maniacs. In fact, a lot of them *are* maniacs. I guess anything in moderation is okay, but these people drink corn constantly. It makes them crazy after a while."

Jerrica paused a moment, as if considering something. "This moonshine stuff is great material for my article, but— Do you think I could get some snapshots of a still, and maybe some 'shiners?"

Charity's frown made no secret of her disapproval. "Jerrica, around here you don't want to even mention it. Don't ask anyone about stills or corn liquor. And don't get any ideas about snooping around the woods trying to find a still. People get shot for that all the time."

"I get the message," Jerrica replied, going a little wide in the eye.

They drove on a ways, the inklings of dusk just beginning to touch the horizon. And, yes, Charity's earlier observation held true. She'd gotten up at five a.m. to leave D.C. by six, had been cooped up in the tiny car with Jerrica for over nine hours, yet she didn't feel fatigued in the least. If anything, she felt revitalized, shot in the arm with a brisk new vim. She supposed it could be attributed to an array of things: fresh country air instead of smog; the vast stretch of field and forest, unpocked by skyscrapers; plus the persistent rekindlement of childhood memory.

"Okay, this is your home, Charity," Jerrica pointed out. "Which way do I go to get to town?"

"Luntville isn't really a town, not as you would think of one. Just old, small houses stretched along the Route and the backroads. There is a main drag, though—Main Street, if you can believe that. Just keep going, then veer left when you see the white church." Charity let her thoughts swim then, clearing her mind of the world behind her. Raddled scarecrows seemed to stare at her from the endless cornfields. More fields of wild pokeweed shimmered in orange dusk, and beyond, sweeping hills offered the distant silhouettes of blooming white dogwoods, hornbeams, and groundcherry trees. The drag of wind caressed her face, like fastidious, cool hands.

Despite the tragedy of this place, the social grimness that reality had racked upon Appalachia, Charity felt the core of her own realities dissipate to nothing. Her admin job where she'd be lucky to get a raise to $15,000, the stifled city and all its impersonality, and—particularly—her absolute failure with men... This generally ran amuck in her thoughts, but not now, not here. *I'm home,* she thought obtusely, for it really was an obtusion. Coming here from the city could be likened to moving from one world to another.

"Here?" Jerrica asked.

Charity focused. The white facade of St. Stephen's Church approached before the orange tint of dusk. "Yes," she said. "Veer left onto Old Chapel Road. If you go right, you'll end up in the boonies."

Jerrica's slim, tanned arm moved adroitly as she downshifted. The car hitched slightly, the engine revving. They passed the church in a smooth sweep, and Charity felt suddenly blitzed by disappointment. St. Stephen's Church, once grand and cleanly white, stood now in something close to ruins. Time and neglect had blistered its pristine paint. The fine, glittering stained-glass windows were either boarded up or punched out, showing only tarnished lead lacings. One of the front double-doors hung off its hinge.

Gone to rot, Charity thought. It was a sad realization; in her childhood, the church had always been a proud landmark. Now, though, it remained only as a symbol of everything else around here. Dilapidated, sucked dry of its blood by ongoing recession and apathy.

Jerrica paid it no mind. "That church—it reminds me. Your aunt said something about a priest coming to stay at the house. To reopen Wroxeter Abbey. Will you—" Her words trailed, softened. "Will you take me there?"

"What? To the abbey?"

"Yeah." Jerrica's blue eyes thinned excitedly. "I'd love to see it."

"I'm sure there's nothing much to see. You heard Aunt Annie; it closed down years ago. It's probably in worse shape than the church we just passed."

Jerrica downshifted through another bend, her hair flying. "So? I'm dying to see it. I need it for my article. Come on. Let's go there now."

"I don't even know where it is, Jerrica. You're forgetting, I left this town over twenty years ago; I don't know anything about the abbey accept what Aunt Annie said. We'll have to ask her for directions tomorrow."

"All right. But I've just *got* to see it. I want to find out all about it. I want to know *everything* about this area."

Charity admired her companion's enthusiasm, however overstated. But why on earth would she want to visit an old abbey, or a still site, for that matter? *I guess this place is as new to her as the city was to me...* "Here we are," she said next. They slowed as the road descended, and just as quickly, "downtown" Luntville was upon them. Main Street looked washed out—uneven, drab buildings to either side. A red light winked from afar. "Luntville's only traffic light," Charity remarked.

"But...there's no traffic."

"Most of the stores close at six."

"But—" Jerrica decelerated before the light, glancing around as if stunted. "There are barely even any stores. Look."

Another sad realization, and more proof of this town's disease. A good many stores along the drag were locked up tight, FOR RENT signs taped to their plate-glass windows. At least Hodge's Farm Market hadn't gone under, nor had Chuck's Diner, which actually seemed to have a few patrons inside.

"Turn here," Charity said, pointing right. The car purred through the turn, proceeded past another block of closed shops. Then Charity, staring aside, muttered, "Oh, no. I don't believe it. Even the school is closed."

Jerrica pulled to a stop, eying the shabby brick building full of broken windows and chained doors. "Did you go there?"

"Yep. Clintwood Elementary. I was just starting the third grade when the state took me."

"Then where do the local kids go to school now?"

Charity made a tiny shrug. "I don't know. I guess they bus them to Filbert or Tylersville."

Jerrica idled on in low. "So far this little trip into town must be real depressing for you. Most of the stores are closed, your school is closed. The whole town looks dead." But then Jerrica gazed over the open top. "Wait—there's something. Those buildings there."

Several three-story buildings faced each other at the end of the street, drab and rundown as everything else, but their windows were full of lights, and within them, hunched figures could be seen.

"Sewing shops," Charity recognized immediately. "Unless you want to run moonshine, this is about the only steady work a person can get around here."

"*Sewing* shops?" Jerrica queried, a bend to her voice. "I don't get it."

Charity explained, "It's been going on since the mines closed. Out of state clothing manufacturers wait till a shop goes under, then rent it for peanuts. Then they hire local women to do the sewing."

"Why don't they just open a plant in their own state, hire their own people?"

"Because they'd have to pay them a lot more. Why hire state residents to sew for seven or eight dollars an hour, when you can truck your fabric here and get women to do it for minimum wage? When people haven't worked for five years, they'll take any wage. I guess anyone would."

"They're sweat shops, you mean?"

"Yep. Round the clock shifts. And no one is allowed to work more than thirty-one hours a week."

Jerrica looked at her. "Why?"

"Because anything more than thirty-one is considered full time. Then the home company would have to pay unemployment insurance and a higher state accident fund."

"Jesus. Corporate America. What a bunch of cheap shits."

"They'll look for any loophole to save money and exploit workers."

Dusk now bled more darkly into the famished recess that was Luntville. Jerrica turned on her headlights, took a pair of lefts, and cruised up the next block, where several more sewing shops stood, interspersed by ruined buildings. But then a lit sign appeared through the murk: DONNA'S ANTIQUES, and even this late, it was obviously open for business, for a lone man went into the front door just that moment. Down the street, several more shadows approached.

"That's about the silliest thing I've ever seen," Jerrica said. "It's going on nine o'clock. Who's going to buy antiques at this hour? And who'd want to open an antique store here in the first place?"

Charity raised her brows. "Well, because it's not really an antique store; that's just a front."

"A front? For what?"

"Donna's Antiques is actually the local bordello."

"You're kidding me? An old-fashioned brothel? A whorehouse?"

"That's right, I'm afraid. There's no police department in Luntville, and since Russell County is uncharted, there's no county police force either. The only real law enforcement we have comes from the State and a small sheriff's department, and they're spread way too thin to begin with. So they look the other way, so to speak, as long as things don't get out of hand."

"Unbelievable." Jerrica sounded astonished.

"There's a bar around here too, or at least there used to be," Charity remembered. "The Crossroads I think it was called, right around the corner."

"Oh, good," Jerrica commented, making the turn. "I hope it's still there, 'cos I could definitely use a drink."

"You're not serious!" Charity startled. "We can't go to the Crossroads!"

"Why not?"

"Well…it's, you know, for men."

Jerrica smirked. "What, bars are only for men?"

"No, but—well, it's not what I'd call…sophisticated at all. It's pretty rowdy, I suspect."

"A redneck watering hole, in other words?"

"Yes! They have dartboards and pool tables."

"Oooo, sounds like bad news to me."

"If we go there, they'll, you know, they'll leer at us. They'll try to pick us up! Really, Jerrica, we shouldn't go in."

Jerrica wasn't listening. "All right!" she celebrated.

Ahead, the high postsign blazed in blue neon: CROSSROADS. A long, squat tavern with tawdry blinking lights. "It's still here," Jerrica rejoiced. The red Miata prowled for a parking space. Music rumbled in the air, rising and falling as the front door opened and closed. Hoots and hollers abounded from within. The gravel lot looked about half full, with pickup trucks and dented hotrods, plus a few poorly-kempt motorcycles.

Jerrica parked the car. Charity struggled not to complain.

"Come on," Jerrica insisted. "We're going in."

Dust eddied up from the wood floor's seams as they marched through an entrance spotted with more garish, blinking lights. Charity followed reluctantly along, but Jerrica felt electrified. Yes, this was a real "slice of life" bar: a dump. Jerrica, of course, was no stranger to bars, but this place? Its frowziness seemed so genuine—its cheap tables and tacky padded booths, its dartboards and pinball machines—and this delighted her. She wanted reality for her article. Well, here it was. A working man's bar in the depths of Appalachia.

She needed her article to be more than just frilly trimmings; she wanted to relate the society beneath the environment, and what better place could that be found than here? From here, The Crossroads, Jerrica could make the most superlative observations as to the beating heart of this rural neverland.

"Oh, God," Charity whispered in a fret, grabbing Jerrica's bare arm. "They're...looking at us!"

"Calm down," Jerrica consoled. But it was true. The second they'd entered, every eye in the place turned to them. Big men in overalls, workboots. Beer mugs paused midsip, talk paused midsentence. Old men, bent and racked by age, young men, broad-shouldered and virile—they were all different yet all crafted from the same arduous mold. The jukebox twanged on in some insipid hybrid of hard rock and C&W. Charity urged them toward the back booths, but Jerrica insisted on pulling up two seats at the bar.

A lean barkeep in suspenders and shortsleeved shirt traipsed toward them.

"Really, Jerrica!" Charity whispered fiercely as ever. "We shouldn't be—"

"What's kin I get ya, ladies?" the keep interrupted with a high, tweaky voice.

"Two Heinekens, please," Jerrica requested.

The keeps eyes shot up. "Heineken? *Hein*eken!" he exclaimed, pronouncing the word as *hahn-a-kern.* "This here's a *American* bar, ladies. We don't carries none'a that foreigner beer."

"Oh, well in that case, two...Buds?"

The keep grinned through cracked teeth. "Comin' right up."

Charity remained sitting nervously on her stool, her hands worrying in her lap. "I feel ridiculous."

Jerrica lit a Salem. "Why?"

"I mean, look at how I'm dressed compared to everyone else. Everyone else is wearing jeans."

"Honestly, Charity. You worry about the silliest things. What difference does it make what you wear to a bar?"

"I just feel uncomfortable." Charity lowered her voice. "And what about all these leering men?"

Jerrica looked around. "What leering men? You're being paranoid. Nobody's looking at us. Nobody's *leering.* Sure, right when we walked in, everyone gave us a glance because they've never seen us before. Now they're back minding their own business. Look."

Charity sheepishly peered down the bar, then behind her. All the other patrons had returned to their conversations. Two men played pool, oblivious to them. "Thank God," she whispered to herself.

Christ, Jerrica thought. *No wonder she has problems keeping a man. No wonder they never call her back.* Did Charity act this anxious everywhere she went? Jerrica, on the other hand, couldn't have felt more engrossed. Amid the music, she could pick up bits of slanged talk. "Blammed plow hit a rock big as a water barrel, it did..." "So's Jory tells me I'se a idjit fer buyin' a D3 with a cast eye-urn engine block in the first place, says I shoulda buyed loominum. Shee-it..." "And when we'se opened that there silo—gawd almighty! Found ourselves three full acres'a grain gone all ta rot on account'a Roy never knowed he hadda leak in the blammed roof!" Two young women, dressed similarly to Jerrica, sat at a back booth, puffing cigarettes. "I'se tell ya, Joycie," one related. "I'se tried real hard ta git my G.E.D., but whens the project bus come 'round, I were so shook up over Druck Watter cheatin' on me, I couldn't even pass the 'quivalency appler-kay-shun." "Well, don'ts feel bad, hon, 'cos those crackers at the state wouldn't let me 'ply fer foodstamps. Says I makes too much money workin' at the sewin' shop! Kin ya believes it?"

Yes, another world it was here. Simple in its truth, and so real in its lack of veneers. Real people with real problems, however unadorned. The typical bar in the city would be full of phony pseudo post-yuppies listening to The Lemonheads and bragging about that new Lexus with the Nakamichi CD player and 12-speaker sound system, or lamenting that the condo fees just went up on the loft on Capitol Hill.

Billiard balls clacked. Darts ticked into cork boards. Then the juke changed songs: "Tar Water," by Charlie Pickett.

Jerrica sat reflecting, sipping her beer. She couldn't wait to get started on her article. There was so much to see, so much to write about...

"I haven't had beer in ages," Charity commented, breaking her anxious silence. "It's pretty good."

At least she was livening up finally. "See? I told you this place wouldn't be so bad." But Jerrica's thoughts, then, began to stray a bit. Perhaps it was the alcohol. They'd be here for two weeks. *Two weeks,* she thought. That was plenty of time to write her article but—

Christ. Can I last?

It was a scary question, and one she'd asked herself before.

"Are you all right?" Charity asked.

Jerrica shook out of the sudden mental freeze. "Oh, yeah. I just...spaced out there for a minute."

"Spaced out about what?"

Wow. What could she say? Oh, I was just wondering if I can go two weeks without getting laid? No, she couldn't say that! Instead, she told a semi-lie. "I was just thinking about my article."

"It must be exciting to write for such a big newspaper, and knowing that hundreds of thousands of people are reading your words."

Indeed, it was exciting, but that part wore off quick. "You get used to it. Believe me, you'll forget about that sort of thing real fast when you've got line editors and production editors and copy editors on your ass every day. Not to mention a boss who's about as amiable as a mad dog. I can't really complain, though. It's a good career."

Charity sipped more beer, loosening up now that she realized the big bad rednecks weren't going to carry her off into the woods. "What are your goals, though, long range goals? What do you want to be doing in ten or twenty years?"

A tricky question. "Well, I don't ever want to be an editor, and I sure don't want to be in the management office." She drew on the thought, lit another cigarette. "I want to be the best feature writer for the *Washington Post.* How's that for modest ambition?" She laughed gently. "And I'll be there one of these days, I know I will... What about you?"

"I don't know," Charity responded. "I've not very career-oriented, I guess. My job's okay, and as long as I'm making enough money to pay my bills, I really don't need anything more than that. I'd like to be an accountant, but— I guess I want more traditional things eventually."

"Like what?"

"You know, marriage, children."

Jerrica shrugged. That certainly wasn't her own agenda, but she could easily respect it. "You'll find the Prince Charming eventually. I'm sure you will."

Charity's chin dropped to her palm. "That's what worries me. I guess I probably will...but when I do I'll probably be too old to have children."

"Don't be ridiculous," Jerrica offered. "What's the rush, anyway?"

"I'm *thirty,* Jerrica. Not exactly a spring chicken."

Jerrica smiled, shook her head. "You've just got a case of the biological clock, Charity. Shit, women can safely have kids up to their early forties. That gives you over ten years."

"That's what worries me, too," Charity gloomily continued. "I've got ten years, but in the *last* ten years, I've never even come close to having a relationship. Like what we were talking about on the drive up. Honest to God, I've never even been asked out by the same man twice."

Jerrica's brow raised unsuspectingly. That *was* a bit odd, and Charity didn't seem the type to exaggerate. She seemed pleasant enough, and intelligent and thoughtful. A little timid, sure, and a little insecure, but traits such as those hardly made a woman anathema. And—

She's certainly good-looking enough, Jerrica quickly considered now. Perhaps *handsome* was more fitting a description. Her face was pretty in a plain, unfrilled way, and though she might be described as large-framed, she wasn't really overweight. A nice curvature, nice legs. And—Jerrica noted fully for the first time—a more than ample bosom riding tight in her dresstop. So ample, in fact, that Jerrica felt a bit envious. She couldn't imagine a single reason why men wouldn't take to her.

"It's like anything," she offered a simple aphorism. "Patience is a virtue. In order to get what you want out of life, you have to be patient."

"Yeah, I guess you're right."

Jerrica wished she had something more promising to say.

But the conversation had long since turned morose, so she got off it. "Excuse me?" she asked of the keep. "Could we have two more beers please?"

"Why shore!" the feisty keep replied.

"I'll be right back," Jerrica said. "Got to make use of the facilities, if you know what I mean."

Charity smiled vaguely, nodding, as Jerrica hopped off her stool to search for the ladies' room. At once, though, her earlier preoccupations reappeared. *I'm a clinical sex addict,* she reminded herself, and she knew she had been since her first orgasm at age fifteen. The teenage boy helping the pool man change the filter at her parent's posh Potomac estate. She'd flirted with him all day in her bikini until he eventually goaded her behind the cedar pump shed. She could've sworn she'd come the instant his roughened fingers touched her sex. Then he'd promptly ruptured her hymen. The pain had been intense but momentary, soon overplayed by waves of pleasure even more intense. The pool boy had been the hook which would change her life. Since that day, sex and orgasm had grown to a pining, even hell-bent need. It wasn't normal, she knew, to be so obsessed, but as hard as she'd tried, she could never help herself. The pining only grew worse over the years, to the extent that it destroyed genuine relationships, like Darren, for example. One man was never enough, not *nearly* enough. Like an alcoholic shaking for a drink, Jerrica Perry shook for sex. Masturbation proved a poor substitute; three times a day for the last decade, and it barely took the edge off her need. Many times she'd rush home after a sexual interlude—often after repeated coital orgasms—only to desperately retrieve her vibrator for what she thought of as her "nightcap." Allaying herself, trying to sluff it off as merely being oversexed, had long since stopped working. After hundreds of men and thousands of acts of intercourse, Jerrica was no closer to controlling her desires than she was over a decade ago, while the sweaty pool boy humped into her aching virginity behind the pump shed...

And now, as she wended her way cross the bar, she caught herself discreetly eying the male patronage, as a man himself might eye centerfolds in *Penthouse.* The younger ones all brandished hard, exciting bodies, somehow made more exciting by unkempt hair, work-calloused hands, and the scent of a day's work. "Hi, boys," she said, stepping between the billiard tables. All eyes immediately left the table and rose to Jerrica, her tanned legs and belly, her jutting breasts in the halter top. "Where's the ladies' room?"

A pause of speechlessness, then one overalled player finally spoke up, "Rat in there, hon," pointing to a dark hall by the payphones.

"Thanks." She could feel the eyes on her back as she proceeded, eyes like needy hands. She liked the simile. The two local girls in the booth glanced dourly at her as she passed, venom in their eyes, and then she arrived at the little hallway, transomed by a neon-red Miller High Life plaque. By the juke, more young, work-hardened men snuck glances at her body; several smiled. She smiled back, noticing the onlookers not as whole men but as parts: tapered backs, broadened chests and shoulders, toned biceps on sunburned arms. The hot visions nearly dizzied her. *Would I really go to bed with any of these guys?* she asked herself. The reply faltered, and perhaps so did her soul.

Of course I would...

"Christ, Jerrica, what is wrong with you?" she muttered subaudibly. FELLAS read a carved board on one door in the dim hallway. Then, GALS.

The bathroom was empty, cleaner than she would expect in a place like this. Cinderblock walls shined pale green from many counts of enamel. *No, no!* she thought, once in the stalls and sitting on the commode. Just seeing that crush of men left her tingling; she wanted to touch herself. *I am not going to masturbate sitting on a toilet in a redneck bar! Get a hold of yourself!*

Without thought, she scratched at her ring finger, then noticed the tan line. Darren's engagement ring—she'd removed it earlier, putting it away in her little travel bag as effectively as she'd put him away. It reminded her of what Charity said, about wanting "traditional" things. *Shit.* The things Charity wanted the most were the same things Jerrica threw away on a regular basis. When she'd stashed the ring, though, she'd noticed the small bag of years-old cocaine stashed there too: a haunting reminder. She'd had a bad habit just out of college, but she'd kicked it, so at least that proved she could kick something. But she kept the cocaine around to prove her resolve, the way an alcoholic keeps an unopened bottle of scotch stowed, knowing he'll never open it.

She sought more diversions as she urinated: the stall's walls. Trace graffiti could be seen, scratched into the paint. CHAD AMBURGY CAN GO STRAIGHT TO HELL! one woman had scrawled. Another: LS & MT 4 EVR with a heart around it, and then a more recent X etched through it. And another, typical: MEN ARE PIGS!

But the diversions didn't work. Jerrica felt flushed, winded by her own hot thoughts. She should've considered this before making the long trip. *What am I going to do!* The fever of her lust throbbed. Sweat began to trickle down her face. *How am I going to last two weeks without getting laid!*

Frustrated to madness, she grit her teeth and finished her business. But as she was pulling up her panties and cutoffs, she noticed a final graffito, scratched right in the middle of the stall door facing her. How could she not have noticed it?

The barely literate inscription read:

THE BIGHEAD'LL GET'CHA
IF YA DON'T
WATCH

1 2 3 4 5 6 7
SIX

SIX

(I)

Fer days now, The Bighead had been outa the Lower Woods, marchin' ever onward through the thickets and forests, yes sir, ever onward an' headin' fer the Outside World. A'corse, he didn't know where the Outside World was 'zactly, he just knowed it was somewhere. Grandpap had said so.

"I ain't yer pappy," the old man had told him so very long ago, just when The Bighead started to understant words. "Just calls me yer grandpap."

The Bighead had no idee-er how old he hisself was; 'n'fact he didn't really even have much of a understandin' 'bout time. He knowed he'd been a l'il tike once, and then he growed big. It were Grandpap who'd raised him up there in the mud'n thatch shack deep in the Lower Woods, and it were Grandpap too who'd told him 'bout how he'd et his way out his mama's cunt. Grandpap was a stinky, crinkly ol' fella, who had but one normal arm. The other arm weren't nothin' but a li'l twig'a flesh with a finger hangin' off it, an' the finger moved! Grandpap said this were so on account of his own maw an' paw was brother an' sister, which Bighead didn't quite understant. But Grandpap, over time, were the one who taught Bighead all he knowed, like words, an' how ta git food, an' how ta bust folks up, et their brains, fuck gals, an' the likes. Grandpap were a fine ol' man he was, and The Bighead had tears in his big lopsided eyes when

Grandpap died last week. Bighead et Grandpap's brains 'fore he buried him by the shack, 'cos he figured Grandpap woulda wanted him to, ta take all that knowler-edge inta hisself. And that's when The Bighead started walkin'. Shore, Grandpaap had taught him lots, but Bighead knowed there were much more ta learn, and that learnin' wouldn't come ta him here in the Lower Woods where he'd been raised, no sir. That learnin' could only come from the Outside World that Grandpap had talked about so often.

"People ain't no good, Bighead," Grandpap had told him shortly 'fore he died. "That's why I'se chose to live out here in the Lower Woods, ta be *away* from people. Don't'cha trust no one, son, 'cos if ya do, they'll'se screw ya over any way they'se can shore's shit. They'll'se *use* ya, Bighead, an' don't'cha let 'em. If ya ever hear anythink I ever said, here this, son. Ya got ta fuck folks up 'fore they fuck you up."

So's it was with this in mind that The Bighead embarked, leavin' Grandpap in the ground, leavin' the shack, an' leavin' the Lower Woods ta embarks upon the Outside World. The Bighead hadda mission, ta fulfill all that Grandpap had told him…

Two days passed and Bighead hadn't come across no folks at all, not since that last gal he'd spunked up an' brain-et. So's he hadda et a groundhog and a coupla possums, oh, yeah, and a big fat hognose snake. He'd chopped off the snake's head an' tail with his handmade knife, an' sucked the snake's guts right outa the hole in the middle. It were good, snake guts. But sometimes he gots ta worryin', likes maybe he should go back ta the Lower Woods, likes maybe he'd never find the Outside World. He didn't even know the way, he didn't! But he kept movin' nonetheless, he did, almost likes he were bein' guided by somethin'. The Bighead, a'corse, wouldn't know what the word *instinct* meant, nor *reminiscence.* He just figgured it was Grandpap's spirit smilin' down on him from heaven, guidin' him the proper way, 'fore Bighead just knowed in his heart that he'd find the Outside World 'ventually.

He wore what he'd always wore: the fine boots Grandpap had made fer him outa tanned deerhide, an' his overalls that Grandpap had stitched up fer him outa canvas sacks, an' the knife. It were a big knife, it were, which Grandpap had alsa made fer him outa shapin' a long piece'a steel an' stone-sharpenin' it real sharp, and whittlin' a real nice handle fer it outa cherrywood. The way Bighead seed it, he didn't need nothin' else.

"A fine, big, young fella such as yerself," Grandpap had said 'fore he died (Grandpap said a lotta things 'fore he died), "it's only natural that you'll wanna git ta wanderin' so's ya kin see the Outside World fer yerself. But 'member what I'se told ya. Don't take no shit offa no one. Ya gotta fuck 'em up 'fore they kin do the same ta you. An' 'memeber this too, son. The Outside World is chock fulla some really bad folks, so's the only ways ya kin git by is ta try real hard ta be badder'n *them.*"

The Bighead did not foresee a problem there.

(II)

She was just a little truckstop whore, a skinny little stringbean with long brown hair an' tiny little titties showin' through her top. See, Tritt Balls Conner and Dicky Caudill had just come off another *big* 'shine run fer Clyde Nale, and they was hungry as horses so's they pulled up at the Bonfire truck stop up near the county line fer some sam-widges, and that's when this little brownie-head whore come up the El Camino. "Hey there's, sweetheart!" Balls greeted, his mouth fulla B,L,T. "Hey," she said back, stoppin' at the open winder on Balls' side. She were kinda twitchy, kinda scratchin' at her arms, and Tritt Balls knowed in a minute that she were a junkie, and Balls noticed too just then how long her hair was, hangin' alls the way down past her little butt!

"I'll suck both you fellas off fer ten bucks each," she offered without hesitatin' a hitch. "Give ya's both the best pecker-suck'a yer lifes, I will. I'll suck yer peckers so hard your buttholes'll inhale."

"Why, hail!" Balls cited. "Hop on in, cutie, 'cos that shore sounds like a right fair deal ta me!"

Dicky, meantimes, kinda rolled his eyes 'cos he knew what Balls really had in mind. She climbed right on in, an' 'fore she could say another word, Balls had his big meat-hook hands 'round her tiny neck, an' lickety-split, he choked her little lights out in all'a ten seconds. "Drive," he said ta Dicky.

Dicky shoulda knowed. He cruised down the Route a ways, an' he didn't have ta worry 'bout cops 'cos they'd already dropped off their load'a hooch. He pulled up one'a the side roads past Miller's Farm, cut the bigblock 427, an' doused the headlights. Then they'se dragged the whore out ta the clearing. Balls fancied this clearing in pah-tick-ah-ler 'cos at night right about this time, the moon'd light up the field right nice an' pretty. Balls tored the gal's top an' shorts right off. Her skin looked kinda pale in the high moonlight, but her nipples were kinda neat, really big'n dark on them little titties. Stunk pretty bad, though, she did, which made sense 'cos no doubt she'd been suckin' dirty cocks all day, an' gettin' humped by unwashed truckers in their cabs. Balls didn't mind though. He flipped her right over onner belly an' started ta out a corn-holin' on her 'fore she'd even woked up.

Dicky stood aside swiggin' a beer. All this ruckin' they was doin', rapin' chicks, killin' folks, it were fun, shore, but more'n more it got ta botherin' Dicky Caudill. It weren't that he was turnin' inta a softie, or some faggot, naw, it were just the law'a averages that he was worried 'bout. Once in a whiles, shore, no big deal, but lately they'd been pullin' ruckin's like this most ever-day. *Sooners or later,* he fretted to hisself, *We'se gonna git caught.*

An gettin' caught'd be a right blammed bummer, it would! Shee-it. Fer what they pulled, they'd git life in the state slam fer shore, an' Dicky knowed plenty'a ex-cons who'd told him what went on. White boys, 'specially white *cracker* boys got turned a might quick. Turned as in turned inta faggots, yes sir! Most fellas in the stone motel, they was city bucks, an they was big, in more ways than one. An' white boys like Dicky'n Balls, why, they be turned inta genn-ral-pop cherries in less time than it took ta blow a snot out'cher nose. Dicky knowed full well that he wouldn't be's able ta hack havin' ta spend the rest'a his God-givin' life gittin' butt-fucked by bucks an' suckin' cock. Uh-uh. So hence were the form-er-lay-shun'a his trep-er-day-shuns. Doin' life in the joint. An' it could even be worse, couldn't it?

Yeahs, it could be worse than just gettin' caught, it could. We could even get ourselfs kilt...

It could happen, shore. Why not? What's ta say one'a these gals they snatched wouldn't pull gun on 'em, an' pop both he an' Balls fulla holler-points, or one night they'se could be jackin' some fella out for his green and they'se could wind up with faces fulla 12-gauge double-ought buck from a sawed-off. This were plain stupid, this was, pullin' shit like this alls the time...

"Hail, Dicky!" Balls guffawed, poundin' away on this poor gal's backside. "She gotta butthole on her bigger'n cow's, I say! Bet she been gettin' assed since she were four! Bet her *daddy* broke her in, creamin' her poop fer years!"

Balls looked intent on drivin' her right down inta the dirt, hard as he was reamin' her. "Aw, lordy ta shee-it!" he eloquented, then pulled his dog out an' shot a good-sized wad right on her back. Just then, though, she came too, groanin' an' droolin', her eyes aflutterin'. But Balls railed, "Aw, what the *hail!*"

"What's wrong, Balls?" Dicky asked.

Balls were there on his knees, his dirty pecker droopin', an' he were lookin' down a might disgusted. "You know what this cracker whore done, Dicky? She done *shit!*"

Dicky frowned; he could see it in the moonlight. Shore enough, she had crapped herself a lumpy, runny shit right there in the dirt.

"Got some on my's leg too, the dirty whore!" Balls grabbed her long hair, shook her head around to rouse her further. "What's wrong with you, girl! Ain't'cha got no manners? Hail, only crackers shit thereselfs whiles their gettin' buttfucked!" He jerked her head some more, whippin' it back an' forth. "An' ya plumb shit on my leg ta boot!"

Then he dragged her around. She groaned steady now, her eyes propped open wide. "Dicky! Git the pliers out the 'Mino! We'se got ta teach this here gal some manners!"

Dicky did so, not even botherin' ta wonder, an' cracked hisself open another beer.

"Eat it, cracker!" Balls demanded of her. He'd forced her face down right in front of her shit. "Eat that poop right up like a good li'l whore."

"No!" she was finally able to respond, hacking.

Balls chuckled. "Somehow I'se thought you'd say that," and then he took those pliers, stuck 'em right in her back, an' pinched up an inch'a skin. He squeezed the pliers hard, givin' a good twist.

The gal screamed so high'n hard, Dicky's hair almost stood on end.

"Eat that shit, girl!"

"Nnnnnnnno! Ya cain't make me!"

"Aw, shore I can, honey." Next, the pliers bit into the back of her thigh, and she screamed again even louder.

"Still ain't gonna eat, huh?" In the moonlight, Tritt Balls' eyes looked devilish, his hair hangin' in front'a his face like a reg-lar red-neck from hell. Next thing he grabbed with them pliers was her pussy lips, an' he clamped down *real* hard this time, he did, and this time the gal screamed an' hollered, "Okay okay, I'll'se do it!"

An' did it she did, all right. She put her face right on down there an' started eatin' her own shit.

"There ya go. Bet it tastes good, huh, whore? Eat it all's up an' swaller it down. Hard-workin' gal likes you *deserves* a good-sized helpin' of hot viddles."

Hackin' an' gaggin', the poor gal et it all up, she did. It weren't much poop, but damned if she didn't lick up the last right up outa the dirt. So's next Balls chuckled some an' said, "Dicky, that shore weren't much of a meal, ya know, an' a growin' gal like her, she needs proper noo-trish-er-un, what with all that hard fuckin' an' cock-suckin' she does ever-day. Comes on's over here an' drop trow. Pinch our li'l cutie pie here a *big* loaf, yes sir!"

Dicky groaned to hisself. "Aw, come ons, Balls, I don't wanna—"

Balls' face glared up mean as a weasel. "What the hail's wrong with you'a late, Dicky! You shore are turnin' inta a big creamcake!"

"Aw..." Dicky smirked an' moseyed on over, droppin' his jeans an' jockeys. He squated an' pushed, bustin' a few farts first, then pinched hisself out a coupla big logs'a poop.

"There ya go, honey," Balls announced, pushing her face down again. "Now *that's* what I'se call a *meal!*"

Her face white as a ghost now, the poor li'l hooker opened her yap an' got ta eatin' again. That first poop she'd made herself weren't nothin' compared to Dicky's big logs! Steam flowed off'a 'em, 'n'fact, an' bite by bite, she et 'em up.

"There, ain't that better now?" Balls made the inquiry. "Probably the first good meal ya had in a long spell, I bet. But now that yer belly's full, I reckon ya'd like a good drink ta warsh all that good food down with, what say?"

Balls flipped her back over and stood up. Her head lolled, her mouth droopin' open, showin' brown teeth. Then Balls leaned back, smilin' like that evil smile'a his, and let rip a long hard piss inta her wide-open yap. "Yeah, sweet thang. Ain't nothin' like a good, cool drink on a hot night, huh?"

Chrast, Dicky thought. *We gotta git outa here.* "Come ons, Balls. Let's roll. Just kill her so's we'se kin be on our way."

Balls was hitchin' up his trousers now, lookin' kinda funky at Dicky. "What'choo talkin' 'bout, boy? What kinda dag bastard ya think I am? Ya think I'd leave a lady here, all alone in the woods? No ways. The least we'se kin do is drive her back down the road, huh?"

Dicky didn't know what Balls meant, until he watched what he did next. Balls grabbed the gal again by her real long hair, he did, an' he dragged her ta the El Camino's rear bumper. Now this gal's hair, as were preev-er-us-lee stated, was, like, *real* long, three foot at least, an' what Balls did next was he tied that hair ta the trailer-hitch, then fixed a big hose-clamp around the knot an' screwed it down good'n tight.

An' what they did then was—

"Yeah boy!" Balls whooped. "We'se gonna have some *big* fun tonight!"

They went fer a *long* drive.

(III)

Charity's earlier reservations—about coming to the bar— diminished quickly with the introduction of alcohol. Instead, her mental involvements shifted back to herself, as they frequently did, to all the things about herself she didn't like, to all her failures. Her spirit felt dwarfed, sitting next to Jerrica...

As the evening deepened, so did the crowd; The Crossroads filled up with more of the same: rural locals. Loud, rowdy, hard-drinking—sure. Every so often, men would cast a glance their way, but Charity suspected that their appraising gazes were more intended for Jerrica than herself. The juke music played on, as did the billiards and dart games, the laughter and drinking and high-spirits.

While Charity's own spirits plummeted.

She tried to maintain the conversation—again, she liked Jerrica very much, and liked talking to her—but now, after five beers, she felt buried by her own reflections. Jerrica ordered another round, then nudged her. "Hey, why so glum all of a sudden?"

"Huh? Oh, I'm sorry," Charity replied, chin in hand. "I was just thinking."

The keep brought two more beers, then emptied Jerrica's ashtray which, by now, sat clogged with butts. As he did so though, Jerrica leaned forward, squinting. "What the hell is—"

"What?" Charity asked.

Jerrica's finger touched the bartop, the space the ashtray had been sitting on. "What is this?"

Now Charity squinted. *Writing,* she realized. Etched vaguely in the varnished wood, by a knife no doubt, were words, like a graffito. "I can't make it out," Charity admitted.

Jerrica squinted harder. "It says, 'The Bighead was here.' And that's weird. Somebody wrote something similar in the bathroom, on the stall door. Who the hell is The Bighead?"

The Bighead? Charity's eyes narrowed, and she remembered as vaguely as the words had been scrawled. The memory seemed a million miles away. "Its like a local legend, I guess."

"What, you mean like 'Kilroy was here'?"

"No, more like a resident bogeyman. I remember hearing the stories from when I was little."

Jerrica's eyes seemed suddenly enthused. "Tell me the stories. I can use them in my article."

Charity half-shrugged, numb now from beer and self-reflection. "I can barely remember, it was so long ago. Just some story about a monster-child who lived in the woods. He had a giant bald head and crooked teeth, and supposedly was a cannibal. It's just a story parents made up to scare their kids, you know, 'Be good or The Bighead'll get you.' Over time it sort of developed into a backwoods myth."

"Ain't no myth, girl, I'se kin tell ya." The rube barkeep's face hovered close as he replaced the emptied ashtray.

"Oh yeah?" Jerrica said. "Tell us about this Bighead."

The old face hardened, an eye cocked. "Ain't a purdy story. Might git you city gals all upset were I ta tell ya."

Jerrica challenged him with a sly smile. "Try us."

A pause, a hand sliding against whiskers, then the barkeep began, "This were long ago, mind ya, but it was outa the woods he came. No one knowed who his parents was, and no one'd wanna know, 'cos The Bighead were about the ugliest kid you could ever 'magine. I seed him once myself, matter'a fact."

Jerrica, obviously, was getting a kick out of this. "You *saw* him? You saw The Bighead?"

"That I did, girl, and I'se wish I hadn't. Wearin' old scrap fer clothes, he was, an' ya coulds smell him a hunnert yards off, I swear. You coulds always tell when he was around too, 'cos the woods'd get real quiet. Any ways, they called this kid The Bighead on account of he hadda real big head, like twice the size'a normal, an' there weren't a single hair on it, an' his eyes—Jimminy Christmas! The Bighead's eyes were big an' crooked, they was, an' reals close together, looked like a coupla hard-boiled eggs pushed inta his face, only one were big an' one were little. An' his teeth? He hadda mouthful'a teeth on him that looked like dog teeth, he did, an' I'se know it's true 'cos, like I said, I seed him myself. I seed him eatin' deerguts in one'a the soybean fields by Luce Creek."

"Gross," Jerrica remarked, paling. "Deerguts?"

"Shore," the old man bantered on. "The Bighead like guts, an' brains too. Liked 'em raw."

"Come on," Jerrica said.

"'S'true, I'se swear." The keep, then, poured himself a shot of whiskey, fired it back neat. "An' it were more'n just animals he et—it were people too. See, it weren't fer but a week 'er so that The Bighead went on his rant. Alls of a sudden lotta folks started findin' their livestock kilt, gutted. We'se all figgured it was a timber wolf 'er somethin', even though there ain't been a wolf in these here parts fer over a century. Then, a'corse, it were more'n livestock we started findin' dead. It were local folks too, all on the north side'a town, toward the ridge. Kath Shade, Vera Abbot, Vicki Slavik an' her husband Martin, shee-it, several more, cain't remember 'em all. So's we all banded together'n went out onna shootin' party, 'cos at that time we still thought it must'a been a wolf or somethin'. 'Corse, we knowed we was wrong once we saw it."

Jerrica lit another cigarette, intrigued. "So other people saw The Bighead, not just you?"

"Shore, plenty'a fellas. Cain't quite think 'zactly who off hand, but we'se saw it, all right. 'N'fact it was me who saw it first, in the soy field eating that poor deer's insides. I chased The Bighead, I did, an' the other fellas caught up ta me, an' we'se started firin'. I thinks we hit it, but I'll never be sure. The blasted thing run off through the woods, an' nobody ever saw it again. Next day we searched the woods fer the body but couldn't find nothin'."

Jerrica was trying hard to contain her amusement. "And you're saying that The Bighead murdered people, townspeople?"

"Shore am," the keep affirmed. "Murdered 'em, et parts of 'em too. Mostly gals. See, The Bighead liked gals even though he were only a kid." The keep's lips turned up. "He kilt a few fellas too, but like I say, it were mostly gals...*blond-hairt* gals at that."

"I guess I better dye my hair," Jerrica laughed.

"Ain't nothin' ta make sport of, missy," the keep replied with no mirth at all. "'Cos like I just got done tellin' ya. We ain't pos-er-tive we kilt it." Another quick whiskey shot was poured, and swallowed fast. "So's who kin tell? The Bighead could still be out there somewhere. All growed up now. An' who's ta say he won't come back?"

"Out*rag*eous!" Jerrica said, cutting the Miata's motor. "That old guy was a trip!"

Charity got out, closed her door, then they headed wearily for the front porch. "Most people around here are like that. They love to tell tall tales."

"The way he sounded, The Bighead was real."

"I hope you don't believe that."

Jerrica chuckled. "Of course not! But what great material for my article—a local myth, a *monster-child!* I can't wait to find out more about it!"

Just then they sky briefly alighted; Jerrica glanced up. Vague lightning flashed on the horizon, bereft of accommodating thunder. "That's weird. A storm's coming but the sky is almost totally clear."

"It's just an electrical storm," Charity cited. "It happens all the time out here in the summer. No rain or thunder, very few clouds. Just silent lightning. It's kind of spooky."

Spooky, hmmm. Well, after that story in the bar, Jerrica figured anything would seem spooky. But she held her gaze a moment more to the sky and watched a few more of the mute, distant flashes. *I'll have to remember to photograph that. It'd make a great time-exposure.*

Only the parlor and stairwell lights were on when they entered the boarding house. *Annie must be asleep,* Jerrica surmised. The grandfather clock in the den tolled twelve times as she closed the front door behind her, and after that: silence.

Jerrica nimbly mounted the steps while Charity more or less trudged behind.

"You look exhausted," Jerrica said on the landing.

"I am. All those beers finally caught up to me."

"Well, get some sleep—" Then Jerrica casually kissed Charity on the cheek. "I'll see you in the morning."

Charity smiled bleakly in her doorway. "Good night." Then her door clicked closed.

Before Jerrica could move on to her own bedroom, she noticed a light on under the door across from hers. *Who's room is that?* she wondered. *Annie's? No, I think she said she sleeps downstairs. Goop's, maybe. At least I'm not the only night owl.* When she went into her own room, she propped upon the windows, smiled with her eyes closed at the mild breeze. More lightning flashed mutely from far off. She didn't understand how she could feel so enlivened, though. It had been a long day for her too, the seemingly endless drive, then six beers at the local tavern. But she didn't feel the least bit tired. It was her assignment, she knew, that prompted this new elan, this vitalization. It was a rare thing when a writer could feel so charged over a project.

She reached into her travel bag, pulled out her Mouse Systems trackball; in doing so, though, she again noticed the small bag of years-old cocaine. This made her smile again, happy with herself. *I don't need it. I don't even want it!* Proof of her victory.

She input some quick notes into her laptop, the white screen aglow in her face; tomorrow, she'd tap out a working outline. It was a multi-part series, so she wouldn't have to fret as much over word-count. *I'll divide it into sections,* she decided. *Locale, history, economy, then the sociological element as a summation.*

Still, though, and late as it was, she felt too energized to go to bed; it would be useless to try. Instead, she took a cool shower, donned a sheer nightgown, and went downstairs. The hardwood floors felt warm under her bare feet as she traipsed through the quiet house. She moved through the parlor, through the dark country kitchen, eyeing the myriad relics and gimcracks. Old quaint portraits hung on the papered walls, faces peering through dark oil paint. The top of an antique high-boy boasted a display of genuine Depression glass, lovely translucent blues and greens. A sparkling corner caddie in the den—of perfectly rounded glass and gold-painted woods—shelved what must've been hundreds of crystal knickknacks. *For a dirt-poor hill woman, Annie's got herself a nice place,* she thought. And the house itself, though old, had been refurbished impeccably. New appliances in the kitchen, a great butcher-block counter that must've cost a bundle. Yes, the boarding house was beautiful.

But the real beauty assailed her when she stepped outside, onto the back porch. Jerrica felt stunned; she peered out into the flowered demesne that was the backyard—she had to actually catch her breath at the vision.

Moonlight shimmered over the trees, tinseling the exploding beds of flowers. A nightbird frolicked at one of many concrete bird baths, and an owl hooted at her from the high trees. Sounds throbbed in an uneven anapest, crickets and peepers sending out their calls of love. That, and of course, the strange lightning and its silent pulses fracturing the twilit horizon. It was a wonderland of sound and moonlit spectacle, a silent tempest. *I've never,* Jerrica realized, *seen anything so beautiful in my life...*

But then—

crunch

Jerrica's eyes darted toward the tiny sound. And then—

creak!

When she turned, her heart nearly ceased. A tall figure like a carven shadow stepped up on the porch and stopped, facing her. Big shadowed claws for hands hung at the figure's sides. Jerrica's sudden fear seemed to close around her head, like jaws, and just before she would scream, the figure said:

"Miss...*Jerrica?* That you?"

Jerrica's sigh of relief heaved out of her. "Jesus *Christ,* Goop! Don't sneak up on people like that!" Her hand opened on her chest, as if in doubt that her heart were still beating. "You scared the living shit out of me!"

Goop Gooder seemed to shudder at the respite, his voice pitched like an upset child's. "Aw, daggit, Miss Jerrica! I'se terrible sorry! I'se-I'se, aw! I'se didn't mean ta—"

Jesus, she thought when she calmed down. *Sounds like he's gonna start crying, for God's sake.* "Don't worry about it, Goop. It was an accident."

"I'se mean," his voice quivered on, gibbering, "I'se had *no idea* yous was out here, no I didn't. I'se *awful* sorry fer scarin' ya."

Jerrica rolled her eyes. "Forget it, Goop. Calm down." It was then, though, as the young handyman made another step, that Jerrica took closer note of him, his body in particular. He was dressed in nothing but jeans, his long dark hair disheveled as though he'd just gotten out of bed. Now his physique caught the moonlight at a delineating angle, and Jerrica could well see its masculine lines, the bundled pectorals and broad, tapered back—a hot lust-sculpture, a chiaroscuro of flesh…

She had to distract herself to say, "What are you doing out here so late, Goop? Surely you don't have chores to do at this hour."

"Aw, no, no, Miss Jerrica." Finally, the boy had simmered down. Jerrica guessed that she'd scared him more than he had her. He drawled on, "I'se, see, I'se forgot ta set the tammers."

Jerrica's brow creased. *Tammers? What the hell is a tammer?*

"Fer the sprinkler system, see. Miss Annie's got sprinklers now fer her flower garden."

"Oh, you mean timers," Jerrica figured out.

"That's right, tammers. She asked me ta change 'em ta make 'em go off earlier now that it's gettin' hot, an' I'se forgot, so's I hadda git outa bed an' do it. Didn't figgure anyone'd be up this hour."

"Charity and I got in late," Jerrica told him. But already she was having trouble concentrating. It always happened this way, didn't it? Her temptations rearing like a slowly rising beast. "We, uh, we went to The Crossroads."

"Ya did!" Goop Gooder seemed amazed. "That's a fine place, ain't it? Fine place fulla fine folks. I'se go there alls the time."

"Well, if we'd known that we would've invited you to join us."

Goop gulped in the silver shadows. "Ya—ya would've? Me?"

"Well of course, Goop. I'm sure we'll be going again soon. We'd love for you to come along."

"Aw, shucks, Miss Jerrica." Goop looked like he'd swallowed a flounder at the suggestion. "That'd shore be great, an' I'd shore be proud ta go *anywheres* with you an' Miss Charity…"

But already the words were fading out, as Jerrica's awareness began to shift into the ever familiar fever. The warm night seemed to lick her skin beneath the gauzy nightgown. Her mind in a swarm, she could only look speechless at him, and could only imagine the most lustful and even indecorous images. She imagined Goop's cock stuck in her mouth to the balls as her fingers handled his testicles like ripe fruit on a vine. She imagine the thick, salt taste of his sperm as he ejaculated, and the viscid texture of it as she swallowed. More imaginings, more images then, in a steady, hot stream. Then she'd sit on his face, let his tongue rove her anxious, open sex. She'd thumb his rectum and suck his cock hard again, and *so hard* it would be, hard as polished wood. Yes, that's what she imagined. And then she'd *impale* herself on it, let herself be skewered. And that would only be the beginning.

This was how it happened every time, for nearly as long as she could remember: her desires running mad in her mind until she could explode, and each dense image acuminating to an awl-sharp point. Back to earth, back to the here and now of this wild, hot night on the back porch of Annie's boarding house, and the stark flesh reality of what was dopily standing before her. Jerrica could guess where Goop's eyes were; where else would they be as she faced him in a nearly see-through nightgown whose hem ended higher than mid-thigh, and with nothing underneath? The night teemed. The moonlight limed his muscled flesh and its traceries of perspiration.

More dead-silent lightning flashed.

Jerrica struggled not to fall. "It's, it's fascinating, isn't it?"

"Whuh—oh, yous mean the lightnin'. Heat lightnin's what it is. Happens lot durin' the summer."

She tried to push her mind away from that awl sharp point of her senses, averting her eyes to the sky. "It's beautiful."

Goop stuttered, "So's-so'so's are you, Miss Jerrica, I means, if ya don't mind me sayin' so."

Her resolve collapsed, the keystone of an arch giving way. Jerrica's nipples felt like hot pebbles against the scant top. Her sex felt soaked.

She took Goop Gooder's hand then, and in a voice that barely even sounded like her own, she said, "It's a beautiful night, Goop. Let's go for a walk."

1 2 3 4 5 6 7 8 9 0
SEVEN
ERIK
1999

SEVEN

(I)

That weird lightnin' flashed an' flashed as The Bighead tried ta sleep. He'd cooped hisself up in the crook of a hillock, his mind racin' with wonderin's. He'd seed the silent lightnin' many times in the past, but never so clearly as this, 'cos livin' in the Lower Woods with Grandpap, the tall trees mostly blocked it out. But now he could see it just fine, and how weird it looked! And— And—

And it reminded him'a somethin', didn't it?

It reminded him'a the dream.

It were a dream he'd been havin' fer longer than he could 'member. Not ever-night but ever so often, and it were always the same.

The Bighead dreamed of a castle, and the castle had angels in it, purdy ones, three or four of 'em alls scurryin' around like they'se was scairt, and they'se was screamin'. There's was old men lyin' around too, faces peerin' up like big dry mushrooms like the kind he'd seed growin' at the bottom'a trees in the dark woods.

The angels was just so purdy, and purdier still by the way they was runnin' around screamin' like that. Then the eye'a the dream showed him two more angels, but buck-nekit they was, an' they'se was takin' baths in one'a the rooms in the castle. Well, Bighead, in the dream mind you, he didn't waste no time layin' some serious peter on 'em. He fucked 'em both an' drowned 'em right there in their purdy smellin' baths. Then busted open their heads an' et their brains, too. Afters that, though, he took ta walkin' round the castle, and tracked down those first four in their angel clothes, and they'se was still screamin' and tryin' ta run away. The Bighead wouldn't stand fer it, no sir, an' he fucked 'em, cornholed 'em, juss like that, left 'em bleedin' ta die, 'cos like Grandpap said, ya gotta fuck with folks 'fore they'se kin fuck with you. Bighead were quite randy in this here dream, an' he had enough spunk fer all of 'em, he did, an' he weren't stingy dolin' it out, neither! Bighead's big hard pecker shore did bust all these angels wide open, it did, an' some of 'em was gushin' blood whiles he were comin' in 'em, an' the ones he cornholed, they bled even more, an' when Bighead were done, they all laid dyin' with their purdy angel faces kinda frozen in fear, their eyes wide open, their mouths wide open too, an' their pussies an' poopholes droolin' blood an' shit an' piss.

So much fer the angels.

Then the dream took him further inta the castle, back ta where he'd seen all them old men layin' 'round. The Bighead guessed that the old men must be angels too, 'cos why else would they be in the angels' castle? It were a lot'a fun twistin' off their ballbags an' pullin' their shriveled old peckers off. Coupla these old angels, he made 'em eat their own peckers, he did, made 'em scarf their own dickmeat right down, yes sir. Bighead popped their eyeballs outa their screamin' faces, jerked their arms outs their sockets, busted their bellies open an' hauled out their guts. When he were gettin' close ta finishin', he found his pecker gettin' hard again, more good spunk buildin' up in his lower parts, so's he buttfucked the last few ta boot an' had hisself a couple more dandy nuts. Shee-it, Bighead must'a come enough ta fill a milkbucket time he was done! But thens he looked arounds an' discovered that alls'a these old men angels was dead now, an' all the gal angels too it looked, an' there weren't no one left movin' in the castle.

The castle were dark, it were, an' it were a dark night, an' Bighead, still in the dream, mind you, sometimes he could barely see 'cept fer the quiet lightnin' flashin' in the winders.

An' when he were shore there weren't no angels left ta fuck an' put a killin' on, he left, an' he stood outside in the middle'a that grand an' fine night an' he looked up inta the sky.

The lightnin' continered ta flash, weirdlike, with no sound, ands then, still in the dream, he heard a voice…

It weren't Grandpap's voice, no sir. It weren't no one's really.

Instead, the voice seemed ta sizzle in his head as he stared out at the lightnin', an' what the voice said was this:

It said, COME.

That were the dream that Bighead had ever so often, and that were what he was thinkin' 'bout right now as he tried to git some sleep by the hillock. What bothert him most weren't all them angels he kilt in the dream, it were the voice he heard sizzlin' like coon meat on the fire.

COME, the voice had said.

But—

Come where?

COME.

The Bighead just couldn't figgure it. Why in tarnations would he have a dream like that? One time Grandpap tolt him that dreams had meanin's, that dreams were like the soul callin' out. But what could this dream mean?

He knowed there weren't much point in tryin' ta sleep, so's he got up an' stretched, an' he pulled a long piss in the bushes, then shat up them possum and coon brains he'd et earlier, an' them dandy snake guts. It were late'n dark, it were, an' the moonlight shined bright in his lopsided eyes. He looked up in the sky and just stared.

An' that's when he heard it. An' he knowed he weren't dreamin', he knowed he was full awake now…

Yet he heard it nonetheless.

He heard the same voice from the dream, an' it said:

COME.

The Bighead, well, he didn't quite understant how he could hear for real somethin' he'd heard inna dream. But he figgured there was only one thing ta do.

Foller the voice…

(II)

The lightning flashed in silent whips across the windshield. *Heat lightning,* Father Tom Alexander recognized. Static electrical charges built up in a high-pressure zone. Common in mountain regions during the summer.

The Mercedes veered down the black road, Route 154. The lime-green dash clock read 12:58 a.m. How could time have gotten away from him so thoroughly? He should've at least called, to let them know he'd be late. *Ah, well. I've slept in tank turrets and rice paddies, in field barracks and pup tents and bivouac perimeters. If the landlady is asleep, it won't kill me to sleep in a fucking Mercedes tonight.*

He lit a cigarette, let the warm night air stream across his face. So far, at least, the place was well marked; there were signs every few miles: ANNIE'S BOARDING HOUSE, and Halford said his room had been paid for in advance.

His gaze strayed as he drove on. *Beats the shit out of Richmond,* he concluded. The countryside was gorgeous, he had to admit, even more so at night. The moon followed him like a gibbous chaperon, racing over treetops. The roads wound and wound; eventually he was there.

Decent looking old place, he'd give it that. A winding lane led to a gravel lot. Two vehicles parked out front, a snappy red Miata convertible and a beaten pickup truck that looked thirty years old. Alexander parked, doused the lights and cut the engine. All day now he'd been sweating in his black slacks, black shirt, and Roman collar. The latter felt like an iron cuff digging into his neck. He grabbed his suitcase and embarked up the steps.

A brass door knocker faced him, strange in that it was a face: just two eyes, yet no mouth, no other features.

Everyone's probably turned in, he felt sure now. But when he tinnily knocked, the door opened nearly at once, and Alexander was let in by a comely, white-haired woman in her sixties, in slippers and an indigo robe. "Father Alexander?"

"Yes, and you must be Miss—"

"Annie, please." Blue eyes beamed at him. "We've been expecting you."

"I'm very sorry for arriving so late," Alexander apologized. "Oh, that's quite all right." She showed him to a faintly lit parlor which was nicely cooled down by crosscurrents from open windows. "Set down your bag. May I offer you some wine?"

"Uh, well sure, thanks." Alexander smiled. *Actually I could use something harder, but wine'll do.* He glanced around in her brief absence. A quaint house, homey and genuine. From somewhere nearby, a clock gently chimed the first quarter hour. Annie returned momentarily with a glass of something dark. "It's raspberry wine, made locally," she said. "I hope you like it."

If it's got alcohol in it, I'll like it. "Thank you," he said. "My boss says I'm paid up for two weeks, correct?"

"Yes, that's right."

"I'll have another check cut soon; it looks like I'll be needing to stay a bit longer than that."

"The longer, the better, Father. We're delighted to have you." They both sat at a leafed table covered by intricate doilies. "So you've already been to the abbey?"

Alexander nodded, sipping the wine which was sweet and refreshing. "It's a mess. Eventually I'll be moving in there to oversee the repair work, and commuting to and from Richmond a few days a week for my regular duties."

"Did you have trouble finding it?"

Alexander stifled a laugh. "Just a bit, but I know the way now." Actually, he'd driven for hours, in search on Tick Neck Road, of all names, which, as it turned out, was not on the county map. "You probably know more about the abbey than I do," he suggested. "The diocese didn't have much to brief me with. Do you know how long it's been closed?"

An expression of brief contemplation crossed Annie's face. "Oh, I'd say they closed it in '75 or so, twenty-some years."

"It looks more like a hundred." During his excursion, he'd found essentially a vast vacant hulk, festooned by cobwebs thick as rigging ropes. It hadn't been anything like he would expect; the word abbey projected a certain image—he imagined a great stone edifice atop a hill, something medieval in appearance. What he'd found instead was a stark, cedar-shingled building with narrow windows and a canted roof, nestled in the midst of a dense forest. Most oddly, the building's actual age was given away by its outer walls: unlikely logs gapped by yellowed mortar, but then Alexander remembered Halford's expeditious briefing—the abbey was first built in the late 1600's, and its original exterior remained. A small bell tower, though, was the only thing "churchlike" about it. Inside proved labyrinthine, a single story of dark halls and boarded up doorways, and Halford wasn't kidding when he'd said there was no electricity. Alexander burned up three sets of flashlights batteries during his excursion, and he saw no evidence even of power lines ever being connected. *A wreck,* he concluded. *And it's my job to fix it up. Yeah, that's what I call God's work. They send* me *to fix up their messes...* Behind the building, in moonlight, a lake glimmered.

"I'll need some supplies rather quickly," he said. He didn't hesitate to light a Lucky when he noted that the old woman had lit a thin white pipe. She'd placed a turtle shell on the table for an ashtray. "I'll need alcohol lamps, flashlights, some minor cleaning supplies, things like that. I trust there's a general store or something like that in the vicinity?"

"Oh, yes. I'm sure Hull's will have everything you need. Goop, my handyman, will take you tomorrow. It's just in town, not far."

"And any list of construction contractors you could provide me with would be most appreciated."

"Father, Luntville's chock fulla fine, strong men who need work, and they'll work their hearts out, I kin guarantee."

Of course. Perhaps that explained the woman's enthusiasm over his being here. This entire region had been racked by grievous unemployment for a decade. Alexander, on the purse of the Church, was bringing jobs to dole out like an ice cream truck full of fudgecicles. The woman intrigued him, though, and he sensed her enthusiasm had deeper roots. Perhaps she was one, like many, who'd retained her sense of faith in a faithless society; to her, Alexander was a symbol of obscure power and truth. And, yes, she was quite attractive for her age: high-bosomed, shapely, keen and lean with no trace of the physical dilapidation that poor rural life heaped typically on the elderly.

She'd aged, instead, in fine grace. Alexander hoped the years would treat him as well.

He finished his wine, stubbed out his butt. "Well, Annie, please know that the Church most appreciates your hospitality and lodgings. And thanks for the wine. I think I'll be turning in now—it's been a long day."

"Well, like I said, Father, it's great ta have ya." She rose spryly, led him to the foot of the stairs. "And ya won't be disturbed none, either. Only other boarders are my niece Charity and her friend Jerrica, who's a big city newspaper reporter." Then she gave him his room number. "And if ya need anything, just come ta Annie."

Alexander smiled. "I will, thanks. And good night."

He trudged up the banistered stairs, passing framed portraits and still lifes. The house seemed to tick in its quietude. He proceeded down the carpeted hall as directed, and paused momentarily at one of the closed doors. He heard—something…

Murmuring, a woman's. Ever faint but undeniable. Modest utterings of what could only be described as…torment.

Someone, he thought without a doubt, *is having a nightmare.*

(III)

Charity's dreams flashed along with the silent lightning in her window. And terror flashed too, like vivid slices of glass-sharp imagery. She tossed in her sleep, routing the sheets, her sweat so profuse that it stuck her nightgown to her skin like damp tissues.

In the dream, men were making love to her, or so she thought. All the men she'd ever been to bed with were in bed with her now, one after another, different bodies, different faces, but each act of love was gruelingly the same, not real love at all but something short-circuited, perfunctory, and always so pale compared to what she expected. Steve, Johnny, Tim, Rick, and all the others, and lastly Nate. In the warm darkness, their faces appeared above her like a flitting deck of cards, and so did their bodies. It always began so nicely at first, always. She could see their penises, wet from her preludial offer of fellatio, each one as different as their faces. Some long, some short, some thick, some thin. And one, Nate's, beautifully large. Each time, Charity knew she was in love, until…

One after another, they entered her. She could barely feel the penetration but she didn't care. She cared about *them*, not the responses of her sexuality. She felt so charged up anyway, and the sensation of a desirous, naked man atop her was all the feeling she needed. They slid their erections into her, began to make love. Then—

It all fell apart.

Each time, they stopped after only moments. It was the look on their faces which startled her most: expressions of sudden perplexion melding to disappointment. What was wrong? One by one, they pulled out of her and left, claiming "Must've drunk too much," or "I guess I've just been too stressed out at work," or "Just not into it tonight," or any other excuse they could concoct. It didn't make sense. Everything up until now had gone wonderfully, and it all turned to rot once in bed. And one after another, they left her there, wan-faced and with tears in her eyes.

Every time.

Then the dream turned to hideous nightmare. The quiet lightning flashed and flashed. More men came, men she'd never met. Men from the future? Was this nightmare some mode of her psyche predicting similar failures to come? Grunting, faceless, they roughly fornicated with her, slapping her, pulling her hair and mauling her breasts, only to similarly abandon the wet confines of her vagina, electing instead to straddle her chest and masturbate. Their hands shucked vigorously up and down over their penises until their sperm jolted out and sopped her face, stung her eyes, fell saltily into her agape mouth. Then, like the others, they left her in the dark.

Charity tossed and turned. The sheets wound about her body like pythons. The lightning continued to flash soundlessly.

And in the nightmare's soundlessness, she began to hear a voice, like someone talking on the other side of a wall, or perhaps on the other side of her soul.

Yes, yes.

A voice…

(IV)

Another dream, in another room. Just images, just words.

Her own words.

The broth...

And her own hands, extruding her breasts.

Thumb and forefinger pinched the nipple, squeezed it…

Geraldine, Geraldine...

The match flared in the grainy dream-darkness…

I'm so sorry...

Then the flame touched the pinched, pink nipple till it began to burn, to sizzle…

(V)

They'd heard voices when they snuck back in. "Shhh," Jerrica whispered to Goop just as he would open his big hick mouth. "We have to be quiet."

The voices were coming from the parlor, she discerned. *It's Annie, and—someone.* But who? And what would Annie be doing up this late anyway? She'd been asleep earlier. But there was another voice, which Jerrica couldn't make out at all.

"Come on," she whispered to Goop, still holding his big redneck hand. *That's all I need,* she thought, *Annie catching me sneaking around her boarding house at one in the morning, after having just fucked her handyman in the bushes.* She grit her teeth, took a breath, then scooted through the den. Goop followed her like an obedient puppy. When they passed the parlor, she noted two shadows of people sitting at the table. She smelled Annie's pipe and cigarette smoke, and also glimpsed half-full wine glasses on he table. Who could Charity's aunt be entertaining at this hour?

She left the thought, and quickly mounted the steps, Goop in tow. *Thank God!* she thought once they got to the top without being seen. Then Goop blurted, "Aw jeeze, Miss Jerrica, that were really—"

"Shhh!" She tugged him quickly down the hall, stopped at his door. "Go to bed now" she continued to whisper, like a mother scolding a child caught up too late. In too many ways, in fact, Goop *was* a child: no depth, infantile sensibilities, no introspection at all. But of course, those weren't exactly the traits she'd been looking for out in the dark back yard…

"Got to bed now, Goop. Goodnight—"

"Aw, Miss Jerrica," he faltered, his big face stamped with a dopey, gushing smile. He affectionately clasped her hands in his own. "Ya knows, you's really do mean a lot ta me, an—"

She pecked him quickly on the lips, pulling away. "It's late! I'll see you tomorrow."

She left him with his lovelorn grin at the door, slipped quickly through her own and closed it.

Shit, she realized, *that big stupid kid has fallen in love with you! What a headache!*

And what a headache it would no doubt continue to be for the rest of her stay. Dealing with it would be no picnic, to be sure. *I'll just have to avoid him, politely put him off—*

At least the sex hadn't been bad, though, but then, to Jerrica, there wasn't really any such thing as *bad* sex. The moment, and its acuity, had overwhelmed her as it always did. All else on her mind had been wiped clean by his sudden shirtless presence on the back porch. She'd seduced him in place, about hauled him into the deeper regions of the moonlit back yard, where they'd fucked in the dirt for an hour, like intent animals. Goop didn't know much, but that scarcely mattered to Jerrica. Her sexual fuse was very short; her legs and sex were quivering before she even got her nightgown off, and her hand, roving up in the darkness, felt that he was already fully erect. She pulled him onto her, into her, her breaths desperate and hot in this brazen immediacy. His corded, muscular weight squashed her into the ground, a precursory sensation she always craved. He whined childlike and came in a matter of a minute or two, but by then Jerrica had already come twice, her drenched sex pulsing off as she groaned and her toes curled in the dirt. "Aw, shucks, Miss Jerrica," he stupidly tried to apologize. "I'se didn't mean ta git off so's fast, I'se just couldn't help—" Her hands pushed up on his massive chest silenced him; she pushed him onto his back, unhesitantly tasting the slick meld of his semen and herself when she admitted his penis into her mouth. She sucked him voraciously, playing with his testicles and perineum as she did so. Leaning over his groin, her ass jutting in the air, she felt the hot wallop of his sperm run out of her vagina and drool down the inside of her leg. She wanted more, more of everything she needed. Her breasts felt like hot rocks, tipped by the burning points of her nipples. His erection bloomed back in her mouth, in only minutes, after which she straddled his groin like a horse saddle, her sex wet and so aching with need she felt tears in her eyes. Goop sported a fair-sized member, which stabbed her at once. She rode him roughly, with wild vigor. They were manic shadows in the night, gulping the humid heat open-mouthed, their nostrils flared at their sexual scents along with the lush aromas of the flowers all about them. Each descent of her spread hips skewered her deeper; his sandpaper hands pawed her back as her breasts swayed, and she came twice more, heaving, her own fluids running like an open tap.

Jerrica was maniacal now; she climbed off to hastily arrange herself in the next position of invitation: hands and knees. Goop's erection pulsed upward with each hard beat of his heart. He was just about to enter her again, when she breathily demanded, "No, in my ass. I want it in my ass." "Buh-buh-b—" Goop stuttered. "Use spit," she ordered. Goop stuttered again, "But, Miss Jerrica, I ain't never done that before. I don'ts really know what ta do." Jerrica frowned annoyed. She spat on her fingers, reached back and lubricated her rectum, then guided his glans to the spot. "Push," she said. "Push it all the way in. Don't be gentle." Her relief came like a snug bottle being corked. Now his more-than-average size felt huge; it made her feel absolutely *stuffed,* and that's how she wanted to feel, that's what she needed. The slow thrusts heightened. One side of Jerrica's face nudged back and forth in the dirt. She reached between her legs and alternately squeezed his testicles and plied her clitoris until the fever of her need rose to a boiling point. The succor of her own fingers combined with his girth crammed to the hilt had her squirming, every muscle flexing. She drooled in the dirt as she came, then sighed at the feel of his own orgasm flooding her bowel…

Goddamn, Jerrica, she thought now, back in her bedroom. *I practically raped him.* She knew it was wrong to seduce a man like that, poising him solely for her own bent needs—especially someone as simple and impressionable as Goop. But that didn't mean she wouldn't do it again. She couldn't trust herself not to.

What a mess, she concluded. She looked at herself in the mirror, her white nightgown badged with dirt. But when she skimmed it off she found her body even more sullied. Soiled hands, feet, and knees, handprints of flowerdirt branding her breasts and belly. More dirt blackened half her face. *Christ, if Annie saw me like this, she'd probably throw me out of the house...*

For the third time since arriving, she showered, let all the detritus of her lust sluice away in the water. Then she finally doused the lights and lay nude in bed, thinking, cooling off. The fever had broken, leaving its familiar afterglow of paling anxiousness. She needed to come again, to buff off the final edge, but this late she didn't dare. Her vibrator could easily be heard with the house this quiet, and even if she used her fingers, she might sigh too loudly or even cry out.

Good God, Jerrica. What is wrong with you?

She tried to objectify, to excuse herself as she always did. *I had an itch and I scratched it,* she reasoned, then, more crudely, *My pussy itched and I scratched it with Goop's cock. Oh, yeah, and I guess my ass itched too.* No, she couldn't excuse herself, not really. Sex addict notwithstanding, she was still a civil human being, and she knew what she'd done was wrong. *I seduced some hick kid who has a crush on me. I* used *him.*

She tried to just forget it, get some sleep. By now, the heat lightning had subsided, leaving her alone in darkness only vaguely patina'd by moonlight. The moisture from the shower turned warm on her skin; her fingers idled through damp pubic hair. Through the wall, she could hear Charity moaning in her sleep. *Nightmare,* Jerrica deduced. *Poor Charity...*

But then she heard something else, not from the other side of the wall but beyond her bedroom door.

Footsteps.

Who's up here now?

She got up, crept nude to the door. The footsteps, unbroken in their pace, passed the door and proceeded. She couldn't resist.

She opened her door just an inch and peered one-eyed down the hall. A figure stood at the end door, a figure in black. It turned momentarily, as if on guard. The exposed white square of the Roman collar glinted.

The priest. He's here.

He glanced vaguely down the hall, shrugged, then entered his room.

Jerrica reclosed her own door, squinting puzzlement in the dark. The priest was here—so what? For some reason, though, the figure's late-night arrival seemed foreboding, bidding a strange undertow of dread. Perhaps God was sending him as an image to remind her of her guilt. Jerrica shrugged herself then. She didn't believe in God anyway.

But she must believe in the devil, if only subconsciously, for what else could explain the dream she had minutes later when she fell asleep?

She dreamed of rising from a tarn of steaming excrement; she'd been close to drowning in it, and when her face finally broke surface, she gagged, hacking up collops of shit. Squab hands were hauling her forth, to a narrow brink of hot, slimy sand. But they were not men who were hauling her out, they were *things,* they were ushers of this demonian realm. With faces of clay and chisel slits for eyes, they looked down at her, grinning, chuckling in suboctave delight. And endless ridge of fire-blackened rock surrounded the tarn. The sky was blood-red, with a black moon beaming down. Jerrica struggled to no avail. The ushers molested her with fervency, their fat three-fingered hands probed her naked, enslimed body, such that in only moments she wished she could be back in the tarn, to drown in feces. The chuckles rose, as did luciferic erections. One usher's hands spread her buttocks, while another's monster-cock bulled unabated into her rectum. Jerrica vomited, screaming. The scream echoed round the chasm like a gunshot. The stout cock in her colon seemed to grow with the tenor of her horror. It grew and grew, yes, extending up threw her guts, until its peach-sized glans was running up her throat, whereupon it eventually exited her mouth.

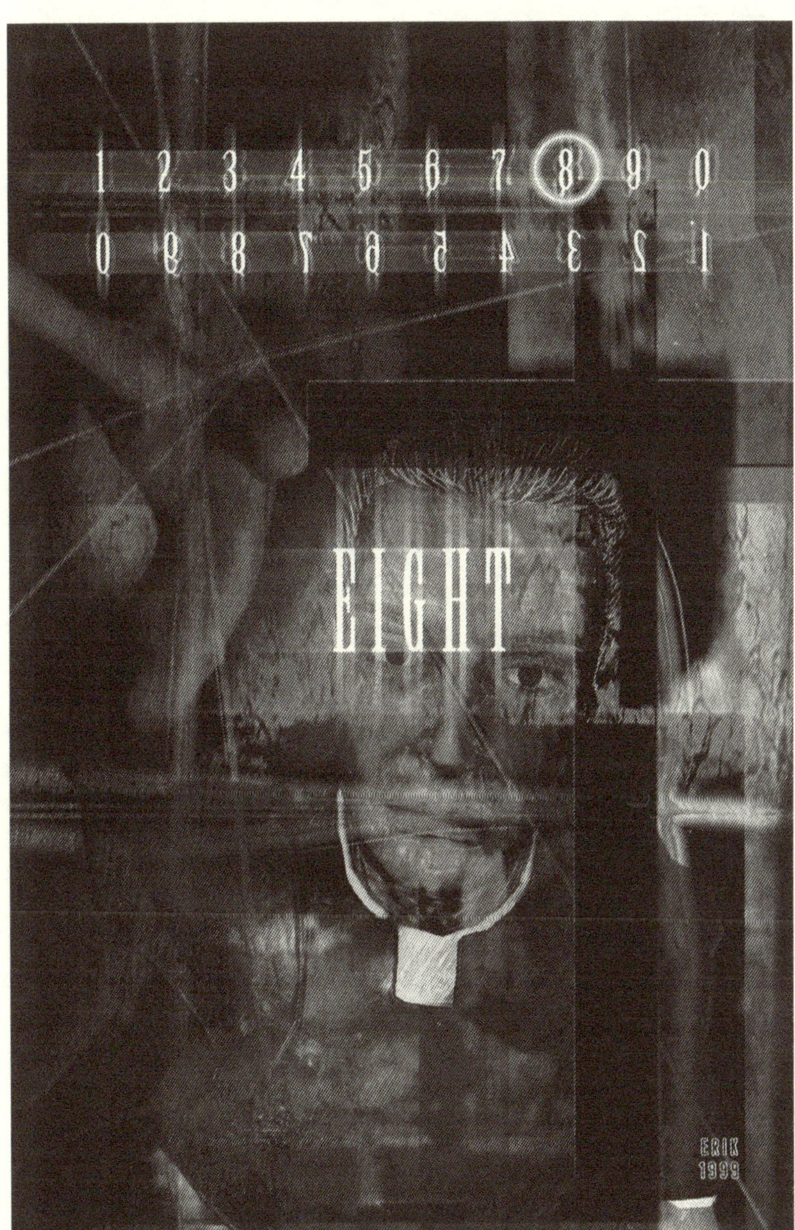
1 2 3 4 5 6 7 8 9 0
EIGHT
ERIK
1999

EIGHT

(I)

tap-tap-tap

Charity's left eye popped open, the right side of her face burrowed in the pillow. *Morning?* she thought. *Already?* Sunlight radiated in the panes of the french doors; birds could be heard, chirping their avian celebration.

tap-tap-tap

"Charity? You awake?"

"Yeah," came her groggy reply. "Come on in."

Jerrica entered through the connecting door, her blond hair tousled from sleep. All she wore was a single bedsheet wrapped about her. "I guess we should rise and shine, as they say."

"Who's *they?*" Charity groaned. "I can't believe it's morning already. It seems like I went to bed about fifteen minutes ago. And—" Her whole face pinched up, and she brought a hand to her forehead. "Boy, did I have a nightmare."

Jerrica laughed. "Don't feel too bad. I'm sure it wasn't as gross as the nightmare *I* had. Shit. I dreamed I went to hell." She made a *yuck* face. "I dreamed that demons were raping me. It was disgusting!"

This made Charity feel a bit better; her own pallid nightmare had been spared, at least, of demons. The rape had been perfunctory.

Jerrica lazily smoked a cigarette. "Oh, and guess what? The priest is here."

Priest. Oh, yeah, Charity recalled now. *Aunt Annie mentioned him yesterday, something about coming to inspect the abbey.*

"Maybe I can talk him to taking me to the abbey."

Charity sat up in bed, rubbed her eyes. "When did he get in?"

"Last night," Jerrica answered. Now she was looking out the french doors, into the garden. "It was about one."

"One! I thought you went right to bed when we got back from the bar. What were you doing up that late?"

Jerrica turned, chewing her lip. "Well, I kind of…"

"What?"

Jerrica huffed a sigh. "I kind of ran into Goop. I went out on the back porch for some fresh air, and he was there adjusting the sprinklers or something, and, well, you know." Charity couldn't quite believe the implication. "Jerrica, you didn't! With *Goop?*"

Jerrica nodded, shame-faced. "It was just one of those things, I guess. He was there, I was there—then one thing led to another."

"Where?"

"In the back yard."

"You're kidding!"

Jerrica shook her head, spewing cigarette smoke.

"But Goop is, like—isn't he retarded?"

"No, he's a little slow, maybe," Jerrica observed. "He's not *retarded,* for God's sake. Kind of a bumpkin is all. And that's not the problem. It's obvious, he's got a bigtime crush on me."

"That *is* a problem," Charity agreed. She still couldn't believe it, though. *Jerrica had sex...with Goop?* Well, she supposed he was attractive, in an earthy, unsophisticated way. But she hadn't even been here one day! "You sure move fast," she said, finally climbing out of bed. She blanched a moment, recalling her lurid dreams. But then the most unusual question occurred to her. "Can I ask you something—personal?"

"Sure." Jerrica half-chuckled. "Personal questions are the best kind."

Charity's voice lowered. "Was it—you know—was it…good?"

"Yeah, actually it was," Jerrica responded without a second's pause. "It was real good. But it was just a one-night thing, you know, and like I was saying before, the kid's hung up on me. It could be a mess."

Charity couldn't argue. "You got that right. A guy like Goop? He'll be following you around like a little poodle."

Jerrica maintained a steady frown at her predicament. "I'll just have to steer clear of him, give him the polite cold shoulder. I don't want to hurt his feelings, but, Christ—" She didn't even bother finishing.

More atypical questions assailed Charity. She couldn't imagine why. *How long did they do it? How many times? Did she...come?*

It simply blurted out of her before she could even think. "Did you come?" she asked.

Jerrica shot her an amused look. She was obviously not the type to be offended by such a query, but it was clear she was a bit surprised. "I just told you it was good. Of course I came. A bunch of times."

Another pang of jealousy. Jerrica's looks, her out-goingness and overall personality already made Charity feel secretly inept. Now this. *I've never had an orgasm in my life,* she thought, *and Jerrica talks about it like she's having another cigarette.*

"Enough of this sex-with-Goop talk," Jerrica proposed. "We better get our butts in gear and get downstairs. Your aunt'll think we're a couple of lazies. And I can't *wait* to meet the priest!"

(II)

The nun was pissing up his ass...

Holy...shit, Alexander thought.

He jerked up in bed, a bad taste in his mouth. Perhaps it was a veritable *night* of dreams, an encampment of nightmares, for Father

Tom Alexander had had a nightmare of his own, from which he'd just wakened. Hideous. Disgusting…

He'd dreamed that he was staked to the ground, naked, on his belly. His wrists and ankles chafed within girds of bristly rope. Who had tied him down? And why? And—

Where am I? his thoughts struggled.

In the dream, a shadow crossed the floor. He craned his neck, to glance up over his shoulder the best he could. Eventually, he spied the figure projecting the shadow.

A nun.

"What the fuck is this?" Alexander demanded in the dream. "Un-fucking-tie me right now, goddamn it!"

Her voice was a whisper, fragile as perfume, and vaguely southern. "Though shalt not take the name of the Lord thy God in vain."

"Yeah?" the priest retorted. "And though shalt not tie fucking *priests* naked to the fucking floor!"

"But it's only a dream," the nun pointed out.

"I don't give a shit," Alexander continued to profane. "I don't like it, so untie me! I feel like a fucking idiot tied naked to the floor in front of a nun!"

But she was a beautiful nun, he noted in time. Her delicate white hands steepled at her bosom, as if reciting a standing prayer. She wore a traditional black habit, but stood in bare feet rather than the expected black clunky shoes. A lean, pretty face seemed mounted in the open oval of her white wimple. It was a sedate face, but wanton. Clear brown eyes beamed down on him, shining in honesty and faith. In reverence to God on high.

So why was Alexander tied up?

"We've been cleansed now," she said. "We've been purged. It feels so good…" Her brown eyes focused more sharply. "Wouldn't you like to be purged?"

"No!" Alexander bellowed. "I'd like to be *un-fucking-tied!* That's what I'd like to be!"

She didn't so much as flinch at his rant. Instead, she smiled ever so faintly, a nun's smile, and then she—

"You gotta be shitting me," Alexander muttered, still peering painfully over his shoulder.

—hiked up the skirt-section of her habit. She wore no typical black legsocks, no linens beneath. The vision, at once, seemed to bark at him. Two slim, pretty legs stood spread above him, joined by a bountiful plot of black pubic hair. Fainter hair trailed wispishly down the insides of her white thighs, while an even fainter lance rose upward, to her navel.

"Ever heard of Lady Remington?" Alexander said.

"The purging is upon us, Father," her dainty voice embarked. "And it's upon *you.*"

Holding the bunched habit above her waistline, she awkwardly stepped forward, behind him. She stood with her feet on either side of his bare hips, her bushy pubis directly above his buttocks.

"Ahhhh," she murmured.

She began to urinate.

"What the FUCK!" Alexander yelled, helpless against his fetters.

She pissed hard. The stream was hot, and firing directly into the cleft of Alexander's clenched buttocks.

"Stop it!" he yelled.

She didn't stop it. Instead, the force of the urine accelerated. It stung, expelling in a pinpoint line to his rectal orifice, and eventually its velocity rose to such an extreme that it was actually entering his anus. Soon he could feel it, he could feel the droll nun's piss forcing its way into his rectal canal. And piss she did, on and on…

"What are you, a fucking race horse!" he shouted.

It seemed to go on for an hour, her urine firing precisely as a laser, jetting from the plush plot of hair.

"Aw, gimme a break!" Alexander groaned. "You're pissing enough to fill a gasoline truck!"

Eventually, and thankfully, the stream abated, dying to a trickle which dribbled onto his calves. But in the aftermath, he could feel it all in there, all that hot urine wobbling, filling his large intestine to the point of distention, and slowly working its way up into his alimentary canal…

"There," the nun said. She dropped her habit. "Doesn't it feel good, Father? Doesn't it feel good to finally be purged?"

The image followed him, like a buzzing pest. When Alexander leapt out of bed, he rushed immediately—if out of reflex—to the bathroom, where he immediately defecated. No urine, of course, was forthcoming, but he felt obliged to do so regardless. Then he showered and shaved, dressed quickly in his black slacks and shirt, affixed his collar. But the image wouldn't leave him.

The nun, he thought.

Christ.

"I should see a psychologist," he considered, then stalled. "Wait a minute. *I'm* a psychologist!" But what could explain such a disgusting dream? Dreams, after all, were born in the psyches of the dreamer. It was *part* of him, in other words… Christ.

Eventually he got moving, went downstairs and looked around. There was no sign of Annie, the proprietor. But when he turned through the kitchen into the dining room, he saw two attractive women sitting at the veneered table, eating. One blond, one brunette. They both glanced up in unison.

"Good morning," he said. "I'm Father Alexander."

"Hi, Father," said the blonde. The brunette smiled curtly and nodded.

"I'm rooming here for awhile."

"We know, Annie told us," said the blonde. "I'm—"

"Don't tell me." Alexander held up his hand. "You're Annie's niece, and you—" he pointed to the brunette. "You must be the newspaper reporter."

"You got it backwards," the blonde told him, laughing. "I'm Jerrica, the reporter, and this is Charity, Annie's niece."

"Nice to meet you both." They all shook hands; Alexander sat down.

"Would you like some funnelcakes, Father?" Charity offered, extending her hand to a plate full of squiggly looking pieces of fried dough beside which sat a small bowl of molasses.

"No thanks. They look great, but I'm never hungry in the morning." Then he looked more closely at both women. Charity was dressed primly in a billowy, flowered summer dress. Jerrica wore cutoff jeans and a white halter. But both their faces, pretty as they were, looked drained somehow, depleted.

Then Jerrica, the blonde, spoke up. "You're probably noticing how ragged out we both look, Father. It's because we both had outrageous nightmares last night."

Alexander felt his brow go rigid. "Well, then, nightmares must be contagious around here, because I had a hum-dinger."

"Oh, yeah? We'll tell ours if you tell yours."

Ho! Alexander thought. *I dreamed that I got a piss-enema from a nun. That's not the kind of thing I really want to tell people about.* "Forget it," he said instead. "One time I dreamed that the Pope and I were playing volleyball, and he was kicking my butt; dreams are a lot of laughs sometimes. But, believe me, this one's worth forgetting."

"Aunt Annie said you're here to rebuild the old abbey," Charity said.

"Not rebuild it, restore it," Alexander corrected.

"It used to be a convalescent home for priests, right?" Jerrica ventured.

Precocious, Alexander thought. "Something like that. What we're going to turn it into now is a rehab center." Alexander knew the rap. Lately the Catholics were getting trashed bigtime. Lots of priests up on allegations of child molestation, drug addiction, gambling. That's all that filled the papers these days, and no doubt Jerrica, a journalist herself, had made the connection. Christ, they were probably going to close down St. Luke's in Suitland, the rap was so hot. The local residents were protesting, said they feared for their children should a sick priest escape.

"I'll be the first to admit," he came clean. "The Catholic Church is looking for remote places to field their rehab centers. Priests are like anyone else: sometimes they get sick. But in the old days, Wroxeter Abbey wasn't a rehab, it was a hospice for dying priests. It was a long time ago, mid-70s. We had a bunch of Epiphanist nuns running the place. They were just back from Africa, and they had nothing to do, so the Pope gives them this gig." Alexander noticed another turtle shell on the table, and lit up. "Cancer, Alzhiemer's, and just plain old age—"

"AIDS too, right?" Jerrica challenged.

He didn't jive her. "Probably, before AIDS was an official diagnosis, sure. Sometimes priests go astray, the Church has never denied that. But when they become terminal, we needed a place to put them that was cheaper than a hospital. So we make hospices, and that's what Wroxeter was."

"But it closed down, didn't it?" Charity asked.

"Yeah. It wasn't very full, and the Pope needed the nuns to go back to Africa, for another famine. So they closed her down."

All this talk of nuns, though…

Nuns, he thought, with a sudden taste like sour milk in his mouth. *The nightmare...* Alexander's stomach involuntarily clenched. Then he looked up to notice Charity pouring iced tea; the trickling sound only reminded him more—of being urinated on. What inside him could summon such a dream? Did he secretly harbor some fear of refinishing Wroxeter? *Do I have a secret fear of nuns?* he wondered. But that couldn't be it; it didn't make sense.

Wouldn't you like to be purged? the nightmare sister had asked…

"Father?"

Alexander looked up. It was Jerrica, casting a sudden look of concern.

"Are you all right?"

"Oh, yeah, sorry. Mind got away from me a minute. Anyway, that's the scoop on the abbey."

"But that's a strange assignment that the Church should give you, isn't it?" Charity inquired next. "What about your regular duties, your parish?"

The $64,000 question. "I don't have a parish," he admitted his pet peeve. "I'm the psychologist for the Richmond Diocese."

"That sounds fascinating," Jerrica offered. "A priest shrink."

"I wouldn't quite call it fascinating, but it beats jacking fries at Burger King." *God, she's beautiful,* he thought to himself. Actually, both women were, Charity's looks remaining more subdued, more prim. But Jerrica, there was something vital about her, something really in-your-face. The striking contrast of her suntanned skin and white-blond hair, blue eyes bright as gems, slender yet curvaceous.

She could pop a stiffer on a bishop, he thought. *It's a good thing I'm celibate, otherwise I'd be all over her like a cheap suit. Christ, twenty years ago? Look out, honey!* At least he could joke about it now; actually, though, celibacy proved easier than he'd thought. It was even relieving. It converted his human lust into much more productive energy. Celibate, he could look at women honestly—*without* lust

—and acknowledge the beauty of their womanhood minus the taint of libidinal hormones. It refreshed him to be able to look at women without wanting anything of what he saw. Besides, in his younger days he'd had his fill, so to speak. If anything, *more* than his fill.

"Is Annie around?" he asked. "I haven't seen her?"

"We haven't seen her either, come to think of it," Charity said. "I don't know where she could be."

Alexander screwed out his butt in the turtle shell. "Last night, she told me there's a handyman?"

"Goop," Charity said.

"What?"

"That's his name," Jerrica added. "Goop."

"Goop. Ah, well. Anyway, where can I find him? Annie said he could take me into town, to the general store. I need some supplies."

Jerrica's eyes lit up. "Oh, forget Goop. Let us take you, Father!"

(III)

More'n more, it seemed, the more Dicky looked at Tritt Balls Conner, the more he started lookin' like the devil's son. Yes sir. A lean fella he were, big, an' with rock-hard muscles in his arms, like apples under his skin, they looked. Black hair hangin' ta his shoulders, anna goatee ta boot. And that blammed John Deere hat. But it weren't all that as much as the gander in his eyes. Steely little eyes, they was, like barrelholes on a long rifle.

"Bored, I'se say," Tritt Balls remarked, ridin' shotgun in the 'Mino. "Bored shee-it-less, I is, Dicky."

"I'se hear that." The El Camino rumbled along Rout 154, sucking down onto the road under about 450 horses. "What we gonna do today, Balls? We ain't got no shine runs till the right now."

"'S'true, Dicky. We'se ain't got no runs, but what we'se do got is a wad'a cash in each our pockets the size of a hamhock. Guess we'se kin find *somethin'* ta do."

"Shore, but what?"

Balls chuckled, strokin' that black goatee. "Well, I'se'll tell ya what I'd *likes* ta do. Like ta cornhole me some bitch so hard my spunk'd be dribblin' out her nose like she just blew a snot, I would."

Dicky frowned at the wheel and Hurst shifter. "Yeah, Balls, but we cain't do that now. 'S'broad daylight, it is. We'se cain't be pullin' no shit like that this early."

"I'se know, Dicky, I'se were just sayin'." Balls frowned hisself just then. "I'se hungry, though. Shee-it, man, I'se so hungry I could et me Mother Ter-ay-shah's pussy, I could, an' her asscrack too, I say. What say we stop on by the diner fer some hash'n eggs?"

"'S'awright by me."

Dicky Caudill didn't even know who Mother Ter-ay-shah was, but he weren't genrally one ta turn down *any* invitation ta eat, bein' as he wore about a waist forty-four, an' had a big gut on him, an' tits like a gal, only his had hair on 'em. But as he undertook the task'a drivin' inta town, he thought again 'bout Balls. Yeah, a devilish dude, we were; problee done stuff, 'n'fact, that the devil'd be proud'a. *Yes, sir,* Dicky thought, *what I gots sittin' right next ta me is problee the son'a Lucifer.*

At least it were unique company…

Yeah, they done some ruckin' in their time. *Bad* shit, it were, but it were fun, even Dicky hadda admit. But then he got ta thinkin' what he were thinkin' 'bout awhiles back, 'bout how one day they'se might pick the wrong folks ta fuck with…

Dicky shrugged, an' let the speck-er-lay-shun pass. Not much point thinkin' 'bout that, now were there?

Music twanged on the radio, good foot-stompin' music. The singer were singin': "I'm gonna buy me a gun just as long as my arm, kill everyone who ever done me harm…"

"Shee-it!" Balls howled. "Now *that's* some lyrics, ain't they? I likes that, I do!" Then Balls Conner burst out laughter. "Only thing is, Dicky, any folks we run into don't live long enough ta do us harm!"

"That's a fact, Balls," Dicky agreet, an' it were pretty much true. Like that one time they was in some roadhouse bar up'n Lockwood. They was just about ta leave, both takin' a piss in the john, an' Balls finished pissin' an' he starts ta walk away fom the toll-et, an' some big redneck dude says, "Hey, man, was ya brought up inna barn? Flush that toll-et when's ya finished pissin' in it. I'se shore don't wanna hafta lookit yer piss."

"Well, ya ain't gotta look at it, brother," Balls proclaimed, with that devil look'n his eyes. At the same times, what he done was he whipped out his buck an', lickety-split, had the blade ta that redneck's throat, he did, an' were bendin' him over with his dick still out. "No sir, ya ain't gotta look at it, but what'cha do gotta do is drink it, huh?"

And damn if that there redneck didn't drink outa that toll-et like a thirsty hound dog! After which Balls cut his throat anys way. Filled that toll-et *right up* with that fella's blood, he did. Then's there were that time, shee-it, coupla years ago? Some white trash chick they'd picked up thumbin' the Route. She's kicked Balls a good one in the rocks, so's Balls'd smacked her a better one in the noogin with his hickory pick handle. When she woked up, her feet was tied to's a tree, an' her hands was tied to the back bumper, an' Dicky popped the clutch. Arms popped right out her shoulders, but Tritt Balls? Naw, he weren't quite satis-er-fied with that. "Dicky," he hollered. "Git the hacksaw out the toolbox," whereupons Balls per-seeded ta saw offs her legs too. Then he humped her hard in the dirt, he did, jibin', "Hail Dicky! I'se bet I'se the first fella in town ta fuck a torso!" They chucked the arms'n legs in the woods when he were through. Then there were this other time last spring, they'd pulled off the Route so's Balls could hang hisself a moonshine piss, an' he spied a jeep, one'a them fancy Jap 4 runners, ands down a ways there were a tent an' campsite an' such. Past the ridge a piece, a fella an' his squeeze was fishin' fer bass off Kohl's Point, they was. City folk, they looked like. The dude had one'a them snort city-queer haircuts with no sideburns, and were wearin' shorts anna button shirt, fer God's sake, an' loafers with no socks, which was about the queerest thing Tritt Balls ever did see. Nice milkers on the chick, though. Plump, they was, an' about the size'a the honeydews at Wally Eberhart's stand, an' Balls could plain see she wore no bra 'neath that pussified Shephard's College t-shirt she wore. "Looks like a coupla happy campers ta me, huh, Dicky?" "Whys yeah, Balls," Dicky agreet. The dude spun at once, droppin' a perfectly good Zebco Lancer with brass works right smack dab inta the water. "Look, guys," he stammered. "We don't want any trouble." Now, Balls, he was a big boy, he was tall'n strong, an' he could put some serious ooompah-pah behind that fine veneered hickory pick handle of his. *Ka-CRACK!* came the sound as the business end swooshed a great arc upside that yuppie, city-queer head. "How's that fer some trouble, City?" Balls politely inquired. The dude lay smack dab flat on his back an' got ta twitchin' real bizarre, half his city-queer head caved in, and City's squeeze got ta screamin' right off, watchin' her fellas twitch like that. Tritt Balls smiled like a great big Hallerween pumpkin, he did, 'cos, see, there were just somethin' about hearin' a gal scream that got him hotter than woodstove at full tilt, and when Balls got a stiffer, he'd turn right imaginative. So's his shucked his big buck ands showed it to the gal, grinnin'. "You git right on down there, sugar plum," he said nicely to the gal. "We wants ta see you do the mouth job on City Boy here." "Feller-ay-shee-oh's what they'se call it in the city, I'se think," Dicky offered up some wisdom. Now this college gal had some really fine blond hair cut perfectly striaght 'bout ear-level, an' bangs, which were kinda cute inna queerified city kinda way, an' if there were one thing about Balls, it were that he *really* liked blondies, an' neithers of 'em could quit ganderin' that fine plump pair'a milkers on her. "But-but-but...he's *dying!*" she protested through insane hitching sobs. "Ain't no matter 'bout that, li'l lady. Just you git on down there an' do it." Dicky pulled down City's yuppie-jocko-homo sports shorts ta his knees, an' the kid kept twitchin' away real fierce like, blood squirtin' out his cracked head. "That's right, git right on down there 'cos, see, if ya do a good job then we'se might let ya live," Balls artick-er-lated, waving that big buck. It were amazing the things folks'd do at knife-point if they'se thought it'd save their lives. "And git that 'dickerlous queer-ass commie college t-shirt off so's we can gander yer tittes whiles yer doin' it." The blond girl obliged, she did, and then, shore enough, she began to assume Balls' demented request, mouth-loving away a country mile a minute like a reg-lar trooper as City's entire body continued to vigorously convulse via the massive nerve damage and cou-counter-cou subderal hematoma inflicted by that big hickory pick handle. Now, this were a sight, all right, City twitchin' whiles his big-titties commie-college girlfriend did the suckjob on his limp pecker. Balls an' Dicky laughed it up real good, they did, right up until City bled out an' died. Somehow, it weren't fun no more, what with the cessation of City's head-trauma convulsions. Dicky whipped out his bone an' began ta wank, ganderin' the gal's milkers, while Balls dropped trow an' did her dogstyle in the dirt, eventually spoogin' all over that big beautiful commie-college-gal backside'a hers. She gots ta screamin' again real fierce once they started ta work on her with their bucks. "I'se said we *might* let ya live," Balls explained the newfound discrepency to her screaminng-blubbering-shuddering face as he sliced long deep purdy lines down her belly. Then, guffawing, he got ta carving on her girlyworks, and that really put some jump in her, and thens he scalped her. "Aw, what the hail?" he remarked next an' began laughing like ta wake all the dead outa Bell Cemetery. Dicky'd finished wanking and were now pulling a good long pee inta City Boy's dead face whiles Balls sliced those big titties right off the college gal. He placed her scalp atop City's head and stuffed them big severed titties up under that queer-ass city-faggot Christian Dior button shirt'a his, wailin', "'Magine the look on the poor fucker's face who finds 'em, Dicky! A gal's hairdo an' titties an' a *pecker* hangin'!" Yes sir, Tritt Balls Conner were on a roll that day! Before headin' back on up ta the 'Mino, he dropped a good-sized healthy farmboy meat'n potato bowel movement on what remained'a the gal an', a'corse, wiped his crack with that commie-college shirt'a hers. Yes sir, big fun it was they had that day. *Big* fun.

So's now they was both sittin' in Chuck's Diner, still bored shee-it-less, havin' thereselfs *big* plates'a hash'n eggs, wonderin' what they'se was gonna do all day, 'cos it were still mornin' right now, it were. Chuck's were Luntville's greasy spoon, good grub fer a good price, but there weren't hardly no one here now, just some ol' duff havin' coffee'n donuts up the counter, ands this big fat cracker chick with ratty hair, in flip-flops, shorts, anna t-shirt big enough fer Dumbo the Elephant. She were eatin' her second plate'a hash'n eggs herself, a reg-lar machine, she were, but Balls'n Dicky didn't pay her much mind on account'a she were so fat, like her buttcheeks was hangin' over each side'a her stool like a seed bag sittin' there, an' she hadda gut on her likes a cow. Insteads, Balls ignort her, reflecterin' ta hisself. "Hail, no shine runs, no ones ta mess with, shee-it. What we gonna do today, Dicky?"

"Dunno," Dicky replied, his mouth steady fulla hash'n eggs. Chuck's Diner, they shore made some great hash'n eggs.

"I'se mean, I *hates* bein' bored, Dicky. We'se lively young fellas, we is, yet we ain't got nothin' ta do on such a fine mornin' as this."

Dicky nodded in agreement, shoveling another fork'a hash in his yap.

Balls leaned forward, "An' I'se kin tell ya, Dicky, I'se so fuckin' *horny!* My dog's been hard since I git up. Shee-it. I'se *swear,* I could fuck this plate'a hash'n eggs."

Aw, don't do that! Dicky Caudill thought. There weren't no putting *nothin'* past Tritt Balls Conner.

"Hail, I coulds even diddle that fat gal sitting up the counter."

Dicky's eyes swelled. "*Her?* You gots ta be shittin' me, man! She's as big as a doublewide!"

Balls crimped his nose at the suggestion. "So's what. What we'll do is we'll wait tills she's done etin', then I'll'se sweet-talk her inta the 'Mino!"

Shee-it, Dicky thought. *We don'ts need this shit this early in the mornin'.*

But wait they did, 'cos the gal ordered *another* plate'a hash'n eggs!

Took her awhiles ta et it all, it did, but when she were done, she hopped off that stool like a pallet'a mason blocks, she did, an' thens she started ta walk out.

"Hey there's, purdy lady!" Balls exclaimed. "Looks like yous leavin' the same time we is! How's 'bout we give ya a ride ta where yas going?"

Her fat blubber face smiled, as though she were real complimentered by Balls referrin' ta her as "purdy," an' she just said "Whys shore, boys!"

That were all it took. No sooner than ten minutes'd passed, Dicky were pullin' up the El Camino inta another dell, right by the river. Balls had already smacked the fat gal out with his homemade jack, an' they'se lugged her outa the 'Mino, they did. "Hail, Dicky!" Balls pointed out. "She plumb weighs more'n yer bigblock 427!"

"That she does," Dicky agreet, haulin her acrost the dell. What they done then was Dicky stood her up, an' Balls tied her upright ta a tree. He took a quick pee onner feet an 'structed Dicky, "Git my hickory pick handle, Dicky!"

Dicky did so, an' passed said hickory pick handle ta Balls, who stood there chucklin', waitin' fer the fat gal ta come fully to. "Hail, Dicky! As much as she et at the diner, I'll'se bet she got enough inner gut ta fill a hog trough!"

"Bet she problee does, Balls," Dicky hesitantly agreet.

An' when she came fully to, Balls reeled the pick handle back way far and—

whap!

—socked her real hard in the belly. Made a sound like slappin' a heifer, it did! Once he did it, an' twice an' then a third time, an' on that third time, her fat face turnt white, an' she lurched forwart as far's her ropes'd permit, an' she just *cut loose*, she did, throwin' up like a reg-lar gusher rights there in the dell. Out all them viddles came up bigtime, they did, blowin' 'least three foot out her yap acrost the leafs. An' it were a *lotta* food!

"Hail, Dicky! 'Chew see all that puke she blowed!"

"That I did, Balls," Dicky, none too pleased, accented.

"Hail! Lookit all them hash'n eggs she blowed out her mouth! Cain't quite believe it! She done et herself enough fer *ten* fellas!"

"That she did, Balls," Dicky repeated.

Balls rapped her in the belly one more time, an' that erped out the last'a it. Her puke—shee-it!—it flew out her mouth four er five feet this time, an' landed with a wet *whap!* in the dirt.

"A fuckin' elephant, she is! Got enough space inner belly ta hold a whole load'a hootch fer Clyde Nale, she does. A fuckin' fat cracker vol*can*o, she is! But.." Balls chuckled dark. "I feels kinda bad, dee-privin' her'a all them good viddles she paid fer. Guess we'se better let her et it all back up, huh?"

Balls, then, cut her down with his buck an' pushed her face down ta that big plume'a puke, just like that whore he'd made eat her own shit, holdin' the knifepoint to her eye. "Et up all that puke, honey, et it up an' swaller. Ain't nothin' but hash'n eggs. Problee tastes better second time around!"

She ate it up, gaggin', she did, and it were *a lot* of hash'n eggs. "See what we done, ya hog?" Balls said. "We done let ya et the same meal twice!"

When this fat gal was done eatin' up her puke, Balls whipped his dick out. He held it rights up ta her face ands said, "Suck it now, slim. Suck it good!"

She had some fiest left inner, Dicky hadda give her that. After pukin' up a storm an' takin' five er six whaps in the belly from Balls' pick handle? Ands then bein' forced to *eat* her own puke? It were a women of resilience who coulds say, after alls that, "You stick that dirty cracker dick in my mouth, an' I *swears* I'll bite if off!"

Guess she were a feminist. Tritt Balls, well, he didn't like no fat splittail sayin' such ugly things ta him, no sir! Not one bit. "Dicky!" he wailed. "Git the pliers out the toolbox!"

Groanin', Dicky did so.

Balls, then, pulled out all her teeth with them Sears Craftsman pliers, he did.

"There, ya fat cow!" Balls celebrated. "Nows ya cain't bite nothin'!"

He turnt her over in the dirt, an' brownholed her right there, humpin' her backside hard till he shot'a load'a peckersnot right up her tail. Then, what he did was this, he flipped her right back over an' wiped his shit-smellin' dog right in her face.

Then he gots ta whittlin'.

Yes sir. Tritt Balls whipped out his buck again an' got ta whittlin' on this fat gal fierce. She were screamin' she were, while Balls whittled off all the skin off her fingers, like they was carrots! Then he whittled alls the skin offer arms, an' off it came like sheets'a wallpaper. Then he sloughed off all the skin offer back an' legs, he did, which made even bigger sheets, an' she were screamin' the whole time like a cat throwed into a combine, she was, as all that fat white skin fell ta the ground, a fat cracker blood-red mess she were! 'Ventually, he got ta whittlin' the skin offer toes'n feet. "Hail, Dicky," he commented. "Lookit these feet, wills ya! Bet she wears a size 12, I'll'se bet! Thems the biggest feet I ever did seen onna gal!" She finally died once he got ta cuttin' on her more. Clipped off her big pale nipples, he did, then he sliced off those big-as-a-baby's-head hooters, an' held 'em up in his hands an' squeezed the blood out 'em like they was big warm wobbly sponges. Dug her eyeballs out her head too, just fer fun, an' popped 'em in his hands like they was big white grapes.

"Come ons, man," Dicky complained. By now, even his stomach were feelin' sick wacthin' this. "She dead, Balls. Let's git on outa here."

"Git outa here, hail!" Balls responded. "My dog's hard again, ands I'll'se be damned if I'se gonna waste it! Gots me a load'a spunk in theres somewhere, an' I'se gonna pop it!"

Tritt Balls, then, began to fornicate with the fat, eyeless, and thoroughly flensed corpse, humpin' her dead girlworks a right fierce, he did, an thens he pulled out'n spooged right inta her agape yap, dead as she were.

Balls, sees, he were't very par-tick-ah-ler 'bout the kinda gal he made whoopee with.

1 2 3 4 5 6 7 8 9 0
NINE
ERIK
1999

NINE

(I)

Morning seemed to blossom into afternoon, akin to the thousands of flowers in the back yard. Charity elected not to join Jerrica and Father Alexander on the trip to the general store; lazing around the house seemed more appealing, and sorting her thoughts and contemplations.

There were many…

For one, the yard itself. It was beautiful, meticulously trimmed and weeded, and tracked by fine fieldstone walkways which must've cost quite a bit. A sub planted sprinkler system, a luxurious kiosk, and an open shed full of groundskeeping equipment: a tiller, a power edger, a hedge trimmer, and a stout rider mower. Aunt Annie was poor. Where did she get the money for all this? And where did she get the money for the boarding house's exorbitant renovations? She even had a hired hand now…

"Hi, there, Ms. Charity!" Goop Gooder, of all people, greeted, coming round the side of the house. He was trundling a wheelbarrow full of pine bark mulch. "I'se say, you're lookin' mighty fine today."

"Thank you, Goop," Charity replied. "That's nice of you to say." But she wondered. Was it really true, or was he just being polite? The paranoia deepened. If she was attractive, what could explain her ceaseless misfires with men? And there was always the image of Jerrica—*more* paranoia. The image nagged at her: Jerrica could be a model in *Swimsuit Illustrated. What could I be?* Charity glumly asked herself now.

And Goop standing there made it even worse. The broad chest and back, the muscled arms, the long hair. An emblem of fresh, vibrant lust. The caricatured "farmboy," country youth and virility. *Jerrica had sex with him last night,* she reminded herself, still mildly shocked at the thought. Was she jealous about that too? *Would I want to have sex with...Goop?* She didn't think so.

So why these incessant dwellings?

It seemed almost as if Jerrica proved the archetype of all the things Charity wished she could be. Yes. Jerrica.

"Have you seen Jerrica, Ms. Charity?" Goop asked next, leaning forward on his wheelbarrow handles, as if to denote secrecy.

"She went to town with Father Alexander," Charity said.

"Oh..."

Don't get jealous, Goop, she nearly wanted to voice. *The man's a Catholic priest.* "He seems like a unique man."

Goop's face blankened, as if he weren't familiar with the word *unique*, which very well may have been true. "I ain't met him yet, but Ms. Annie tolds me he came in last night."

"Oh, I'm sure you'll like him, Goop. And, by the way, where *is* Aunt Annie?"

"Off on hers walk, I 'spect. She goes fer a walk'n the woods ever afternoon."

Charity remembered this; she'd seen her aunt wandering into the treeline yesterday, with twin bundles of flowers. And, now that she thought of it, two decades ago, when Charity had lived here, her aunt had done the same thing everyday, hadn't she? Where did she go?

"She'll be around," Goop assured. But the tint of hurt in his face shone baldly—he was thinking of Jerrica. "Well, I gots ta go now, talks to ya later. 'Bye."

"'Bye, Goop."

She watched him push away behind the wheelbarrow, and wend toward the rear flowerbeds. *Poor Goop,* she thought. *Don't you know that you were just a one-night stand?* What a cruel truth Charity was privy to. The poor dumb kid was propping himself up for a heartbreak.

But that thought made her think ever more incisively about herself. *That's what my entire adult life has been: one string of one-night stands...*

"Charity!"

She glanced away, into the opposite end of the back yard's shaded spaciousness. There was her aunt, barely seen, waving to her.

Charity, smiling, walked the stone aisles, passing great eruptions of flowers. "I was wondering where you were."

"Oh, I'm just picking my daily flowers," her aunt replied, bending over a flank of multi-colored paintedcups and delicate bluecurls.

Charity stood with the sun warming her bare shoulders. Her aunt was wearing a sundress nearly identical to her own: a blank, pastel chartreuse. "I remember now," she said. "From when I was little. Every day you'd gather flowers and go for a long walk in the woods behind the house. Where do you go?"

"Well..." Annie stood up, smiled indistinctly at her niece. "After all these years, I guess it's time you found out, now, ain't it?"

Charity didn't query; instead, she followed her aunt into the thickening woods. The dense trees—a conglomeration of Blackjack Oaks, Red Maples, and tall, tall Mockernuts—made it seem cool as evening, and as dark. The fieldstone path led on and on, leaving Charity again to wonder where the money had come from to lay it. "Aunt Annie?" she couldn't resist. "I'm really curious about something—"

"Let me guess, hon," her aunt came back. "You wanna know where I got the money."

Was the fine old woman psychic? Or was it a question she'd expected all along? The latter, of course. "Well, yes, if you don't mind my asking," Charity admitted. "I don't remember a whole lot about the time I lived with you, but...you know, the house was run down, there were no fieldstone paths—things were tight. I mean, that's why the state took me away from you, isn't it? Because they felt you didn't have enough money to raise me?"

Annie seemed to wilt, her pace feebling. Around the next bend came a sitting area, with facing white-painted iron benches, and, dejectedly then, she sat down, bidding with her hand for Charity to do the same. "Sometimes I just feels like luck ain't on my side, like there's a blight on me, honey. But yer right, that's why the state 'thorities took ya from me, 'cos they deemed I didn't have enough money ta raise ya proper. Guess it were true. I only hopes ya kin fergive me."

"Aunt Annie!" Charity exclaimed. "It wasn't your fault!"

"I hope it weren't, honey. All I can say is I did my best with what I had."

"Of course you did!"

"An' I feel mighty bad 'bout only writin' ya letters all these years, an' never invitin' ya out, but the reason I didn't is 'cos things never seemed ta change. Yer ol' Aunt Annie just kept gettin' poorer, and the house kept gettin' more run down." Annie brushed a tear from her eye. "I was just too ashamed ta invite ya back home. But then..."

Charity waited, poised on the hard metal bench.

"What happened were like a gift from the Lord. A class-action suit's what they call it. Turns out that my land an' 'bout a thousand acres either way were what they called Schedule E Mineral Property. And goin' back ta way back when, Northeast Carbide was pipin' natural gas without tellin' no one—offa *our* land! Makin' millions a year, they were, and, well, some fancy lawyer from Roanoke got wind of it and he took the case. Proved in federal court that those Carbide bastards were stealin' from us, takin' gas from our land an' not payin'. An' this lawyer, well, he won his case. So me an' a whole bunch'a others 'round here got paid what they call a pro-rata settlement, based on the number'a acres we each had a deed to. Most of 'em, you know how fellas are, they blew all their money on gambling an' such. But I used mine to make repairs and for signs. That lawyer took a third'a the total take, but it was worth it. My end was close ta half a million dollars. Got most of it socked away still, but I used some ta fix the place up, and post all them signs."

"Signs?" Charity asked.

"The roadsigns, honey, like the ones you saw on yer way with yer city friend. Folks on the highway see the signs and pull in. We're a good place to stop fer those headin' south, and there's some fine tourist attractions, the Boone National Forest, Kohls Point, best fishing spot in the state. And, a'corse, the woods themselfs. An' ya know what? It worked. Every fall an' spring 'specially, I gotta full house, makin' an actual profit. That's how I kin afford to have Goop, and fixin' up the flowerbeds. An' I make a couple thousand a month from bank interest from what I got left. But—" Annie's graceful face turned down, the flowers in her lap like something stillborn. "It just makes me feel so bad..."

Charity couldn't for the life of her understand. "Aunt Annie! That's wonderful! There's no reason to feel bad."

Annie's eyes welled with tears. "I feel bad, dear, on account'a I can't understand why it took so long. If this'd happened all them years ago, then I'd'a never lost ya. I feel like I let ya down..."

Charity got up and sat down next to her aunt, put her arm about her. "Don't cry, Aunt Annie. That's just the way things happen sometimes."

"But that ain't good enough," Annie whimpered. "Yer mama dyin' so awful by her own hand, not a year after she gave birth to ya—she was my sister. I felt obliged to take care'a ya, but I couldn't. The damn state took ya away from me."

Charity stroked her aunt's shoulder. "It wasn't your fault, Aunt Annie. You did the best you could, and that's better than most. And, look at it this way. You're doing fine now with the boarding house, and I'm doing fine with my career and my night classes. It's like they say—"

For some reason, Charity thought instantly of the priest.

"God works in strange ways," she said.

(II)

"God works in miraculous ways," Alexander stated matter-of-factly, behind the wheel of the Diocesan Mercedes. He'd been answering a common question, of Jerrica's. *If there's God, how come there's war? How come there's ethnic cleansing and murder and rape and child abuse...* Typical questions of a non-believer.

"God does not own the title deed to the earth," he said. "The devil does, and he has since Eve put her choppers to that apple. All God has here is His holy influence, and His love of mankind."

"But what's miraculous about war and genocide and rape and everything else?" Jerrica challenged.

"Nothing. It's God's love for his kingdom that's the miraculous part. I can't judge you personally," he said, steering around another sweeping, wooded bend, "but I can promise you that you'll know what I'm talking about when you die."

Jerrica hitched up her halter, awe-faced. "You really...believe all that, don't you?"

Alexander glanced at her, lit a cigarette. "Yeah. I believe it because it's true." Then he quoted *Psalms.* "'I have chosen the way of truth.' And as for genocide, rape, murder, war?" *Romans.* "'The whole creation groaneth and travaileth in pain together until now.'" And, finally, from *Isaiah,* "'I have chosen thee in the furnace of adversity.'"

"I—" Jerrica blinked. "I guess I see your meaning."

"But you don't believe a word of it," Alexander challenged her now. "You're appeasing me."

"No, I'm not!"

"Sure you are." He chuckled at the wheel. "But don't worry. You will see the light before your life on earth is over. You will arise to the Kingdom of God."

Now Jerrica smiled. "Oh, yeah? How do you know? Are you psychic? Did God whisper that in your ear?"

Alexander's glance turned blank as a carved wood totem. "Yeah," he said. "As a matter of fact, He did."

They drove on for a spell, in silence. *That got her thinking,* Alexander felt sure. *Good. That's my fuckin' job. That's what God is paying me for.*

They'd already gone to Hull's, the general store, where Alexander purchased flashlights, batteries, several alcohol lanterns, work gloves, and cleaning supplies. Then they'd driven slowly about town—*Not much of a town,* the priest noted—where Jerrica pointed out the local bar, the diner, then took him down the block and explained the "sewing shop" enterprises. Evidently it was common for non-resident clothing companies to come here and employ women at a minimum wage. Oppression, he knew, was relative. And more oppression passed them when they turned and headed out. "And there's Donna's Antiques," she said, pointing to the high clapboard building. "It's really a brothel."

"Oh yeah? I ought to walk in there and ask them if they have any 1820 Sheraton bow-front chests in Hepplewhite walnut. Can you imagine the looks on their faces?" Alexander laughed behind the padded wheel. "A priest? Walking into a whorehouse?"

Jerrica shared the hilarity of the image. "Somehow I can't quite picture that."

"Wouldn't be the first whorehouse I've walked into."

"You're kidding me?"

"I haven't always been a priest, you know," Alexander admitted. He'd visited, in fact, several such establishments in Saigon, sex for a ten, blowjobs for a buck. It was even cheaper in the field. God had a knack for payback; three times Alexander had been sent to the med unit with cases of the clap so virulent he felt like he'd been plugged into a mobile generator. *You live and learn,* he thought. Before he'd been embraced by the priesthood, the sins of the flesh hadn't been foreign to him. Some of the things he'd seen in The Nam bordellos, as a non-participant, were appalling: "Butt-bangs" and "fletch parties," 20-man blowjob galas, G.I.'s paying 12-year-old hookers to fornicate with dogs. If anything, the sorority girls in college were as bad. Sex and drugs and rock and roll, and if you had to let your English proff sodomize you in order to pass—well, hey! And a little coke money never hurt anyone, right? Once Alexander had TA'd a philosophy course and was astounded by the number of girls who'd offered themselves for higher grades, and he'd been even more astounded by the things they'd offer to do. Evil was everywhere, and it had a lot of different faces. Seeing it was how one learned about the world, and sometimes learning hurt. But Alexander, unlike most priests, had no problem admitting his less-than-saintly days; denial was as false as lying bold-faced. "No, I haven't always been a living model of Christian thesis." He laughed again. "But at least I am now, so I guess that's all that matters."

Jerrica didn't get the joke. She seemed very focused right now, full of questions she wasn't sure if she could ask. Alexander had seen it many times: women were fascinated by the notion of celibacy.

"If you—" Jerrica stumbled. "—don't mind my asking, when, uh, when was the last…time?"

"1977," he answered without even having to think. He'd almost married that one, hadn't he? They'd had sex seven times in one night. *Talk about getting things out of your system.* Yes, he'd considered marrying her, but right now he couldn't even remember her name.

Jerrica looked pale. "That's over…*twenty years.*"

"Uh-huh," then, just as brazenly, "And, no, I haven't masturbated since then either. That's usually the next question."

"Good God," Jerrica whispered.

"Yeah, He is."

They both laughed at the remark. He could tell she had many more questions bubbling in her, but she wouldn't ask now. *Christ, people think priests are made of tissue paper,* he thought. And he knew he was no exception; before the priesthood, they'd been on par with the Marquis de Sade. He could tell, too—just by *looking* at her—that Jerrica Perry was no stranger to the sins of the flesh. Maybe it was her aura…

They passed an old, steepled church. Alexander, with a cigarette dangling from his lips, crossed himself.

"Don't bother," Jerrica said. "Charity told me that church is closed."

"So?" He shrugged. "It's still the house of God, full of the presence of God."

She shook her head, smiling. "Where are we going now?" He'd been heading out of town actually, back to Route 154. "Well, I guess I better drop you off back at the house," he said. "I've got a lot of work to do at the abbey."

Jerrica turned briskly in the Mercedes' leather sat, her face suddenly alight. "Oh, Father, please! I'm dying to see the abbey. Let me go with you."

"Out of the question. It's dirty, it's dangerous. I've got a lot of grubby work to do—"

"*Please,* Father! I'll help you."

"No way."

She leaned forward, her breasts compressed in the bright-white halter. Alexander could smell the lovely scent of her herbal shampoo.

"*Pleeeease,* Father," she nearly whined. And her smile escalated to something bright as the glare of the sun.

Alexander frowned. *Christ, what a sucker for a pretty face.*

He pitched his butt, lit another, waved a hand.

"Oh, all right," he agreed.

(III)

She were preggers, this one. Red-hairt, she were, an' skin so smooth'n white likes nothin' he ever seed. Big high tits, *twice* the size'a his fists, an', a'corse, that big preggered belly.

The Bighead licked his chops.

He'd walked miles since mornin', crunchin' along, thinkin' 'bout his dreams'a the castle, the angels, an' the Voice he'd heard, sayin': COME. An' that's when he come upon this li'l red-hairt thing. She were buck nekit, warshin' herself in a creek. That were about the only cause'a Bighead's object-shure-uns: that she were warshin'. See, Bighead liked his gals *stinky,* 'cos it occurred ta him that bein' stinky were part'a bein' real. Bighead hisself, fer example, he were a *might* stinky, on account'a he ain't took a bath since the day he were born. Didn't see no reason ta. When The Bighead walked through the woods, see, he'd bring a stink alongs with him that'd make a buzzard puke. An', yeah, he hisself *liked* the smell'a shit an' piss an' buttcrack, an' b.o. Liked ta taste it too. Somehows, tastin' up a gal who'd just warshed were like ettin' a possum-gut stew with no spice.

Were kinda bland, it were...

Anyways, this red-hairt preggered gal, Bighead were watchin' her from behind a fat tree, and she were bendin' over just then, warshin' her backside, an' when she done so, Bighead could see her pie, he could. An' it's were a *big* pie, that red fur goin' round the slit, an' the slit bein' bigger'n a groundhog hole. So's that's when Bighead got ta thinkin'. So far he'd hadda problem havin' a proper fuck with a gal on account'a their poons weren't never big enough ta take alla his pipe. But this gal here, with that yawnin' baby-hole onner? This might be somethin', yes sir!

That might be just the pocket ta take alla Bighead's meat...

She screamed ta high heavens, she did, when The Bighead walked out from behind that fat tree, showin' his big warped head, an' the eyes in his face, one biger'n the other an' lower, an' a'corse that big smilin' yap fulla long crooked teeth like a dog's. He hauled her up a'shore. She screamed so loud she did, 'n'fact, he thought she might break her voice. He socked her groggy with his fist, thens went down onner, suckin' that purdy red pussy'a hers, ands at first she tasted kinda creeky-clean, but once he gots ta suckin' hard, a bunch'a cheesy stuff came out her hole, reals tangy-like, an' that just made The Bighead's day. Wished he had some'a ol' Grandpap's flatbreads or cattail pancakes, he did, ta wipe that girlcheese onto. Then he's started fuckin' her right there in the creek mud, after hockin' a big loogie onner hole, ands at first her pussy were a might accommodatin', even fer Bighead's big pole. He humped her fierce, he did, whiles she just lay back screamin' inta the big, bright afternoon sky, an' there were milk sprayin' out her big titties whiles he humped her, which Bighead thought were kinda neat. Just li'l sprays like mist, they was, an' white as a spiderweb. Bighead, 'n'fact, were so intrigued by this that he leant over an' sucked hard on them big milk-filled titties, whiles he continered fuckin' her. He musta sucked a *bucketful*'a milk, he musta, and's it tasted warm'n sweet, an' he could'a swored her titties was about half the size once he were done, him havin' sucked out all that good mama's milk. Sucked 'em dry was about what he did, till there's was nothin' left in 'em. But lo's an' behold—

He was humpin' her so fine'n dandy, pluggin' his 14 inchers'a cock in an' out that big slippery red-hairt puss, when she just started ta bust up, just like the rest'a 'em. His dickknob felt her insides startin' ta pop, an' things breakin' inner, an' he could'a swored he felt his big pecker pop that baby right in the eye, an' thens she broke her water, which Bighead cupped in his hand and dranked, an' it were warm an' good, but it were no con-ser-lay-shun. With all the gals

Bighead'd fucked, not one of 'em hadda poon big enough take alla his meat, not even this red-hairt with the biggest poon he'd seed yet. She started bleedin' like the time he bit the head off that weasel, she did, only she weren't bleedin' out her neck stump. Turnt the water red, it did, all that blood, gushin' out her like a tap, an' she just murmurt with her green eyes flutterin', an' she died.

Bighead were depressed, he were. Once—just *once*—he wished he could finda gal with a poon big enough fer him ta come proper. He's comed right in that baby's face, he supposed, thens pulled out, an' he figgurt he oughta bust her noggin' open an' et her brain, but then he's got another idea.

See, this gal was preggered, as in *real* preggered, like she were about ta drop that crumb-snatcher any day. So's he just got back right down on that bloody red-hairt pussy'a hers, ands he started suckin' The Bighead sucked hard, he did, and 'ventually he started hearin' somethin' tear inside'a her, ands he sucked an' sucked an' sucked till—damn!—that baby inner belly started comin' out.

Bighead, in his mind, began ta rejoice, he did.

He hauled that baby outa there an' held it upta the sun…

It begun ta cry, it did.

And Bighead smiled.

'Cos although he'd et a lotta adult brains in his time, never once had he ever had the opportunity ta et a baby's brains.

No sir!

Them baby's brains?

He bit a whole in that soft skull, an' he sucked them brains right out that baby's l'il head, he did, like suckin' a duck egg the way Grandpap'd taught him.

An' they was good, they was.

Yes sir!. Them baby's brains was *real* good.

They hadda tang'a salt, like a adult's, but they was real warm too, an' had somethin' of a sweet taste along with it, likes they'se had sugar in 'em…

(IV)

"The administration office was sealed," Alexander said, peering at a photocopy of the first-floor blueprints. Upon arriving at Wroxeter Abbey, he'd immediately knocked the boards off the windows on either side of the long central hall, to let in light.

"They *sealed* it?" Jerrica didn't understand. "Isn't that strange?"

"No, not really," the priest replied. "Diocesan laziness. Wroxeter was a hospice for dying priests, like I was telling you and Charity this morning. Obscure, out of the way. The in-patient records weren't deemed critical, so the Church decided to just leave them here rather than go to the expense of transporting and filing them in Richmond. The chances of those records ever being needed are a million to one. So they simply transferred the few remaining in-patients and had the office sealed." Alexander peered up from the blueprints. "And I'd say that the office has to be somewhere along this wall."

Red, mortared bricks—surprisingly unfaded—composed most of the north interior wall, while half-paneled sheetrock formed the south wall. A strange design, but then, Jerrica noted, so was the entirety of the building itself. Inside and out, it completely defied what she expected. Abbeys brought with them a certain connotation; in her mind she pictured a great edifice, slate-roofed, made of stone, something medieval and churchlike. Wroxeter, instead, proved to be more akin to an lodge, centuries old, or a vast cabin. A bell tower, bereft of bell, reminded Jerrica of something headless.

But the diversity of building materials were plain; the outer walls, she saw with astonishment, were made fróm long, stout trees stripped of their bark, stained, and lain lengthwise, seamed with mortar, and ancient cedar shingles crusted the slanted roof. An old Colonial design, which Alexander verified upon arrival. "The abbey was built in the late 1600's, in case you're curious about the logs. But the interior is totally different, due to several overhauls. Wroxeter is actually one of the oldest Church properties in the state."

Fascinating. Like a log cabin on a larger scale. It sat nestled fully in the grips of the forest, at the end of a long, rising dirt lane. From what Jerrica could discern, the elevated terrain ended abruptly, as if

Wroxeter were erected on a wooded precipice which descended shortly past the building's rearmost limits.

"So you can see," the priest had gone on, "why the Church wants to use it for a rehab facility. Way out here in the woods, all this peace and quiet."

"Yes," she agreed. Well, sort of anyway. "It's a beautiful area. It's just that the abbey itself looks so bizarre. I expected something huge, something with turrets and stonework, high windows and all that. But this place is only one story. It just looks so...weird."

Alexander laughed, hoisting a box full of tools from the Mercedes. "The Catholic Church doesn't give a squat about what it looks like. All they care about is the price, and the price is right: free."

Jerrica picked up the supplies they'd bought in town, and followed the priest. Inside proved even more peculiar, an obtuse collision of designs. The entry and vestibule stood tall and dark in tudor stone archways, sconces, and lancet windows which once had no doubt been inset with stained glass, but only lead webbings remained now. A slate floor proceeded to the central hall, carpeted literally by an inch of dust. Rotten rugs, whose original color was anyone's guess, led down the main corridor.

"Just like Trump Towers, huh?" Alexander joked. Then he'd whipped out his xeroxes of the floor layouts, began to scrutinize them.

"I can't believe how hot it is," Jerrica commented, sweating profusely already.

"Yeah? You should've been here yesterday, before I had a chance to break out the planks nailed over the windows at each end of the main hall. It was like a sauna. At least now we've got a little bit of a cross-breeze."

A little bit was right. "How did you break the window planks out?" Jerrica asked, for lack of anything else.

"Trusty old twenty-pound sledge," the priest answered, and hoisted its haft from the toolbox.

Jerrica giggled lightly. "Somehow, it's hard for me to picture a priest knocking out window planks with a sledge hammer."

"Well, when I find out where the admin office is, you're gonna get to see a priest knock down a brick wall with one." His eyes tarried over the blueprint copies. “This is gotta be it,” he supposed. “Right here. Take a look. Doesn’t this look like new brickwork to you?”

Jerrica felt flattered he’d asked her opinion. Generally, men relegated her as a party host and a bedmate. But when she glanced at the indicated area, she saw what he meant. Newer, darker-hued brick filled a gap between the older work. “I’m sure you’re right,” she acknowledged, brushing sweat from her brow with her forearm. “Why else would that newer brick be there?”

Alexander nodded in ascent, then grabbed the sledge. “Only one way to find out.”

Jerrica started at each steady impact, priest suddenly becoming construction worker, or *de*struction worker in this case. Alexander wielding the long-handled hammer with something akin to expertise—not exactly what she would’ve expected.

chink-chink-chink!

The hammer smacked on and on as she watched, and it wasn’t long before some of the darker emplacements of brick began to give, sifting powdered mortar from their seams.

chink-chink-chink!

He stopped a moment, to wipe his own brow. “Thank God this is slipshod brick-laying; these bricks are coming out pretty fast. Like they were set in putty.” Then he sighed, wiped his brow again, and slipped out the white Roman collar. “Christ, you’re right. It’s hot as hell in here.” Then he took off the black cotton shirt.

chink-chink-chink!

Jerrica watched on, no longer interested in the man’s deftness with a sledge hammer. Instead, she couldn’t take her eyes off his body…

He was nude now from the waist up; Jerrica found him ever more attractive. Tight, modest muscles flexing beneath tighter skin. No body fat at all. He was not possessed of the extended musculature of Goop, of course, but Father Tom Alexander was nonetheless not lacking in physical definition. A faint crucifix of hair crossed his denuded chest. But—

“Wait,” she asked without thinking. A flurry of pocks graced his lower side. “What’s that?”

The priest lit a cigarette, leaning on the hammer's haft. "Shrapnel scars," he answered without a flinch. His fingers brushed over the slightly darkened pits. "I was on a LRRP, that's long-range-reconnaissance patrol; I was backing up the point man, a buddy of mine. Anyway, he tripped a Russian-made APERS."

"APERS?" Jerrica, fascinated, asked next.

"Anti-personnel mine. Not much more than a grenade hanging in the bush. My buddy tripped it, bought the farm—" Alexander crossed himself. "I lucked out and caught a few pieces in the side. Actually it's the best thing that ever happened to me because I got airlifted out by some pure-ass crazy warrant officer, and I sat in a med-unit while the Tet Offensive was going on that year. If that shrapnel hadn't hit me, there'd be some other over-the-hill priest banging this brick wall."

"You're not over the hill!" Jerrica immediately objected.

"Hey, I'm pushing fifty and probably look sixty."

Jerrica's eyes rose, a breath stalled in her bosom. "Believe me, you look *good.*"

Alexander smiled, the cigarette hanging. "Oh, yeah? Well, thanks for the compliment. Hey, how about doing me a favor. See if the access is blocked to the bell tower, for one. And see if there's a basement. The blueprints aren't clear on that."

"Uh, okay," Jerrica agreed. She knew she would agree to anything he asked. And she also knew this: *He cut that off real fast because he knows I think he's hot.* Why else would he thank her for the compliment, then send her off?

Didn't matter, though. *Shit, he's a priest,* she reminded herself. After a few moments of scuttling through dust down the north end of the hall, she found a door which led up to the bell tower. There were several unsealed rooms down this end, dorm rooms they looked like: stripped cots, old wall lockers. *The nuns must've slept here,* she reasoned. A larger dorm contained half a dozen stripped convalescent beds: the in-patient area. All pretty boring stuff.

But next she found another door in the same stairwell leading down to the basement. When she hurried back and reported this to Alexander, she saw that he'd knocked out all the new bricks, which lay now in a sifting heap at his feet. "Shit," he remarked. "I could lay better brick than that! Let's go in."

Another boarded up room, stuffy nearly to the point of suffocation. The priest's sledge hammer—*Ka-CRACK!*—promptly knocked out the planks, filling the office with sunlight and fresh air. Alexander's lean muscles flexed when he yanked open the first of many rusted file cabinets, celebrating, "Halford was right. All the records are still here."

"That's great," Jerrica said, simply just to agree with him.

And her eyes reopened on the man, relishing his hard flesh. Even the darkened pits of his war scars seemed erotic to her…

She leaned against the wall, a hot breath growing hotter in her chest. Her vision shifted to the most treacherous deceit: in her mind, then, she saw the two of them making love, right there in the inch-thick dust on the floor, groveling over each other, licking each other's sweat. Her eyes widened but she saw the fantasy as if they were closed and she were dreaming. She was desperately yanking down his priestly black slacks, admitting his penis to her mouth. Then she was sitting on his face, going cross-eyed as his tongue tended her clitoris and his fingers entered her sex. First one finger, then two, then…four. It was another of her countless fantasies: to be fisted till her throat felt full, till she couldn't see straight. And here he was, the goodly Father Alexander, doing just that in the scape of her scurrilous mind… Fisting her. Moaning for her as she sucked him. His muscles clenching. She sucked him harder, felt his penis throb and his testicles draw up. Then all that pent-up come, from so many years of celibacy, jettisoned out to flood the back of her throat. She swallowed it all like warm, salty soup as she came, screaming aloud…

"Hey. Jerrica. Where you at? The Twilight Zone?"

She snapped to, probably blushed. "Oh, I was just… thinking."

"Thinking, huh?" Did he suspect her forbidden thoughts? Could he tell? His frown melded to half-smile. "Look at this. Isn't this off-the-wall?" He'd opened all the desk drawers, which remained full of office supplies and even some personal effects: letters, a locket, a monogrammed prayer book, an old bracelet that read JOYCLYN in cursive engraving.

"And check this out."

Jerrica turned. Along the wall sat a glass-paned metal cabinet. She tried to turn the handle but found it locked. The priest wiped dust off the panes, peering in. "This is amazing. There are still pharmaceuticals in there."

"Pharmaceuticals?"

"Remember, this place served as a hospice for terminal priests. I'm sure most of them were on some sort of medication or another, and this is obviously where they kept them, in the abbess' office."

"That really *is* bizarre," Jerrica noted. "Medications, drugs? You would think the Church would've taken them all out of there when the abbey closed."

"Yeah," Alexander agreed, scratching his head. He shrugged.

"Let's go check out the basement, see what's down there."

She followed him sheepishly. He redonned his black shirt but didn't button it back up. *He knows,* she feared, digging her fingernails into her thigh. *Why else would he have put his shirt back on? He knows I'm staring at him, he knows I'm fantasizing.*

His black priest shoes snapped echoes up into the hollow staircase. She followed him down. Her nipples tingled, she knew they must be standing out like points through her white halter. At least Alexander seemed distracted now, flipping through more blueprint copies.

At the landing, they turned, followed down a dark, hot hall of bare cement flooring.

"Unexcavated," the priest murmured.

"What?"

"That's what these plans say. They say the entire basement is unexcavated."

"I don't...quite follow you."

He lit another cigarette, the insides of his pectorals showing in the opened black shirt. "These plans are pure garbage. I can't believe Halford would do this to me."

"They must be out of date," she guessed.

"*Fucked up,* is what they are," the priest obscened. "Pardon my language, but this is par for the course of the Catholic Church. What kind of bullshit is this?"

"I still don't understand," Jerrica said.

He frowned up at her then, the cigarette fuming. "We're standing in the basement, right?"

"Right."

"Well, according to these blueprints, there *is* no basement."

Jerrica shrugged. Big deal, they were old blueprints. Her fantasies, though, continued to drag at her, like undertow. More dices of sunlit flesh, more prurient images: Now she lay naked with her legs parted so thoroughly her tendons hurt. But the pain only added to the pleasure. He was on top of her, thrusting into her…

"That son of a bitchin' Halford," Alexander remarked.

His cock stuck up her so far she imagined she could feel it bumping her stomach…

"Don't ask me why I think this, but I'll bet my benefice pay that that goddamn guy *knows* that these blueprints aren't updated. Shit, it says right in the corner frame: 1921!"

Come in me! Come in me! she was thinking, feeling each thrust. That, for whatever arcane reason, was the only thing she wanted in the world: his semen in her. *His come in my pussy,* the thought groaned. The fantasy jumbled on. His arms girded her back like iron braces, his mouth sucked her tongue, and that's when she felt it all pouring into her, like viscid broth, like warm wax.

Oh, shit, she thought. *I fucking love you...*

"I'd like to kick that wussy's ass up and down the fucking street," the priest eloqueneted. "That stick-in-the-mud crusty, lying motherfucker sent me all the way out here and didn't even bother to get me new floorplans."

"Father," Jerrica said, finally surfaced from the dream. "Do priests use language like that?"

"Fucking-A right they do, honey." He was visibly outraged, tumultuous. "When our superiors treat us like fucking subordinate idiots, you're *goddamned* right we use language like. That shit-for-brains lazy motherfucker…"

Jerrica was appalled yet fascinated. She considered it an honor to witness a priest with his dander up, to the extent of profanity. It seemed to break a sacred rule, it shattered what she envisioned as the mold of the priesthood. But then—

Something caught her eye.

She had to agree: the basement seemed bizarre, even useless. It existed as a single corridor, walled by bricks on either side. There were no doors, no rooms, nothing. Only a few broken footing windows offered light. She would've expected to find at least a utility room down here, a mechanical room, a fuse closet.

"Nothing," Alexander griped. "Not one room down here; it doesn't make sense. There's never even been electricity in this joint; otherwise there'd be some kind of transformer, and it would have to be down here. But look." He pointed upward. The stucco'd ceiling seemed filmed with carbon-black soot. "Same as upstairs. For the whole time this place was open, they were using oil lamps, for shit's sake."

Jerrica noted the oddity, but still didn't quite understand the priest's irritation. *Why should he care?*

That, however, was not the cause of her query, when she squinted along the wall, pointed, and said, "What's this?"

"You gotta be shitting me," the priest murmured.

Another line of brick-demarcation. It was plain to see. A wedge of newer bricks filled in a block-space in the wall, as though a doorway had been there years ago but had been filled in. It was just like the obstruction upstairs, at the admin office. Only there was one difference:

"What the..*fuck?*" Alexander profaned once more, staring at the incongruently that Jerrica had already noticed.

"It looks like," she began, but even her own bewilderment choking out the rest of the words.

The newer insertion of bricks looked, well—

That's the strangest thing, Jerrica pondered.

—as though they'd been impacted by some kind of tool.

As though someone had tried to break them down.

1 2 3 4 5 6 7 8 9 0
TEN
ERIK
1999

TEN

(I)

A cemetery, Charity thought. *Of course...*

The heat of afternoon quickly burned off the late morning's haze. But the interior woods remained cool in dappled shade, breaking only periodically. Winding footpaths through the brambles took them away. Aunt Annie had calmed down by now, almost as if the bunches of flowers in her hand gave her solace. Charity felt horrible, though, finally aware of the weight of guilt the graceful old woman had been carrying all these years. Certainly her previous poverty wasn't her fault, nor was it her fault that the mineral settlement had come so late. Charity tried to reckon what it must be like for her Annie, trodding onward with all these broken pieces and bad luck...

"Here we are," Annie said, just as the sun dazzled the shade away. The trail ended, emptied into a long, open dell. Spiring trees flanked to either side, in surprising symmetry; lush, high grass made a carpet pocked by simple gravestones, crudely carved.

"This is the family cemetery," Annie related. She seemed to stare in thwarted awe, as if reminding herself that she, too, would someday be interred here.

"It's very nice," Charity said. "It seems much more honest than typical cemeteries, much more real."

But Aunt Annie acted as though she hadn't heard her, too caught up in more personal reflections. Charity gazed out into the sunlit dell; it was oblong, like a coffin. *Appropriate,* she thought. Bees buzzed, hopping from one wildflower to the next, bundling pollen. Small birds watched them from the high Mockernuts. The scent of honeysuckle and hickory was delightfully overpowering, it made Charity high, in a sense. But eventually, this preliminary sensory impact lagged behind. *She brought me here for some reason,* she remembered. And that could only mean one thing:

She brought me here to show me a specific grave...

Charity had a good idea whose.

"I've never showed ya your mother's grave, Charity," the elder spoke. "And I never told ya the whole details. You was too young, at least that's how I saw it."

"I understand, Aunt Annie."

"But now it's time ya saw, an' heard it all."

Charity followed the old woman's fragile form straight out into the burning sunlight. The ends of the high grass sifted; the flower-scents stirred. Around the graveyard's peripheries, she noticed wild roses, stalks of lupines, sunflowers with great dropping heads. Their feet followed the path beat down by Annie's feet day after day; Charity could see it, swarming forward around the unsophisticated stones. And just then it occurred to Charity how long this little jaunt had taken—it must've been a good two miles from the boarding house. *No wonder she's in such good shape for her age!* Making this walk on a daily basis would keep anyone in shape.

Annie stopped at a pale granite stone. The inscription, obviously carved by hand, read: SISSY.

That was all.

At its foot lay a dried cache of yellow coneflowers and tarweeds. *Yesterday's offerings,* Charity speculated.

"This is your mother's grave, dear," finally revealed. "My sister."

Charity already knew the gist of the details: her mother had committed suicide shortly after her birth, and shortly after that, her husband—Charity's father—had been killed in a mine explosion. Charity had never even seen a picture of her mother. Everyone out here back then was too poor to even own a camera.

Aunt Annie was stifling tears. "I'm just so sorry, Charity, things did'nt work out like they shoulda," she sobbed. "I hope you know that, and I hope Sissy knows it."

"Of course she does, Aunt Annie," Charity consoled. "You did the very best you could to raise me. The state taking me wasn't your fault."

But Charity could scarcely think of more to offer. This was difficult. *I'm standing before my own mother's grave,* she told herself. It was a bizarre realization.

Annie took up the old dried flowers and replaced them with new ones. But the second new bundle remained in her arms.

"She was a wonderful gal, your mother," Annie elaborated. "A fine woman and a good mother. But she just let the bad things get to her..."

Charity burned, however sadly, with the next question. "How—how did she commit suicide?"

Annie blinked, staring down at the sparsely marked grave. "I cain't talk about it right now, sweetheart. But I'se realize ya got a right ta know about yer mama, and I'll tell ya all about it later, back the house."

"That's fine, Aunt Annie."

But the woman looked crestfallen, she looked like a sleek, grand vine hammered too intently by the sun. "Charity, dear, what I'd like ya to do if ya don't mind is take these old flowers and wait fer me back by the path. I'll just be a minute."

"Sure, Aunt Annie," Charity agreed, taking yesterday's dried bundle of flowers.

"There's...another grave I need ta stop by," the elderly woman said.

Charity did as instructed, secretly grateful to be out of the fierce blade of the sun. She couldn't see much of her aunt for that time, just the vague shape of the woman's billowy dress moving down the rows. Then she seemed to stop, gazing down with more regret in her eyes.

She was standing in front of another grave, weeping.

Whose...grave? Charity struggled to wonder.

Did Annie have more relatives out here? Well—of course she did; she'd said this was the *family* graveyard. But Charity's question itched at her like a fresh patch of mosquito bites under anxious fingernails. *Whose grave?* she wondered. *Whose grave?*

She blinked, staring into the torrid sun. The question would not cease to form on her lips.

(II)

"So what do you think?" Jerrica asked. The Mercedes' open windows let in voluminous wind. "Don't you think that was strange?"

"The whole place is strange," Father Alexander tacked on. "My boss is strange. The whole Catholic Church is strange."

He was sideswiping the question, something, she'd learned, that he was very good at.

"Come on, Father! Bricking up the administration office is one thing. But that room downstairs?"

"We don't even know that it *is* a room," he reminded her. As he'd done upstairs, he'd tried to break into the basement anomaly, via the sledgehammer. He'd failed. *Whoever set these bricks,* he'd said, *weren't the same crew who did the pissant job upstairs on the admin office.*

He'd barely dented the face of new bricks.

"And what's weirder is the blueprints," she added. "What was it they said? Undesignated?"

"Un*excavated,*" he corrected. "And I ain't arguing with you. You'd think my friggin' monsignor would've given me updated blueprints. According to these, there isn't even a goddamn basement. What kind of shit is that?"

Again, Jerrica felt oddly charged by the demeanor of this profane priest. Just something about hearing such words come so casually from a clerical mouth.

Evening drained into the valley, with the beginnings of more of last night's heat lightning. It had been a long day, but not once did Jerrica regret asking to go to the abbey with the priest.

They'd happened upon several other oddities too. Upstairs, along the long hall, they examined the nuns' sleeping quarters, arranged almost like military barracks. Each room possessed a cot, a wall locker, and a spartan metal nightstand. The cots were stripped of their bedding, which made perfect sense, but the wall lockers and nightstands, however dust-laden, still seemed to contain a minutia of personal effects: letters, writing materials, rosaries, wind-up alarm clocks. And more personal effects were found in the nightstands in what must've been the in-patient dorm, where the sick priests were kept. Yes, it was strange, and Jerrica easily sensed that these loose ends bothered the priest.

"So what's this you're writing for the *Post?*" he asked, steering down Route 154. It was almost as though he'd asked this sudden question as a distraction, to change topics. As though he didn't want to talk about the abbey anymore. "An article on rural communities, something like that?"

"A *series* of articles, three *Weekenders* in a row. The societal symptomologies of the modern Blue Ridge Mountain culture," she tried to embellish as articulately as she could. "I want the works. The people, the economy, the history, even the folklore."

"Sounds like an interesting piece," Alexander said, sticking a butt in his mouth.

Jerrica, with a cupped hand, lit the cigarette for him, then lit one for herself. "It'll be more than interesting, it'll be a step up the ladder. I could kick myself, though, for not bringing my camera."

"What?" The priest frowned. "To the abbey?"

"Of course. The abbey's as much a part of this place as anything: the sewing shops and the whorehouse and the moonshiners. If it's part of the truth of this town, I've got to write about it."

"I wish I could tell you more, but I don't know that much. All the diocese gave me to go on were those blueprints, and the notarized closure statement."

"But you do know about the nuns themselves, and that'd make a great addition to my article." Jerrica felt on a professional roll now, she felt inspired. Perhaps her forbidden attraction to the priest gave fuel to her creativity. She knew she could be as attracted as she wanted—she still couldn't have him, and *that* seemed more exciting than anything else.

"I can't believe how much time passed while we were out there," Alexander cited. "Sorry for taking up your whole day, but, hell, you were the one who asked to come."

"I had a great time, Father," she allayed him. "It was invigorating. And I can't wait for you to tell me about the nuns."

Alexander laughed. "Not much to tell unless you want a lesson in austerity." When they passed the old, closed church again, he crossed himself. More dedication, more faith. Christ, she admired that, without even knowing why. In all her life, Jerrica had never been to church, had never even believed in God as anything more than the Easter Bunny. She blinked, then, shook her head. What had he said?

"What were you saying? Something about austerity?"

At once, the priest seemed anxious, on edge. "I'll tell you all about them, but— Earlier, didn't you point out a tavern in town?"

"Yeah. The Crossroads. Charity and I went there last night, as a matter of fact. Just turn here," she guided, pointing to the veer-off to Main Street, "and you're there."

"Outstanding," he said. "How about you let this busted, over-the-hill priest buy you a drink?"

Jerrica felt lit up. "Sounds fine by me."

(III)

"Hail, Dicky," Tritt Balls Conner elucidated, rubbin' his crotch ta boot. "That fuckin' job we did on the fat gal's still got my dog a'hoppin."

Aw, man, Dicky groaned to himself. *This guy's a psy-ker-path.* "What say we just cool it fer now, huh, Balls? We done enough today, ain't we? Tells ya what. I could use me's a cold beer."

Tritt Balls, stroked that devil goatee'a his, lookin' speculatively out the winder-shield. "Ya knows somethin', Dicky? Hail. I'se thinks yer right. A tall, cold one'd do the job a might nice right now. Let's git us a few."

Thank God. Balls could be some mean trouble, yes sir! And that fat chick they'd busted up today? Boppin' her in the belly an' makin' her puke? That had got Balls' dander up a right fierce—afters, he'd jacked hiself off in the 'Mino ta boot! Dicky didn't wanna be part'a no more ruckin', no he didn't, an' he were glad as glad could be when Balls agreet ta havin' a beer.

So's Dicky, what he did just then was he pulled that El Camino'a his right inta the parkin' lot'a The Crossroads. But 'fore he could do so fully, he glanced over an' complained, "Aw, shee-it, Balls! Cain't ya ever git enough?"

Balls Conner grinnned back like a tomcat, his jeans pulled down his ankles. Whuppin' his willy fierce he was, an' not even mindin' that gal's shit still on his dick, an' just then he spooged hisself big-time. Looked like a load'a Elmer's Glue, it did, sittin' there on his belly.

"Told ya, Dicky, cornholin' an' killin' that fat beaver back there got my dog'a barkin'. But now that I'se hadda good come, I'se *really* ready fer a beer, I is! So's let's go!"

(IV)

A few heads turned, naturally, when Jerrica entered The Crossroads with Father Alexander; the moment seemed to freeze, faces locking up, the clack of billiards balls halting, hands cocked back at the dart boards. "And my broker isn't even E.F. Hutton," the priest joked. But in less than another moment, the tavern's conventions returned. Jerrica and the priest took a far booth.

"Howdy, Father, miss," greeted the floor waitress, a cherubic brunette in cutoffs and a pink tubetop. Her bellybutton peeked over the snap of her shorts. "What can I git yawl?"

"A pitcher of beer, please," Alexander said. "Don't care what kind as long as it's cold."

"Comin' right up."

Above them, ceiling fans roved lazily, breaking the hot air, and when the beer arrived, it sluiced right down their parched throats.Alexander leaned back, sighed. The day's labors had finally caught up with him, but Jerrica herself felt kindled. She knew what it was: it was him. His presence enlivened her, recharged her.

"God, that's good," he remarked, taking another big sip of beer.

"Yeah. After all that hot work all day?" Jerrica sipped her own; her concentration, however, remained fixed on Father Alexander. He didn't look like a priest at all; he looked more like a refined tough guy, wearing the Roman collar for kicks. She'd seen his body from the waist up—his face seemed the same. Lean, even incised. Intense.

Her fascination wouldn't let go.

"So how far along are you with your article?" he asked.

"Just notes—I brought my laptop, so I can work on the road; I've only been here two days. But it's coming along well. This piece is going to kick butt."

"Don't forget to mention me," he joked.

"Oh, don't worry." She smiled bright. "I will… But you promised to tell me about the nuns."

The comment seemed amusing. Alexander lit a cigarette, sighing smoke. "The Sisters of the Heavenly Spring," he recalled. "They're an order of cloistered nuns that make lye soap look like Ivory. Very hardcore, so to speak. They even wear habits."

"But I thought all nuns wore habits," Jerrica ventured.

"No. Misconception. The Second Vatican Council lightened up on all the rules, cut a lot of slack. But the Sisters of the Heavenly Spring? They didn't care, they didn't want to hear it. They're Epiphanists, kind of like the French Foreign Legion of nuns. The hardest, grubbiest, crappiest work that the Church has to offer—they volunteer. They believe in the *severity* of faith."

"Well, what about you?" Jerrica dared to ask. "Aren't all priests severe?"

Alexander chuckled. "Depends on how you define the word."

"Well, I mean—" She knew she shouldn't ask this, but her curiosity wouldn't release its grip. "Priests are celibate. Isn't celibacy severe?"

"Oh, no, that's the easy part," he answered. "That's cake."

"But..." More hesitation. She couldn't help it. "Isn't sex something God created, for people to enjoy?"

"For those in Christian wedlock to enjoy within the realms of procreative love. But God didn't create it to be exploited, which is what's going on now. Just because it feels good doesn't mean one has carte blanche. Heroin feels good too, but it's still evil. The devil's everywhere, twisting the minds of the faithful, and those who would be faithful. It's a card game."

Jerrica stared at the man's words. They sounded so antiquated–*Those who would be faithful*—but the conviction behind the words seemed to make them real. "Do you really believe...in the devil?"

"Of course," Alexander replied without reluctance. "Some priests will duck that question, with metaphors. They'll tell you that the devil is just a symbol of the failings of humanity, but they know it's more than that. There really is a devil, sitting on some abyssal throne in the blackest guts of the earth. And he's smiling bigtime. He's kicking serious ass, and he loves it."

This was getting too deep. She didn't want to challenge him, because she sensed that if she did, he would bury her with thesis she could not argue. She didn't want to argue. She just wanted *to know*. "Okay, back to celibacy. Why go through all that hardship?"

"It's not hardship, it's a gift."

"Why go through all that abstention and frustration when you don't have to?"

"I *don't* have to, that's the point. I do it because it's my call. It's my call to not have sex. I've had plenty of sex in my younger years. When I was a teenager, when I was in the army. But for all that time I knew there was something else more important waiting for me, and it excluded sex. So I stopped. Simple."

"But *why?*" she nearly whined in confusion.

The priest leaned back in the booth, one arm up, his beer in his other hand. The cigarette jiggled in his mouth as he answered: "I'm celibate because it's a sign of the Kingdom where no one will be given or taken in marriage and our love will be universal as God is universal. I'm celibate because it makes me more available to the people of God, who themselves constitute the Church, which is the Body of Christ." He shrugged lackadaisically, dragged his cigarette, spewed smoke. "I'm celibate in the imitation of Jesus, who elected to be bound to no one in *particular* so that he might be embraced by *all*, in an eternal covenant of living sacrifice."

Jerrica stared.

"See?" he said. "It's that simple." Then he laughed. "Shit. It ain't for everyone, and it ain't supposed to be. It's another mystery of faith."

The words seemed to disperse, like glitter in the air.

"But you're so much in opposite," she said next. "I mean, you're a priest, but you smoke, you drink, you even *cuss*."

"Smoking and drinking, hell, we're allowed to. It's about the only thing the Pope hasn't jacked out from under our feet. And as far as cussing goes—well, communication is communication. If I say 'Holy Father, I beg thee to forgive my transgressions and my offenses against thee,' that means the same thing as saying, 'Holy shit, God, I fucked up and I'm really sorry, so how about giving me a break?' Same thing. God doesn't care what words you use. Shit. He only cares what you mean."

Fascinating. He was a *uniqueness.*

"But the Church does," the priest rattled on. "And that's where I have some big problems. That's why I ain't got my own joint."

"Your own...*joint?*"

"My own parish. 'Joint' is priest-jabber for 'parish.' I cuss too much. I speak my mind too readily. And I don't kiss ass. It's employment harassment, you ask me. But I don't give a shit. It's God's will, and that's good enough for me. If God would rather have me psychotherapizing clerical nutcases and reopening abbeys in the boondocks, then that's what I'm gonna do. He must have a reason, and I ain't gonna get in a pissing contest with God. I'll do what He fucking tells me and I'll like it."

This continued conviction, however colloquial, did not cease to invigorate her. It only made him more fantastic, more out of the mold. *I've never met anyone so interesting in my life...*

"But enough of this religious talk," he urged. "Tell me more about you."

The inquest shocked her. "I—I don't know," she stammered. "There's really not that much to say."

"Well, maybe there isn't—not now. But there will come a time when you'll have a lot to say. One day you'll see *your own* call to God."

She didn't even believe in God, but she couldn't tell him that, could she? Then again, though, she sensed very strongly that he already knew this, that he could tell.

So what did he mean?

Her own notice of herself changed the topic, which was probably a good time to do so. She ran her hand down her forearm and saw it come away faintly smudged. "I can't believe how dirty I got at the abbey."

"I told you it was a grubby place. Hot, dank, dusty. But no one's fled the bar yet, so I guess that means we don't stink too bad."

Jerrica couldn't help but laugh at his remarks, her fingers unconsciously rubbing her own bodily grit. "It was *so hot* in there." And then her visions swept away; suddenly she drifted in the midst of her fantasies again. The afternoon heat of the abbey, the sweat drenching out of them, and the priest's own sweat glistening on his naked chest like veneer as he swung the sledgehammer time and time again. Yes, the humid heat smothered her as she watched; it sucked on her skin, and the rising dust stuck to her like glue. Suddenly she was in the shower—with the priest. The cool torrent pouring down on them, revitalizing them. He stood behind her, his hands on her breasts, rubbing the soap to a thick lather. Then the bar lowered to her pubis, circled her hair, and brazenly slid across her vaginal lips back through the cleft of her buttocks. The sensation brought her to her tiptoes as his strong, callused hand worked the lather more thickly. An inquisitive finger probed the slit of her sex, then delved further, and sunk into her anus. Her nipples, suddenly, felt like nails sticking out of her skin; the brink of her orgasm threatened. So she turned, to stave it off, not ready to come yet. She likewise lathered him up with suds, letting the soap and the cascade of cool water wash away the day's work of grime. She knelt before him, sudsing his pubic hair and penis. The penis came alive, a separate entity, when she sucked the glans into her mouth; at once it hardened to a good seven inches, nudged her tonsils. She sucked it very precisely and very hard, at the same time allowing one hand to slide around his buttocks, sink a finger deep into his ass to massage his prostate. He shuddered and came almost instantaneously, launching one string of hot-salt semen into her mouth after the next. And in the suffix of the act, she sucked him down gently, milking out the last drop, swallowing the warm lump in her throat, and sighing. But she nearly shrieked at what he did next—he grabbed her hair, knelt himself, and hauled her roughly to the shower floor. Her neck jammed against the wall, and he was awkwardly pushing her knees into her face, extruding her vagina. At once the priest's mouth was on her, eating her like a rich meal, his index finger on her g-spot, his pinky up her ass, and then she came like some sort of underground demolition, her fluids releasing as he sucked them all out, sucked her orgasm out of her like fresh juice from a crushed fruit…

She reeled in the fantasy. *Stop it!* she yelled at herself. *You're with a priest!* She struggled to put back the pieces of her thoughts, remembered what she'd been talking about. "When you guys finally fix the abbey up, I hope you get air-conditioning."

"Oh, I'm sure we will. The Church will dump decent scratch into the place. They want to turn it into a state-of-the-art rehab center."

Her struggles began to ease, more pieces refitting. "It's still interesting, though. You know. The bricked up office, and all those personal effects still in the nuns' dorm rooms. And what about that strange wall downstairs where there shouldn't even *be* a downstairs? Someone tried to break through that wall. I wonder why."

"We'll find out soon," Alexander promised her. And just the simple fact that he'd used the pronoun "we'll" delighted her. It meant that he was *including* her.

"My tired old ass couldn't bust through it, fine. Then I'll rent a goddamn jackhammer, bust through it with that. Ten to one, though, we'll be disappointed. Probably just an empty room back there. 'Unexcavated,' just like the prints said—" The priest paused then, as if startled. All at once he seemed to be squinting at the wood-plank side of the booth. "Hey, what's this?"

Jerrica leaned over the table, knowing that she shouldn't—for the drastic incline of her upper body only highlighted her cleavage. Some devilish part of her wanted more notice out of his celibate self, wanted him to see her attributes. *Does he fantasize?* she wondered. *Are priests allowed to do that? Does he wish he could go to bed with me if he weren't celibate?* She leaned further, her hardened nipples poking through the sweat-damp white haltertop. But—

The cruel inducement collapsed.

What was he looking at?

She saw scratches faintly carved into the side of the wooden booth. "What's it say?" she asked.

"'The Bighead Was Here,'" he recited. "What the hell is that?"

"Oh!" Jerrica celebrated. Finally there was something she could tell *him*. "The Bighead," she said. "It's, like, a local myth. Charity was telling me about it last night, and so was some old guy at the bar. It's some child-monster that supposedly roams the woods, looking for people to eat."

Alexander refilled his beer mug. "What? And this *myth* is supposed to be true?"

"Well, no of course it can't be true. But it's part of the culture out here. All cultures have their legends."

The priest rubbed his chin, his eyes thinned. "Well, there's something about legends that always seem to have some root in fact. Vampirism and porphyria, for example. Lycanthropy and lupine hebephrenic syndrome. Schizophrenics who believe they're possessed by demons, aliens, what have you. My point is, however far-fetched, there are quite a few 'myths' that actually harbor more truth than fabrication."

It was an interesting point, but Jerrica couldn't help but laugh nonetheless. "I don't think we have to worry about a hill-bred monster-child trying to eat us."

"Hope you're right," Alexander said. "I'm sure I'd leave a bad taste in his mouth, dirty as I am right now."

Jerrica laughed again, tipsily now. Er, perhaps, a bit more than that. She'd only had a few beers thus far, but now she realized how thoroughly they'd snuck up on her. And it was no wonder. She hadn't eaten all day, she'd been out in the sun, working in the abbey's furnace-like heat. Of course alcohol would impact her more than usual. Suddenly her better judgment, if she even had any to begin with, slipped away. Her boldness surged as it frequently did. Her old self never failed her. She always knew when she was about to say something she'd regret, immediately before she said it.

"Father," she said. Aw, Christ, the beer was whacking her now, dizzying her. She quickly jerked her head. "Can I—uh, would you mind if I asked a personal question."

"Hey, personal questions are the best kind," the priest said, and with that, Jerrica repressed another laugh; she'd told Charity the same exact thing just yesterday, during their conversation about Goop.

"I mean, you don't have to answer, I mean, you know, if it puts you on the spot or anything, but—" She blinked hard, to clear her head. *What on earth is wrong with you, Jerrica!* she hollered at herself. *You can't ask a priest something like that!*

Of course she couldn't. But she asked anyway.

"If you weren't a priest, would you, you know… Would you be attracted to me?"

After the words left her mouth, the regret fell on her head like a cave-in.

But Father Alexander shot a sly smile. "Hey, if I weren't a priest, I'd be all over you like black on a bible," he said.

What an answer! Jerrica blushed, and that wasn't easy.

He laughed outright at her expression, poured them two more beers. "But I don't want you to think I'm teasing you, so I'll give you the whole gist." Shit. He was getting serious now. "You're a beautiful woman, Jerrica, and the grace of God allows me to perceive and admire and acknowledge the beauty of women, and of all people. But that's where the buck stops, just to set the record straight. I got holy vows that I've made to God, and I ain't gonna break 'em for no one."

"Oh, but I didn't mean th—"

"I know you didn't, I'm just saying. I can't look at a woman in lust, I can't look at a woman in sexual desire. I'm not allowed to, so I don't. I admire your beauty because God gave it to you, and anything God gives is beautiful."

She tried not to show her disappointment with this vocal appendix, and she knew it was ridiculous to be disappointed at any rate. He was a priest, for God's sake! What was she thinking?

Thankfully, he broke the ice of the silence, laughing, "And besides, you should've seen the stuff I was doing when I was a teenager. I made Bill Clinton look like Mr. Rogers."

She laughed it off. Of course she did. She couldn't possibly have been thinking—

"Hey there, blondie," a sudden voice intruded. "I'se say, you're about the purdiest thing I ever did see. You's make my whistle blow, shee-it!"

Both Jerrica and the priest looked up at the same time. Some tall lean redneck, with long stringy hair, a tractor hat, and a sparse goatee had stepped right up to the front of their booth. Beer reeked in the wake of his voice, and some fat kid stood right behind him.

Alexander didn't falter. "Hey, man, bug off. Can't you see the lady and I are having a private conversation? Private means you ain't invited."

"Hail, holy man, who're you, huh?" The guy leaned back, hands on hips, and laughed. "I'se ain't talkin' to you, I'se talkin' ta her."

"Yeah?" Alexander mocked, "Well's lemme tell ya somethin', Einstein, *I'se* talkin' ta you, an' *I'se* tellin' ya ta beat feet an' mind yer own business."

The bearded kid grinned. The grin was menacing, His pecs flexed beneath a black t-shirt that read showed a Care Bear proffering a middle finger. "I'll'se do you a big favor, priest, an' pretends I'se didn't hear that. I'se talkin' ta the lady, see, and a lady this hot *is* my business."

"Fuck off," Jerrica said, her face crimped with distaste.

The kid and his fat sidekick laughed. "Don't'cha know no respect? Cain't be sayin' words like that'n front of a priest."

"Fuck off," Alexander said.

"My, ain't you somethin'! What'cha gonna do, Father? Shoo me off with that collar'a yours."

"I'll kick your ass up and down the street," Alexander said very coolly, "if you don't grow up, get a life, and leave us alone."

Silence descended on the bar as though the roof had fallen in.

Still faces peered. Alexander recognized the situation: a redneck stalemate. But something was going to happen, and it was the bearded kid who'd have to make the first move.

The kid rubbed the crotch of his jeans, smiling sharp as ever. "What's a purdy thing like you doin' in a bar with a holy man anyway, sweetcakes? He fuckin' you? You suckin' his cock? Hail, I'se thought priests weren't supposed ta do stuff like that, 'cept ta each other, ain't that right, Dicky?"

"Uh, that's right Balls," the fat kid said, hefting his gut. "An' would ya git'a load'a the titties on 'er? Shee-it! I thinks I just gotta have me a squeeze on 'em, an' I'se think this old man priest here ain't got the nuts to do nothin' 'bout it."

Alexander stubbed out his butt. "If you touch her, I'll smack you in the head so hard you'll see stars."

"Yeah?" Another guffaw. "We'll'se see 'bout that." The grin held, dark eyes slitted over it. Then—

"You better not," Alexander calmly warned.

Then this bearded, long-haired kid reached down very quickly and grabbed Jerrica's left breast. She winced, squealed, and—

SMACK!

—Alexander punched the kid in the side of the head so hard he saw stars. The kid reeled back, arms reeling, landed on a table and broke it. Then he slid to the floor.

Alexander stood up, fists clenched but with a look of total peace on his face. "How about you, fat boy," he inquired of the other. "You want some too?"

The fat kid stammered, took a hesitant step forward. "I'se—I'se'll bust yer head, priest! I'se—"

Alexander nearly smiled. His left hand darted, grabbed the kid's lovehandle and pinched down like a claw. The kid wailed. Then Alexander's right fist collided solidly with the kid's jaw.

SMACK!

A strange sound, like a bat striking a cement floor. Pain contorted the fat kid's dumpling face as he, too, reeled backward and fell.

"You boys get out of here before you start to bother me," Alexander said, then kicked the first guy in the butt as he was crawling up. "You don't want to be late for bedcheck at the reform school, do you?"

Both of them stumbled away, grumbling and wobbling for the door. Patrons laughed and applauded.

"That was...wonderful!" Jerrica celebrated.

"Not for my hand it wasn't," Alexander replied, shaking it. "Like punching a couple of big rocks. Those boys must have concrete where their brains should be." Then he looked dismally at the broken table, groaned, and whipped out his diocesan checkbook. "Sorry about the damage," he apologized to the crusty keep at the bar. "The Catholic Church will be more than happy to reimburse—"

"Forget it, Father." The keep was chuckling. "Believe me, it's worth the price'a fixin' a table to finally see someone kick tail on those two punks. Gracie! Git the father and his friend here another pitcher—on the house."

"Hey, thanks," Alexander delighted. He sat back down with Jerrica. "That's damn nice of him, slipping us a free pitcher."

But Jerrica remained astonished by his previous feat. "You really are a trip. I can't believe it, I just got to watch a Catholic priest beat up two rednecks."

Alexander lit up again, shrugged. "Sometimes you gotta break bad on these kids—it's the only way they'll learn. But I'll tell you, when I was their age, the bad guys were a hell of a lot badder than that."

Outside, a heavy motor could be heard rumbling. Then tires squealed out of the lot.

Alexander chuckle under his breath. "Naw, I don't think we'll have to worry about those fellas anymore."

1 2 3 4 5 6 7 8 9 0
ELEVEN
ERIK
1999

ELEVEN

(II)

The Bighead were gittin' horny again, an' hungry. It'd been a long day hikin' through the woods an' over the hills'n dales, an' bys now, the Lower Woods where Grandpap raised him seemed farthers away ta him than the moon.

Yeah, the Lower Woods, they was behind him now. They weren't his home no more.

The Outside World—*that* were his home now...

The sun were dippin', takin' its fine bright light from the sky. Darkness were comin', it were. And as The Bighead clopped along, through bushes'n vines'n the thicket, he was rememberin' his Grandpap an' alls the things the old man taughts him. Fer years, old Grandpap had hisself a truck, an' he'd drive out fer a spell ever now'n then, ands come back with some rube gal he'd picked up hitcher-hikin' er somethin', an' that's how Bighead learnt 'bout the birds'n bees an' 'bout how ta bust a gal's poon an have a nut. A'corse, it never worked out quite like the way Bighead thought it'd. "Tarnations, boy!" Grandpap'd wailed once, after watchin' The Bighead bust a chick. "God shore did hang a pecker on you, He did! Big as Grandma Meyer's rollin' pin it is! Problee ain't *never* gonna git ta come proper hangin' a pecker that big! S'post ta fuck 'em an' come in 'em, Bighead, ands give 'em a baby! Ain't s'post ta kill 'em!" The Bighead were confused by this; he wanted ta do what were right, but it didn't look like he were doin' it, no sir. His dick so big it were killin' gals, that weren't the way it was s'post ta be, not accordin' ta Grandpap. But what could he do!

He thoughts then again 'bout that big boomin' Voice he'd heard, tellin' him ta COME. Bighead weren't one ta clearly see a whole lotta meanin' in life but he figgurt it cain't hurt ta foller the Voice like he been tolt. An' that's just what he been doin'! Walkin' fer miles ever day, not knowin' at all where he were goin' but goin' just the same. "The meanin' of life'll call ya someday, Bighead," Grandpap'd tolt him shortly 'fore he died. "An' ya gots ta foller that meanin'."

Just a bit'a heat lightnin' crackled just above him, an' The Bighead heard the Voice again.

COME, it said.

An', well, Bighead were'a comin', but he was gittin' ta need to come in another way, ya know, an' he were terrible hungry.

An' that's when he saw that there li'l farmhouse…

(II)

"That's a good girl, that's my baby…"

Ned cowered in the dark of his room, listening.

"Ow, Daddy!" his sister fairly screamed. "It hurts!"

"Aw, now, darlin'," came their father's voice. "What'cha gots ta learn is that some things in life'll smart a little. Ain't nothin'. You'll'se git used ta it."

It happened most every night: Daddy'd come off the farm with the big green seed drill or the baler, and he'd sit and sip his shine till the moon came out. And that's when it always happened.

Ned was thirteen, Melissa was twelve. Their Mommy had died a few years back, some kind of cancer, the doctor told them. And ever since then, things just hadn't been right.

Young Ned *knew* they weren't right, because he listened to the other kids at the middle school, and none of them ever talked about such things happening. So Ned kept quiet about it, didn't want his friends to think his family wasn't normal.

But it just kept going on and on…

Daddy'd always start with Melissa first. Ned never actually saw, but he could guess. "It's Daddytime, Melissa," Daddy'd always say. They could smell that awful shine on his breath. Ned would wait in his room till it was his time. He'd hear what went on, though, and sometimes Daddy'd get a right nasty—Ned could hear the sharp wet *slaps!* That would be Daddy cracking Melissa in the face when she whined or didn't go along. Ned knew, because he got the same treatment too.

"That's it, sweetheart," Daddy was saying now on the other side of the wall. "All I wants is ta git ready fer yer brother, that's all."

She cried some more, like she was trying to swallow her sobs. Daddy made Melissa bleed most of the time, and that wasn't surprising, because it made Ned bleed too.

"Good girl. That's Daddy's *good* little girl. The smartin's over, honey. Daddy's all finished."

Oh, no, Ned thought. Because when Daddy said that, it meant it was Ned's turn.

Ned did the only proper thing he knew to do: he prayed to God. "'Trust ye in the Lord forever,'" Father Karpins would say every Sunday at church, before the church closed down. "'Believe in God, and He will help thee.'" Well, dammit, Ned *did* believe in God, and he prayed every night, but not once since mama died had God ever answered one of Ned's prayers.

The door clicked open. The hall light lanced into the room, landing on Ned's face.

"It's Daddytime, son…"

He'd long since stopped trying to fight it; Daddy hit him when he did. "You know what to do," Daddy said.

His thing was sticking out, kind of bobbing, as he stepped forward.

"Be a good boy, now, and do good to yer Daddy."

Naked, shivering, Ned leaned forward. He didn't want to do it, but, God!, he didn't want to get hit. Daddy hit hard.

"Good boy. That's a good son…"

Ned had it in his mouth now, just the way Daddy had showed

else…stopped.

Daddy, suddenly, was off of him, and when Ned turned to see, he couldn't see much on account of the room was so dark. But he saw a shadow there, a *giant* shadow, lifting Daddy up by his head.

Then Daddy got thrown down onto the floor, and that big shadow was all over him. There was a fierce stink in the room, and an ugly thunking sound which Ned guessed were his Daddy's feet kicking the floor.

Then Daddy screamed…

A chill bolted right up Ned's spine. The door swung open further and Melissa rushed in—her little white nightgown had a red spot in the front—and she squealed when she looked down.

"Melissa! Come here!" Ned shouted.

His sister rushed to him and he put his arm around her to try to comfort her. It was so dark they couldn't really see what was happening, but they knew it wasn't good for Daddy, the way he was screaming there on the floor with that big shadow lying on top of him.

Melissa blurted sobs. "Who—who *is* it?"

"I think it's God," Ned said, tightening his grip about his sister's shoulder. "I prayed ta God ta make it stop, and it did! That big shadder walked in an' grabbed Daddy an' it stopped!"

"It's—" Melissa swallowed another sob. "It's…*God?*"

"I—I don'ts know fer shore, but I thinks so."

The room rocked with Daddy's screams. It was louder and sounded worse than the time the power-tedder pulled up that big rock in the field and fed it into the works. No, Daddy's screams didn't hardly sound human.

But then they stopped, and then there were sounds like dry twigs snapping, but they could still see that big shadow lying on top of Daddy, humping like, and then there was a grunt and something like a sigh.

Then another sound, something crunching, like walnuts maybe, and then a wet eating sound.

And then the shadow stood up…

It must've been eight foot tall, and its face stepped right into the moonlight beaming in from the window. And Ned and Melissa—they *saw* that face.

"That ain't God!" Melissa screamed.

No, Ned reckoned, *I guess it ain't.*

"God don't look like that! He's a nice peaceful man sittin' onna throne, ands he got long white hair'n a white beard!"

But what they were looking at right then was a face nothing like what Melissa just said. The head looked bigger than a watermelon, and the eyes in the face…

Ned nearly screamed.

One eye was big as a grapefruit, and the other small as a grape. And the mouth… The mouth looked like a black hole full of broken glass.

"It ain't God, Ned!" his sister shrieked. "It's the devil!"

The devil? But that didn't make any sense! Ned had prayed to *God* for help. Not the devil.

"It's the devil," Melissa sobbed. "An' he's gonna do the same ta us that he just done ta Daddy!"

But Ned couldn't believe it. He *wouldn't* believe it. *Naw, no way!* God wouldn't do something so mean like that, would He? Let the devil hump their heinies after saving them from Daddy doing the same? No! No way! Ned *refused* to believe God could be such a right son-of-a-bitch to let something like that happen!

So he did what he always did. He prayed.

Please, God. Me'n my sister, we ain't done no one no wrong. And we'se know You wouldn't let the devil do them things ta us. I thank Ya with all my heart fer savin' me from Daddy, but now I'se prayin' again, just like Father Karpins said ta. I'm prayin' fer Ya ta make the devil go away.

The devil drooled, staring at them, and that's when young Ned took note of the size of his thing. It was *huge,* and—

Aw, no!

It was getting hard again.

It'd kill them both, Ned could tell just by looking at the size of the thing. *No way!* he thought again. *No way God's gonna let this happen ta us!*

Melissa was gibbering. The devil's shadow moved closer…

Please, God! Ned prayed with his eyes squeezed shut. *Please!*

Make the devil go away! I'm BEGGIN' ya!

And then that awful stink left the room. Melissa shuddered in his arm.

When Ned opened his eyes back up, he saw that the devil had done just what he'd asked God for it to do.

The devil had gone away.

(III)

Shee-it. They was just tots, they was! The Bighead stomped off away from the house, inta the darkness. He'd had hisself a fine nut up the father's ass, an' he'd busted open his noggin an' et some *fine* brains, he did, an' filled his belly like it needed ta be filled. An' then he were hard again fast, too. But when he saw them there kids—shee-it!

So's little they was. Weren't no point in fuckin' 'em. Shee-it, big as The Bighead were, he problee couldn't even git it *in* 'em. Best ta just leave.

Yes sir. That's what he felt were best ta do. 'Sides, he were feelin' grateful, he were. Hadda good nut, got hisself a good bellyfull'a good hot brains. It were time ta move on now.

'Cos if there were one thing The Bighead felt more strongly than anything, it were that he hadda move on. He hadda mission, he did. Didn't know what it was, but he still had it.

An' above him just then, in that big black sky, more'a that weird silent lightnin' flashed, an' when it flashed, he heard that one familiar word in his head:

COME.

(IV)

"It was *outrageous!*" Jerrica bragged at the parlor table. She sat next to Father Alexander, and opposite them were Charity and Aunt Annie. Annie had poured raspberry wine and set out a plate of funnelcakes and homemade molasses. Jerrica, more than half-drunk now, rambled onward, "These two guys, you should've seen them. Lowlife punks to the max. And when they started giving us a hard time, Father Alexander threw it right back in their faces! The bearded guy touched me, and when he did, it made my skin crawl. But a second later, the guy was flying across the bar! Father punched him right in the face!"

Alexander tried not to show his smirk. Yeah, he'd kicked ass on a couple of guys that needed it, but now, after some thinking, he didn't feel too cool about it. A line of Scripture kept occurring to him, from the Gospel of Matthew. '*All they that take the sword shall perish by the sword.*' And another, far more important: *He who smite thee on the right cheek, turn to him the other also.* Alexander, despite Jerrica's celebration, spewed smoke in self-disgust. *The guy grabbed her,* he tried to rationalize. *He touched her. For Christ sake, he squeezed her breast. I had to do something, didn't I?*

But he wondered now, if God approved of what he'd done. *Gee, why do I have this funny feeling that he doesn't?*

"That's amazing, Father," Charity said. "A priest, taking on local hoodlums."

"It was no big deal," he tried to sluff it off. "Just one of those things. I probably should've tried to handle it better."

"Handle it better?" Jerrica questioned. "It was you or them. The law of the jungle, you know."

Alexander poised a smiled, nodded. *Yeah, honey, but I'm a priest. I go by a different law...*

A minute pause gave him the opportunity to switch subjects. *Thank God!* He glanced over to Charity and her aunt. "So what did you two do today?"

"Well, Father," the wonderful old woman began, "I felt it was high time to take Charity to her mother's grave. She was my sister—Sissy, I called her—as fine a woman as you'd ever meet. I just feel kinda bad, fer takin' so long."

"Oh, Aunt Annie, please," Charity heartfully objected. "There's *nothing* to feel bad about!"

Alexander interjected, with some Scripture. "Time means nothing," he said. "'Who can number the sand of the sea, and the drops of rain, and the days of eternity?' 'That which hath been is now, and that which is to be hath already been.'"

A tear came to Annie's eye at the condolence.

Yeah, Alexander considered, looking at her. *When she was young, I'll bet she turned enough heads to cause an epidemic of whiplash.* A fine woman, and an attractive one, age regardless. Sometimes you could just tell, without ever even knowing someone. Charity's aunt was good people.

"Oh!" Jerrica exclaimed once more, after another sip of wine. "You'll love this, Charity! Father and I were sitting in the bar—before those two punks put upon us—and guess what Father saw?"

Charity peered quizzically. "I can't imagine—"

"Right there, carved into the wooden side of the booth. Just like what we saw last night! BIGHEAD WAS HERE, someone wrote."

"Oh, God!" Charity dismissed.

"Bighead?" Aunt Annie asked.

"Oh, yeah. Some guy at the bar told us all about the local legend," Jerrica was more than happy to recall, with the help of the cool dark wine. "It's fascinating. I can't wait to write about it in my article. A rural legend, a *monster-child* born in the woods, a cannibal!"

"You best write about more important things," Annie suggested. "Ain't no call ta be insultin' our community with such stuff."

Jerrica seemed to shrivel. "Oh, I'm sorry, Annie. I didn't mean any harm. I just—"

"Don't worry about it, hon. It's just my opinion. You wanna write about our land, it's my reckonin' that you won't wanna add all that rubbish."

"Oh, I won't, Annie, I promise," Jerrica pleaded. *Christ, she's drunk,* Alexander noted. The babbled on, "Really, I meant no offense. I wasn't thinking—"

"I think," Alexander butt in, "that it's been an interesting day, and it's getting real late." By now, they were all getting on each other's nerves anyway. Best to close down now. He swigged the rest of his wine, stubbed out his 'rette in the turtle shell, and suggested, "Why don't we all turn in and get some sleep?"

"That's a great idea, Father," Charity agreed. Annie and Jerrica, reluctantly, agreed too.

"I'll see you all in the morning," the priest bid. "And as far as Bighead goes, I don't think we have to worry about him knocking on the door."

The women laughed in unison. But then—

Rap-rap-rap!

All heads turned in the parlor's dim lamplight.

Rap-rap-rap!

Someone was knocking on the door.

A sudden warm breeze gusted into the house when Annie opened the front door. *Who the hell could be calling at this hour?* Alexander wondered. A tourist looking for a late room? Someone whose car broke down? The priest squinted, Charity and Jerrica standing right behind him. Twilight, and intermittent whiplashes of far-off lightning, turned the figure at the doorstep into a strobic silhouette. A *tall* figure, big, brawny…

"Can I…help you?" Annie inquired, her eyes wide open. Her fingers curled about the door edge.

But then Alexander noticed something flash on the figure's chest, and behind him, in the circular drive, more lightning elucidated a shiny white car with a visibar, a gunrack, a crest on the door.

A cop, the priest realized.

"Sorry to disturb yawl, I know it's a might late," the man said. "I'm Sergeant Russell Mullen, Virginia State Police." The voice seemed canted in a typical drawl. Police came out as *poe-leece.*

"Is anything wrong, Officer?" Charity spoke up, her own voice meekened not only by curiosity but also by something close to apprehension.

"Well…" Officer Mullen stalled, one hand on his hip. "Please know that it ain't my intention to scare yawl, but what I wanna know is if any of ya seen any suspicious folks about, er I should say not folks but a man, a *big* man, like maybe peepin' in windows, hangin' about? A stranger walkin' down the road? Anything like that?"

They all replied in the negative, pausing themselves now at the unsettling inquiry. The priest's eyes narrowed, while the women's widened.

"There've been a couple murders, folks," the cop finally had out with it. "There's no cause fer alarm, I just—"

"*Murders* are no cause for alarm?" Jerrica testily remarked. "Well, ma'am, a'corse they are, but these murders've all been committed quite south'a here. Spread out as this area is, and bein' that Luntville don't have a police department of its own, it's takin' us a while to talk ta folks. Just a precaution is all, ta be on the safe side. You know how folks can be 'round here, don't feel it necessary to lock their doors an' windows an' all. I'm just here to advise ya ta do so."

"Just as a precaution," Jerrica mocked.

"That's right, ma'am."

Alexander asked, "Could you give us any details relative to the murders, Sergeant?"

"Well, Father, I really cain't do that," Mullen replied, more heat lightning flashing at his back, "'cos it's confidential. All I'm allowed ta say is that over the past coupla weeks some women have been found dead a right nastily. Just hill girls mostly, an' mountain gals."

Hill girls, Alexander considered. *Mountain gals.* "Were the murders sexually motivated?"

"Uh, yeah thcy was, sir, er I mean Father." Mullen flinched as if chilled. "The crime scenes was all really bad is what I was told."

"Any witnesses?"

"Not until tonight, Father. What happened tonight is the killer attacked a farmer in his home, murdered the poor guy right there while his kids watched. Thank the Lord he didn't turn on the kids, too. And them poor kids, they was understandably hysterical, not much useful they could give us fer a description, 'cept that the killer was big."

Alexander felt obliged to ask the next pique of his curiosity. "Was there also evidence of sexual assault with this latest victim, the man?"

Mullen grimly nodded. "An' I'm afraid that's about all I'm authorized ta say regardin' the details, Father."

"But where did this happen?" Charity asked. "You can tell us that, can't you?"

"The one tonight? Cain't tell ya the victim's name, but he'n his kids lived in an old farmhouse just outside'a Crick City."

Aunt Annie, at once, seemed relieved, a hand to her bosom. "That's close to fifty miles away."

"Yes ma'am, so you can see, like I said, there's no real cause fer alarm. Just want'cha ta be careful fer the time bein', until we catch this guy. You know, like I was saying, lock yer doors an' windows, an' keep an eye out."

"We will, Sergeant," Alexander offered, "and thanks for coming out."

"But wait a minute," Charity's next question leapt ahead. "What about the other murders, the women? Where did they occur? Where they further away?"

"Yes, ma'am, they was, all in the next county to be exact." But then the trooper faltered again, shifted uncomfortably. "And that's actually the main reason we're notifyin' folks in the Luntville area."

Alexander peered quizzically. It didn't make much sense; it seemed, even, like a poor judgment call on the part of the state police commander, or some grievous over-reaction. "I don't get it," the priest challenged. "If these murders happened that far away, why notify Luntville residents?"

Another shift, another pause. The cop was a grim silhouette before them. "The first coupla murder victims were found just north'a the Boone National Forest and Game Preserve. Then we found another one near Stearns. Two more between Bristol an' Lockwood, an' two more after that between Lockwood an' Rocky Top."

Annie gasped. "And the one today, the farmer. Just outside'a Crick City, ain't that what you said, Officer?"

"That's right, ma'am," the trooper replied in his darkest tone yet.

"My God," Charity said.

But Alexander looked around, examining the sudden severity of their faces. "I don't get it. What's the big deal?"

Lightning crackled in silence; the warm air stirred. "See, Father," the trooper began, "based on where we've found the bodies of the victims, the killer seems ta be movin'...in a straight line—"

"Straight for Luntville," Charity whispered. And—

"Annie!" Jerrica squealed.

Confusion diced the moment. *What the hell?* Alexander thought, but then he heard *thunk!* and he blinked and darted forward. The state cop rushed to assist.

Aunt Annie had fainted instantly, and collapsed to the floor.

1 2 3 4 5 6 7 8 9 0
TWELVE
ERIK
1999

TWELVE

(I)

Alexander and the cop carried Annie into the parlor, and lay her out on the old crushed-velvet scroll couch. Charity and Jerrica briskly fanned her face, with straw fans from the highboy. Alexander elevated her feet. "I better radio fer an ambulance," Sergeant Mullen said.

"Wait, I—" Alexander leaned over, peering down and holding the elder woman's hand. It felt cool, fragile. "She's coming to."

In time, Annie's eyes opened fully. She looked wilted lying there, and stark when she realized what had happened. "My… gracious," she whispered. She squeezed the priest's hand. "I… just got so light-headed for a moment."

"You fainted, Aunt Annie," Charity said, she and Jerrica still waving the fans.

"Are you all right?" Jerrica asked. "The officer can call an ambulance."

"Goodness no." Her eyes fluttered, then she seemed to pinken with embarrassment. She sat up then, validating her recovery. "I'm fine, really. I'm so sorry to be such a burden."

"It's no trouble, ma'am," Mullen offered. "You're sure you're all right?"

"Oh, yes, of course. Thank you, thank you all. I feel much better."

"Let's get you to bed," Jerrica suggested, whereupon she and Charity aided the woman to her feet. "You've had a busy day."

"*Too* busy," Charity added. "All that walking today in the hot sun, and this beastly humidity." They both gently guided Annie out of the parlor and down the hall for her room.

Alexander walked outside with the cop.

"I really am sorry to cause all this ruckus, Father," Mullen apologized." The heat lightning continued to whiplash when they got out to the car. "Guess there ain't no subtle way to tell folks that a killer might be headin' fer their town."

"Hey, you're just doing your job," the priest said, and lit a cigarette. "We appreciate you taking the time to come out. Annie'll be all right. I guess it was just a combination of the news of the murders and all this heat." Alexander paused to reflect, dragging his Lucky. "But it seems strange, doesn't it—these murders, I mean? A laid-back, remote area like this, I'd think that there'd be almost no crime at all."

"'Round here, shore," Mullen agreed. "Originally, I was thinkin' that maybe the murders are spillover, but they ain't 'cos the m.o.'s so different, and they're coming from the wrong direction."

"Wrong direction? *Spillover?* What do you mean?"

Mullen shrugged, lit a cigarette himself. "You'd be surprised by the murder rate along the state line forty, fifty miles west'a here. ATF's always findin' bodies, hooch-related."

Hooch? the priest wondered, but then he considered, *ATF, Bureau of Alcohol, Tobacco, and Firearms.* "You mean moonshine, unlicensed whiskey."

"Right, Father. Them shine-runners off each other two a week, and a right dag bunch'a sick'n crazy bastards they all are. But most'a them all happen on the other side'a the line, an' they ain't nothin' like these murders I came to tell yawl about. You're right, murders *round here,* 'specially sexual murders, *never* happen."

"And now all of a sudden you've got—what?—half a dozen?"

"A few more'n that, Father, if ya wanna know the truth. I ain't seen none'a the bodies myself, but we all read the alert-fax from HQ at the substation. This boy makes them 'shiners look like a bunch'a toddlers. Right sick what he done to them gals, and that farmer. Real devilish work, Father."

Devilish. Yes, the devils were everywhere these days, right around every corner, the priest knew. *Human* devils. Psychopaths. It was sad to recognize that the world's evil reached out even this far. "Any leads?" he lamely asked.

"Naw, I shore wish I could tell ya otherwise, but so far our forensics unit ain't got squat. We'll get him though, whoever this sick son of a bitch is—an' pardon my language, Father."

"Think nothing of it. And good luck." *I hope you bust him and break his balls,* he thought. *Crack that motherfucker's chops...* "I better get back in to check on Annie."

"Good night, Father. An' again, sorry ta disturb yer night like this."

"Don't worry about it. Take care."

Mullen pulled off in his shiny cruiser. Alexander watched the ruby-like taillights fade around the bend. *Christ, what a night,* he thought. Then he closed the great oak door.

And locked it.

"She's asleep," Charity announced, gently closing Annie's bedroom door. "Went out like a light."

"Good," Alexander said. "Rest is exactly what she needs."

"The poor thing," Jerrica added. "I guess everything just caught up with her at once."

Alexander nodded. "Yeah. A long, hot day, plus that heavy wine on top of it, and then a cop coming by with reports of murders—"

"And me bringing up that creepy Bighead story probably only made it worse. Me and my big mouth."

"Don't blame yourself—it was nobody's fault," the priest asserted. "The important thing is she's all right. I'm sure all she needs is a good night's sleep."

"That's what I need too," Charity said, caught in a yawn.

"That's what we *all* need," the priest finished.

"Goodnight all," Charity bid and headed up the stairs. Alexander made to do the same, but then Jerrica touched his arm. "Care to join me in a last glass of wine?"

He considered it, then shook his head. "No thanks. I've had my fill; any more alcohol for me and I'd be the next one fainting." She seemed disappointed, though, when he'd said this, and she also seemed…fidgety. "You okay?"

"Sure," she said but her mind seemed elsewhere. She followed him up the stairs, and once they arrived on the landing, she appeared even more distracted, rubbing her arms, her eyes down cast.

The priest's brow cocked. "You *sure* you're all right, Jerrica?"

"Yeah, yeah. I guess all the excitement's still got me a little wound up. Good night, Father."

He passed her, down to his own door. "Good night."

"Oh, and Father?" She offered a final smile. "Thanks for saving me from those thugs at the bar."

Alexander laughed. "All in a priestly day's work." Then he heard her door clicking shut as he shut his own. He rubbed his chin, thinking. Yes, something was wrong; all at once Jerrica seemed on edge, hyper even.

I wonder what's eating her all of a sudden? he thought.

(II)

"A cool shower, Jerrica, that's what you need," she muttered aloud to herself. She wouldn't think about the sudden fear, which had nothing whatever to do with those silly Bighead stories, nor even the grim revelations made by the police officer. It was a fear of herself that suddenly seized her.

And a familiar one.

But if it wasn't one thing, it was something else. That mean, irresistible edge began to rear. It had been a while, hadn't it? She thought she'd lost it…

So instead she took flight in her muse of flesh. Once naked and in the shower, she let her visions claim her; again, she fantasized of the two of them there, together, in the cool sprinkle.

Herself and the priest…

Their bodies pressing. Their hands lathering each other into suits of cool, white froth. She couldn't stop thinking about him, she couldn't stop imagining…

Damn, she thought, touching herself as the water sprayed down on her face.

Yes, if it wasn't one thing, it was something else.

And she knew what the something else was, all too well…

No, she told herself. *I will not.*

Yet she toweled off in haste, haphazardly, then walked naked across the bedroom. Her laptop, sitting there like a bored mascot, didn't even occur to her, nor did the idea that she might type in some more notes, get some work done. After all, that's why she was here: to work.

Her heart began to race; she could feel the blood thumping hotly in her breasts. Her sex felt inflamed and her hands shook. *Habituated personality,* the counselor had said. *Conative fixation-disorder. You're a sex-addict, Jerrica, and when you can't get sex, you seek your escape elsewhere.*

"I. Will. Not," came her slow staccato murmur. Her hard eyes fixed down on the travel bag. "I won't. I…promised."

It had been so long—it had been *years.* The only reason she even brought it was to remind her of her resolve—

She began to masturbate, flooding her mind with the images of her desires with the image of the priest. Her fingers slickened herself, her eyes were rolling back in her head nearly at once—a minute was all it took. *Oh, God,* she thought. She imagined his cock in her, stuck up right to the balls, while his mouth sucked her tongue as though it were a cock itself. But she'd already opened the tiny tin…

Oh, God…

It was something she learned from some nameless former lover, some one-night-stand. She'd been fellating him—his was quite large, as she recalled; perhaps that was the only way to remember men, not by their faces or their names but by their penises—and upon the brink of his orgasm, he lit a small glass pipe full of cocaine. Jerrica's hips tremored at just that moment, her breasts seemed to rush forward in the sensations. She dipped the fingers of her other hand into the tin of pearlescent powder, brought them hastily to her nostril, and sniffed—

—and came at the same time.

It rocked her. It racked her. The delectable feeling seemed to squeeze the juice out of her brain, a wet sponge in a pail.

It seemed to take forever to wind down, to finish. Next thing she knew, though, she was leaned raw-breasted over the tin, dying for more.

"I. Will. Not," she avowed to herself, as she had so many times. "No. No. No. Enough."

Then she upended the tin onto her travel mirror—

I hate myself, she thought.

I should kill myself.

Then she began to cut the rest up into lines.

(III)

She dreamed of hot, licking lights and fertile air. She could *smell* the fecundity.

The broth, she thought.

She dreamed of herself, standing in worried wait before the bed. The bed's host, another woman, flinched with her legs spread, her face a stamp of pain, her gown pushed up over the distended belly.

They'd told her what to expect, hadn't they?

That's why—

The broth...

The broth.

The broth...

What had she done? She couldn't remember now, not even in her dreams. Or maybe she only *thought* she couldn't.

Maybe it was something she dared never to remember.

The host's breasts began to bleed a film of milk. The raw vagina spread, like a maw unhinging its jaw and widening to eject some huge, unearthly contents.

"Get ready," came another voice, some man's. "Ain't gonna have this. No we'se ain't."

She opened her hands before the painfully spread legs. *Please, please,* she thought. *Let her git through this...*

But then blood began to pour.

She screamed.

And she saw.

Teeth like shredders grinding tender meat—

—then the dream traversed—

Geraldine, she thought, with tears pouring.

Geraldine?

Geraldine...

—she thought once more as she lit the match and brought it to her nipple—

—and, again, the dream prolapsed—

—she was somewhere else—

—she was naked and sweating in some moonlit field of thatch, her own wilted desires forcing the fantasy. *No, no,* she thought. *I can't allow this, not even in a dream...*

The priest was fucking her, sucking her nipples as he fastidiously humped. *I love you. I love you, bitch,* he said to her in his thoughts. Then he bit her nipple, till blood gave. She screamed in ecstacy.

Yes, of course. It was just a fantasy now, not a retelling. It was the fantasy of her forbidden attraction.

Slap me.

He slapped her, hard, in the face.

Bite me again.

He bit her so hard on the nipple, it almost came off.

Choke me.

His hand grabbed her throat, squeezed, as his hips continued to steadily pump. He squeezed, let go, squeezed, let go, like that for some time, her brain flashing right along with her running sex. He squeezed, let go, squeezed, let go—

Squeezed.

This time, he *didn't* let go. His grip clamped off the blood to her brain as effectively as a hemostat. Her tongue extruded, her eyes drawing to wanton slits. As her vision darkened, a delicious buzz filled her brain, then began to spread. Soon she felt disembodied; she could still feel the priest's cock tilling her sex, yet she seemed to be watching it. She watched her body starfish beneath the frenetic, humping figure; her face was a twisted mask of lined, dark-pink flesh, grinning hideously. He squeezed harder, fucked her harder. She began to orgasm in clutching, jerking salvoes…

He let go just before she would die, her consciousness rising back through the blackened buzz, her skin electric, her nipples erect as if plucked at with pliers.

Come hard. Fuck me hard. Fuck me till I bleed.

He did so, without reservation. She was *still* coming.

I love you so much, my precious bitch.

He pulled his musky cock out, jerked it, squirted his semen right into her eye where the sharp stinging sang to her heart. She drooled out of her mouth, coming like a tap—swallowing demented pleasure like a snake swallowing goose eggs.

Suck it up.

She sucked it into her mouth, sucked out the final, finest drops—wicked salt on her tongue.

But then the dream changed again, a noxious deception. It wasn't the priest at all lying atop her. It was someone else, someone so dark he nearly wasn't there at all. Someone hideous.

The malformed teeth glinted in moonlight.

The giant hand stroked Annie's cheek.

I love you so much, my precious aunt…

(IV)

Charity dreamed as well, just as she had last night. Her skin felt lit with pleasure, anticipation. She parted her legs for any number of the lovers of her past. Her nipples kindled, her face flushed with heat that spread like a lance to her sex. Her sex *oozed…*

The cock dipped into her, her suitor's body pressing her down. She didn't feel much but she didn't need to. All she needed was the contact, the passion, the vivid idea that a man was excited over her.

His hips thrust several times, eager at first, then faltering. Even in the dark, she could see the capitulation on his face.

"I'm sorry. This just…isn't working."

Charity's passion turned to compost.

She watched him climb off, put his clothes back on in haste, and leave.

(V)

And the priest dreamed too, though not quite so deceptively. *My violence! My sin!* he thought, tears in his dreaming eyes. *God Almighty. Forgive me.*

Those two punks, those two assholes. He'd beaten them, thrashed them. Jesus was standing in the middle of his dream, frowning, and—yes—smoking a cigarette. "'Ye who smite thee on the right cheek, turn to him the other also,'" Then: "You fucked up, priest. I'm so pissed at you, I could puke," Christ the King told him. "What the hell is wrong with you? I oughta rip that fuckin' collar right off and shove it down your phony throat, 'cos you ain't fit to wear it, brother. And that ain't just a dream talkin'. That's the King of Kings. That's *Jesus Christ* talkin', pal, and you better get your shit together 'cos if you don't, even *I* can't save your rag-tag over-the-hill Viet Nam ass. The Morning Star will bury you so deep in primeval shit, even God Himself ain't gonna have a shovel big enough to dig you out. And *keep* your goddamn eyes off that blonde, you pious hypocrite. You got any idea how that makes us look? You ain't some field grunt anymore, boffing Saigon whores on Tudo Street and pulling out your pecker for quickie blowjobs in some goddamn alley! You're a *priest!* You're a *priest!*"

Alexander wept openly. "I'm so fuckin' sorry, Lord! I shouldn't have beat those guys up! I've disgraced you! I'm ashamed!" He choked on his own snot. "Forgive me, Jesus, I beg of thee..."

Jesus flicked his butt, shrugged, lit another. "I forgive you." Then he leaned abruptly forward. "Asshole! *Shithead!* But hear me out, 'cos I ain't fuckin' around with you no more. If you don't get your shit together, killer, the devil's gonna step on your dick a hell of a lot harder than I can! You wanna drown in blood and sperm and steaming shit every night for eternity? It can be arranged, and you're doing a dynamite fucking job arranging it right now!" Then Jesus' mean-spirited cast turned clement. "I cannot take you into the Kingdom of Heaven unless you are worthy."

"I know!" Alexander screamed so hard his throat erupted blood.

"Wear that monkey suit like you gotta pair."

"I will!"

The King of Kings, then, grit his fine, white, perfect teeth in exasperation. "And *keep* your goddamn eyes off that blonde! You wanna save her, then save her, 'cos we got a lotta room. But quit looking at her like she's some goddamn ten-buck trick, 'cos if you don't I'll put My foot so far up your ass you'll be able to give me a pedicure with your teeth!"

Alexander bit the tip of his tongue off, to prove his resolve. "I will do as You bid, my Lord. Save me."

Jesus frowned at the cigarette, as though it were too weak. A Doral, a Kent Ultra Light. "I can save you, if you fit the bill, paisan. All that Calvinism shit is bullshit–*we* don't know. But I gotta good feeling about you, dickbrain." Then Jesus' face lit up, like white neon. "I can save you."

"Please, Son of *God!* Save me!"

"I probably will. I can save your soul. Heaven ain't a bad crib, lemme tell you. You read the Bible. The Book of Daniel? Heaven is 1500 miles long, 1500 miles deep, and 1500 miles high, with a river running through it and lots of fruit trees, so there's always grub, and it's gotta 150-foot-high fence made of pure jade encircling it. Beats the shit out of some waterfront condo or a suite at the Mayflower, no lie." Jesus inadvertently stroked his beard, nodded. "Yeah, man, I can save your soul—" Then, viciously, the Son of God grabbed Alexander's throat and shook his head like a ball on a fuckin' spring. "But I can't save you from your dreams!"

Alexander blinked, swallowed more snot. *Jesus is telling me I'm on thin ice. I better quit fucking around...* But— What else did He say? Something about...*dreams?*

Jesus, then, very quickly, turned into Steven Tyler, his hand wrapped around a multi-colored kerchief cloaking a microphone.

"Dream on," He, or she, said. "Dream until your dreams come true."

Forgive me for my sins, God, forgive me for my sins, God, forgive me for my—

The nightmare popped, like the head of a pus-filled boil.

Suddenly, Father Tom Alexander, ordained Catholic priest and deputy psychologist of the Richmond Catholic Diocese, found himself again staked down naked to a dirty cement floor. But unlike the first perverse dream, he was this time bound on his back. Candles flittered from afar in dusty darkness, humid heat rose. His penis seemed so shriveled it felt like a bloodworm died in the sun.

Wake up, he pleaded with himself. Somehow, he knew who would appear next. *Wake up and get out of this fucked-up dream.* But, indeed, there was no relent, and in only moments she *did* appear. The nun, becloaked in heavy habit, wimple, and veil, walked barefoot to where he lay on the cold, bare floor.

"Father, I beg thee," she said.

Alexander smirked, wrists and ankles lashed to iron pegs sunk into the floor. "Beg me *what?*" he testily asked.

She said nothing just then in response. She hoisted the skirt of her black habit, brandishing, again, the plenteous pubic mound, bristled thick and clean as slivers of coal. "I'm the nun who pissed up your ass last night."

"Believe me," he countered. "I remember!"

"But before you can be purged, you must first be filled."

Alexander wished for a cigarette. "I think you did a pretty good job of filling me up *last* night."

"Not good enough," she said in her gentle southern drawl, and smiled with a blinding innocence. It was only then, though, that the priest noticed the plastic tube, clear, like an air-line for a fishtank, tweezed daintily between her thumb and index finger. She smiled again, and then—

"No!" he yelled. "You sick *bitch!*"

—lubricated its end with saliva and began—

"NO!"

—to insert it into his urethra.

Down and down it slid, Alexander's nude hips jerking at the blade-sharp sensation. "In you go," the nun proclaimed, "All the way down..."

Alexander's eyes felt like they'd launch from his head. But what could he do? This was a dream! "I'll kick your Epiphanist ass if you don't stop that!" he warned.

"You're not going to be kicking anything, Father. You're paralyzed. You're staked to the floor." Then she reimmersed herself in her current duties. "Yes, yes," the nun remarked, working the tube ever deeper. "That's a good boy."

Alexander felt something give, way back near his bowel—the tube-end popping through his urethral sphincter.

"Yeah…"

Squatting, still, the nun leaned back with a cast of deep satisfaction on her face, and only then did the priest notice exactly where the *other* end of the tube went. The nun had already previously catheterized *herself…*

"Ahhhhhh," she moaned, eyes closed, face toward the ceiling.

Alexander felt the hot flood entering him. He squirmed.

"Ahhhh, yeah. Last night I pissed up your ass, tonight I'm pissing into your bladder…"

Alexander reeled at the sensation, his eyes clamped closed so hard he thought the seams might heal together. *She's pissing into my dick!* he realized quite grimly. *What kind of a dream is this?*

But that thought caused him to think. Jesus had told him He couldn't save him from his dreams, hadn't He?

And my dreams, the priest thought, *come from …me.*

"Ahhhhh, ahhhhh," the nun went on, emptying her bladder into his.

"Why are you doing this!" Alexander, helpless, screamed.

"Ahhhh," came her answer, and with that another nun appeared, just as lovely, just as innocent. *Oh, no,* Alexander thought, though, when he took a closer look. *You gotta be shitting me.*

When this second nun raised her habit-skirt, he saw that she too had been catheterized, only *this* catheter was substantially thicker than the first nun's. A half-inch thick in diameter, to be exact. Smiling reverently, she squatted over his face, then deftly began to insert the other end of the thick plastic tube into his mouth.

Alexander remained helpless…

"Down you go," the second nun sedately announced. "All the way down into Father's stomach." Then—

"Ahhhhh," she moaned, just in unison with he first nun: "Ahhhhhhhhhhhhhhhhhhhhhh—"

They were filling him up.

They were nuns, and he was a priest, and the were—

Filling me up with their piss! he thought, since he could no longer actually say it, oh no, not with a half-inch-thick piss-catheter running down his throat.

His belly and bowel, simultaneously, began to inflate. He could feel the hot water slushing. Filling him up, yes, until he felt like a goddamn medicine ball fit to burst.

"All right," the first nun directed. And with that they both—

"Owww! Shit!"

—yanked out their respective catheter tubes.

"It's your fault," said the first nun.

"What you let happen to us," added the second.

"What! I didn't do shit to either of you!" Alexander yelled.

"We're…dead."

His eyes, once more, widened to slug-size.

"The Pope sent you back to Africa, for a famine! I can't help what happened to you there!"

"We never went back," said Nun Number One.

But before Alexander, urine-filled and sloshing, could even reply, the first nun went on: "How does it feel to be purged?"

Purged? Perhaps Alexander had a misconception of the word. "Purged!" he bellowed. "You two psychos just did the opposite! You didn't purge me! You *filled* me!"

"Of course," she said, still reverent-eyed, still so sedate her entire form was scarcely a whisper.

The second nun: "Before you can be purged, you must be binged."

The first nun gazed down. "Don't you know what that symbolizes?"

Alexander didn't have a fucking clue, and he didn't care.

"Supplantation, Father. Transcension…"

"Transposition…"

But when he looked again, they were gone, and so was he. The stone-cold floor and the heavy lashings were gone, and he lay again in darkness.

And in that darkness, Jesus reappeared. Jesus' face, that is, dressed as Steven Tyler of Aerosmith.

"Oh, and dickhead?" Jesus inquired of him. "One last thing I forgot to tell you."

"What, my Lord?"

Jesus cleared his throat, lit a butt. "Listen, Tom, and listen good."

"Yes, my Lord!"

Jesus, for the last time, grinned, and wiped His brow with the multi-colored kerchief. Then He said this:

"The Bighead'll get you if you don't watch out."

(VI)

Aw, man, he's mad, Dicky thought. *This ain't good, no sir!* They'd hidden out down the block, waited, then followed them at a distance. An old white Mercedes it looked like they was drivin', an' they'se pulled up at that boarding house on the edge'a town. ANNIE'S it was called, the place with all them ad signs up'n down the Route an' 23.

"Come on, Balls," Dicky pleaded. "Just let's ferget it."

"Ferget it, hail." Tritt Balls' eyes looked crossed he was so mad. "Ain't no man on this green earth gonna whup Tritt Balls Conner, 'specially no holy man…"

Dicky idled the El Camino just at the entrance. He gulped, then dared ta ask, "So's…what you figgure on doin'?"

"I'se gonna *kill* that there priest, Dicky Boy, I am," Balls assured from his shotgun seat, his eyes glarin' up that road like a jackal's onna big, fat chicken. "An' that blondie bitch he were with?" Balls made a sound like a chuckle. "I'se gonna fuck her ass so hard my dick'll come out her bellybutton. Yes sir. I'se gonna *bust* her hole…"

Dicky gulped again, sweat tricklin'. Yeah, he knowed Balls quite well, he did, and he knowed how crazy he could git once he were riled. Knowin' Balls, he'd bust right inta that boarding house right now an' put a ruckin' an' killin' on ever-one there, then they'd problee wind up gettin' caught an' goin' to the slam fer the rest'a their lifes. Balls weren't one ta think things smartways whens he were this mad.

"Please, Balls," Dicky pleaded. "We cain't just march on in there an starts killin'—"

"*Shire* we'se can, Dicky!"

"But that priest," he reminded, "he whupped us good, an' he's might whups us agin."

"Naw, no way, Dicky Boy." Another chuckle, another leer up the dark road. Then Balls reached under the seat and—

Awwwwwww, no, Dicky thought.

—pulled out his dear dead Daddy's big-ass Webley .455 revolver. He brandished the weapon, weighed it in his hand, keeping that grin'a his. "He may'a whupped us once, Dicky. But he ain't gonna whup us agin, that's fer *dag* shore!"

"Not tonight, Balls," Dicky about begged, his fear frantic as a caged field ferret. "Please, not tonight."

And then this weird diffusion passed over Ball's face'n eyes. The bill'a his John Deere cap turnt his face dead black. He was starin' up that road, to where the boarding house was.

"Naw," hc whispered. "Not tonight, my man. What we'll'se do is wait fer the time ta be *perfect.*" He turned his head. The wicked grin beamed. "Then we'll'se have us some *big* fun…"

1 2 3 4 5 6 7 8 9 0
0 9 8 7 6 5 4 3 2 1
THIRTEEN
ERIK
1999

THIRTEEN

(I)

In the morning, something seemed strange. *Leftovers from last night,* Charity guessed. *Murders. Heading our way.* Not that she herself was terribly concerned—these murders the trooper had mentioned were so far away, she felt certain the killer would be caught soon. The police were working on it fulltime. *They'll catch him...*

But Aunt Annie looked awful. She looked depleted, pale, as she feebly served breakfast.

"Let us do that, Annie," Jerrica volunteered, taking the pan of hoecakes and sorghum syrup. "You look so tired."

"I am," Annie admitted and sat down at the table. "I didn't sleep at all. Kept havin' awful dreams."

The comment reminded Charity of her own dreams: the recurring dream of her own insolvencies in love. It was a cryptogram, or perhaps only a cruel replay of her life. *The minute I get into bed with a man, he's turned off completely. Why?*

"I had awful dreams," Father Alexander announced, appearing at the dining room entry. "Second night in a row. I feel like I didn't get any sleep at all."

"You and me both, Father," Aunt Annie said.

"Maybe my brain is just having a bad reaction to all this clean air," he joked. He poured himself orange juice from the iced pitcher, lit a cigarette. "I'm used to Richmond smog."

Jerrica's eyes seemed to go alight at the sudden presence of the priest; Charity duly noted this. But she noted something else. *Jerrica,* she thought quizzically. Her friend didn't seem herself. She seemed on edge, wired.

"And speaking of Richmond," the priest continued, "I have to drive back today."

"What!" Jerrica exclaimed. "I thought you were staying here to reopen the abbey."

"I am," he told her. "But those papers I found in the administration office yesterday? They're really messed up, can't make hide nor hair of 'em. I'm going to have to show this stuff to my boss, see what he can make of them. I'll be back in a few hours."

And Charity, then, couldn't help but notice the way Jerrica was suddenly squirming in her seat…

"Goop, my handyman, should be back this afternoon, Father," Annie said. "He can drive you if you like."

"No, that's not necessary." Alexander paused over his orange juice. "Where did he go, by the way?"

"Yes, Aunt Annie," Charity added. "Come to think of it, I haven't seen him since yesterday morning."

"That's because I sent him to Roanoke last night, to buy some vinyl trim," Annie revealed.

Which didn't make sense to Charity. "You sent him to Roanoke at *night?*"

"Well, I didn't need to, and I don't really even need the trim," her aunt began to explain. "I sent him last night deliberately."

"Why?" Jerrica asked.

"Well, hon, because I wanted to make sure he stayed there overnight. Goop Gooder's a wonderful, helpful young man, but he can also be quite a gadfly—as far as women are concerned, I mean. I couldn't help but notice what a likin' he's taken ta you, Jerrica. So I thought I'd send him out'a town fer a day, keep him out'a yer hair."

Jerrica blushed. "Oh, Annie, you didn't have to do that. It's no big deal."

"It shore is if ya ask me. You're a guest, after all, and a friend'a my niece. I can't have my handyman houndin' ya."

Alexander raised another brow, but Charity couldn't help but smile. “When are you leaving for Richmond, Father?”

“Right now,” he said and stood right back up. “I’ll be back late afternoon or early evening. See you all later.”

“Bye, Father,” Annie and Charity said nearly at the same time. But Jerrica jumped up and chased him into the foyer. Charity tried not to appear that she was eavesdropping, but she couldn’t help it. “Father!” Jerrica said from the other room. “Let me go with you!”

A pause. “Sure,” the priest agreed.

Then they were out the front door.

“Poor girl,” Annie said. “She’s taken an awful fancy to Father.”

“It seems so,” Charity said.

“But I gotta admit, I find him a might attractive myself, an’ even more so on account’a his faith.”

`”Priests always have that effect. I guess because they’re off-limits, so to speak.”

“You got that right, dear. Ain’t nothin’ more attractive than a man ya cain’t have.”

Charity sat still, thought about that. *Why can’t I have a man?* she wondered. *How come everything goes to pot, and I don’t even know why?* She felt inclined to talk further on the topic, maybe even take her aunt into confidence. But what point would there be in that? All she’d do is make herself look foolish.

“But let me ask you somethin’, Charity. Is it my ’magination or does Jerrica look a bit funny?’

She noticed too, Charity thought. But what could she say? “I think you’re right. She seems…anxious. But it’s probably just because this is so different for her,” she excused. “She’s a city girl. She’s not used to the country.”

Annie nodded. “Never thought’a that.”

Charity changed the subject. “Would you like to gather some flowers now, walk out to the cemetery?”

Her aunt canted her head, put a hand to her brow. “It ain’t reglar that I miss a day, but honestly, Charity, I feel so pooped out, what I’m gonna do right now is take a nap, if ya don’t mind.”

“You should,” Charity agreed. “With all that excitement last night? Go get some rest. I’ll be fine.”

"You shore?"

"Of course, Aunt Annie. Go take a nap, and we'll talk later."

"You're such a dear." Annie got up, heading for her room. "But I promise, tonight I'll fix us up a supper like you won't believe."

"Okay, Aunt Annie. Rest well."

Charity watched her aunt trudge off. Then she found herself alone, wondering what she would do today.

Then—

Her eyes opened wide.

I know, she thought.

(II)

"Out with it," Alexander demanded.

"What?" Jerrica said, buckling her seatbelt as the Mercedes turned off the exit to 23.

"Don't give me that *what* shit. You're high. You're fucked up, Jerrica. You're acting like you're sitting on the third rail to the fucking Metro." The priest scowled. "What is it? Coke? Flake? Speed? You're on something."

Her head could not have hung lower. "Coke."

"Asshole! I *knew* it!" Alexander came close to shouting. "I won't even bother with the lecture, Jerrica—you've heard it a hundred times. All I'll say is this. Life is a fuckin' gift from God...and look at what you're doing with it."

She sobbed silently; she knew it was all true. "I—" she began. How could she explain it? How could she tell him about her curse, and how if it isn't one thing, it's another? He'd bury her. So all she said was this: "I have some problems."

"Oh give me a break!" he bellowed. "Let me rosin up my fucking violin, Paganini! *You* have problems. Shit, Jerrica, *everybody* has problems, but they don't use those problems as an excuse to be a drug addict."

The term—*drug addict*—chinked, like a hammer to stone. *I'm a drug addict*, she realized, but deep down, even for the years she hadn't touched the coke, she knew that. The priest was simply infuriating. "I stopped for years," she said, her throat hitching. "I didn't want to do it again until I met you."

"Oh, so it's *my* fault you're a cokehead, huh?"

Her teeth clacked shut, her fists clenched. "It's because I fell in love with you!"

Now he really went off. "Are you *out of your mind?* I'm a fucking PRIEST, Jerrica! I can't be in love with you or anybody! The only person I'm in love with is JESUS CHRIST! What, some cute blond says she loves me and I'm supposed to throw my collar out the fucking window, forsake my vows to God, and piss it all away?"

"I'm just telling you how I feel!" she shrieked.

"Yeah? Well how you feel is fucked up! You just sit there and shut up and you don't say a word for the rest of the trip!"

"God, you're an asshole!"

Alexander lit a Lucky, laughed. "That's right, baby. I'm an asshole. Asshole is my middle name. But you want to know what *your* middle name is?" For a moment, he looked like he might actually strike her. "*Your* middle name is junkie." And with that, he slammed the brakes, screeched to a halt on the sunny shoulder. "I'll bet you're *carrying* that shit, aren't you? Give it to me. Where is it?"

Her throat felt so thick she could barely speak. "I-I-I—"

"I-I-I *what!*" hc bcllowed.

"I don't have it!"

"BULLshit!"

"I don't! I swear! I used it all up last night! I was just telling you how I feel!"

He shot her a look, then, of such disdain, she felt like she might dry up right there in the car seat, like a little puddle.

"Just keep your face shut for the rest of the drive," he repeated, and pulled back onto the road. "If you don't, I'll kick your ass right out of the car and let you hitchhike back to D.C. or Luntville or Coke City or anywhere else you might want to take your busted, fucked up life. But *don't talk! Don't* say a word to me!" He settled back down behind the wheel.

"Because I don't talk to *junkies,*" he said.

(III)

It was so hot, so humid! *How does she stand doing this every day?* Charity asked herself. *I'm thirty years younger than her and* I *can't stand it.*

And hot it was, even in the shaded forest walkways. The heat was *teeming.* Gnats and mosquitoes buzzed about her face and arms, which she swatted at with a vengeance. Light and billowy as her organdy summer dress may have been, she was drenched in sweat in only moments; all of her skin seemed to *trickle.* Sweat even dripped from her eyebrows to her cheeks.

But she strode on, her own inquiry seducing her as effectively as the pseudo-lovers she'd dreamed of last night. Thickets snapped beneath her sandals. The dapples of sunlight through the trees, like radiant brushmarks, guided her further.

Something's wrong with Jerrica, she thought, trying to divert her mind from the stifling heat. But there could be no denying it. At breakfast, Jerrica hadn't eaten a thing; instead she'd just sat there, almost shaking. She couldn't have been upset about Goop; Charity knew that she *dreaded* seeing Goop again, after her quick fling with him. So what was it? The priest? *I hope not,* Charity thought. True, Jerrica had openly revealed her rampant sexual longings on the drive up, which surprised her, but even an inveterate nymphomaniac should know the futility of desiring a priest.

Then her thoughts flywheeled. *The trooper,* she recalled. *The murders...* But that was silly to worry about. Like the officer had said, it was just a precaution. She couldn't imagine a murderer running rampant in *Luntville* of all places; it was absurd. *I'm just distracted,* she thought. *I'm hot.*

After what seemed miles, the humid forest path opened up. It was stunning, despite the heat: the flowing, sunlit view of the cemetery. Wild weeds swayed in the warm breeze. Heads of Queen Ann's lace bobbed. Charity walked directly to the spot of her mother's grave. Solemnly she gazed down, her hands clasped. All the simple, faded stone read was: SISSY. *My mother. Annie's sister.* She committed suicide when Charity's father had died in the mine explosion; Annie had told her everything. It was strange, though, standing like this over her own mother's grave, a woman she never knew.

Rest in peace, Mother, she thought.

Then she moved on. It wasn't only her mother's grave she'd come to see. She couldn't escape the recollection of yesterday. How bizarre it had been. After Aunt Annie had placed the flowers on Sissy's grave, she'd asked Charity to retreat back to the woods, and wait. And Charity saw where her aunt had gone.

To another grave at the far corner of the cemetery, with a *second* bundle of flowers.

Who? she thought. *Who?*

The far corner, yes, nearly beyond the actual limits of the graveyard itself. Charity followed her memory, and at once she was there. She knew this was the right plot because of the flowers her aunt had left only yesterday, a string-tied bunch from her own backyard garden. And there they were.

She stared down at them, shielding her eyes from the sun.

The flowers had baked already, such heat. But the plot looked so stark. Tiny. And—

This is so odd...

A perfectly blank gravestone.

It was old, she noted, stained by years of rain and weather. But its typical rounded face offered no inscription.

Unless—

Charity dropped to her knees. There was something, wasn't there? Just at the grassline?

She pushed the grass down at the base of the stone. Squinted in effort then pushed harder. Her fingers could feel...*something.*

But it was too deep!

She stood again, grabbed either side of the stone with both hands, intent now on finding out. No one would see, would they? This was a family cemetery, and who would be out here on a day so scorching? *Just me,* she thought and almost laughed.

She worked the stone back and forth. At first it didn't budge at all, but eventually—

Yes!

—it began to give a little. Then a little more, then…a lot more.

Soon the stone was so loose it wobbled.

All right, Charity thought, profuse with sweat now, but just as profuse with determination.

She hoisted the stone upward, and—

Ughhhh!

It pulled up and fell down.

(IV)

I should never have come, she thought, her head cast down so long now, she had a stiff neck. *I should've stayed at the house with Charity, worked on my article, anything…*

Alexander parked the Mercedes behind a small, drab complex of brick buildings, what she guessed was the diocesan center. Jerrica didn't know much about Richmond, had scarcely ever even seen the city before. They'd driven past ghettos, rows of squalid tenements, abandoned streets still with litter. Was the whole city in such disrepair?

As ordered, she hadn't said a word since his outburst. How could she? Jerrica had felt a lot of shame in her life, but not like today, not like now. *He's right,* she condemned herself. *I'm a junkie, I'm a fuck up. He must be...disgusted.*

"All right," he finally said, parked now, the motor off. Then he began with difficulty, "Listen, Jerrica. I'm sorry for yelling at you back there."

She looked up peevishly; this was the last thing she expected to hear. *He's…sorry?*

"I said some pretty shitty things to you, things I didn't mean, and I'm sorry. You hearing me?"

She nodded. Dried tears crusted her cheeks.

"I'm a behavioral psychologist, that's my training. I came down on you hard because you're in a lot of trouble. I said those things to you because you're important to me, and I care about you. You understand?"

She nodded again, confused.

"If I *didn't* care about you, then I wouldn't have said a word. Your life is your business. I just don't want to see you blow it."

"I know," she peeped, her hands in her lap.

"You're gonna have to get yourself squared away. We'll talk about it, okay? I'll help you. Okay? Do you want me to help you?"

"Yes!" she suddenly blurted out, and all at once she was crying again, hugging him, sobbing. "I'm sorry! I don't know what's wrong with me, I don't know why I do the things I do! I feel so ashamed!" Her tears ran freely, dampening his shirt.

He paused, held her, gave her a few moments to calm down. "It's a tough world, I know, and a lot of times it just doesn't seem fair. But in the end, and I think you know this, it's all up to us as individuals to make things right. Now, I'll be inside for an hour or so, with my boss. In the meantime, I want you to think about things, and we'll talk when I'm through. Okay?"

She nodded one more time, took her face off his shoulder. "I want to. I want to get fixed up."

"And you will," he assured.

They got out of the car. The sun beat down on them. Alexander went on, "You probably noticed that the diocesan center isn't exactly located in the posh part of town. Don't go off the property, all right?" He pointed past a brick fence with an iron gate. "There's a courtyard back there. Wait for me there."

"Okay," she said.

He smiled in the sun. "Everything's gonna be fine." Then, briefcase in hand, he walked toward the building and entered through a side door.

Jerrica watched after him, wiping her eyes. Nothing could properly describe the way she felt, but it was the way she *always* felt, wasn't it?

If it wasn't one thing, it was something else.

Why now? The old demons were back, but why? She struggled in the glare, to find any scapegoat, but there were none.

Only myself.

The enclosed courtyard appeared fairly well-kept: trimmed

hedges, brick paths. Heavy boughs of trees hung overhead, giving shade. Yes, the courtyard looked like a nice place to sit and think, as the priest had advised, but—

Already she knew.

I. Will. Not, she struggled, and the more she struggled, the more diluted she became. Sex, drugs—it didn't matter. It was always the same. One way or another, she was lost, and she always had been.

And she always would be.

Her eternal excuse: she couldn't help it. She turned quickly away from the sanctuary of the courtyard and scurried away.

For the bad part of town.

(V)

"Tom! What a surprise!" Monsignor Halford greeted with genuine enthusiasm. He had his feet up on the fine teak desk, reading the *Catholic Review.*

"Somehow I knew you'd be working hard, Bob," Alexander remarked, afrown. "No rest for the faithful."

"So, what brings you back? What's going on with Wroxeter?"

"Bullshit in a crock pot." Alexander snapped open his briefcase on the coffee table. "*Dick.* That's what's going on."

Halford pinched the bridge of his nose, closed his eyes. "Aw, come on, Tom. I've asked you to put a lid on the foul language, huh? I ask you a simple question and you're already spouting profanity."

"Gorilla turds—that's what's going on at Wroxeter, Bob. Shit balls in a buttcrack."

"Come on, Tom!"

Alexander waved the folder full of the operating logs from the abbey. "Somebody's pulling bigtime wool over my eyes, and I got a funny feeling it's you."

Halford sterned up. "I resent that, Tom. What gives you the right—"

"There is *no administrative record* of Wroxeter Abbey ever closing," Alexander enlightened. "These logs show in-patient records, duty rosters, and supply inventories all active until July of '76. That closure statement file you laid on me states that the place closed in April."

"A clerical error—"

"My ass," the priest shot back. "Come on, Bob, the abbess' office is *untouched.* It's still even full of her personal effects, and so are the nuns' dorms." Alexander began to watch the monsignor very closely, paying particular attention to the eyes, the face, hand gestures. "The bedstands in the in-patient dorm are full of personal effects too. And the med station is still loaded up with drugs that are over *twenty years old.* What, the diocese closes up the abbey but they leave controlled pharmaceuticals on the premise? This doesn't jibe, Bob. It's almost like everyone disappeared over night, and the Church sent some flunky out there the next day to seal the place up before anybody could get wise. And why would I suspect such a thing? Yesterday I called the goddamn office of land records for Russell County—"

"Goddamn it, Tom!" Halford, quite out of the ordinary, yelled. "You have no right to obstruct Church business!"

"Church business, no. Monkey business, yes." Alexander smiled, lit up a Lucky. "I knew that would put some fire up your crack. And I don't have to tell you, the county recorder of deeds claims that the Church never filed the closure statement."

"We filed it with the state!"

"But that's illegal, Bob."

"Not with a waiver, smart boy!"

"Why get a waiver?" Alexander kept on him. He was getting everything he suspected, just by watching the monsignor. "Why not file the closure notice properly? What's the big deal? The only reason you'd apply for a records waiver is to either beat property taxes for an actively occupied building, or to prevent a county inspection. And I don't have to remind you that the Catholic Church is exempt from all property taxes."

Halford was not pleased. He was livid. "I don't appreciate being called a liar, Tom."

"Then stop lying. Christ, Bob, I'm a trained psychologist. I'm *trained* to be able to tell when people are lying. Ever heard of tasal plate fluctuation, negative-impulse kinestetics, opposite-eye opposite-hand deflection? You're doing it all right in front of me, Bob. I'll bet my benefice that you're lying to my face."

"You son of a bitch," Halford muttered, then confessed, "All right, I'll level with you. But I wasn't lying. Just call it a minor circumvention of facts."

"Great. Bullshit by any other name is still—"

"I ought to fuckin' transfer you!" Halford suddenly jumped up, pounded his fist, and bellowed.

"Watch that foul language, Bob."

"You're *way* out of line pulling a stunt like this!"

"Relax." Alexander shrugged in his seat, puffed his smoke. "Just tell me the real scoop, will ya?"

Halford sat back down, fuming. "We waived filing with the county so they wouldn't send an inspector. We didn't want a county inspector out there because the fiscal year ends in April. We said we closed the place in April instead of July because we didn't want to have to pay hospice taxes for the following year. The Church isn't tax-exempt on everything, boy genius."

"All right, I can dig that," Alexander agreed. "But there's more, so just have out with it. Hospice taxes, I'll admit, I didn't know about those, but I *do* know that the transport of intensive-care patients, such as *terminally ill priests,* must be legally filed with the county health commissioners office. I called them too, Bob. You guys never filed shit."

Halford's shoulders slumped, like a poker player whose bluff had been called.

"What's the real reason, Bob? There's no record of any of Wroxeter's in-patients being moved after the place was closed. You guys did this waiver bit, not to beat *hospice* taxes, but to prevent a county inspector from going out there, because you were afraid he'd see something. I want to know what it was you didn't want him to see."

Halford was grinding his teeth, wringing his hands. "There was still evidence on the premise. We didn't want a county title inspector going out there and filing a police report."

Alexander gaped. "A police report?"

"A *homicide* report. Christ, Tom. Why can't you just do what you're told? I sent you out there to get the place ready to reopen. Twenty years is long enough that no one's going to ask questions. But back then? That's just not the kind of thing that the Catholic Church could afford being publicized."

Now Alexander was lost. "You couldn't afford to have *what* publicized?"

Halford threw his hands up in disgust. "The nuns were murdered," he said.

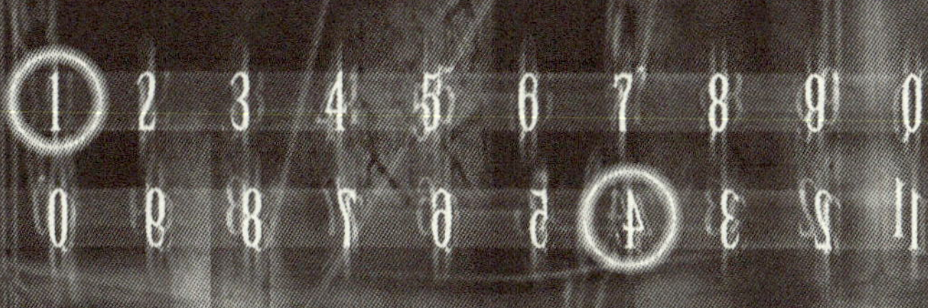
1 2 3 4 5 6 7 8 9 0
FOURTEEN
ERIK
1999

FOURTEEN

(I)

"Make me wanna holler!" the voice cracked.

Jerrica shirked in the sun. Yes, this was the bad part of town, all right. *What am I doing? I must be crazy.*

Federal Street existed as a vanishing point into desolation and strewn bits of litter; the street itself reeked, and Jerrica thought she could even *see* its fetor wafting off the asphalt with the heat waves. Dark faces peered at her from rowhouse porches.

Jerrica was terrified.

"Uh-*huh.* Yeah." The black man approached from an alley that seemed to gush a distilled stench of urine. He was tall, lanky, but with biceps like veined baseballs, shoulders like sculpture. Jeans, a tight t-shirt that read NWA. Quite uncharacteristically, though, he wore a huge afro, like something from the 70s. Uh-*huh,*" he repeated. "I say she just make me wanna holler 'cos I ain't *never* see a white woman so fine-lookin'."

"Hi," Jerrica said rather stupidly. Only now did she imagine how preposterous this must look, how crazy. A young white woman, in cutoffs and a halter, walking alone through a ghetto.

"I'se kin tell, sho'," he said. He squinted at her, cut a smile like a knife blade. "I'se kin tell whats you need."

"Yeah?" she said, trying to sound unafraid.

"I'se kin tell juss by lookin' at yo eyes, and what'choo want, lets me guess. Ice, you want Ice, I gots it, have you flyin' fo' ten hours. Or how's about some top-dro' Rock? A ten-piece, a twenty? I gots it."

This truth wilted her even more, that he could *see* the desperation in her eyes. "I want blow," she said. "I've got two hundred dollars."

The smile beamed. The big hands rubbed together, like black ferrets tussling. "An' I'se got blow too, lots of it. Come on, over here ta mys office."

Jerrica quailed; his hand bid the alley. "Can't we just do it right here?"

"You crazy, bitch? You wanna buy drugs from me in the middle'a the street? Shee-it."

The man had a point. "All right," she agreed, and then they walked off the sun-drenched street.

What am I doing, what am I doing, what am I... The thought tossed round and round in her head. She'd never bought drugs in such an environ, but— She knew she didn't care. She needed it. The alley's darkness enshrouded her but lent no relief to the heat. The piss-stench slapped her in the face; she had to breathe through her mouth.

A hand went to his pocket. "Gots ta hold yo' green first."

Unhesitantly, she gave him the money, and then out came his hand.

Oh, God.

Suddenly she felt as though she'd chugged scalding water: burning fear bloating her belly, spreading. It was a small gun that filled his hand now, not the cocaine she craved. The realization smacked tangily as the urine-fetor. *I'm going to be robbed, raped, murdered...*

"Please," was the only word she could say.

His knife-grin never abated. His eyes looked like white lights set into the dark face. "When a white junkie bitch come into *my* town fo' blow, well, that what she gotta do, catch my drift? She gotta *blow.*"

"I'm begging you," she croaked. Her mouth, in an instant, felt devoid of all moisture. "Just, please, don't—"

The gun raised its interruption. "What kind'a dumb white

bitch're you anyshow? *I'm* the Mack Daddy on this street. This *my* 'hood, baby, and you *my* bitch right now. I bust a cap in a nigger's ass juss fo' *lookin'* at me crooked. But a *white* bitch? Shee-it? Get down on them white knees an' suck."

He already had it out. In the alley's gulf of shadow, it looked like a dropping snake, a faint shiny line down its side. Trembling, Jerrica lowered to her knees, touched it, and nearly gagged. Now the alley's stench of urine seemed like perfume; instead, the man's crotch seemed to bark with a stench of its own. He mustn't have washed in a week or more. Jerrica wanted to bend over right then and there, and vomit.

The gun nudged her head. "This li'l thing? It don't make no noise." He cocked it. "Suck. Tredell need a *good* suck."

The stench was evil, but the taste was worse: sweat and dirt and old semen from previous engagements. She took it into her mouth; it felt feverishly hot. "Mmmmmm, yo," he remarked. Breathing through her nose only amplified this crude horror. Had she ever smelled anything so revolting in her life? Probably not. But that's what this was all about—her life. She could lose her life…

It came erect quickly, a hair-trigger reflex; suddenly that drooping snake had sprung alive, fat in her mouth. She felt divided immediately: terror versus resolve. *If I want to have any hope at all of being alive an hour from now, I better suck this guy's cock real good,* she told herself. Not an easy task, though, with the barrel of a gun to one's head. It was all she could do not to retch when her lips encircled the glans, sucked it up, and pushed down. There was a significant foreskin, she noted right off, and it was *filled* with pockets of bitter smegma. "Lotta cheese in there fo' ya, honey," he commented, chuckling. "Don'ts worry, a li'l cheese ain't gonna hurt ya." She sucked it all off, squeezed her eyes tighter than brick-seams, and let the human paste dissolve in her mouth. *Don't puke, Jerrica. Don't puke.* "Yeah, that's straightup knob-polishin', fo' a white ho," this Tredell was kind enough to compliment. "Shit, goddamn, git off yo' ass an' jam!"

Jerrica felt like she was dying. This would be her hell, wouldn't it? To eat the smegma out of this dope-dealer's foreskin for all time. The crotch-stench steamed into her flared nostrils; then he instructed,

"Get a finger up my asshole, bitch. Make me come better."

Repulsed, she didn't hesitate. The gun barrel was drawing circles in her hair. She wiped some drool off her lips onto her middle finger, then burrowed the finger up the rank cleft, slipped it up his anus.

"Yeah, baby. Yeah..."

Her political correctness as a journalist fractured. *You mother-fucking dirty criminal nigger. I wish I had the balls to bite this black cock off and spit it in your face!*

Fantasy, though. Of course.

He came rather quickly, but to Jerrica it seemed more like an hour of this. The gun barrel raked her head as his hips flinched. "Suck that whip, baby. Suck out all that spunk..."

Jerrica, in her expertise regarding male sexual anatomy, had long since noted that, like all people, all men were different when they came. Some spurted abruptly, some shot the freight of their loins in long, long strings, while others merely dribbled. Tredell, instead, *oozed*—not hot shots to the back of her throat—slowly pouring a voluminous ration of semen onto her tongue, one spurtle after the next. When it was over, she felt as though she had a mouthful of curdled egg-drop soup. She couldn't wait to spit it out, but—

"Swallows it all up, ho. See, Tredell like the idea'a all that good gangsta niggah spunk deep in yo' white-bitch gut."

Her eyes crossed at the order. *Just...do it.* And then her throat audibly clicked when she opened her throat, gulped, and forced it all down like so much thin snot. *Don't puke,* she pleaded with herself again. She fell back against the alley's brick wall, her finger slipping out of his rectum, her other hand uncaringly landing in some unnamed slime. A shadow, to her left, skittered: a rat. She didn't care. Something like a long, runny worm seemed to settle in her belly.

"Yeah, that a good li'l white bitch." Her accomplice, then, stepped forward and wiped his cock off in her pristine blond hair. "Tredell always live large," he said. "Boo-ya."

It was over now, but was it really? What next? He could kill her back here and no one would ever know.

"Please," she hacked. "Please don't kill me."

"Shee-it," he said, standing high above her. "I ain'ts gonna kill ya, baby. You a good customer." His smile never faded; it seemed to actually cut into the alley's hot dark. Then he tossed her a small plastic bag of cocaine.

"Come back when you need some mo'. Ask fo' Tredell."

(II)

"All of them," Halford said. Now he lit a cigarette himself, rare for the monsignor. A tendril of smoke coiled up. "Nuns, for God's sake. Murdered."

Alexander knew something was fishy about this whole mess—*now* he knew what it was. "How come you didn't tell me?"

"No need to, Tom—"

"No *need*?"

"No." Halford's response was adamant. "You're just like me, Tom, just like all of us. We serve the Church as the Church sees fit. We don't ask questions. Am I right or wrong?"

Alexander bobbed his head. "You're right, fine. But... shit. *Murder?* And what about the in-pats?"

"There were only four or five in-patients at the time, all terminal priests, and they were all murdered too, quite violently."

Alexander didn't ask for the details. But there was one detail he *had* to ask. "The nuns, the sisters. Was their evidence of sexual assault?"

"They were raped in a big way," the monsignor replied, more colloquially. "All of them. But there's one thing..."

"What?"

"Two of the nuns, the abbess as a matter of fact, and her Sister Superior, their names were Joyclyn and Grace, respectively—"

Alexander frowned. *What, I care what their names were?* Halford had a talent for making a short story long. "What about them?"

"What I want you to know—hell, Tom—I was younger than you are now when all this went down, I was intineraire for the monsignor, hadn't been out of the seminary five years. In other words, I didn't go to Wroxeter myself, but I overheard the consultation at the time. It wasn't good. And I also read the diocesan file."

"What!" Alexander barked.

Halford's eyes turned dark and very sad. "Joyclyn, the abbess, and Sister Grace—"

"What, for God's sake. Quit jerking me!" Alexander yelled.

"They both survived, for a very short time," the monsignor admitted.

"How long?"

"Oh just a few hours after they were found. They died before we could even get an ambulance up there. But a few hours was long enough..."

"Long enough for what?"

"To talk, Tom. What I'm saying is they lived long enough to report an identical description of the killer."

Alexander's voice rattled when he said, "Tell me."

"It was the strangest thing—I doubt that even I would put any stock in it. Keep in mind, these were *cloistered nuns,* Epiphanists, for God's sake, and they'd been viciously assaulted and raped by the perpetrator."

"Bob, if you keep jerking my chain, I'm gonna kick your butt from here to St. Peter's Cathedral."

Halford believed it. "Before they died, they both rendered descriptions of the rapist." Halford abstractedly stroked his cheek. "They said it was a child."

Alexander's faced crimped up. "A *child?* Come on, Bob!"

"That's what they said. When the diocesan counselor asked what age, they said the perpetrator looked to be about ten years old. A child, Tom. A child."

"You expect me to believe that a child killed an abbey full of nuns and priests?"

"That's not all they said, though. But of course, after a trauma like that? I'm sure they were delusional." Then a question lit the monsignor's eyes. "Are delusions ever shared? Or hallucinations? Can two people have the same hallucination, Tom?"

"Yeah, sometimes," Alexander replied, exasperated. He wanted answers, not clinical questions. "But it's rare. It's called *Folie a` deux,* there's plenty of documentation to make it credible. Multiple-hysterical viewpoints, di-exocathesis. But these are *psychopathic* labels. Maybe they all went nuts up there."

"Unlikely," Halford said. He seemed to be squinting past Alexander, back at the calamity of over twenty years ago. "Downing went up there every month to check on things."

"Downing?"

"He had your job then, the shrink for the diocese." Halford paused. "He's the one who discovered the bodies."

"But if he was checking on them every month—a psychologist, mind you—he would've known in an instant if any of the nuns were displaying signs of psychopathy, or any other serious mental disease mechanism. So that rules out your shared delusions theory."

"Yes, yes," Halford vaguely muttered. "It seems so."

"I give up!" Alexander's glare felt honed to the sharpness of a scratch awl. "This a game? I'm supposed to guess? What the hell are you talking about, Bob? What was the goddamn delusion?"

"They didn't just say it was a child, Tom." Halford's eyes went astray. "They said it was a *monster*-child..."

(III)

"What's the matter with you?" Alexander asked. "You're practically shaking, you're jittery."

"I'm fine," Jerrica complained in response.

"Fine, huh? You look like you're having withdrawal symptoms. If you are, I'll take you to the hospital."

"Get off my back," Jerrica sniped. "Just take me back to Annie's boarding house."

"All right. You don't want to talk about it, fine. That's your business. But I thought we were gonna talk about things."

"I don't feel like talking right now," she said. And she didn't. What could she say? I just sucked a drug dealer's cock for cocaine? I swallowed his sperm?

"How was your meeting with your boss?" she asked instead.

"Enlightening. But it's confidential so don't ask."

Jerrica slumped. She felt like a piece of thread twisted out strand by strand. Part of her could only think of how badly she wanted to get back, to fulfill her need. Another part could only recognize that Father Alexander himself was the cure. Still another part reminded her how useless it all was.

If it's not one thing, it's something else...

She came very close to putting her face in her hands and crying. *I love you! Can't you see that!*

But what difference did it make? He was a priest.

They drove back to Luntville in silence. All she could be reminded of was the acrid taste of sperm in her mouth, and the feel of the small plastic bag in her hip pocket.

(IV)

The Bighead, he could smell it, he could. Now he knowed somethin' were up. All this time since he'd left the Lower Woods, that Voice'd been callin' ta him durin' the night. It had been leadin' him somewheres, ain't it?

He stopped at the edge'a the trees.

Couldn't help hisself. He whupped it out right then'n there, thinkin' 'bout all that fine splittail he busted in his time. Hot, wet li'l holes he could sink his pecker in. Too bad he'd never hadda proper nut in any of 'em. They was all too small! But he thinked about it anyways, an' jacked hisself off a *dandy* load'a dicksnot, which landed inna clump'a weeds. Felt good, it did. A *might* good!

But then he got backs ta thinkin'. This place...

He knowed, he did!

This was one place the Voice'd been leadin' him too, weren't it?. A place fer puttin' folks'n the ground. Slabs'a stone stuck out 'round the grass. He knowed what this was, 'cos Grandpap'd tolt him.

This shore's shit were a cemetery.

1 2 3 4 5 6 7 8 9 0
FIFTEEN
ERIK
1999

FIFTEEN

(I)

"Are you feeling better, Aunt Annie?"

"Oh, yes, hon, much better now that I've had a lie-down." She looked rested and chipper as she diced spring onions on the kitchen's great butcher block. "Slept the whole day away, though—gracious! I'll be late getting supper ready!"

"Don't worry about it," Charity said. "Father Alexander and Jerrica aren't even back from Richmond yet."

"I've just got this burnin' desire to impress Father with some real mountain cookin'. Red Beet Eggs, Spoonbread, and my famous Squirrel Pasties—how's that for a supper?"

Squirrel. Pasties. Charity's College Park instinct at first recoiled, but then she remembered, from her childhood, how good squirrel was. *Just so long as I don't have to see her skin and butcher the squirrel,* she thought. "That sounds great, Aunt Annie. Is there anything I can do to help?"

"No, no, dear. You just leave the viddles to me." A "pastie" was one of many makeshift aspects of southern mountain cuisine, something akin to a burrito: meat and vegetables wrapped in soda dough, then baked. As Charity recalled they were delicious, and so was Annie's sweetened spoonbread, which she also remembered. Red Beet Eggs were simply hard-boiled hen's eggs marinated for several days in beet juice—also delicious. Just thinking of these treats sparked Charity's appetite.

"So what did you do today?" Annie asked.

"I— I went to the cemetery."

The kitchen momentarily hushed. "Well, I thought it only fitting and proper that you see your mama's restin' place."

"Yes," Charity replied, clumsily. "I have so many questions all of a sudden."

"Now's not the time, dear; let me get supper on. These pasties take an hour and a half ta bake. Low heat or else the dough cooks faster than the insides. But I promise ya, tonight I'll tell all about yer wonderful ma..."

Sissy, Charity thought. *Annie's sister. My mother.* What was she like? These questions had scarcely ever occurred to her, but now?

Now they burned.

Proximity—that must be it. Charity, after so long, was back home, so naturally the questions would come. But—

"Charity!" Annie exclaimed, her knife poised mid-chop over the turnips and onions. "Your hand!"

Charity's muse roused; she'd been scratching at the bandage on her hand. She didn't dare mention to her aunt the entails of what she'd done today—she'd need more time to ask about the unmarked grave. And she just couldn't see herself saying: Well, Aunt Annie, when I went to the cemetery today, I didn't just visit my mother's grave. I also looked at that second grave you put flowers on yesterday. The grave you didn't want me to see. Oh, and I pulled that unmarked stone...out of the ground.

This she had indeed done, having noticed something like etching below the base of the stone. *R.I.P* was inscribed, in crude fashion, as if by an untrained hand with a stone chisel. And: *Geraldine, forgive me.*

But when she'd been setting the stone back in place, she'd scraped some skin off her hand, which had bled rather profusely.

"It's nothing, Aunt Annie," she excused. "I just scraped my hand today..." Then she lied. "On the back fence. I've got it bandaged up fine."

"You shore, hon? Maybe some iodine'd help."

"No, really. It's fine."

Charity's thoughts, then, strayed. *R.I.P,* she remembered. Why inscribed such a thing *under* the stone? *Country ways,* she considered. *Strange ways.* And who was Geraldine?

"Whuh-why, hi, Miss Charity!"

Charity turned, to notice Goop Gooder standing in the kitchen entry. The boy was attractive, Charity had to admit: tall, well-muscled, something close to a *GQ* face, and obviously, via hard work, bathed in sweat. But still— *Not my type.* However, she could now understand how Jerrica had found him desirable, if not however crudely. "Hello, Goop," she answered. "How are you today?"

"I'se fine, Miss Charity," he told her with spark and enthusiasm. "I'se just outside hammerin' up the vinyl trim thats Miss Annie sended me ta Roanoke fer yesterday. Say, you know where Miss Jerrica is?"

"Goop!" Annie interrupted. "Are you done hangin' that trim?"

Goop Gooder stalled. "Whuh-well, no, not yets, Miss Annie."

"Then git back to it! An' don't'cha be botherin' Charity's fine friend. Ya just leave her be an' git about yer business."

"Yuh-yuh-yes, Miss Annie."

Goop, then, disappeared out the back door, slumped in dejection.

"Do you need to be so hard on him?" Charity ventured.

Annie went back to her chopping. "What'cha gotta understand, hon, is that I know full well Goop's a fine, fine boy. But he kin get ta be a pain in the you-know-what, when it comes ta lady folk guests. I love him dearly, I do, but sometimes I just gotta keep on him. I cain't have yer dear friend Jerrica bein' pestered by Goop."

"It's just a young man's crush," Charity pointed out, but her next thoughts added, *Yes, Aunt Annie, it's just a crush. To the extent that Jerrica had sex with him in your garden the other night!* "I'm sure he won't bother her," she said in replacement.

"I shore hope yer right, Charity, 'cos I cain't bear the thought'a yer friend goin' back ta the city thinkin' we'se all a bunch'a hayseeds."

"Oh, Aunt Annie, you're impossible!"

Still, though, she wondered. Goop obviously had no interest in Charity herself. *Why her and not me?* her insecurities made her wonder.

(II)

Dinner was fabulous, the food exquisite. But one thing Charity couldn't help but notice was this: Jerrica and Father Alexander scarcely spoke. Jerrica seemed flattened, while the priest appeared distracted, muddled. Not like them at all. Then, rather early, in fact, they both retired to their rooms.

"I wonder what's wrong with them?" Annie queried. "My gracious. I hope they liked the Squirrel Pasties!"

"So." Annie lounged back at the big table in the parlor. She lit her acrid meerschaum pipe, and Charity immediately thought, *If you're worried about people thinking you're a hayseed, Annie...lose the pipe.*

"Just you an' me now, ever-one else is in bed, an' it's late an' it's actually even kinda cool."

Charity waited, listened.

"Perfect time, hon, fer me ta tell you 'bout yer ma."

"I want to hear about her," Charity said, nearly without breath.

"I called her Sissy, she were my younger sister, an' a *fine* woman she was. An' she married a fine fella named Jere, from Filbert he was, fine a man as you'd ever meet. Started at a rock-pickin' job at the mine and worked his way up ta shift supervisor, he did. A fine, fine man."

Yes, I heard you. A fine man, Charity's thoughts complained. But she knew she must give the old woman her due. The elderly had a way of relating a story—the roundabout way—and that was usually the best way.

"Yer daddy, hon, he was not only a fine, lovin' husband, he was almost problee the handsomest man in the ridge. Lotta hearts was broke when he married yer ma, but that were fine by God 'cos Sissy were a blessed woman. Things was goin' just fine, they was. Yer mamma was pregnant with you, yer daddy climbin' the ladder at the mine—just fine they was. Until one day..."

My father died, Charity knew.

"Yer daddy, hon, he died. Weren't slow was what the inspectors said, so don'ts ya worry 'bout that. Kilt instantly, they claimed. See, a prop stull busted in the main shaft, all that coal in the ridge came a'tumblin' down on yer daddy and a bunch'a other fine men." Annie poured two glasses of the dark raspberry wine, then repeated, "Kilt instantly, they was."

"But my mother," Charity began.

"Yer mama, hon, she was a fine woman, like I'se said, but also a awful unstable one. Only thing kept her alive, I 'spect, was her bein' pregnant with you. So's she waited, she did, gettin' bigger ever day, till she had out with ya. An' I kin say, Charity, you was the most beautiful li'l baby girl I ever did see. See, I was the midwife these parts, an' I saw 'em all. But you?" Annie sipped her dark wine, trembled, closed her eyes. "You was just the cutest li'l thing. 'N'fact, that's why we'se called ya Charity, 'cos you were a charity from God..."

Charity wasn't very impressed. She wanted to know the rest, down to every last detail. She had a right to know, didn't she?

"But it weren't long after," Aunt Annie went on, "that yer ma just couldn't tolerate it n more." Annie gulped, poured more wine. "It pains me ta say it, hon, but one night yer mama took up one'a Jere's shotguns and—"

"Tell me," Charity insisted. She'd never feel complete if she didn't hear it all. "What...happened? Exactly?"

"Yer mama, dear—she blowed her head off with that shotgun."

The vision of the trauma assailed her. Charity couldn't imagine the strength of the depression to drive someone to do such a thing. *Shotgun,* she thought. *In the head.* Did she feel pain? What were her final thoughts?

Did she think about me?

"So that's the story, hon. I never tolt ya all of it 'cos they took ya from me when ya were so young. Didn't think it fittin' ta tell ya everthing, when ya were just eight. I'se don't feel good about it at all."

"Annie, stop. You did the right thing. An eight-year-old is too young to hear such details."

Aunt Annie slugged more wine, obviously not at ease. "But I feel a tad better now, just knowin' that I finally told ya. Please, hon, fergive me..."

(III)

Joyclyn, he thought. *The abbess. And Grace, the sister superior...*

He looked at their old photos, from the file that Halford had given up. Attractive women, for sure. The abbess, lean and smiling, with short sable-hued hair. And the sister superior: raving, clear green eyes; smiling angelically, with a headful of bright red hair...

Both dead. Over twenty years ago. Raped and butchered by a madman.

Or, as Halford had inferred, a mad*child.*

Shared delusions. Shared hallucinosis. Alexander considered this. Folie a` deux? But Downing, the resident psychologist, would've tagged that in a heartbeat. *Crazy nuns? It would be obvious to even a novice or a newbie.*

So what bothered him?

The record was filled with death-quotes. *A monster-child,* Joyclyn had said. *The devil's brood.* And Sister Grace, more delineated: *Ten years old or thereabouts. Hideous. A huge head, big as a watermelon, Father Downing, and eyes...God save me. One eye big as an apple, and one... smaller than the end of my thumb, Father! It was the devil's child that came in there that night!*

Then she went into a coma and, shortly thereafter, died.

Alexander closed the files. He sputtered and smoked. Last night, Annie had told the tall tale of The Bighead, the "monster-child." A local *myth.*

And, according to this secret archival record, that's exactly what Abbess Joyclyn and Sister Superior Grace had described as the attacker of Wroxeter Abbey.

A monster-child.

The priest squinted at the window. Heat lightning flashed, followed by eerie silence. He took off his black shirt and slacks and prepared to shower.

A monster-child?

No.

Just, he thought and struggled with the idea. *Just...a coincidence.*

(IV)

Goop, laved in sweat, went to his bedroom after he'd put the tools away. Vinyl trim, new caulking? The house didn't need any of that, and Annie sure didn't need to send Goop to Roanoke to get it. It almost seemed as though his employer had concocted the excursion solely to keep him out of the house. He hadn't even *seen* Jerrica for a full day!

Dag it, he grumbled to himself. He knew what was going on; it was a cah-spear-ah-see!

Annie's tryin' ta keep me away from Jerrica...

Vinyl trim. New caulk. The boarding house looked just fine, and a lot of it was because Goop had worked so hard; Annie was just spendin' money on account'a she had it now from that ass-klaction suit or whatever it was. He tried ta calm hisself down, an' 'ventually did.

But he couldn't help what he done next.

He slipped inta his closet, took out the panel an' went in. Shee-it, if Annie ever fount out 'bout this, she'd have his hide! Down the narrow corridor he went, feelin' his way mostly 'cos there were no light. But he'd done it so many times...he knowed his way fairly well. First he passed Charity's room. The hole glowed, and Goop Gooder put his eye to it. Miss Charity were sitting on the bed wearin' this really fine-lookin' teddy—er at least that's what Goop thought it was called. Had some fine, purdy white legs onner, and that musty dark hair hangin' ta her shoulders. Purdy face. But what Goop's eyes took to mostly were that set'a boobs onner, fillin' up that teddy top the way a couple'a big summertime melons'll fill a pick-sack. *Lordy!* Goop thought. But Miss Charity's face, purdy as it were, hadda look to it...

Confused, kinda. An' maybe even sad. Like she were thinkin' 'bout things that not only got her down but things also that she couldn't figgure.

No nudie action here, fer shore. She'd ob-ver-us-lee already hadda shower an' were fixin' ta bed down. Goop moved on.

The very next hole— Goop stopped, stuck his eye right up.

An' there she were.

Nekit, like the first time he seed her, an' touchin herself. Goop had to touch *hisself* just lookin', purdy as she were. *I loves her so much,* he thought, pressin' his hand against his pants front. *I'd marries her inna heartbeat, an' be a good husband ta boot...*

His eye, a'corse, didn't have a whole lotta mobility, peepin' inta that wall-hole, but he coulds see just the same. There were some funky li'l computer-thing sittin' with its lid up on the desk, but Miss Jerrica herself...

She were layin' on the big, high bed an' moanin' an' squirmin' as her hand played with her girly parts. *I loves her,* he thought again, squeezin' his own crotch whiles he were watchin'. Ever-thing about her were just beautiful. Them pretty tits onner, them long tan legs and trim tummy. Her bush—swear ta God!—were the same fine bright-blond color as her hair. Shiny as silk, it were!

Then Goop thought: *Wonders what she thinkin' 'bout whiles she doin' it. I wonder if she thinkin' 'bout me...*

She were done, though, in another minute 'er so, so loud enough fer Goop ta hear through that wall. Her face turnt a kinda soft-pink, then her tensed-up body went just as soft. Then she laid there fer a few, her chest goin' up'n down. An' then—

She leaned up, turnt over onner side. That vision just there—Jerrica half rolled over—almost made Goop shoot a wad right in his pants, it did! 'Cos he could see her li'l beaver pressed 'tween her cheeks as she done so, like a li'l blond chipmunk like the kind that run 'round in back, in Miss Annie's flowers. Cutest li'l thing...

But—

What'n tarnations she doin' now? he thought.

She was leanin' over ta the nightstand, fishin' somethin' out. Hadda lady's compact mirror open an' were pourin' somethin' onta it, then choppin' it up with what looked like a razor blade.

What the—

Then he knowed.

Miss Jerrica, what she done then was she brought that li'l mirror upta her face an' started sniffin'...

Drugs, Goop thought. He'd heard about it from folks. *The devil's toy,* Miss Annie'd said once, commentin' 'bout it. It were this city stuff, this white powder, that folks'd sniff inta their noses an' mess 'em alls up. Mess up their heads, it would was what Annie'd said, make 'em git close ta the devil. *She's doin' drugs,* Goop realized, his unblinkin' eye pressed hard against that hole. *The devil's gotta hard bite on her!*

She sniffed that evil stuff up a coupla times, then lay back with a tiny grin onner face. Then—

She got up, slipped onna nightgown an' left the room.

Goop had no idea where she might be goin' at this hour, but he didn't care. All he knowed was this: *I loves her, an' I gots ta help her fight that devil-made ah-dik-sher-un she got...*

Goop, frantic now, paced back down the unlit corridors until he got back to his own room.

Then he raced out.

(V)

Charity couldn't sleep. She tossed amid the sheets, audibly whining. Each time she started to nod off, some awful dream would plague her, mostly dreams of her past men, the men who had rejected her and never said why. *What's wrong with* me? *Why do I repulse men every time I'm with them?*

Familiar questions, and familiarly unanswered. *Mental block,* she always told herself. Some aspect of her subconscious, perhaps, was blocking her capacity for sensation.

Then, she'd keep waking up.

But was that what really bothered her?

No...

She knew what it was. That grave. That little stone.

R.I.P. scratched onto it, below the base.

Geraldine, forgive me.

Whose grave was it? Why did her aunt go there?

My aunt...

Maybe she'd thus far kept the ultimate question out of her mind. It was something secret.

Why had Annie not mentioned this second grave—this *unmarked* grave?

And maybe it was her imagination, but—

Though this was the first time in two decades that Charity had actually seen her aunt, she had, in fact, received many letters from her over the years. Hundreds of letters—

And now she couldn't help but think about that.

The etched scrawl at the bottom of the gravestone…

It must be my imagination, she thought.

But the etched scrawl at the bottom of the gravestone reminded her of Aunt Annie's penmanship.

(VI)

"Miss Jerrica?"

Goop slid out of the shadows with caution. He didn't want to scare her like he done the other night. She was traipsin' about in the moonlight, back by the kiosk in the garden.

But she didn't seem startled at all when she turned. "Goop? Hi!" she greeted as thought she were really glad to see him. "I haven't seen you since yesterday!"

"I knows," he said. "I hadda go ta Roanoke, spend the night there inna motel, an' git some trim'n stuff fer Annie. But—"

She wasn't herself, her could see that. *Them drugs,* he realized. *It's them drugs she been sniffin' upper nose.*

The sight'a her, though, seemed to lock in his head: her standin' there in the dark, that big bright smile'a hers, an' that body livin' an' breathin' beneath that nightgown.

"I'm glad you're here," she said, her voice just as soft as the color'a her hair. "I missed you."

Missed me. Keee-riiist. Goop doubted that he'd been missed by any gal he'd ever knowed, not that there'd been many. But here was Jerrica, sayin' just that, an' lookin' sweet as ever.

"I—I missed you too, Miss Jerrica," he said, tryin' not ta tremble. "I'se been thinkin' 'bout you a lot."

Her nightgown fell to her feet, and then— There it all was, all that wonderful, tanned city body, them hooters onner, all pure white against the tan, an' nice hard-lookin' nipples stickin' out the color'a radishes... Then her hand reached out, cupped his crotch.

"Awwwww, Miss Jerrica," he nearly stuttered. "There's somethin' I gots ta—I gots ta—talk ta ya about—"

"Talk later." Her voice was like a warm breeze, her smile lighting up the dark flower garden. Above them, the heat lightning flashed, lighting her up ever more so. More fer him ta see. More fer him ta love.

"I need you real bad," she whispered, and squeezed harder.

But this weren't right, was it? *Them drugs,* he thought, thinkin' agin 'bout the evil of 'em. *I gots ta talk ta her 'bout them drugs...*

She was kissing him, working her hot tongue into his mouth, and working her hand into his pants. "Christ," she whispered even more faintly. "I want that big farm-boy cock in me so bad—"

Keeeeeeee-riiiiiist...

She grabbed his hand, placed it right into the middle of her soft, blond pussy, She pressed his finger into its wetness, then retracted it. Next thing, she was sucking his finger.

"I'm gonna suck your come out into my mouth," she breathed. "Would you like that, Goop? Hmmm? Would you like that?"

What could he say? What would *any* guy say?

"I— I shore would, Miss Jerrica. That'd be a might—"

She didn't let him finished. She was rubbing her body against him now, embracing him. Her thigh raised up, rubbing the bottom of his crotch. *Aw, aw,* he thought. He were about ta come right then'n there!

"I gonna sit on your face and suck your cock at the same time..."

She tried to haul him down to the ground, just like the other night, her tits pressing, her pussy leaving a warm wet spot on his pants leg. It was all Goop could do to steady hisself. Somethin' weren't right, that was fer shore. She weren't herself.

Them drugs, he thought. *Them drugs...*

"Miss Jerrica, I gots ta tell ya somethin'."

"Tell me later." Her fingers gently encircled his balls, gently squeezed them. "I want your come in me first, then you can tell me anything you want." Then she squeezed his shaft, and again he almost came. "I want you to fuck me, Goop, and squirt all that hot come right up into my pussy. I wanna feel it..."

"I saw what you was doin'," he flinched and finally said. "But I wants ya ta know, it's all right. I'll'se help ya."

"What are you talking about, Goop?"

"I saw..." He clenched his eyes close, swallowed. "I saw ya doin' them drugs."

Her kisses pulled back. Her hand slipped out of his pants. "What...do...you mean?"

He grit his teeth. He *hadda* tell her! "I saw ya, Miss Jerrica. Don't ask me how—that don't matter none. But I saw ya doin' them devil-made drugs an' they ain't no good fer ya. I wanna *help* ya."

In the moonlight, her face seemed to twist up. "You—*what?* Why you— You were *peeping* in my window?"

"Naw, Miss Jerrica, but it don't matter—"

"You motherfucking redneck slime!" Suddenly her face was a slice of hatred. "You've been *peeping* on me! You goddamn redneck moron piece of *shit!*"

"Aw, no, Miss Jerrica! Ya gotta understand!"

At once she was hauling her nightgown back on. "I understand that you're a fucking backwoods pervert, spying on people! What gives you the right to do something like that! Jesus Christ, I'd have better luck with that goddamn priest! You're a piece of shit, Goop! A scumbag, no-account, imbecile, retarded *piece of shit!*"

Goop stared at the words as if they could actually be seen. *Naw, naw, what've I done?* "Please, Miss Jerrica! All we'se gotta do is talk!"

"Fuck you!" she shouted. A moment later, the back door slammed. She was gone, back in the house, far away from him.

Naw naw naw, he thought. *She don't mean them mean things she said. It were just them evil city drugs makin' her say them things.* He knowed full well; there were only one thing ta do. Go up, right now, ta her room, an' *talk.* Talk ta her 'bout this thing. And Goop Gooder turned to do just that, when—

"Hey, cracker."

Goop stopped, turned. Didn't quite reckon who'd said it, but didn't care. Didn't like ta be called a cracker by no one. The moon shined in his eyes when he turned. He clenched his fist, fixin' ta kick some serious ass, blinked—

Smack!

Goop went down. Somethin' hit him so hard upside the head he could barely see a second later. Alls he could do was huff an' feel the hard ground 'neath his back.

"Lookit this big cracker! Hey, Gomer Pyle!"

"We'se gonna kill him right here?"

"Naw, no way. We'se gonna have some fun first!"

Goop's vision struggled somethin' fierce. Two blobs'a faces looked down, two fellas, but that's 'bout all he could make out.

And Goop couldn't move…

"Lets me tell ya something, ya big cracker," the one grabbed his collar an' said. "That prissy priest-lovin' city blond ya got yer eye on? We'se gonna ass-fuck her so hard she gonna shit blood. Then I'se gonna jack my dicksnot up her nose an' cut her skin off real slow like, ya hear? I'se gonna kill me that city bitch, core her ass out like a apple an' make her eat her own shit an' thens bury her." A chuckle in the dark. "An ya knows what, cracker? Ain't nothin' you gonna be able ta do about it."

Goop heaved, summoned every ounce'a strength his big body had ever called. But that whack on the head—

He couldn't move barely a muscle.

"Drag him back the 'Mino, Dicky," the voice said. "Hail, let's do a job on him 'fore we dump his cracker body in the woods," A thumb and index finger squeezed his face. "Hear me, cracker! We'se gonna do a job on you like ta make the devil puke!"

1 2 3 4 5 6 7 8 9 0
SIXTEEN
ERIK
1999

SIXTEEN

(I)

"There are a whole lot of people you can piss off and it doesn't mean shit," Jesus said in the dream. "But one of 'em isn't THE SON OF GOD!"

Alexander trembled. *What did I do now?*

"What do you think I am, some kind of an asshole? Some rube moron out of the hills? Didn't you and I have a big talk last night?"

"What have I done, Lord? Forgive me in my ignorance, but what have I done wrong now?"

Jesus took the pack of Lucky's out of Alexander's shirt pocket, tapped one out, lit it. But the King of Kings was wearing not only a crown of thorns but a Danzig t-shirt: black, in white letters. He smoked deep.

"You may be able to bullshit the little people, priest," Jesus said, "but you can't bullshit Me. I'm Hosanna the Highest, I'm the *Messiah* for My sake!"

"I'm not bullshitting, Lord," Alexander spake back. "Please, I beg of Thee. Tell me what's wrong?"

Jesus tapped an ash. "You're still lusting after that blonde and you know it."

"I swear to You on high, I WILL NEVER LAY A HAND ON HER."

"That doesn't matter!" Jesus bellowed. "If the sin is in the heart, it's as good as if it's been committed! *You* know *that!* Didn't you read the Jimmy Carter interview in *Playboy?* He wasn't much on foreign policy or the deficit, but at least the guy had the balls to admit his Christian sins!"

"Forgive me, Lord."

"*Keep* your goddamn eyes off that blonde! She's a cokehead and a nympho! And what are you? Christ, man. You're a *priest.* That's *My* black cloth you're wearing, *My* collar of faith around your turkey neck. The Morning Star is laughing so hard at Me, I can hear him all the way from the goddamn abyss! You're making me look like a *schmuck!*"

Alexander croaked, "I will do anything in reparation, my God. Anything. I swear."

Jesus' long dark hair hung in His face. "You wanna do something for *Me?* Then do *this!* Stop being a hypocritical dickbrain!"

"Yes, Lord!"

The Messiah's face inclined forward, shaggy hair and beard. "You got any idea what hell is like, any idea at all? I've *been there,* man. And it ain't no picnic. You should see the shit that motherfucker pulls down there. You want *that?*"

"No, my Lord!"

Jesus took a last toke of the Lucky, jerked His head. "Then get your shit square, brother." He flicked the butt.

"Yes, yes! I will, I swear!"

"Swearing to Me doesn't mean *crap,* man, unless you mean it to yourself. You got any idea how many broken promises I hear? Shit, if I had a nickel for every one, I'd make Bill Gates look like a fucking toilet attendant."

"Everything I say to You is from my heart."

"Then make *damn sure* it is." Jesus' holy face turned clement; He'd simmered down. "Because if you don't, you're lost."

Alexander nodded with such vigor he thought his neck might become dislocated. "Your will will be done."

"Thanks for the butt, man. I gotta book. But—"

"But *what,* my Lord?"

Jesus' lips screwed up. "The ghosts are back. They want to see you again, and there ain't nothing I can do. So all I can say is just suffer, like Job, you know? Hack it. Walk it like you got a pair."

The nightmare sailed, into blackness. And then—

"Supplantation."

"Ever comes the morrow."

"You are such a silly little priest!"

"Must still be thinking about that blonde drug addict."

"Or maybe the old lady!"

"Unto you, Father, I commend my spirit."

"Really, Grace! What you should say is this: Unto you, I commend my fist!"

Laughter, evil chittering…

Now two more visitors were at hand. His night-suitors had a face now—*faces*. Abbess Joyclyn and Sister Superior Grace. "It feels so good to be purged," Joyclyn said. "It feels so good to transpose…"

Grace leaned over, grinning. "Shit, you're a psychologist. Haven't you ever read Freud or Jung?"

Alexander moaned, pinned naked now on his back. The voices, and faces, blended together then, like wax under high heat.

"Where's that lube?"

"Right there."

"Give it here. I'm gonna fist this pious fucker. I've always wanted to fist a priest…"

Alexander, pinned as he was, tried to push his mind away, to some other place. He knew that this was just a dream—all the stress of his life building up, added to Halford's deceptions about the abbey, plus the specific revelation regarding the murders.

Not simply a child, he recalled the monsignor's testimony.

A *monster*-child.

A fist glistened in the lamplight, like a hand dipped into glycerin. The priest's legs were abruptly parted.

First one finger, then two, then three…

Into his rectum they wormed.

Then four…

Christ Almighty, stop it!

Then all five.

The entire fist seemed to fill his bowel like a big fruit. It urged back and forth, twisted around.

"All priests are actually queer," one nun said. "That's why they flee the world for the priesthood, to deny what they know of themselves. They're really queer. They love to have things stuffed up their asses."

"I'm not queer!" Alexander bellowed, snapping against his bonds. "And I don't want *anything* stuffed up my ass!"

"A Freudian contradiction. People always deny what they really are..."

"Oh, *fuck you!*" Alexander screamed. "I'm sick of hearing that liberal bullshit!"

Chuckles. Giggles. "Then how come you're getting hard?"

Was he? So what! This was a demented, stress-related nightmare. He couldn't be held responsible...

The small, greased fist churned in his bowel, pummeling his prostate. "Yeah," one of the nuns cooed. "This is great, isn't it? I'm fist-fucking a priest up the ass. Always wanted to do it, used to finger myself thinking about it. And that schmuck Downing? Shit. I wish I had a dick so I could stick it all the way up his ass and come."

"I was lying on the abbey floor bleeding to fucking death and I swear that asshole was undressing me with his eyes."

"All priests do."

"I'm surprised he didn't fuck both of us."

"Who would've known? No one."

"Shit, maybe he did and we just don't remember."

"I'll bet he did! I'll bet that old crevice-faced motherfucker fucked us!"

Alexander, though, was missing most of the conversation. After all, it was hard for a priest to maintain much of an attention span while an Epiphanist nun was fist-fucking his ass. He winced as he felt the hand open and close inside of him, stroking the inside of his large intestine.

"He fornicated with prostitutes in Viet Nam."

"Bad boy!"

"And you know what else he did? He killed people."

"A killer priest, oh my! Well how do you like *this*... killer?"

Alexander's stomach quaked; he felt as though some brutal, living thing were inhabiting his bowel...

"Blow him."

The priest shouted, "No!"

"Make him break those phony vows. Make him come."

The fist continued to eddy in and out. The other nun's mouth descended, engulfed his half-hard penis. It wasn't half-hard for long though; in perhaps ten seconds it had fully enlivened in the confines of the nun's mouth.

"Can you imagine?" the fister queried. "This guy hasn't fucked in years. Can you imagine how much spunk has built up?"

"He probably jerks off three times a day," the fellatrice paused long enough to remark.

"I don't jerk off!" Alexander bellowed. "I haven't jerked off in over a decade!"

"Yeah, right. Just like you didn't kill kids in Viet Nam."

"I didn't kill kids! I killed the enemy! I killed NVAs because if I didn't, they would've killed me!"

"Murder is an impediment to the priesthood, asshole."

"I didn't murder anyone! It was justifiable homicide! It says so in Vatican II!"

And with that, Alexander's hips convulsed. A vaguely familiar sensation arose: something rising to escape—

"Jerk him now."

The hand opened and closed inside. Another hand grasped his spit-slick shaft and stroked. When Alexander opened his mouth to moan, hot jets of semen flew into it.

"Out*rag*eous! We just made a priest come in his own mouth!" I wonder if he's even aware of the existential symbology of that. I wonder if he knows what that means."

"He's too stupid. He's too hung-up on that cocaine blonde."

Alexander spat his own semen out of his mouth, to rebel. "I am not hung up on—"

"Shut up, asshole." Then—

schlap!

Alexander barked a shout as the fist was quickly withdrawn.

"Should we shit in his mouth?"

"Naw, no time. Christ, we've only got so much time."

"You're right."

"But I gotta pee. And he likes to be peed on."

"Let 'er rip."

The priest's head rolled back and forth in the midst of this outrage. One of the nuns hoisted her habit-skirt, bared the ever-familiar pubic bush. And then it came, the amber cascade, spurtling in a gentle arc directly into his mouth.

Alexander gagged, his face pouring warm liquid. It stung his eyes. *I'm going to drown in a nun's piss...*

The stream moved, forcing itself into his nostrils. He felt the heat jet up his sinuses, as if seeking his brain.

"Yeah, Sartre would love this!"

When the cascade subsided, the other nun cackled like a witch, and wiped her smeary hand off on his face, a gelatinous conglomeration of Noxema and his own excrement.

"We're ghosts, Father. Did you know that?"

"I had an idea," Alexander gasped.

"You think that because you're faithful, you'll go to heaven?"

"Yes! I know I will!"

"Stop being so selfish, killer. We were faithful too, and look where *we* are."

Alexander got the point.

The figures began to dissolve. Alexander could taste hot urine dipping down his nasal passage to his tongue.

"Watch out for The Bighead," one of them said.

The voices drifted, like distant surf.

The macabre light of nightmare dimmed.

"Don't go in the basement, Father..."

(II)

"Dicky! Git the strap wrench!"

Dicky squatted in the bushes, his pants down, his bulbous buttocks jutting like twin moons. "Aw, Balls, gimme a sec, I'se takin' me a dump!"

"Wells hurry up!" Balls called back. "And that coil'a rope too, the heavy stuff."

Whatever it was Tritt Balls Conner planned ta do, Dicky knew it wouldn't be purdy. They'd been stakin' the boarding house when they jacked the big kid out with Balls' homemade jack, throwed him in the back'a the 'Mino, an' drove here, the bluff on the other side'a Kohl's Point. Boone River could be heard a-gushin' a hunnert feet down.

"And bring yer shitrag, too, Dicky!"

My— "Aw," Dicky moaned. Frownin', he wiped his crack with an old oil rag, then jacked his jeans back up. Walkin' back ta the dell, he complained, "Balls, what'n tarnations ya want my shitrag fer?"

Balls cut a grin in the moonlight, pointed down. "Gag that cracker."

"Aw—"

"Just do it! An' git that other stuff I tolt ya."

They'd stripped the big kid nekit and hog-tied him. He were just comin' to when Dicky, quite a look'a distaste on his face, stuffed that shitrag in the fella's mouth an' tied it in with some twine. Then he went back to the El Camino ta hunt down the rope and the strap-wrench. *What he wanna strap-wrench fer anyway?* he wondered. Gawd knew! Whiles rummagin' through the tool box, though, he could hear Balls already gittin' ta work on the kid, a real weird muffled sound as the poor kid got ta screamin' beneath that shitrag gag. "Ooooo-doggie!" Balls celebrated. "An' Dicky? Bring them loppin' shears too."

Dicky rolled his eyes. *Balls in another'a his crazy moods,* he realized. Weren't no talkin' him out of it neither. Dicky found the strap-wrench and then the loppin' shears, which he kept in the box fer when they needed ta cut the metal bands on the pallets'a moonshine. He alsa found the rope, fifty-foot worth problee.

And that hog-tied kid were floppin' fierce in the dirt when Dicky came back. "What'cha do, Balls?"

"Dug his eyes out with my buck. Lookit!"

Dicky winced. Two bloody eyeballs looked up at him from the ground, and it were a weird feelin'. "Hi, cracker!" Balls exclaimed, wavin' at them eyeballs. A reglar comedian, he were. Then he stomped on the eyes hard with his boot. The eyeballs popped.

Balls shook the kid's head around by the hair. "I just stepped on yer eyeballs, cracker! How you like that?" In the moonlight, Dicky could barely make out the sight'a the kid's gagged face, two holes where his eyes'd been. Balls grabbed the loppin' shears then, and—

snick! snick! snick!

—took ta clippin' off the kid's toes'n fingers. Each *snick* of them shears caused the kid ta jerk against his tied wrists'n ankles.

snick! snick! snick!

"Lordy, this is fun!" After a lot more snickin', all them fingers'n toes'd been clipped right off, an' Dicky could see 'em sittin' there on the ground. Weren't much blood, though, on account'a how tight Balls'd tied the wrists'n ankles.

"Lookit! The big dumb cracker's passin' out."

"Shee-it, Balls. Maybe he up'n died. Why not just cut his throat so's we kin git outa here."

"Hail, Dicky, quit bein' such a wuss all the time. He ain't dead. This a big *strong* cracker. Got a lotta spark left in him. Nows gimme that there strap-wrench."

Dicky did so an' watched, still not quite dee-duckter-ive enough to figger what Balls had in mind fer his fun. Balls were kneelin' now, an' what he done next was he wrapped that thick canvas strap right around the kid's dick'n balls, and Balls hisself, he didn't flinch 'bout handlin' another fella's privates, no sir. He slipped the end'a the canvas strap through the latch-slot, then started a'crankin'. "Balls?" Dicky asked, still kinda mystified. "What'choo doin'?" "You'll see," he were told through Tritt Balls' grin. Soon he'd cranked that strap so hard, this big fella's cock'n balls was locked so tight over that wrench strap they was stickin' out and *throbbin'*, they was. Balls'd fixed that wrench ta the fella's works so tight that *nothin'* would be's able ta pull it off. But then he took the end'a that rope an' fed it through the hole on the wrench handle.

And then—

"Dicky, ties the other end'a the rope ta that there tree over yonder."

Now Dicky were beginnin' ta see. He did as tolt, tyin' a hard knot, the rope leadin' back ta the strap-wrench clamped hard ta this big fella's pecker. Balls were slappin' him in the face.

"Wakes up, cracker! Ya don'ts wanna miss the fun now, do ya?" He slapped harder, an' then the fella's eyeless head started ta move. "I dugs yer eyes out, ya dumbass 'Ginia cornhole, an' I'se clipped off yer fingers'n toes. An' it were *fun!*" Balls throwed his head back an' laughed so hard Dicky coulda swored the trees shook overhead. "Nows it's time fer ya ta be on yer way," he said next, still shakin' this poor kid's head back'n forth, "I wants ya ta know that I'll'se give that purdy city blondie yer regards when I'm'se yankin' her guts out her cunt!"

By now, with the bluff just a few yards away, Dicky knew full well what it were Balls had planned. He an' Balls, then, picked the convulsin' kid up on either end ands carried him ta the edge. Dicky looked down just once, he did, an' could see the churnin' river an' rocks in the moonlight.

"One!" Balls shouted. "Two! Three!"

Ands right then'n there, they throwed that big cracker fella right off the edge'a the bluff. A coupla seconds passed, then—

twang!

—the rope sprung, drew real taut, then—

snap!

It broke, ands when it broke, there were no doubt that it did so on account'a the fella's cock'n balls snappin' off his body, wheres-upon he fell smack-dab onta them shaller rocks in the river a hunnert feet below.

Balls wiped his hands, noddin'. "What ya think, Dicky? Ya thinks we done a good'nuff job on that fella?"

Dicky reeled up the rope an'—shore enough—there were the fella's cock'n balls still stuck ta the strap-wrench. "Ya shore strapped 'er down tight, Balls," he commented.

"'Corse I did. *Real* tight. Ands ya kin see I dids it so tight it didn't pop out."

"But what we gonna do with it now?"

Balls cackled. He grabbed the strap-wrench outa Dicky's hands an' yanked them there dick'n balls right out.

"Feed the fish, that's what we'se gonna do."

Then he throwed them severed geni-ter-als over the bluff where they 'ventually splashed inta the Boone River.

1 2 3 4 5 6 7 8 9 0
SEVENTEEN
ERIK
1999

SEVENTEEN

(I)

"I'm going to the abbey now," Alexander said in the foyer. "You wanna go with me?"

Jerrica's eyes cast down. "No, I—"

"Come on. I could use your help."

"No, I shouldn't, I—"

The priest made a face. "Look, I said I was sorry about yesterday. We can talk about it, and I promise not to be an asshole this time. Come on. Don't be a candyass."

Even Jerrica had to smile. "All right."

But it *wasn't* all right, was it? *I'm a drug addict.* Father Alexander knew, and now, somehow, so did Goop.

First thing was first. She had to talk to Goop.

"I mean, I'll go, but not right now," she said. "I know how to get there; I'll come in my own car a little later, okay?"

"All right," the priest conceded. "I guess you need some time to work on your article."

The very words made her struggle not to shrivel into herself. *Who am I kidding?* She'd barely worked at all on her article, and that was the reason she'd come here in the first place. *Too busy fucking Goop and snorting coke and falling in love with a goddamn priest who's probably twenty years older than me...*

"Anyway," the priest went on. "I'll see you a little later then." He gently touched her shoulder. "'Bye."

She gulped, watched him walk out the front door. Then she peeked through the sidelight window and saw him pull off in the white Mercedes.

She felt nervous, agitated. She walked back into the house and up the stairs, then, her mind rising with each step. Something in her psyche cringed; she had the new dope in the pocket of her shorts, but she refused to acknowledge it. She *must* try, she *had* to try.

Only some things weren't so easy.

In fact, *nothing* was…

Her hand came away from her pocket. *I'll talk to Goop, get things straightened out. Apologize for the things I said last night—*

But Goop…wasn't there.

His bedroom door stood open, but no Goop inside. Earlier, she'd looked around the house, to see if he was working on the trim or in the yard. And—

No Goop. And his truck was still out front.

Where is he?

She stood in the middle of his room, dumbfounded. It was a spartan room—no surprise, as Goop was a simple person. Just a bed, a dresser, a chair, a small desk that looked untouched. And—

The closet, she saw.

Ordinarily there'd be no big deal about a closet in a handyman's room, but *this* closet…

"What the *hell* is *that?*" she muttered aloud.

The closet door stood open, yes, but *within* the closet—

She inched forward, peering.

There seemed to be another door. Or, not so much a door but a panel out of place, as though the closet's back wall were actually an exit.

Jerrica stood still a moment, blinked, then walked in.

(II)

Charity slept late, and as usual, she had essentially the same dream that she'd been having since she arrived at the boarding house.

Men fucking her, their faces suddenly collapsing in disappointment, then getting up and leaving. One hard cock after another, stroking into her vagina a few times, then wilting, then pulling out. She lay there like a hot starfish, looking tearily up as each of them left without a word.

Always the same, always the same…

When she awoke, the slats of sunlight from the blinds seemed to rake her eyes. But she still felt distant, wobbly. She wasn't sure if she was actually awake or not…

Am I awake? she wondered.

A voice pounded in her head.

COME, it said, or seemed to.

Am I awake?

COME.

No, no.

Charity leaned up, rubbed her face.

Of course. It must have been a dream.

(III)

A passageway…

Yes, that's exactly what it was. Behind that open door in Goop's clothes closet was a *passageway.*

Curiosity killed the cat, Jerrica considered, but she went ahead anyway. The first leg of the passage was pitch-dark, but then she turned and saw…

Dots.

Bright white dots of light, like spires, like lances poking out into the darkness.

Holes, she realized.

She soft-footed up to the first hole, put her eye to it, and saw—

Charity's room…

Goop *was* a goddamn peeping tom! Jerrica was gazing right in now, and *looking* at Charity as she leaned up in bed, rubbing her eyes. The next hole of light was even more tell-tale—

My room!

So that was how Goop knew about Jerrica's cocaine-use. *He was looking in at me the whole time. God knows what else he saw!*

All the other rooms were empty, she knew—no tenants, and Father Alexander had already left for the abbey. She walked a bit further, though, and found…

A ladder.

Right there, at the end of the passage, a ladder descended. She could barely see but she could see enough, for all of the spiring holes of light.

A ladder. Leading down.

She placed her sandaled feet, began to descend, until she found yet another passageway on what was no doubt the first floor. One hole showed her the kitchen, another the den, and yet another—

Annie's room…

And there she was: Annie.

At first, what Jerrica saw shocked her to the extent of disbelief. *My…God. What is she doing?*

Annie sat naked on the edge of her bed; another shock to Jerrica was how attractive the woman had remained for her years. Tan arms and legs, trim, large round breasts that hadn't sagged much at all, with nipples as dark and pert as Jerrica's own.

But it was what Annie was doing that shocked Jerrica most.

She's…burning herself…

Tears flowed down the old woman's face. "I'm sorry, I'm so sorry," she quietly wept, applying the flame of her cigarette lighter to the inside of her thigh. "Oh, Geraldine, I'm so sorry…"

Geraldine? Jerrica wondered.

But then she winced.

"Not enough, I know!" Annie whispered her next exclamation. "Nothing can ever give me forgiveness…"

Then—as Jerrica nearly shrieked behind the wall, Annie pinched her right nipple between thumb and index finger, distended it—

"Forgive me…"

—and then raised the lighter's flame to the dark-pink tip.

Jerrica's teeth clacked shut at the sight. The lighter's flame remained on the nipple-end for what seemed a full minute. Eventually the pain sent Annie reeling back on the bed.

What is she doing! Why! Why!

It was sick. It was demented. The woman was *cooking* her own nipple. Jerrica couldn't imagine the pain. And now, as she looked closer, she could see that the old woman had been doing this for some time: both nipples were nothing but scar tissue.

But the nipples weren't the only things she was burning…

"Not enough," Annie whispered with a tear-drenched face. "I could never punish myself enough for what I did…"

And next—

No, no, no!

—the old woman stood up, parted her legs—

NO!

—grit her teeth, bared her furred sex with her fingers, and squeezed her eyes closed as she held the flame of the lighter to her—

FOR GOD'S SAKE, NO!

—clitoris.

(II)

The heat inside the abbey socked him in the face like a flying brick. *Christ,* Alexander thought. So much for the crossbreeze through the windows he'd broken open. Less than an hour after showering and changing into clean blacks, he felt enslimed with sweat. But he strode on, down the vacant main hall, his footsteps echoing. One hand hung free. The other hung heavily as it gasped the sledgehammer. He passed the admin office, recently unsealed, and proceeded to the end.

The stairwell to the basement.

Whatever's behind that goddamn wall, I'm gonna find out what it is, he avowed.

He lit several alcohol lamps, waited for his eyes to adjust. The long brick wall downstairs extended on. The bricks looked ancient they were so faded, save for the newer segment he'd seen the other day. *Yeah,* he realized. *There's a room behind this, and someone bricked it up.*

But why? To seal more records as they'd done upstairs? Not likely. Even in the poor artificial light, this brickwork was obviously much older but much better set. The brick job on the admin office had been half-assed; Alexander had busted through that stuff in a few minutes. And, again, he couldn't help but notice the strike-marks already there. Inch-deep gouges, eye level or so. The implication couldn't be dispelled.

Someone, long ago, had already tried to break through these bricks.

I ain't no fuckin' muscleman, the priest told himself, *but I'm sure as shit gonna bust through this wall...*

He readied himself. As he raised the hammer, though, he inadvertently glanced aside, to the far end of the stuffy corridor, and what he saw was...

(III)

"God*damn* it's hot!"

Jerrica parked her red Miata in front of the abbey. Father Alexander's car sat parked to the side, like a waiting pet.

The abbey loomed before her.

So strange. Jerrica stared abstractedly, lighting a cigarette. The abbey's cedar-shingled roof and old log walls seemed so out of place against the brick front. The odd bell-tower, without a bell. The gun-slit windows.

All stuck back here in the boondocks...

She tried to shake off the infernal heat as she disembarked from the car. It was summer now, sure, and it was supposed to be hot. But *this* hot? *It must be close to a hundred degrees!* she guessed. She felt icky already, her scant clothing adhered to her. The vermillion halter had become a cotton sponge, soaking her perspiration, making the material cling to her breasts like second skin.

Something kept fighting to regain her attention, a fist pounding on a door. She knew what it was. Annie.

Jerrica shivered recounting the image. But what could she say? *Nothing,* she realized. What, admit that she'd been peeping at the old woman through a hole in the wall? Get Goop fired? No, she couldn't do that. *Geraldine,* she remembered. The name Annie had been speaking during her self-punishment. But why had she been punishing herself in the first place? And who was Geraldine? *She'd never mentioned that name before.*

One thing was obvious, though. Annie had a problem, a *big* problem. Self-effacement was a horrible thing, like people who cut themselves to relieve the stress of depression. It sickened her to see the fine, elderly woman put fire to her skin. But—

There's nothing I can do about it. I can't possibly admit that I saw it. And it's none of my business anyway..

Hard as it was, she'd have to leave it at that...

Dust swirled in a tiny dervish when she pulled open the abbey's great front doors. No sign of Father Alexander when she glanced down, just a few alcohol lamps alighted. *Maybe he's in the administration office,* she ventured. Her steps took her down the dusty hall. The building felt so empty, but when she turned into the office, whose bricked-up front the priest had knocked down just two days ago, she saw him sitting up on the desk, smoking. His black shirt, again, was off, his modest muscles lean and honed beneath his skin. But he looked up at her almost as if mystified.

"Hi," Jerrica greeted. "Told you I'd come."

He nodded dejectedly. "Hi."

"Somebody shoot your dog?" she tried to joke.

The priest shrugged. "I've been working my ass off downstairs, trying to sledgehammer my way through those newer bricks we saw two days ago. It's rough."

But was that it? Jerrica didn't think so.

"Well," he added, "and I found something."

"What?"

He shrugged again, stood up. His pectorals glazed in sweat. "Come on. I'll show you."

Dumbly, she followed him, down the main hall to the end-room with the stairs. Along the way, she couldn't help but notice his back:

tight skin over lined muscles, the shrapnel scars poking around one side like haphazard stitches. She forced herself to look away; when she did so, however, a sharp glint caught her eye. "Wait. What's that?"

There was a lancet window in the stairwell, broken out like most of the others. It faced the woods behind the abbey, and the declining ridge. Along the decline, though, through the trees, she deciphered the glint.

"That looks like water," she observed.

"It is. It's the lake," Alexander said with no interest at all. What was bothering him?

"Damn, I forgot to bring my camera again. I'd love to get a picture of it."

"Later," he said dully. "Right now let me show you this."

She followed him the rest of the way down, into sudden darkness. Smears of lights fluttered down the hall: alcohol lamps where the priest had been working. He picked one up, held it closer to the wall.

As she remembered, the segment of newer bricks faced her, as though this had once been a doorway and someone, for whatever reason, had sealed it up. "See these strike-marks in these newer bricks?" he said pointing to the inch-deep gouges.

"Yeah, but we saw those first time we came. Someone—"

"Right," he interrupted. "And someone tried to break through them, probably a long time ago. We've already established that."

Jerrica's lips pursed. What was the big revelation? But then the priest picked something up. "Take a look," he said. "I found this in the corner."

It was a pick ax.

"We didn't notice it the other day because it was literally cocooned in cobwebs. I'll bet this thing's been lying here for decades. And check this out." Alexander hefted the tool. One end of the head was a narrow adzeblade, the other a long, sharp spike. The priest fitted the spike-end into several of the gouges in the wall.

"Fits perfectly," Jerrica noted. But she still didn't see the mystery. "All right, that's the same tool that someone used to try and break down the wall. So what?"

"Look harder. You're not thinking."

Jerrica frowned. She still didn't get it.

"I'm six-foot even, a normal sized adult male," the priest said. "Watch." Then he mocked the act of taking a swing at the bricks with the pick ax. The point of the ax landed several feet higher than the original impact marks.

"If a normal-sized adult had tried to knock down this wall, the marks would be higher, up here, see? But they're two, maybe two and a half feet lower. Get it?"

Now Jerrica realized what he was saying.

Alexander lit a cigarette in the wobbling darkness. "So unless it was a midget down here all those years ago, trying to bust these bricks, it must've been—"

"A child," Jerrica slowly realized.

1 2 3 4 5 6 7 8 9 0
EIGHTEEN
ERIK
1999

EIGHTEEN

(I)

The Bighead sat under a mockernut tree, med-er-tate-in', thinkin' 'bout his psychical placement in the you-ner-verse, he were. Somethin' were...*weird.* Bighead, see, he hadn't et in two days, nor had he had hisself a nut since he corn-holed that ay-dult in the farmhouse, who was punkin' his kids. Usually, see, The Bighead scarfed brains'n guts'n what not as much as he coulds, an' any chance he had ta bust a nut—well, he'd be alls over that like like stink on toe-cheese.

He just weren't interested right now, no sir.

What were it? The Voice? The reck-er-lecktions of his fine ol' grandpap? His filler-soff-ical ass-sen-sure-un into the exer-sten-shull domain? Or were it a comber-nation'a those thingies?

Bighead didn't know! He didn't know doodly-squat! He were a deformed, woods-rompin', brain-eatin', pussy-bustin' retart!

Didn't matter, though, 'cos even deformed, woods-rompin', brain-eatin' pussy-bustin' retarts experienced moments'a surmisin' their state'a self-ack-sure-ull-ization. Like Abraham Masloe's hierarchy'a needs, Bighead were realizin' there were more important things ta life than eatin' an' havin' a come.

Yesterday, when he'd found the cemetery, he'd been even more confused'n fog-headed. It were almost like somethin' had *guided* him there, it were. But why? Why? A cemetery? A place where folks in the Outer World buried dead folks under the ground when they up'n died?

Just one more thing, it were. One more thing that didn't make a lick'a sense!

He'd slept there till mornin' then moved on.

Ands now he were restin' under that mockernut tree, starin' inta the woods, anna big toad hopped forward, but The Bighead didn't even kill it. Any other time, shore, he'd'a squished the guts outa that toad an' sucked 'em right up, but not today. Ands even with no pussy or cornhole ta bust, he'd'a jacked two, three nuts out his pecker by now.

But not today.

Yeah, somethin' were weird, an' gittin' weirder. His head felt all stuffed up with fog, it did, confusin' him like, causin' him ta wonder 'bout things he didn't even understant. Shee-it, how he wished Grandpap were still alive! Bighead missed the stinky, crackly, white-bearded old fuck, and that deformed li'l twig of a left arm flippin' 'round when Grandpap were riled about somethin'. *We'se all put on this here earth fer somethin', Bighead,* the old man had said many'a time. *And I knows now that I was put here fer one reason: ta raise you. Think about that, boy. That's what* I'se *was put here for. Ands one'a these days you'll'se realize what* you *was put here for...*

But that were the problem, see.

How woulds The Bighead ever come ta know 'zactly *what* his purpose were? Grandpap couldn't tell him nothin'—Grandpap were dead.

But then he remembert somethin' else the ol' man said 'fore he died.

You'll'se know, son, when the time is fit'n proper. It'll'se come to ya when ya least 'spect it to. Grandpap coughed, hackin' up a big black goober. *It'll come to ya like a voice whisperin' in yer head...*

The Bighead stood up then, his aura'a godawful stink risin' with him. He walked on, with deliberation, he did. Fer miles. His big feet crunchin' through the brambles, crackin' falled limbs'n branches. The heat beat down on him like hard rain, but after awhiles, he stopped.

His one big eye an' one li'l eye stared though the trees, never blinkin', and that's when he heards it again:

The Voice:

COME.

And that's when he sawwed it too:

The house.

(II)

chink-chink-chink!

"What can I do to help?"

"Huh?" Alexander glanced, if a bit testily, over his shoulder before the next swing of the pick ax. Jerrica looked bored, and drenched in sweat, standing there in the dim lamplight. "I guess I shouldn't have asked you to come out; you look like you're about to keel over from the heat."

"I don't mind," she replied, too politely.

The priest rested the pick-ax head on the floor, exhaled. Not much headway, but at least with the pick ax he was closer to breaking the brick than with the sledgehammer. "This is gonna take me a lot longer than I thought. I'll probably be down here for hours. Why don't you just go back to Annie's? There's no point in both of us burning up."

"No, I'd rather hang around and wait for you. Maybe I'll go for a walk around the grounds."

"Good idea, get out of his heat. I'll be up in a while."

He wiped sweat off his face with his handkerchief, which by now had become saturated. Jerrica moodily disappeared down the dark corridor and up the stairs.

What am I going to do with her? he wondered. *She's got more problems than Holy Trinity's got prayerbooks.* He'd just have to slowly work on her, use his priest-shrink savvy to get her into counseling and treatment.

Soon the heat down here would suck him dry. It was no joke; he wasn't a kid anymore, he'd have to be careful.

chink-chink-chink! he began again with the pick ax. Mortar dust billowed in gusts, bits of brick stung his face.

chink-chink-chink!

He paused to rest again. *Damn it, Spock! I'm a priest, not a jackhammer!* He was picking along the outline, where the newer brickwork had been set in to seal the entry; it stood to reason that this oblong perimeter would offer the weakest point.

I'll bust these bricks, goddamn it! I will!

He wiped more sweat, hefted the pick ax, and began again:

chink-chink-chink!

(III)

The heat was infernal. Even outside now, walking down behind the abbey, Jerrica's sweat poured, her wet arms grained by basement dust. How did the priest stand it downstairs where it was even hotter, wielding the pick ax against the wall?

A lovely, if overgrown, trail led down the ridge. Bright fungi, like scabs of day-glow orange, red, and yellow, adhered to tree roots. Heads of colorful flowers burst forth through teeming weeds. Halfway down the trail, though, she stopped suspiciously, glanced back up the incline. The abbey could no longer be seen. Why be suspicious then? Why be paranoid? Certainly the priest couldn't see her now, not unless he had x-ray vision that could bore through the hard earth of the ridge.

Her hand touched daintily her cutoff shorts. The stuffed front pocket. *No,* she thought, steeling herself. *I. Will. Not.* There was no end to it. *Just a little?* another part of her suggested. *Look what you had to go through to get it.* Her guts flinched, remembering.

Just a little wouldn't hurt, would it?

I. Will. Not.

She needed a diversion, something to get her mind off the cocaine she'd risked her life and swallowed a drug-dealer's semen to get. That's why she'd elected to go for a walk in the first place, but it wasn't working. What? What now?

A sharp glimmer blazed at her through the trees.

The lake!

Yes! Now there was a diversion! In this heat?

She scurried the rest of the way down the trail, as though the silver surface of the lake proffered some temporary salvation. In a moment, she was standing on the grassy shore, looking out. The sunlight raved; the water looked pristine, so pristine in fact, it looked unreal. In D.C., looking at the Potomac River, she'd been spoiled by reality. In this lake, there was no pollution, no floating garbage, no shining rainbow spectrums of oil film on the water. The lake was beautiful. Next thing Jerrica knew, she was taking off her clothes.

Why not? she considered. She wanted diversion—here it was. It was so hot out, and so humid, she could barely breathe. What better way to get her mind off her problems than a nice, cool skinny-dip?

And who would see? Way out here, in the sticks?

Her sweat-damp clothes fell to her feet.

And next, she was sighing to the sky, stepping into the cool water. The water washed away all her sweat, and also all her misgivings, her insecurities, as well as her addictions.

All gone in the cool flow.

I wonder how deep this lake is? she wondered. Silt squished between her toes; she walked further, relishing the unique *coolness.* The water level rose. Mid-thigh, then to her belly. Then to her bare bosom. Then to her chin. And then—

*What is...*that?

She stepped on—

(IV)

The afternoon burned on, then out. Thank God it was cooling down. Annie had been putting flowers on her mother's grave for thirty years, *It's high time I did too,* Charity thought, and picked some out in the wild garden. She picked a pretty bundle of Cardinals and Beebalms, a nice flux of reds and pinks. When Aunt Annie had invited her to go to the cemetery with her, Charity didn't even think of refusing.

"It's *so* hot," Annie remarked down the treed path. She wore a great white sun hat and a light pastel dress. Oddly, though, Charity couldn't help but notice how her aunt, every so often, brought her free hand to her bosom and rubbed, as though her nipples itched. Charity herself, for a change, wore shorts and a lime midriff blouse. And her aunt was right: it was *hot,* even this late in the day.

"I can't imagine were Goop is," Annie said. "I haven't seen him, not in the yard, not in the house. I suppose he's mad at me for sending him off to Roanoke. He must know I did it to keep him out of Jerrica's hair."

"I wouldn't worry about it, Aunt Annie. He's off doing something, but—"

Charity's thoughts bumbled to a halt. What was she going to say? The question had been rasping at her, like a rash. "I have to ask you something."

"What, hon?"

The sun baked Charity's cheeks. Weeds fell under her sandals. "I want to know about the second grave. The unmarked one I saw you put flowers on the other day."

Silence. The two of them marched on down the path. Charity waited, until her aunt finally answered, "It's just…something. Don't'cha worry 'bout it none,."

Not much of an answer at all.

And then Annie, obviously changing subjects, said, "I can't wait till Jerrica and Father come back. I *love* cooking for folks. Tonight I'm gonna serve Crawdad Purloo, Buttermilk Soda Biscuits, steamed Pokeweed shoots, and Pear Upside-Down Cake fer dessert. Father'll love it."

"He's a wonderful man, isn't he?"

"Oh, yes, a fine, fine man'a God."

But Charity could traipse through all this small-talk forever. She wanted to ask again, about the unmarked grave, but figured it would be best not to, not right now. *She'll tell me in her own time…*

Eventually they arrived at the cemetery, its high grasses bright in the sun. When the trail emptied into the graveyard's basin, Charity's foot tripped on a root, and she stumbled, dropping her flower bundle. "Oh, I've got to rearrange these!" she griped aloud. "Go on to the graves, Aunt Annie, and I'll be there in a minute."

Her aunt walked on, seeming almost to disappear in the glare of sun. Charity stooped to retrieve her flowers, paused to refit the arrangement, and—

Heard a scream.

She jerked up, froze, then called out: "Aunt Annie!"

The only response was another scream.

Charity ran, stepping on graveplots. She sprinted out to the far corner of the yard, and saw her aunt collapsed on the ground.

She also saw something else:

The graves of her mother, and also the odd second unmarked grave—

My God!

—dug up.

NINETEEN
ERIK
1999

NINETEEN

(I)

Where the hell is she? Alexander wondered. He'd given up on the wall downstairs; there was only so much of him. He'd have to come back tomorrow, and finish knocking the rest of the bricks out. *An old fuck priest like me—shit. I gotta take it one step at a time.*

But where was Jerrica?

Bad scene, he knew. That heavy ration of shit he'd lain on her yesterday? He was surprised she was still talking to him. *Get a life, Tom,* he told himself. *People have flaws, give 'em a break.*

Still shirtless, and revitalized now in the fresh air, he walked around the circumference of the abbey. Tall trees hovered, laden with heavy green branches; honeysuckle scents nearly intoxicated him, and birds squawked. But Jerrica wasn't to be found.

He lit a Lucky, wended down the path behind the building. "Jerrica!" he shouted. "Where are you?" But then he thought, *Oh, no,* when he arrived at the end of the trail, at the lake's shore. Her sandals, blouse, and shorts lay in a heap. *She's in the water—can't say that I blame her, as hot as it is.* But—

I oughta kick her ass, he thought next. He noticed the bag-corner sticking out of her shorts' pocket, inspected it. More cocaine. *Shit...*

He glanced out over the lake. One thing he didn't need to see—even though a solid part of his pre-priest self did—was Jerrica rising nude from the water. But she had to be somewhere. His eyes scanned and roved the entire perimeter of the lake. Floating sunlight glared, a pane of wobbling glare. Shore to shore, though, he checked, but there was no sign of her. Until—

"Jerrica!" he called out.

There she was. On the other side. He could see her coming out of the water—

"Jerrica!"

Tiny as she was, she didn't turn, or even acknowledge his call. Certainly she'd heard him…

"Jerrica!"

She disappeared into the trees at the other side of the lake.

(II)

Charity struggled frantically. *Heat stroke,* she feared. An old woman like that? Christ, she could die! She pulled her aunt across the fringe of the graveyard, to the cooler shade of the woods.

Too many images piled up at once. Her aunt lying unconscious before her. But also—

The graves…

She'd seen them, only at a glance. But a glance was enough. Someone had dug them up.

Animals? Perhaps. But why just *those two graves?* Sissy's

—her mother's—and the smaller unmarked plot nearby…

Both dug up, as effectively as if by a trencher.

First thing was first, though. Aunt Annie. Her face looked pale, so Charity raised her aunt's feet with a rotten log, remembering from a first-aid class in the orphanage, If the face is red, raise the head, if the face is pale, raise the tail. But with Aunt Annie's legs inclined now, her sunskirt fell down…

Oh, my…God!

Charity couldn't help but see the scars. Right there, burned into the insides of the old woman's thighs. Fat, reddened worms of scars, like burns, abundant. Charity's thoughts came to another guillotine halt, though, when she looked up. One breast had slipped out of the dresstop…

The nipple a crust of burn scars.

"The broth," Annie muttered, still unconscious.

"Aunt Annie! Wake up!"

The old woman's throat wobbled. "Geraldine...forgive me. It was the only way..."

The Annie fell silent again, still succumbed to her faint.

Let her lay still, out of the sun, Charity advised herself. *Let her breathe...*

She strayed, then, back to the lots, high, dry grass collapsing beneath her steps. The sun's heat crushed her, but eventually she made her way back to the grave plots.

Yes, it was no trick of vision. Both plots had been dug up, heaps of soil lying on either side. This was backwoods, rural—no grave liners, in other words, were implemented for burials. But the coffins had been pulled out, their lids unseated and flung open.

Charity, her lower lip trembling, dropped on one knee and saw—

(III)

Jerrica was gone, ignoring him as she walked away naked into the opposing woods, but that was no real surprise. Alexander, however, as he turned, felt his vision snagged, by—something.

He stood at the lake's edge, squinting, the sun-glare on the water bright as the white-phosphorous they'd pump into VC gun nests back in The Nam, with their M-79s. Get a load of white phosphorous—willy-pete, as they called it—into a covered MG nest, and the stuff would burn so fast, it would suck all the oxygen out. The rest was a turkey shoot.

The priest shielded his eyes, leaning forward. *What is...*

There was something...

But the sun was blinding him. The only way he'd be able to get a clearer view was by going to a higher vantage point...

The tower, he realized. *The abbey's bell tower...*

A quick jog took him back to the building. A tougher jog took him up the tower's winding stairwell, decades' old dust puffing beneath his footfalls. *Christ, quit smoking, you asshole,* he warned himself once he got up top. The bell tower's open air rushed his face; he leaned back, gasping, cursing his multi-pack-a-day habit.

And, as do most smokers, he lit another cigarette.

Then he turned, gazed out, and—

Hoooooly motherfucking shit..., the priest thought when he looked again at the lake.

(IV)

It was disgusting, hideous. How could somebody do such a thing in the first place? Charity felt flensed, the skin of her reason peeling back at the loss of what she conceived of as sanity.

Annie partially roused, enough to walk. "Come on! Come on!" Charity barked, her breasts swaying in her top. "We've got to get you back to the house!"

"The broth," her aunt replied insensibly. "Geraldine..."

Who was Geraldine? And what was the broth? Charity stripped it from her pondering for now, more concerned with getting her aunt back to the house alive. But concerned—*very* concerned—also by what she'd seen at the disinterred plots. SISSY read the large stone. Its pried open coffin revealed a mere skeleton. And there was a tiny skeleton, brown-boned, lying in the smaller coffin—just a small crate—of the other unearthed plot.

A child's grave, Charity knew now.

But it wasn't so much the infant's skeleton itself as it was the scrawl of inscription inside.

BIGHEAD, it read. BURN IN HELL.

(V)

"Who is Bighead?"

Annie's eyes drooped.

Charity slapped her aunt in the face. "Who is Bighead? It's supposed to be a myth, a fable. Why did someone write *Bighead* inside the lid of that coffin?"

"One of the men, probably, one of the Ketchum boys, I think," Aunt Annie mumbled as though her mouth were full of frogs. "The men got the coffin—it was just a little packing crate."

"And what about Sissy's grave!" Charity was hot, riled. She wanted answers. "You said she shot herself in the head with a shotgun when my father died in the coal mine..."

Annie's face went gelid, a frozen, old mask. Her eyes locked up...

"Tell me, damn it! The skull in that coffin was intact! What's going on!"

Dusk was seeping into the windows now, the heat abating however slightly. It had taken Charity forever to walk her aunt back to the boarding house.

"What are those scars on your legs, and your nipples?" she demanded next, unable to sort her questions.

"Geraldine. Forgive me."

"Who is *Geraldine!*"

This was no use. Aunt Annie was out of it. Her consciousness seemed to lapse, in and out, her eyes opening and closing.

"Aunt Annie!"

No, it was no use.

Charity's senses pinwheeled. So many questions, yet no answers. And why would someone dig up those graves?

And who?

Charity jolted at the sudden, tremendous sound. A great, wood-splintering *CRACK!*

The front door! she realized.

Someone had just kicked in the front door!

Annie's mouth hung open. Drool shined. Her fingers feebled upward.

"It's him," she whispered.

(VI)

They'd just come offa run, Tritt "Balls" Conner an' Dicky Caudill, that is, takin' their yoo-sher-al couple hunnert gallons'a Clyde Nale's high-octane moonshine up ta them crackers 'cross the state line. Smooth as tit-skin, the job went. As yoo-sher-al.

And, as yoo-sher-al, upon leavin', they'd plucked thereselfs one'a them li'l white-trash alkie cutie-pies who were hitchin' down the mountain road. She screamed like a weasel inna tredder, she did, once Balls jumped out the 'Mino an' got on her, but she didn't scream fer long, no sir. Just one crack upside the head with his homemade jack an' she were out fer the count. Alls it took, then, were a minute'er two ta tie her up in the tarp'n throw her cracker ass in back.

This pleased Dicky a might, it did, 'cos Balls'd ob-ver-iss-lee forgot all about the hot blonde an' the priest who'd whupped 'em the other night at the bar. Dicky didn't want nothin' ta do with killin' no priest, an' if that were still on Tritt Balls' mind, then why'd he even bother jackin' out this mountain gal? *Yeah, Balls done forgot all about it. Good.* That blonde an' the priest—doin' a job on them were just too risky. Shee-it, goin' ta that boardin' house? All them people around? Naw, that were bad news. They'd wind up fer shore gettin' caught an' chucked in the clink. Dicky thanked the Good Lord, he did, fer lettin' Balls ferget all 'bout that scene.

"*Keeee-rist*, Dicky," Balls commented from the shotgun seat. He were hittin' onna li'l flask'a shine, an' he were rubbin' the crotch'a his pants too. "My dick's so hard feels like it's gonna start bawlin'. Hurrys up an' find us a place, huh?"

"Relax, Balls," Dicky assured behind the wheel, sippin' a beer. "We'se almost home now. I'll'se find us a good place'a right quick."

"Keee-rist." Balls whooped. "I can'ts wait ta cornhole me that Kentucky trash in back. Dick been jumpin' all day, dyin' fer a nut. Hurrys up'n park!" Balls continued rubbin' his cock through his pants. "You don't find us a place soon, I'se'll have to jerk off right here in the 'Mino!"

Dicky rolled his eyes, he did. "Don't'cha be doin' that, Balls. Last tmme ya done it, ya got'cher jizz all overs the pole-stree."

"Then hurrys up!"

God, he were insister-ent tonight. Dicky veered the El Camino off the Route then, an' turnt uppa old loggin' road. Soon he were dousin' the headlights, an' parkin' their rod in one'a the side dells they'd used before. Balls were outa the 'Mino like his butt were on fire, openin' the tailgate, an' haulin' that mountain gal out the tarp. Dicky watched in the moonlight, sippin' his beer.

"High *heaven,* I'se horny!" Balls hauled her dirty shorts right off, an' had his cock out his pants faster'n corn-feed through a hog. Then he pushed her knees back inner face, hocked lickety-split inner crack, ands got ta cornholin' hard. "Stinky bitch, ooo-eee!" Balls remarked, thrustin' away. "I'se like that!" His arms propped hisself up over her whiles he were humpin'. But gettin' it so fast an' so hard up the butt roused the gal a right quick, it did, and all at once she come to an' were screamin' again. "Ooo-eee!" Balls repeated. "I'se just *love* ta hear 'em scream like that! Somethin' 'bout these Kentucky crackers, Dicky, ain't there? They got throats on 'em! Fiesty li'l bitches, they is! So's much better rapin' a Kentucky bitch than a 'Ginia bitch! Hows you like it, honey? Hows you like me fuckin' yer shit?"Balls' hard steady thrusts rode right along with her screams, an' right along too with his laughin', but then—

"Owwwwwwww!"

He jerked up in pain, put a hand ta his forearm. "The cracker *bit me,* Dicky! Bit a *chunk* right outa my *arm!*"

This were not good. Nor were it good when she started a'cussin''n kickin' at Balls. "Gits away from me, ya dirty shit!" she shrieked in a voice that sounded like the time Dicky's 'Mino throwed a rod on the Route. An' she were fightin' she were, kickin' an' cussin' an' shriekin' away.

Balls' big fist 'mediately clouted her in the jaw—SMACK!—ands she were out again. His anger were plain on his face. "These crackers never learn, doos they? Kickin' me, bitin' me, callin' me a *shit!*" He was haulin' her up then, draggin' her by the hair ta the front'a the 'Mino. "Dicky! Git the copin' saw!" he ordered.

Dicky's shoulders slumped. *Here we'se go again.* Dicky could scarsely even contermplate what manner'a industrious dispatch Balls had on his mind. But then, comin' 'round the front, he saw that Balls had the gal lyin' onner back, on the hood. "What'cha fixin' ta do, Balls?" he queried.

"Gonna hump me her neck's what I'se fixin'!" He snatched the coping saw from Dicky. "Hail! I'll'se teach this cracker cunt a thing'r two! I'se gonna fuck her *neck,* I'se say!"

Dicky raised a brow in puzzlement. "Fuck her *neck,* Balls? That what you said?" Dicky, a'corse, knowed full well that Tritt Balls Conner were capable'a great feats' a madge-er-nay-shun, 'specially when he got his dander up. But— *Fuck her neck?* Dicky wondered. *How's he fixin' ta do that?*

Then came the gritty, coarse sound'a Balls gittin' ta work with the saw. It were an ugly sound indeed, causin' Dicky ta grind his teeth. See, Balls took a might quick ta sawwin' that gal's head off just at the jawline, right above her aderms apple, an' his shitty dick were still hard'n stickin' out his pants as he were doin' it.

Didn't take long neither, not fer that coping saw ta do the job. The gal's head fell right to the dirt, whiles her body remaindered lyin' on her hood'a 'Mino, blood fairly *pourin'* out her neck. Then Balls stepped right up, poppin' his peter right inta the stump on her purdy shoulders. "See, Dicky, I'se gonna have me a come right down her hatch inta her breadbasket."

"Jeeeeesus," Dicky remarked. Even he was a tad appalled. "Yous shore are one sick pup, Balls."

"Dag straight, Dicky." Balls was holdin' the dead gal's hooters whiles he continnered steadily humpin'. "Feels good, it does, Dicky. Feels *real good* ta fuck this white-trash cracker neck. Kin even feel her tonsils!"

It were the strangest thing Dicky ever sawwed, a fella fuckin' a gal's *neck. Leave it ta Balls,* he thought.

"Ah, yeah, git it!" Balls reveled, quickenin' up his thrusts. "Git it, git it–*ahhhhhhh!*" Balls hips slowed, then stopped, his back arched as he were smilin' up ta the night sky. "Yes sir, that were one *dandy* nut I just had. Shot me a *big* wad'a the cocksnot in her, I did!"

Dicky just shook his head, cracked open another beer. "You shore showed her, Balls," he tried to approve.

"Dag right, an' I'll'se show her some more..."

Dicky's face, then, pinched up in more confusion. Balls, see, even though he'd just had his nut, he weren't quite finished. He pulled his peter out and leaned over, pickin' up the gal's severed head. Her face had turnt a kinda queer white color, her peepers closed and her mouth'n tongue hangin' out. Balls hocked on his bone, strokin' it a bit ta git back a woody.

"Balls? What'choo doin' now?"

What Balls done, see, is he stick his dick in the sawwed side'a the gal's head so's the end'a his peter were stickin' out he mouth! Ands then—

"Ahhhhhhhhh!" Balls moaned.

—he began voidin' his bladder.

"I'se havin' a pee, Dicky," he finally got ta responderin' ta his colleague's query. "Been havin' ta take me a whizz fer a spell now, so's I figgure I mights as well take like this. Ahhhhhhhh, yeah! What'ch think, Dicky? Think I'se the first fella in histree ta take a pee outa gal's mouth?"

"I-I suppose ya shorely are, Balls."

Yeah, Tritt Balls Conner shore were somethin' doin' such a thing. *Oh, well,* Dicky thought. *Least it gots his mind offa that blonde'n the priest.*

Balls' beer'n-moonshine urine were just a'gushin' out the gal's mouth, an' Balls were hard enough that he didn't even need ta hold it there. Instead' he were just standin' with his hands on his hips, peein' away out her yap and laughin' ta high heaven. Looked so weird, it did, not just the end'a his peter stickin' out 'tween the gal's lips, but her head—Looked like her head were growin' out'a Tritt Balls Conner's groin, it did! An' he weren't joshin' when he said he had ta pee bad. Musta stood there five full minutes pissin' out this gal's mouth, he musta. 'Ventually, though, he finished, then offered the head. "Feel like takin' a pee, Dicky?"

"Ah, gee, no thanks, Balls."

"Toos bad. I say that's the *best* pee I ever had!" Balls kicked the head inta the woods, then rolled the dead chick off the hood and made fer the 'Mino. "Let's roll!"

"Shore, Balls."

Dicky drove over the headless gal's corpse whens he backed up'n pulled out the dell. He could hear her bones poppin' under the 'Mino's big L50 tires. A minute later, he were back cruisin' down the Route, headin' home. "Gittin' late, ain't it, Balls? An' we'se shore had outselfs a big day, takin' that big run'a hooch 'cross the line. Good time ta git home'n git some sleep, huh?"

"*Bad* time, Dicky," Balls countered. "It ain't late—shee-it. We'se got *plenty'*a time fer some fun."

"Aw, come on, Balls. We done enough fer tonight—"

"Who you kiddin', Dicky?" Balls were chucklin'. "You thinks that 'cos I just had me a nut down that cracker whore's neck'n then peed out her mouth that I done fergot alls about that holy man and that blond city bitch stayin' up the boardin' house? Well, I ain't. Ands that's where we'se goin' now, Dicky."

"Aw, come on, Balls!"

Tritt Balls' face shined that bad-news-grin'a his in the moonlight. "Just shut up an' drive, Dicky. You drive this rod straight ta that fuckin' boardin' house..."

(V)

Charity's heart felt like a squirming bag fit to explode. She whisked Annie up the stairs just as footfalls akin to cinderblocks pounded through the foyer. *It's him,* Charity remembered her aunt's half-conscious words. *It's The Bighead.*

But how could that be? Even if The Bighead were more than a local legend—an inbred born into monstrosity, a monster-child—Charity had just seen its grave...

So what was this mammoth *thing* suddenly walking through the house?

"Up, up!" came Charity's blade-sharp whisper. "Come on, Aunt Annie, up the stairs and down the hall!"

They were halfway down the second-floor corridor, in fact, when Charity heard:

THUNK! THUNK! THUNK!

Something—huge—coming up the stairs.

She ducked into the first available room, dragging her lethargic aunt. She took a breath, clicked shut the door as quietly as she could. But she could still hear it:

THUNK! THUNK! THUNK!

The footsteps getting closer.

"Shhhhh!" Charity whispered, a finger to her lips. "Don't say a word, don't even make a noise..."

"It's him," her aunt groggily replied.

THUNK! THUNK! THUNK!

Now the footsteps were coming down the hall. *He knows we're in here,* Charity deduced. Now she could smell something absolutely awful, like pork fat rotting in the bottom of a garbage can. The thunderous footfalls continued down, then stopped.

Right outside the door.

A quick glance showed her that this must be Goop's room: overalls lain over a chair, work clothes piled on the floor, etc. But none of that mattered at all. Charity's eyes bugged at the doorknob.

The doorknob was *turning.*

She pulled her aunt into the closet, closed the door, then nearly fainted in the realization of what she had done. *I've trapped us both in here. There's no way out.*

Then she heard the bedroom door squeal open, and then—

THUNK! THUNK! THUNK!

The thing—whatever it was—was in the room now, looking for them.

Charity, with her arm around her aunt's bosom, stepped back in the closet's darkness. There was nowhere to go now, no escape—

What?

Behind her, now, she noticed—

What the hell...

She noticed that the back wall to the closet wasn't a wall at all but...an opening...

An open wall panel...

A passageway.

She pulled her aunt into the opening, closed the secret panel. She couldn't imagine why this would be here, and she didn't care. It was an escape! But now, in total darkness, she fumbled forward. There seemed to be a narrow corridor behind the wall. Where did it lead? "Come on, Aunt Annie! Come on!" her hot whispers ensued. "Move forward!"

They did so in absolute clumsiness, Charity biting her lower lip at the sounds they must be making. But only then did she notice—

Spires? White lines?

Yes, lines of white light, thread-thin, seemed to perforate the passageway's gloom. They were holes in the walls.

Again, the *why* did not occur to her. But she knew this: they were peepholes. And she could still hear the monstrous *thunking.*

The footfalls, she guessed, had circled Goop's bedroom, then made their exit. *THUNK! THUNK! THUNK!*

Then they wound around to the next room.

Charity put her eye to the bright hole.

The priest's room, it must be, she thought. A simple piece of luggage. Black slacks and shirts in the closet. A Bible and prayer book on the night stand. And—

Charity's heart skipped a beat.

The vantage point of what she could see was very limited: the sidewall of the priest's bedroom. But something, suddenly, was *moving* there—

A shadow.

A *huge* shadow.

It washed across the wall, the great, heavy footfalls resounding in accompaniment. It seemed to waver, a hulking silhouette, and Charity, even through the tiny peephole, could smell the earthy, rotten-meat stench.

Then the figure came into view.

Just its back…

It stood what must've been over seven feet tall. It was wearing overalls, vermiculated with rot, shoulder muscles so large and defined they looked like tumors beneath the dark-tan skin.

Then…it turned…

Charity fainted dead-away when she saw the thing's face…

(VI)

"What did you think? What did you think? You think it'd be pretty?"

Now it was Annie, slapping Charity awake.

My God. This is all my fault, Annie thought. *I shoulda knowed it'd all come back ta me someday.*

And come back it did, with a vengeance.

Far as she knew now, though, the thing'd left. Crouched back there behind in the wall, she'd seen it thunk its way out of the room, then out of the house.

The Bighead.

Yeah, I shoulda knowed, Annie realized.

She pulled Charity back into Goop's room. Goop—Christ—it had been Goop who'd done this, finding the walkways behind the walls, drillin' holes so's he could peep on guests. *So help me, I'll tan his hide next time I see him...*

"Charity? Charity?" Annie shook her niece fierce.

No response.

"Come on, sweetie! We gotta get outa here!"

Nothing.

One look was all it took, and was Annie surprised? No. No. She'd never seen it fer herself, 'cept fer that one time, but she could imagine what it looked like now.

A shudder traveled through her at the thought.

"What—was—that...*thing?*" Charity finally roused, murmuring up through a fallow face. Her eyes were shock-white.

"You know." Annie patted her niece's forehead with a handkerchief. "You know now. It was The Bighead. Come back after all these years."

1 2 3 4 5 6 7 8 9 0
TWENTY
ERIK
1999

TWENTY

(I)

"I just don't understand," Charity nearly wept. Exit was their priority now, escape. The only thing that would keep them alive was getting as far away from Luntville as quickly as possible. Once Charity had recovered from her faint of shock, Annie had gotten her out of the house and into the pickup truck. There was no time to look for Goop. There was no time to do anything but leave.

Annie spun wheels out of the front lot, peeling away. The right rear fender banged against a tree when she turned off onto the Route and accelerated.

Charity's consciousness seemed to sift back into some semblance of accordance, like the focusing ring on a lens. But again, instantly, too many images and questions delved into her at once. "Those scars," she said, a hand to her brow as she sat slumped in the pickup's bench seat. "Those awful scars on your nipples and thighs… What happened?"

Annie's determined face remained locked on the road as she drove. "Punishment, honey. Sometimes ya just cain't live with things unless ya hurt yerself. I been punishin' myself fer a long time now."

Punishment? "Why?"

When her aunt refrained from answering, Charity's mouth opened to ask the next of a flurry of questions, but the query stalled when she remembered…

When she remembered exactly what she'd seen in that peephole.

Hideous. Huge. And, yes, a *monster.*

A great shiny bald head, elongated like some strange, warped squash. Hands the size of packing hooks. But when the thing had turned, she was able to glimpse its face, and the recollection, now, nearly caused her to pass out again.

Its face...

Lop-sided, bundled ears. A squashed nose like two dried figs pressed together. One eye large as a tennis ball, the other tiny as a cherry tomato. But the mouth...

Charity shuddered again, her stomach captured by a sudden series of convulsions so intense she thought she might vomit out the truck window—

A huge stone jaw underpinned a mouth akin to a chasm, full of teeth like carpet needles.

"Where are we going?" she asked.

"Out of here. Anyplace that isn't here," Aunt Annie said.

"We...can't," Charity insisted, letting her senses surface further. "Jerrica and the priest. They're still at the abbey. We can't just *drive away* and forget about them. That thing... If it cut across the ridge—it could be at the abbey in less than a half hour. We have to go pick up Jerrica and Father Alexander."

Annie seemed stricken by this suggestion, though she didn't outright object. "We could die, hon, you know that, don't you?"

Charity's teeth ground. "We're *not* leaving them! We have to at least warn them!"

"All right." Annie's voice grated like rusted metal abrading. "We'll go by the abbey. But don't blame me if we never make it out of there."

"Fine." But Charity's mind swirled in more queries. "You have to explain something to me. That...*thing*—that thing I saw through the peephole. It was The Bighead, wasn't it?"

"Yes," Annie answered, heading down the dark road.

"But I saw the grave. Someone had dug it up. And someone had scratched on the coffin top, BIGHEAD, BURN IN HELL. If The Bighead was dead and buried as an infant, how on earth could we have just seen it?"

(II)

It was a question Annie should've expected. By now? After what poor Charity had seen?

The steering wheel felt like slick bone on her hand. "I'll tell you, Charity. Only 'cos you gotta right to know."

"What!"

And Annie's mind fogged away.

Back, back…

Back to that day thirty years ago…

(III)

The townsmen had taken care of the thing, nine months previous. But it hadn't mattered, not for Annie's sister. The men had shot it, killed it. Taken care of it, she thought.

But that still left Sissy, didn't it?

Annie was the town midwife, never could have a child'a her own on account of some problem in her belly. But her sister...

Her sister lay before her now, on the table, her legs spread wide. Her face flushed with the pain of labor, her vagina distending. Large, ripe breasts sweated out a sheen of milk.

Annie continued with her ministrations, her hands outspread below her sister's parted thighs. It's coming, it's coming, she thought.

But what would it be?

"My GOD!"

It wasn't coming out right. It was coming out...through the belly...

It was eating its way out of her sister's womb...

(IV)

"What ya have ta understand is that this all happened a year after you were born, Charity. What I told ya about yer mama committin' suicide with the shotgun—that was just a fib. She died during childbirth. My darlin' sister Sissy, yer wonderful mama," Annie stoically related. She drove the pickup steadfast, through town, toward the far ridge where the abbey was.

"Yeah, a year or so after yer mama had you," Annie continued. "Somethin' happened, that next winter… It was yer mama who gave birth to The Bighead. And when she was done havin' him, she was dead…"

(V)

It shredded its way out.

It ate its way out of Sissy's bloated stomach.

Gnawing, swallowing, teeth glinting…

"We knows what it really is!" one of the townsmen shouted. "It ain't natt-trull! It gotta be kilt!"

And it was then that the thing shouldered its way out of the front of her sister's abdomen…

(VI)

"It was yer mama…who gave birth to The Bighead," Annie admitted.

Charity glared forward. "But I just saw The Bighead's *grave!* It was dug up! It had obviously died as an infant!"

Something so large sunk down Annie's throat. For a moment she couldn't speak. What could she say? How could she admit such a thing?

She felt made of stone when she said, "It wasn't The Bighead that was in that grave you saw dug up at the cemetery. It was…some other child."

"Some other child! What are you talking about!"

"It was a stillborn," Annie went on. "It was Geraldine's. Larkins'…"

(VII)

Annie'd already heard about it. Poor Geraldine Larkins had wanted a baby so bad...

But it was stillborn.

Too much inbreedin', they'd said. Too much moonshine-drinkin' and bad-livin'. Geraldine'd given birth to a beautiful baby boy—

But it was a dead *baby boy.*

They'd buried it shallow in the woods, and Annie'd seen 'em on one'a her walks. She'd seen 'em buryin' that poor li'l dead baby.

So what she done was—

(VIII)

"I dug it up," Annie confessed. "I dug Geraldine Larkins' poor dead baby boy up…and I switched it.."

"You…*switched* it?

"I switched it. 'Cos I just didn't have the heart to do what them townsmen said. They knew where The Bighead come from, and they wanted to kill it. But I told 'em *I would.*"

Charity's face bloomed in question, like a night flower. "You told them you would do *what?*"

"I told 'em *I* would kill it. I told 'em I would kill Sissy's baby, The Bighead. But what I done instead was switch The Bighead with Geraldine's stillborn critter. And what I did then was I…I crushed that dead baby's head with a skillet, and all'a them townsmen seen it. And they believed it…"

"You switched babies," Charity realized. "You switched a live baby for a dead one—"

"That's right!" Annie shrieked, her guilt finally pounding down on her. "I made 'em think it was The Bighead whose head I crushed, but it was really a baby who were already dead!"

"Calm down, calm down," Charity attempted to console. But—

"Annie," Charity said. "I need to know what happened to the *live* baby. I need to know what happened to the *real* Bighead—"

(IX)

She'd had to hurry. Before the men came back, she had to stow the living child that had eaten its way out of her sister's womb. But it wasn't the child's fault, was it? How could it be? How could any newborn child, forbearance notwithstanding, be held responsible for its deeds?

It's not the baby's fault...

She meant to leave the living baby in the woods and pick it up later. But that's when the old rattling truck had come down the road. It stopped. And it's driver had seen her. The driver had seen what she was doing: dumping a baby in the woods...

A crackly old cracker, an old creeker. Inbred. Only had one full arm—the other wasn't nothin' but a little stem'a flesh with fingers wrigglin' out.

"It's prover-dence," the man said. "Here I is, drivin' away from the world without the one thing I'se wanted most, an' heres you are, dumpin' the same thing."

"I—I wasn't dumping it!" a young Annie tried to explain. "I was going to come back for it later!"

"Ands do what, hon?"

"Well, I—I—" Annie blinked at the inbred man. "I don't rightly know, but I shore's hail wasn't gonna let it sit ta die!"

"Give me that baby, hon," the inbred man said. "I'll'se raise it like God planned. Ain't had nothin' in my life work right so's far. But I'se kin swear to ya, I'll'se raise that baby so fine..."

Annie stood stock still, staring at the man's eyes. What would she do with the baby? Honestly, how could she possibly raise such a hideous child without any of the townsmen knowing?

So maybe it was God. Maybe this was God's way'a makin' a miracle.

"Take good care'a this child, I beg ya," Annie said. "It's ugly, but it ain't its fault. So...please. Take good care'a it, and raise it proper."

The man in the truck was crying at the gift. "I'se will! I'se will! I'se promise ya!"

Annie, then, not thirty years old herself, handed the monstrous infant over to the stranger.

And watched him drive away with it.

(X)

"I gave it to a man—"

"A *man! What* man!"

"Some ole inbred fella, said he was dyin' ta raise a kid hisself. There was nothin' else I could do."

Charity's throat made audible clicks. "You substituted a dead baby for The Bighead, and you gave the *real* Bighead to some *man* driving down the road?"

Annie's knuckles turned white on the steering wheel. "When the men come back an' looked in, they saw Geraldine's stillborn baby on the kitchen table, with its head crushed. They thought it were The Bighead. I told 'em I drugged the baby's broth and done it, smacked its head with the skillet, smashed it flat, and they believed it was The Bighead. And then I went out'n buried it. But the real Bighead was already bein' droved off by that inbred fella. And that's when I stopped thinkin' 'bout it…an' started punishin' myself fer it. Burnin' myself. Hatin' myself for the fact that maybe I done the wrong thing." Annie, then, her cheeks wet, looked over at her niece. "I couldn't think'a nothin' else ta do."

(XI)

But what then?

There was more, wasn't there?

God Almighty have mercy on me fer what I done! Annie thought to herself.

There was still more to tell—

About the abbey.

(XII)

"That's why I ain't too keen 'bout going back ta the abbey, to pick up the priest and yer friend," Annie continued.

"I don't get it," Charity said.

"'Cos that's shorely where The Bighead's headed right now."

"The abbey? Why would he specifically be heading for the abbey?"

She couldn't tell it all, could she? *No!* But she could at least tell some.

"It weren't like Father Alexander said," she explained. "The abbey never closed because the nuns were sent ta Africa. The abbey closed 'cos the nuns died."

"Died? How?"

"They was all murdered. By The Bighead. It was over twenty years ago, just a few years after the Church reopened the abbey ta take care'a dying priests. Before that, it was closed fer years'n years, since the fifties. It was, I don't know, early seventies maybe that the nuns moved in ta make the hospice. Couple years after that, though, The Bighead came back. Couldn't'a been more'n ten years old when he done so. Ands he kilt all them poor nuns and the dyin' priests ta boot. The young boy must'a wandered off from where the inbred ol' man raised him, and that's what The Bighead done when he returned to the abbey."

"But I don't understand, Aunt Annie." Charity's expression was flushed with incongruenty. "*Returned* to the abbey? What do you mean? What was he returning to?"

(XIII)

Charity stared through the windshield; the heat lightning throbbed, so far away it scarcely looked real. But Charity's life didn't seem real either. Her mother hadn't committed suicide at all; she'd died giving birth to that *thing,* a year after Charity herself had been born. But what had happened in that year? Something horrible. Something that had to do with the abbey.

What was it? she tensely wondered, numb now in all that had been related to her. *What happened?*

"Yer mama, dear—" Annie was choking on stifled sobs. "You

weren't probably but three months old at the time. Yer mama an' I, we'd go fer long walks through the woods, and one night when we were doin' so we found that we'd moseyed on up to the abbey. We didn't go in, a'corse, 'cos at the time the building was sealed up, had been for years. It wasn't fer ten years after that the nuns moved in and got ta runnin' their hospice fer priests dyin'a cancer and such. But—"

Charity grabbed her aunt's arm. "What—*happened?*"

Annie's eyes gazed forward, as though the lids were stitched open on the memory. "There was a man..." Her voice waved. "A man come outa the woods behind the abbey..."

(XIV)

It happened so fast. One moment she and Sissy were strolling along by the lake, and the next moment...Sissy was screaming.

It was fate that the man had chosen Sissy rather than Annie; at first all Annie could do was stand pinned to a tree and watch in horror, paralyzed. The shadow loomed, engulfed her sister like a cloak, tore her clothes off her body in one motion.

The hulking figure's body pinned Sissy to the ground, raped her right there on the lake's mucky shore. Each thrust of the rapist's hips sent a scream exploding from Sissy's throat, a sound like a cat on fire. In the dim light of the winter dusk, all Annie could see of her sister were her arms and legs jutting out from under the man's humping body. But soon Sissy's screams ground down; she lost consciousness. Yet the sick wet sounds of rape continued as the assailant's hips pumped onward, in and out, in and out, for what seemed forever.

A guttering grunt rose up. The rapist withdrew a softening penis that looked large as a tube of cookie dough. Sissy lay still beneath him—Annie thought she was dead until her head lolled once and her eyes fluttered. But it was then that Annie's paresis broke.

The figure stood up, was beginning to turn—

Annie screamed and ran off into the woods.

(XV)

"Yer mama was raped, hon," Annie went on. "Right there in the mud. Raped worse than you'd ever think rape could be. I shoulda done somethin', I shoulda tried to fight him but—but I was just too scared. So I ran, I ran all the way back to town an' stormed into the old Sallee Place. It was the grace'a God that a lot of the townsmen was there, havin' a card game, Wayne'n Brian, Johnnie Pelan, the Ketchum boys, and that nice bearded fella, Davy Barnett, I think his name was. I told 'em what'd happened and they was outa there like gangbusters, grabbin' their rifles'n shotguns an' tearin' down to the abbey fast as they could..."

(XVI)

Annie followed them, barely able to keep up, her lungs aching. It was close to full dark when they got to the lake, and sure enough, he was still there, having another go at Sissy, humping her nearly to death in the mud. The men's exclamations were not surprising. "Tarnations!" "What'n holy hail?" "Punch'm up fulla holes, boys! Ain't no sick som-bitch gonna do this ta one'a our womanfolk!" The figure rose halfway when the shooting started, ear-splitting claps in the night. One volley after another until the bullets picked it up and dropped it dead. But Sissy—

(XVII)

"They killed him, they did, but yer mama—" Annie's choked out sobs broke into full crying. "Yer poor mama was so tore up from bein' raped. Tore up *real* bad, you know, down inner private place. We got her back the house and Doc Nutman come over, said it were a miracle she was still alive. But she never really recovered. Partial comatose was what the doc said. Fer the next nine months Sissy just lay in bed, never sayin' a word. Just starin' at the wallpaper'n gittin' bigger ever day."

There. Finally. After all these years, Annie had finally had out with the truth of that horrid December night, and the even more horrid scene that took place nine months later. Wasn't fair that Charity should learn what really happened to her mama like this, but sometimes that's just how things worked out.

Annie drove the truck up off the Route, up the entry road. She thought that telling the truth would make her feel better, but it didn't.

It didn't, she knew, because there was still a little more truth to tell. The fine details she could *never* tell.

And before she could even think of it anymore, the abbey's odd brick front shone grainily in the headlights.

1 2 3 44 55 66 77 88 99 00
0 9 8 7 6 5 4 3 2 1
TWENTY
ONE
ERIK
1999

TWENTY-ONE

(I)

chink! chink! chink!

A familiar sound to Alexander, and with each report, he took another step down, shirtless, his black cleric slacks still damp with—

chink! chink! chink!

—lake water.

Zombified, that's how he felt, walking back up the trail and through the lamp-lit abbey the same way he'd walked back to the firebase, coming in from beaucoup shit with Charlie Comm in the field. The man with the thousand-yard stare…

No, nothing would surprise him now; hence it came as no surprise at all, once he descended to the basement, to discover the identity of the pick-ax wielder.

Jerrica.

"Jerrica?" he asked.

She remained stark-naked but maniacal now—

chink! chink! chink!

—as she heaved the pick ax time and time again into the gouged wall, bits of mortar and brick exploding out of each strike, spraying her cheeks, stinging her face, all to no effect.

The lit elements in the alcohol lamps looked like phosphoric halos. The strange light licked the priest's face, his bare chest.

"Jerrica!"

chink! chink! chink!

She didn't hear him, her task all consuming. She'd made quite a bit of headway, though: she'd perforated the wall completely, and was now digging out around the rim of the hole.

"JERRICA!" his throat belted out the name.

chink—

She stopped mid-swipe, turned. Mad blue eyes shined wide-open.

Her nudity raved in the alcohol light.

"Where have you been?" came her coy query.

"I think you know," he answered, stern-voiced. "I saw you, Jerrica. I saw you coming out of the lake."

Her grin shone brightly as the lamplight, brightly as the profuse sweat on her nude body. "What's wrong with a quick skinny-dip, huh, Father? I was…*hot.*" One hand idled up her flat belly, daintily touched a breast.

"This place is haunted," she said.

Haunted, he thought. Maybe it was. Maybe it *really* was.

"And I've seen the ghosts, Father. The…nuns."

Alexander's eyes fixed. *Evil,* he deduced. *Yes, there's something evil here, I can feel it. And whatever it is—it's got her…*

"Abbess Joyclyn? And the Sister Superior? I've seen them, I've talked to them. They really got the hots for you, Father."

Alexander gulped as if swallowing sand.

"But then," she finished, her grin knife-sharp, "so do I."

Christ. *Get back to the point!* "I saw you coming out of the lake. So I went to the bell tower; I looked out. And I saw it, Jerrica. And you know what I did then?"

"You probably jerked off," came the naked blonde's reply. "Thinking about me. Thinking about how bad you wanna fuck me."

"Not quite." He plucked up a pack of cigarettes from the floor, lit up. "I went for a little swim myself."

"Oh, really?"

"Yeah, I saw it, and you saw it too."

Her wicked grin flattened. "Did you touch it?"

What a question. *Odd.* But no, no, he actually hadn't, had he? He swum up to it, fighting bizarre currents, saw it, then was pushed away. "No," he said.

"You should have, like I did. There's something still alive in there, some…power. I don't know. But it made me see a lot of things. It gave some of its power to me—" She gestured the pick ax leaning against the wall, then the wall itself. "—for this."

"What is it?" his throat ground out the words. But he guessed he already knew: things he wasn't comfortable with, things he was supposed to even believe in but didn't want to acknowlege. '*Though shalt worship no other God but me,*' his faith slapped him. Who knew, though, what he believed in now, if anything.

"I believe in God," he affirmed. "Nothing else."

"But you believe in devils too, you told me in the bar. If you believe in God, you must believe in His counterparts."

"Yes!" he shouted. "Yes, devils, yes! Demons! Lucifer! The Morning Star and the Fucking Lord of the Air and the Lord of Lies—YES!" The priest's teeth ground. "But…they're not…supposed…to be…here!"

"Open your mind." Now both her hands caressed her breasts. The big dark nipples distended. "Don't be so draconian. Not all devils are from hell."

The sentence ran echoes in his head as she neared. Her bare footfalls encroached, her grin cut so lewd now, her sex aglint. He just stood there and watched her and did nothing.

She grabbed him by the throat, hauled him to the dust-caked concrete floor. He tried to resist but found her strength paranormal, emboldened by whatever manifestation of evil she had encountered in the lake. Her body, at once, was all over him, her vigorous sweat sliding along with her fine skin across his face, his tensed chest. *Sixty-nine,* some obscure thought mocked, *the beast with two backs.* He read it in *National Lampoon* or some shit. She opened his lake-damp pants, exonerated his cock, while the light fur of her sex sat on his nose. He pushed up, for all he was worth, but nothing happened. He might as well have been pushing against the back deck of an M60 tank.

"Priest," she moaned. She grabbed his balls, squeezed them so hard he flinched. Her thighs spread over his face. "Lick my ass," she commanded. "Lick my ass like a good little priest or so help me I'll squash these two little peanuts to pulp."

The grip tightened; his body flexed at the threatening pain. And out his tongue came, ever so dutifully, and began to lick the flesh-crevice of her buttocks.

He smelled the scent of creeky lakewater, stiffened by bristly ass-sweat. He tasted salt, grime, pasty skin.

"Suck it." His balls in her hand could've been starfruit; just a little more pressure and they would burst to seedy mush. "Stick your tongue in. *All* the way in."

Her anus opened, a willing aperture. Now it was more than salt he tasted, it was the remnants of her last defecation, the reeking, digested oddments of Aunt Annie's funnel cakes and molasses and squirrel pasties and soda-baked biscuits. He was tasting her shit.

"Now suck it, suck it out. Suck my shit out of my ass, suck it into your mouth and swallow it or I'll pop your balls and gouge out your eyes and haul your guts out. Where's your goddamn God now, you pious fuck? Suck my shit or I'll strangle you with your own intestines."

Alexander believed her, his balls about to crack in her clench. And you know what he did then? The man of faith? The man without fear in the grace of God?

He did exactly as she instructed. He sucked her shit.

He sucked it right out of the blossomed pucker. He thought of a soft ice-cream machine with its tap open, only this ice cream was warm, vaguely sweet and salty at the same time. And he swallowed it, just like a good little priest.

"Yeah," she breathed. "You little kinko. First you drink nuns' piss, and now you're eating a coke addict's shit. Taste good, Father? Better than rectory food?"

Now her own face now crooked down into the cleft of his ass. The vertebra of her neck seemed to come unattached, so she could wrench her mouth down further at an angle that would only be described as impossible. But further impossibilities ensued: her tongue.

Her tongue burrowed into his anus, then seemed to elongate like hot, pink taffy. First it slithered up, a supernatural snake trailing up his large intestine, deep, deep, up into the heat of his waste. Eventually he could feel it squirming in his stomach, whereupon it retracted, reverted to a globulous pad that cupped his prostate, sucking, sucking, until her mouth had successfully morphed into his rectum, to suck the intricate gland like a cock. Her hand released his testicles, rose to the shaft…

All it took was three or four strokes and out it came: twenty years of celibate semen jettisoning feet into the air. It looked, in fact, like white yarn shooting out, landing on his heaving stomach, in her wet blonde hair, on the floor. And next… Next, she was licking it all up.

"That's a good, good priest. So much cum!" she rejoiced. "Priest cum is so much thicker, it's like cottage cheese, and it tastes so much better!"

Alexander turned his head and soundlessly puked, urping up the ration of her shit that he'd seen fit to swallow.

"And now the real fun begins," she promised, her voice hot as a car hood in August, her blood-filled tits swaying. "Your priestly cock hasn't been in real pussy for how long? Since college? Since all those Viet Nam whores? Must be twenty, twenty-five years." She expectorated on his half deflated cock, slicked it up with spit; it hardened instantly. Then she was straddling him, and her hand clamped his throat like a steel cusp, squeezed so hard he thought he'd surely pass out. "You're gonna fuck me now, Father."

He couldn't speak, of course, but nor could he even think, as though her supernatural hand were also squeezing off his thoughts. Then her free hand grabbed his penis, prepared to insert it—

BAM!

—when the door at the end of the hall broke down.

(II)

"Where—where are they?"

"God, this is one creepy place," Charity observed. They'd parked the truck, entered the abbey. She knew they were here because both Jerrica's Miata and the priest's old Mercedes were parked out front. But the main hall was so dark. Only a pair of silent alcohol lamps lit the corridor. Several rooms passed them; when they looked in they saw only file cabinets, stripped beds, night stands covered literally by inches of dust. "They ain't here, Charity," Annie proclaimed. "We best git out."

"No. We're not leaving till we find them. Dead or alive, we're not leaving..."

"They must be outside then. Come on."

Charity followed her aunt back out the way they came.

(III)

wing!

That was what it sounded like: a hard, solid whack with a bell-like ring behind it—

Jerrica fell off.

Two figures loomed in the lit shadows. Chuckles cracked. Black silhouette hands rubbed together in feisty eagerness.

"Told ya we'd find 'em, Dicky!" And then—

wing!

Alexander went numb. He knew now what they'd hit Jerrica in the head with: a tire iron, the same thing they just hit *him* in the head with.

The two kids from the bar, he struggled to think. But that was about it. He was fading in and out.

"I'm gonna cornhole me this city blonde so hard she'll be pukin' my spunk!" one voice reveled.

"Aw, come on, Balls. This ain't no good. We'se gonna git caught and then they'll'se throw us in the joint fer life!"

"Hail, yer such a pussy, Dicky! We ain't come all this way just ta leave." A dark face floated above the priest: the long hair, the tractor hat, the goatee and the leering grin. It looked like Lucifer. "Hey, holy man, ya wanna know how we found ya?"

Alexander couldn't answer. He was beginning to suspect that the blow to the head might be fatal, that this was the Golden Hour right now. *Fractured cranial vault, subdural hematoma... I could be dead in minutes.* But would God let that happen? *Christ, after all I've been through in my life, I'm gonna die at the hands of two redneck dopes?*

It didn't seem fair.

Help me God, I beg of Thee. Hear my prayer.

"Cut his cock off, Dicky! Make him eat it!" Balls threw the fat kid a buck knife. "Then cut his throat slow. Meantimes, I'se gonna have me a party with this blond city bitch here."

The priest's eyes moved; a gruelling sideglance showed him the scene. The fat kid was reluctantly opening the knife while his colleague, jeans down to his knees, was vigorously sodomizing Jerrica. And he could discern this too: Jerrica was dead.

The tire iron had lain open the side of her head. Pieces of brains were falling out of the hole…

"You are in a world of shit, man," a familiar voice addressed him. A man's voice, but the priest knew it wasn't either of the rednecks. Alexander squinted upward, ordered his eyes to focus beyond the ramrod pain in his head, and he saw who had spoken the words.

It was his lord, Jesus Christ. The King of Kings.

(IV)

COME. COME. COME.

The words were like a creak in her head, a hinge keening. But Charity had heard it before, hadn't she?

"Did you…hear that?" she asked.

Aunt Annie frowned at her. "Hear what? I don't hear nothin', hon. Come on, we gotta find 'em, so's we kin git outa here."

They descended the ridge and now stood at the shoreline of the lake. The moon turned the lake into a great mirror; from all around them came the throbbing cascade of crickets.

COME.

No, Annie wasn't hearing it. *Just me, only me,* Charity realized. *Why?* Something was calling her but what? It even began to occur to her that she was being beckoned specifically to this place…

But why should she think that?

More heat lightning flashed, then:

COME.

The voice seemed to be issuing from behind them, from the abbey itself atop the ridge. But there was something about the lake, though, some arcane curiosity itching at her…

They'd walked half the circumference of the lake yet couldn't find hide nor hair of Jerrica or the priest. "What's this?" Charity asked, pointing. All wall of stones melded with crude mortar seemed piled up between against the still, shiny water.

"A dam-plug," Annie answered with little interest. "The lake been dammed up since before anyone can remember. Some say it were the Conoye Indians who done it a thousand years ago. No one knows who built it, and no one knows 'zactly what it is, just that it's cursed is what they say. So don't git near that plug. Old as it is it could break."

"Then the lake would empty?"

"That's right, hon. The whole thing'd empty right down the rest'a the ridge. It's no matter, we got other things ta worry about." Annie glanced far down the other side of the lake. "I don't seen 'em no where, Charity. I don't know where they could be, an' I hate ta ditch 'em but we really gotta git outa here."

Charity supposed her aunt was right. "Maybe they're in the abbey."

"Hon, we just done checked the abbey—"

"I mean maybe there's a basement or something."

"All right," Annie agreed. "We'll go check one more time but then we leave."

Charity nodded, turned and followed her aunt back along the moon-lit edge of the lake when—

They both jumped at the sudden white light and tumult. No heat lightning this time—it was *real* lightning, as though the sky were splitting open and shedding pieces. Charity grabbed her aunt's arm at the start. The electric spear from the sky bolted down, exploding at the base of a tall tree on the other side of the lake. The tree shivered, then crackled, then fell—

"Storm's comin', hon!" Annie shouted over the crash. "We best run back to the abbey fer cover!"

But—

WAIT.

"Charity! Come on! What'choo standin' there fer? We could get hit by lightnin'!"

Charity didn't care. The lake was rippling, a sudden wind whipped her hair, billowed her sundress. She been told to wait, hadn't she? *I...will...wait...*

But what was she waiting for?

Annie shrieked, pressed her hands over her ears. The thunderclap exploded—the sky lit up again. Ludicrously, the hair on both of their heads suddenly stood on end in a flux of static electricity, tiny hairs on their arms and necks too, when this second mammoth bolt of lightning tore out of the sky and touched down—

Charity, bathed in static, gazed out.

The lightning struck the dam-plug just thirty or so yards away. Petrified stones flew off in explosive white light—

Then came a great gushing—

A great, mad siphoning sound—

And then, very quickly, the lake began to drain.

(V)

"Don't be such a baby!" Jesus leaned over tauntingly. "What kind of a man are you?"

What a cosmic ripoff...

By now Alexander had come to grips with the very high order of probability that he was dying from a massive cranial trauma. He'd been a good priest, he'd tried very hard. Sure, he'd made some mistakes, he'd cast his share of sins, but—holy shit!—he'd done his job to the best of his ability. And now, as reward, he had this:

Jesus Christ, in a black Joy Division t-shirt, giving him enough shit to sink the Lusitania.

It's just a dream, he realized, though that was hardly a consolation. The brain of a dying man dreaming its last dream.

And he'd dreamed of Jesus before, hadn't he?

I'm dying, yeah. This is just a dream.

"You're not dying, dickhead!" Jesus told him. "Christ, Tom, you're not a quitter, you never have been. But you're quitting on me now? Blow me, brother! I won't have it!"

Alexander winced, still paralyzed. Yes, Jesus stood in the basement hall but, of course, neither of the two rednecks saw Him.

"You think you're checking out?" Jesus continued to taunt. "What, because some cracker hit you in the head with a tire iron? Gimme a break! Your skull's too thick for that, Tom. Listen to Me, will ya? You're NOT dying!"

Not...dying, the priest thought.

Jesus calmed for a moment, reaching down for the pack of cigarettes on the floor. "Hey, man, can I bum a Lucky?"

Alexander shrugged. "Yes," he said. After all, when Jesus Christ asked for a smoke, there was only one thing to say. *Yes.* But the priest said more than that. "Tell me, Lord, I beg your guidance. What should I do?"

"I gotta tell you *everything?*" Jesus seemed pissed again. "The first thing you gotta do is find a pair of balls. I mean, I know you got 'em 'cos I can see 'em. Look at you, man, you're lying there on the floor with your *dick out!* Halford would laugh his wizened ass off. Oh, poor Tommy got hit in the head by big bad rednecks. Get up! This fucking fat walrus-looking punk is about to CUT YOUR DICK OFF and you're not doing shit about it. And that other asshole? He's raping that blond bimbo WHILE SHE'S DEAD! Do something!"

"Help me," Alexander begged.

Jesus held His hands out, the Lucky in his mouth. "I can't. You know how it is. I'm just here for occasional walking around. Believe me, brother, I'd like nothing more than to help you kick the living shit out of these two waste products, but it ain't allowed. You gotta do it yourself."

Alexander blinked. "So... I'm...*not* dying?"

"No, peabrain! I just got done telling you that! I'm *Jesus,* for Christ's sake. *Jesus doesn't lie!*"

The fat kid leaned forward, oblivious to the presence of the Son of Man. He'd already opened the knife, was lowering it—

"He's gonna cut your pecker off!" Jesus rooted. "Don't just lie there! Do something! Show him you got a brass set!"

When the fat kid leaned down closer, Alexander's arm shot up, grabbed the back of the kid's neck, and pulled. Before the knife could be put to any use, Alexander was biting Dicky Caudill's nose, and he bit down *hard.* The fat kid was screaming, as the priest's teeth sunk deep. Next thing Alexander knew he was spitting out the kid's nose.

"Balls! Balls!" Dicky was shrieking like a terrified woman. A fat hand uselessly caressed his face, as if to stem the copious flow of blood. "The priest done bit off my *nose!*"

Tritt Conner's frenetic sodomy ceased; he glanced over his shoulder, then up to the crying, screaming Dicky. He stood up, put his dick back in his pants, and then—

Aw, fuck, Alexander thought.

—from somewhere produced a revolver that could only be described as *huge.* "Yer such a pussy, Dicky. Looks like I'm gonna have ta take care'a the holy man myself."

"Get ready," Jesus warned. "This is serious bizz."

Alexander leaned up, but only barely. His head rang with pain, and his limbs scarcely responded to his will.

Jesus, savoring the Lucky Strike filterless, went on, "Remember that disarm technique they taught you in the Marines."

"I wasn't in the Marines, I was an Army Ranger."

Jesus rolled his eyes. "Marines, Army, who the fuck cares? Just remember what they taught you, 'cos, believe, man, you're gonna need it in about two seconds."

The disarm technique that the King of Kings was referring to was actually brutally simple and very effective.

Tritt Balls Conner approached, cocking what looked to be an antique Webley-Fosbery .455 automatic revolver, something the Brits had invented to take on drug-crazed natives in the Boer War, or some fucked up war like that.

"I'm'se gonna blow yer holy brain alls over this here floor, priest. Then I'm'se gonna finish havin' my nut up blondie's dead ass. What'choo gotta say 'bout that?"

"Blow me, that's what I have to say," and as Alexander said it, his hands shot upward, the right grabbing the revolver's rear receiver, the left pushing out against the barrel. Less than a second was all it took, just like the drill sergeants at Benning had promised. A quick twist, then, and Alexander had wrenched the weapon out of Tritt Balls' hand, without a single shot being discharged.

"Good fuckin' job!" Jesus celebrated. "Hardcore, man! *Outstanding*! Shit, even *I* couldn't have pulled that off!"

Thanks, Alexander thought. He rose to his feet as Balls and Dicky stepped back. Dicky, crying like an open tap, turned and fled down the hall. But Balls' remained, knees shaking but still talking the bad mouth. "Go ahead, priest! You ain't got the balls!"

"Don't say that," Alexander warned.

The grin bloomed within the satanic goatee. "Look at you, man! You cain't do it! You're a *priest!* Priests ain't allowed ta kill folks."

"Don't test me, asshole." He had the heavy gun sighted now, one eye closed, the other focused down the clunky sights. But the kid was right, wasn't he? *I'm a priest. I'm not allowed to kill people, am I? Not even sick, twisted murderers like this?*

"Lord," Alexander asked of his King. "I beg your permission. Can I kill this guy?"

Jesus looked disconsolate, flicking the Lucky butt. "I'm sorry, man. It's all about free will in the light of the Father. I can't advise you."

Shit!

"Fuck you!" the bearded redneck spat. Then he turned laughing, and walked toward the stairs.

Alexander clenched his teeth, watching the kid's back disappear in the sights. *Shit!* he thought again. The kid was gone. Alexander uncocked the hammer and let it reset.

Then he turned, looked down at Jerrica with sudden tears in his eyes. She was dead, yes—stone dead. Alexander looked to Jesus for some answer. "Why, Lord? This is fucked up!"

"I know, man, but that's the way the cards fall sometimes."

"She didn't deserved to die!"

Jesus jerked back at the exclamation. "Hey, bro, nobody does, but that's just the way it is."

"Is she…saved?" the priest dared ask next.

Jesus Christ gave a nonchalant shrug. "Don't know off hand. Can't tell you. But I *can* tell you this. You better get your shit square real fast, because you got a world of hurt comin' right down your alley. Bigtime trouble, Tom. And all you got to fight it is that big piece of shit British revolver and the two nuts God gave ya."

Alexander stared, uncomprehending.

"Get out of here," Jesus said. "Get ready for some shit."

The priest took His word for it—what else could he do? He turned to for the stairs, but then Christ briefly interrupted. "Hey, Tom, hold up a sec."

"Yeah?" Alexander said.

Jesus had picked up the pack of Luckys off the floor. "You mind if I bum one more?"

"How many left in the pack?" Alexander dared to question Jesus Christ the Righteous.

"Two, man."

"Take one, give me the other."

"Right on." Jesus stuck one cigarette in His own mouth, stuck the other in Alexander's. Then He lit the lighter, fired up the priest's.

Alexander stared at the incredulity. *Jesus Christ just lit my cigarette for me...*

Jesus smiled then, and winked. "Good luck, Tom," He said.

(VI)

Annie was on her knees now in the shoreline mud, bellowing sobs. The lake drained and drained in rippling moonlight. It only took a few minutes before something *huge* broke the surface.

Charity's eyes felt peeled to the scene, the diminishing static letting her hair fall back down.

Something sat in the lake like a giant white oval, a hundred yards long.

A spaceship...

"I want answers, Aunt Annie," she demanded. "You haven't told me everything, but you know. I *know* you know! What is going on here! What is that *thing!*"

Annie wept on, hitching. "Yer right—God fergive me—yer right! I *haven't* told ya ever-thing—I lied!"

"Lied about what? Tell me."

Snot fell in strings from the old woman's nose; her tears shellacked her cheeks. "That man that raped yer mama, right here where I'm kneelin' right now! It weren't no man!"

Much more calmly now, Charity deduced, "It came from that thing in the lake, you mean?"

"Yes!"

"What else?" Charity asked, certain there was more. "What else haven't you told me?"

More weeping, more snot. "I'm so sorry, Charity!"

"WHAT!"

"I'se lied too 'bout somethin' else! I told ya you were born a year before the rape—but that was a lie! Yer mama got raped by that thing that come out the lake, an' nine months later gave birth ta the Bighead! But after the Bighead et its way out yer mama's belly, I'se heard somethin'. I'se heard *another* baby cryin' from inside, so's I looked inta yer mama's poor dead remains and I pulled *you* out!"

Charity's features didn't change at the revelation. *Twins.* Somehow, now, she already knew most of it.

"The Bighead's father and my father are the same," she said.

"Yes!" Annie squealed. "The Bighead was a monster, but you were perfect, a perfect little baby girl! But ya both come from the same womb, from the same loins'a the devilish thing that come out the lake thirty years ago and raped Sissy whiles I watched!"

More pieces fit, flying together. Charity's mind felt plugged in to someone else's know, and she had a good idea who that someone else was...

Even the full brunt of the truth came as no real surprise now:

My father was an alien...

But...

More.

And The Bighead...is my brother...

(VII)

Alexander raced up the steps, following the footfalls of the pieces of human shit who'd killed Jerrica. But Christ had warned him of something else…

He couldn't imagine what that might be, yet his old Army LRRP instincts switched on. He was ready, in other words—or at least as ready as he could possibly be, considering.

The main hall upstairs had dimmed, the alcohol lamps running low on fuel. But at the far end, toward the entry, he could see Dicky and Balls scrambling to make their exit, Dicky still screaming at the rude insult Alexander's teeth had paid to his nose. But then—

The entire abbey shuddered—

A titan *CRACK!* filled the hallway—

And so did throat-flaying screams.

The priest stopped in his tracks. Stared. His mouth open in bewilderment and horror—

Jesus was right. There's a world of hurt coming right down my alley…

Because at that same moment, Alexander got a good, hard look at what had knocked down the door.

(VIII)

Dicky threw up when he saw it. A monster, yes sir, with a head big as a propane tank, an' fucked up eyes, an' a mouth like a hole fulla nails. He fell pukin' ta the floor when the thing roared, brought both forearms down so hard on his back that alls his ribs along the back'a his spine broke lickety split. Then he felt his pants bein' tored off, and then—

Dicky, a'corse, was too out of it now ta really know what were bein' done, but what were bein' done shorely weren't good. The monster poked two big fingers right up his butt, then two more, then the thumb. Dicky were screamin' holy hail, he were, knowin' he was dyin' but not carin'. He just screamed an' screamed as the monster grabbed a hold'a the end'a his spine inside his butt, then pulled, and that were about it fer Dicky Caudill.

The monster, cackling like a rooster, pulled Dicky's spine clear out his asshole. And, a'corse, what were connected ta the other end'a his spine was his head, an' the monster pulled *that* out Dicky's asshole too.

One *hail* of a job…

Then, the monster, The Bighead, turnt ta face Balls.

And you know what The Bighead done just then?

Shee-it.

He looked at Balls, thens he looked at the priest at the other end'a the hall.

And then—

The Bighead sniffed the air.

And walked back out the door.

(IX)

"God saved you," Alexander said, sighting the pistol on Tritt Balls Conners' face. "Why I don't know, 'cos you are about the most worthless piece of shit to ever walk the earth. Give praise and thanks to God, for saving your sociopathic mother-fuckin', trailer park ass."

"Fuck you, priest," Balls Conner had the audacity to spit back. "It weren't yer fuckin' God that done saved me. It were that thing. It were The Bighead."

The Bighead, Alexander thought. *Yes. Of course. What else could it be?* He'd heard the stories, he'd seen the giant disc in the lake, and now—he'd seen the monster itself.

The Bighead.

"Get thee behind me…"

"Shee-it, holy man. Ya smelt me out that fast? But I'se ain't Satan, I'se just one'a his friends, made human on earth to walk amongst ya…" But as Tritt Balls Conner continued to speak, his voice descended to suboctaves that vibrated in Alexander's diaphragm and guts. And he lost the redneck, white-trash drawl. "I am a myrmidon of the Morning Star. I am his vassal, his holy servant. There are many like me, Father. Too many for you to fight. Give up and admit your defeat. Throw your weapon down and join us..."

"I'd rather burn in hell forever," Alexander said. But he was convinced. *Demons. Devils.* There were all kinds. They were everywhere. And sometimes...they were human.

I'll just kill myself, get this over with, he reckoned. *I don't need this shit. I've been through too much as it is.*

"Join us, priest, and live with us forever," Balls bid in his new, majestic locution. The voice was timeless and pristine, articulate and strangely *honest.*

"That thing which just left–it matters not where it came from. It is as much my brethren as you are. Open thine eyes and behold the light of truth. Join us. Come with us, man of faith."

"Eat my fuckin' shit-stained shorts, you ass-motherfucking-*hole,*" Alexander spake after a bit of consideration. He cocked the Webley's hammer, then dropped it—*BAM!*—and watched the imposture's kneecap explode in blood. Balls fell, laughing.

"I believe in God," Alexander said. "Sometimes I don't really know why, but that's tough. If I'm wrong, if I'm gonna burn in hell or rot in my grave with my entire life wasted...then I don't really give a flying fuck. All I know is this, scumbag. I'm blowing your shit away."

Balls' familiar drawl returned posthaste, the real demon in him making an expeditious exit. "Fuck you! Ands fuck God'n Jesus'n the Holy Fuckin' Ghost'n the Virgin Mary ta boot! I'll'se cornhole all of 'em, I will, I'll fuck 'em all so's hard my dick'll be stickin' out their mouths! I'll'se *fist-fuck* yer God, an' pop yer Virgin Mary's cherry, an' I'll'se make yer damn Jesus lick the shit off my stick. So's help me, holy man, I'll'se pop a wad'a my peckersnot right in yer God's face, then I'll'se piss up His ass!"

"You ain't doing nothing except dying, shithead," Alexander guaranteed. He'd taken all the blaspheming he cared to, thank you. His finger gently retracted; the hammer fell again.

BAM!

The big bullet took the top off Tritt Balls Conners' head clean off, and spectacularly redeposited the contents of his cranium onto the abbey's slate foyer.

"Fuck it," Alexander said.

(X)

"The men," Annie explained, "the townsmen. They shot the thing dead right back there on the shoreline, and then they'se throwed it into a room in the abbey's basement, and bricked the room up!"

Charity paused to glance back in the direction of the lake, remembering the muck-splotched thing she'd seen in it.

Then:

COME, she heard.

"It come from that thing in the lake. It was your father! And the Bighead's too!"

COME.

Annie sobbed on as they made their way back up the wooded trail. But her sobs cessated only when the great hook hand snapped out of the wavering trees.

The voice in Charity's head now struck like a bell—

COME. COME. COME.

Annie's screams alternated with more explanation, as the hulk of shadow ripped off her clothes and hauled her down into pockets of darkness. "Why you think no man ever wanted ya? Why you think all them men left ya in yer bed? It's 'cos you ain't like normal folk, Charity!"

Charity stood and did nothing as the great shadow continued to maul her beloved aunt. And all those memories, then, replayed in her mind. All the men putting their penises into her, then getting up to leave without even finishing. Leaving her so unfulfilled she thought she would die.

Because I'm not like them, she realized now. *I'm not even fully human..*

Annie gagged in the weedy darkness. "There ain't but one man on this earth who'll love ya, Charity, an' it ain't no man!"

Then she gagged some more, screamed amid a wet tearing sound.

"Yer brother!"

Charity stared.

"Kill yerself, darlin'! It's the only way! Kill yerself 'fore he kin git ya!"

But Charity just watched, what little she could see. The moonlight revealed only snatches: the old scarred breasts, the white abdomen, scarred thighs being pushed apart as the inhuman buttocks pumped on.

"Kill yerself 'fore he kin git ya, 'cos—'cos—"

A crackling of bones finished the exclamation. The shadow grunted and came. A further crunching sound showed Aunt Annie's head being palmed open, large pieces of skull falling like broken nutshells, brains being calmly stuffed into the black-gash mouth.

Then The Bighead stood up.

It grinned, the same primeval face she'd seen in the peephole. Its foot-long-and-then-some cock remained hard, throbbing upward, a line of semen like white string depending from a puckered piss-slit. The gargantuan penis pointed at Charity as if in accusation.

The Bighead's great hook hands reached out.

Charity collapsed.

(XI)

He knew it was coming. Jesus had told him. *Why bust my ass looking for it?* Alexander reasoned. *I'll just wait. I'll let it come to* me. And what was there to be afraid of? It was only a birth-defected alien hybrid. God was on Alexander's side, or: *At least He better be, otherwise I'm in a hopper of shit.*

So the priest sat and waited, and he knew exactly where to wait. Why hadn't it occurred to him before? The basement—the wanly lit warren in which he now stood—was the focal point of everything, wasn't it? Tonight, and twenty-some years ago when the nuns had been raped and slaughtered, when dying priests had been eviscerated and sodomized where they lay, and when the ten-year-old version of what now stalked the shadows had fitfully tried to break down the cryptic brickwork. Two decades ago it had tried and failed. Tonight, though, it would return—older now, and stronger—to finish the job.

Yeah, let Bighead do the work. 'Cos I gotta see what's behind that goddamn wall...

Alexander hid at the far end of the corridor; it reminded him of waiting in the bush behind an Stoner machine gun and a defensive perimeter of integrated Claymores. Waiting and waiting, scratching your crotch-rot, digging at bug-bites the size of bullet holes, and waiting some more. You *knew* Charlie was coming, you just didn't know when.

The alcohol lamps guttered, painting the walls with an appropriate eeriness. He hefted the clunky gun in his hand, flipped open the antiquated receiver. *Four bullets left. If you can't do the job with four, you got no business trying.* He flicked his butt, felt a pang of regret realizing he had no more.

An odd, even impossible wind blew through the corridor; the lamp flames nearly blew out. At once, Alexander felt prickly in a static caress, and cool in spite of the heat.

Then, as he knew, the footsteps approached, thudding down the stairs to the basement.

(XII)

It weren't a dream at all, no sir! No, The Bighead remembert! The dream'a the castle'n the angels'n the crusty, dyin' ol' men. An' Bighead ruckin' 'em all up…

It weren't no dream. It were *real.*

Back a long times ago when he were just a tike…

He remembert it all now.

Ands he remembert somethin' else:

He remembert walkin' down these self-same stairs…

Follerin' the Voice…

(XIII)

Get ready, Alexander thought. Old themes from the Army haunted him. *Cover, concealment, suppression, teamwork...* But all that wouldn't do dick for him now—he was alone...

The thing—The Bighead—stepped into the hall. It was grosser than he'd remembered from his glimpse upstairs. It was naked now, veneered in sweat. Its cock was more than obvious.

Easily over a foot long, half-hard, slicked with blood that was going crusty as dried tempera paint.

And the stench...

Alexander almost heaved-ho. The smell of the thing overpowered him: a meld of offense—something akin to ass sweat, month-old underarm b.o., old shit and stale piss and halitosis and dick-stink and God knew what else, all distilled down by the heat of the earth to launch into the priest's face like a chain-mailed fist.

Wait, wait, he thought. *Don't do anything...*

Its warped shadow crossed the hall, stopped, looked at the wall. Then it picked up the pick ax it had no doubt picked up twenty years ago, raised it, and—

Dropped it.

Instead, it stuck its hand into the hole that Jerrica had generated, pulled, gusted a single breath, and—

The wall toppled like Leggo blocks.

Then the thing entered the new-formed entry.

Alexander already had the Webley revolver cocked, ready to go. He thought a moment about what Jesus said, about his need to "grow" a "pair of balls." Alexander grew them, then walked into the rough-hewn aperture..

The Bighead stood before a clump of...something, its arms out-stretched, its hideous face gazing high. Then Alexander took a look at the clump...

Shit...

It was a raddled, desiccated corpse, or so he thought. A whey-faced *thing*. Dry as wicker—a body composed of something semblant of corn husks—all coagulated against the wall in a crisp meld. A shroud of cobwebs veiled its form like a caul.

It was dead...but...somehow, still vaguely alive.

Maybe its body was dead, but its mind had remained alive all these years, to call its progeny back.

But— *Why?* the priest wondered. *For what purpose?*

It was talking to him—talking to The Bighead.

It was feeding thoughts into its son's malformed head.

But what thoughts?

"Hey! Bighead!" Alexander shouted.

The thing twirled at the shout. Alexander got another good, hard look at its face, and that was all it took. He fired—

BAM!

—right into the face.

The big bullet plowed into the wedgelike forehead. The head jerked back—

Then the thing smiled, raised its thumb and index finger and plucked the puny bullet out of its forehead. The big raw-clam eye winked.

"My ass is grass," Alexander figured.

youareofnoconsequencesowewillnotwasteourenergy...

The priest, expecting to die, watched speechless, looking at the face of the thing that had occupied this room for two decades. The face seemed frozen in a yawn of anhydrous rot, and it looked back at him with hole-punch eyes.

And blinked.

(XIV)

wecouldkillyouwithourmerestbreathwecouldruptureyourorgansjustbylookingatyouwecouldinhaleyourbrainlikeascentofbuttercupsbutwewillnot. wedonothavetime.

wemustgo.

(XV)

The priest sensed the strangest thing: it wasn't the monster talking into his head, it was the dry-rot corpse, the dead body but the live brain...

The Bighead threw the corpse over its shoulder and left.

(XVI)

Alexander followed, grabbing one of the alcohol lamps. One bullet had mushroomed on the thing's forehead; he only had three left—he had to make them count. The thing didn't seem to care, though. It must know that Alexander was following it with a weapon, but *it didn't care.*

Not good, the priest thought. It had been sired by an alien life form–maybe it *couldn't* be killed.

But he had to give it his best.

Think, priest. Remember, he heard.

All the men he'd killed in the field—*dozens.* All the whores he'd fucked.

No! I am forgiven!

Are you?

Yes!

The thing walked on with its vermiculated father slung over its back like a sack of horse-feed. It was walking down the ridge-trail.

It was walking toward the lake...

On the shoreline, the priest saw, Charity lay still.

She looked fine, untouched, unmolested. When The Bighead walked to the edge of the water, Alexander knelt at Charity, swaying the lamp forward. *No, no, she's all right.* Christ, he'd seen the size of The Bighead's cock—like the business-end of a softball bat. If The Bighead had raped her, she'd be ground to pulp now, bleeding like a tap. But—

There was nothing.

Charity, in other words, was all right. There was only The

Bighead to contend with.

In shimmering moonlight, the thing walked on. But only then did the priest see that the lake had…drained.

The vast white disk lay settled there, askew, mottled with algae and silt, festooned with aquatic vegetation.

The Bighead was walking towards it, through the reduced muck of the lakefloor.

It was taking its father back.

Alexander ran after it.

"Hey, melon-head! Ya fuckin' ugly motherfuckin' nibblenuts freak. Take me on! You can't leave before you kick my ass, can you!"

The Bighead came to a momentary halt, then continued.

"Deformed cracker demon bastard! You chicken? You got no balls? What, you're only man enough to fuck with *nuns?* Well, grow ourself a pair and fuck with *me!*"

Another falter, another pause. Then it continued.

"Yeah, you're great when it comes to raping women and butt-fucking old men! But—look at you!—I'm giving you a fight and you're *walking away!* You got no guts. I've seen kindergarten kids with more balls than you, you pissant walking alien shit-heap!" Then Alexander took a wild shot with the Webley—*BAM!*—and hit Bighead's husk-dry progenitor in the back. Dust sprayed out.

The Bighead stopped. He dropped his father in the lake slime and turned—

The bulb-face glared. Needle teeth shimmering like tinsel. The great hook hands upraised, and the penis dangled like a flap of raw porterhouse.

"You are one panty-waist, creamcake, homo, dick-lickin' wuss! I've seen scarier baby toys!"

The Bighead sloshed closer.

"Hope ya don't like it and want to do something about it, you ball-less little nun-raper! Come on over here and kick my ass…*if* you can, twinkie! Yeah, big bad alien crossbreed tough guy. Don't make me laugh!"

Alexander knew he only had two bullets left now. He drew a bead down the Webley's barrel. He remembered how that first shot had mushroomed on the thing's thick head… *Gotta get to the brain,* he realized, and there was only one way to do that.

Through the eye.

"That's right, you tip-toein'-through-the-tulips fairy motherfucker! Hey, Tinker Bell! Come and take your whuppin' like a man!"

Steady, steady. The priest's eye opened wide behind the sights.

"I'll bet your dad wears a tutu back on Planet X, huh? I'll bet he's got one waitin' for you too!"

Alexander drew in a breath, then let half of it out, just like the D.I.s in Army had taught him. Then—

He dropped hammer.

BAM!

And again.

BAM!

The Webley's twin slugs socked right into The Bighead's big eye, punched through the back of his head. Clumps of greenish-white brains flew like little parakeets, then slapped hard into the drained muck of the lake.

The Bighead stared at him with a fury in its other tiny eye. He roared a quick objection, quaked, then—

Thank you, God.

—then fell backward and collapsed.

SLAP!

Dead.

It was only then that Alexander realized he'd shit and pissed his black cleric slacks simultaneously.

Epilogue

"You sure you're all right?" Alexander asked.

"I'm fine," Charity replied. "Tired, shocked—"

"Understandable."

"—but I'm not hurt. Not a scratch."

Dawn was just breaking, Luntville twenty miles behind them now. Charity's dark-brunette hair sifted intricately in the breeze from the Mercedes' open windows.

"It killed everything that moved," Alexander reflected, one hand on the wheel, the other lighting a Lucky Strike, "and it raped every woman that crossed its path. But it didn't so much as even *touch* you. I wonder why."

Because it knew that I was its sister, Charity answered in thought. *It couldn't hurt its sister, its own blood.*

But, of course, she couldn't tell the priest that. She could never tell anyone. All she said in reply, instead, was, "Who knows? I guess God was with me."

"I hear that. He was with both of us."

"But what do we say? What do we tell people, about what happened back there?"

"We don't tell anybody anything," Alexander sternly suggested. "I'll make an anonymous call to the Virginia National Guard and the state cops. Eventually they'll find the thing in the lake, and the bodies of The Bighead and his father. Let the authorities worry about it."

"Yes, I suppose that's the best thing to do," Charity agreed, resting back in the leather seat. The Appalachian Mountains passed serenely to their left, dawn-tinged, wide-open fields and pastures to their right. She closed her eyes, let the wind run like fast water over her face.

Then the car…began to weave.

Charity looked up, confused. "Father?" But the priest, cigarette dangling, seemed to be clenching the steering wheel, his face beet-red and crimped in pain.

"Father Alexander! What's wr—"

The Mercedes swerved back and forth, rubber screeching. The priest's right hand pawed haplessly at his left shoulder, and the left side of his chest.

And all Charity had time to do after that was scream.

What the—, Alexander thought. *What…happened?*

"You wrecked the fucking car, that's what happened," came the reply. But it wasn't Charity who'd said it.

No, it was Jesus.

Bewildered, the priest cast a questioning glance. Yes, it was Jesus again, this time dressed in beige Dockers and yet another black t-shirt, this one emblazoned with face of The Three Stooges. He was sipping from a bottle of Yoo Hoo. And He chuckled, "Yeah, man, Halford's gonna be pissed. Look what you did to his Merc! Man, it's a good thing you're a priest, 'cos you'd never make it as a driving instructor."

Alexander looked. The Mercedes had indeed crashed, its clean, white front end crushed, wrapped around a tree. Steam gently eddied from the bashed grill. Pale green antifreeze spurtled onto the shoulder.

"Charity!" he shouted, and rushed to the wreckage where he could see her lying still in the passenger seat.

"Forget it," Jesus said.

Alexander turned, outraged. "No! Don't tell me she's dead! She *can't* be dead!"

"Relax, Mario Andretti. She's not dead. She's not even seriously injured. Just a little conk on the head. She'll come to in a few minutes."

"Well, Christ—er, pardon me, Lord—I should at least get her out of the car—"

"Forget it," Jesus repeated. The Son of God finished his Yoo Hoo and pitched the bottle into the woods. "She was wearing her seatbelt, you weren't. *Comprende?*"

"Huh?"

"Still don't savvy. That's how it usually works." Jesus frustratedly pushed his long hair back. "You had a heart attack. You wrecked the car. You died."

Alexander's expression went agape. "I—"

"You're dead, man. You bought the farm. But, shit, what did you expect? All that booze, all those cigarettes for all those years. Still don't believe Me? Take a peek."

In slow dread, the priest gazed back into the car, this time looking past Charity. And there, in the driver's seat, he saw… himself.

Neck broken. A little blood on his forehead. But— *Jesus isn't jiving. That's my body in there. I'm dead.*

Yes. Here he was, Father Thomas Alexander, standing in the middle of Route 23 just as the blushing sun rose, and he was looking at his own dead body.

Jesus was taking the pack of cigarettes off Alexander's body. "Too bad about her, though, huh?" He said.

Alexander flinched. "What do You mean? You just got done telling me she's not hurt."

"Oh, she's not *hurt,* but she's sure as shit *pregnant.*"

"That's impossible!" the priest countered Jesus. "That thing last night couldn't *possibly* have raped her. It would've torn her up; its genitals were *huge.*"

"The Bighead," Jesus explained, lighting up a Lucky, "was Charity's brother. You didn't know that, did you?"

"Her…*brother?*"

"That's right, chief, and, yeah, he had a giant dick, just like his alien daddy. But you know what *she* had?

Alexander couldn't contemplate an answer.

"A big pussy," Jesus said.

Somehow, hearing Jesus Christ make such colloquial references to sexual anatomy rubbed him the wrong way. But— *What's He talking about?*

"Come here," his Lord beckoned with a finger. He opened the passenger door, parted Charity's legs, and pulled up her skirt. She was pantiless beneath. Jesus pointed. "See? You ever seen a pussy that big in your life?"

Alexander stared from the street. Christ was right; Charity vaginal inlet was immense...

"She was the only woman on earth who could take all of The Bighead's cock. Stands to reason. Being brother and sister, they both have the same alien reproductive genes."

Alexander continued to stare.

"So," Jesus rubbed his hands together. "Chalk up another one for us."

"What do You..." The priest's words shimmied. "What do You mean?"

But by then he thought he already knew.

Jesus grinned, cigarette in mouth. "Took you awhile to figure it out, huh? I'm surprised."

Alexander's voice raddled. "You motherfucker," he said to Jesus Christ the Righteous. "You lying piece of shit..."

"Hey, look, it's just my job. I do my job, you do yours. Thing is, I do mine better." And with that, the masquerade began to corrode, the great pointed horns already beginning to surface from the imposture's forehead. "Come on, man. Jesus doesn't walk around the earth. He lost that gig two thousand years ago. But me? Shit, I can do anything I fucking want. Blame Eve."

The Morning Star, came the thought like a bad hinge gringing in his head. *Lucifer*— The priest began, "Get thee behind me—"

The horned figure frowned. "Aw, give it a rest, man. Homey don't play that tune. Ya fucked up, Tom."

"I do not deserve to go to hell!" Alexander bellowed.

"There you go, right there. The first thing you think of is yourself. You blew it. Not enough brownie points. Shit, man. Lust, greed, avarice, profanity, indulgence—God don't want ya, Tom, and I can't say that I blame him. But that's fine. Another tenant for *my* boarding house."

"FUCK YOU!"

The Devil smiled. "Time for you to go, Tom. And they're all waiting to see you: all those slopes you killed in The Nam, the old lady, Dicky, Tritt Balls Conner, not to mention Jerrica, your squeeze. Give 'em all my regards."

The road jolted, then split wide open. Flames wafted from the rent as Alexander teetered on the edge.

"But I arranged a very special escort for you, buddy," Satan added. "They'll be giving you the twenty-five-cent tour personally."

Screaming, Alexander was dragged down into the pit, feverish hands pulling at his ankles.

"Oh, and Tom?" the Devil finished, grinning down. "Thanks for the cigarettes."

Down, down. The split hardtop of Route 23 resealed like a wound healing. The priest squirmed, his blood already boiling as his slacks, shirt, and collar were expeditiously torn off by the nimble hot hands.

The nuns rejoiced, cackling over their claim.

Charity regained consciousness several moments later.

The priest was dead.

She unfastened her seatbelt and got out, looked up at the blooming, pink sky, breathed deep.

She felt so confused, but it was only now that she realized what she must do…

It was providence. She could never return to the world; she wasn't meant to. Like a snake shedding skin, it was time to slough off her old life, and walk happily into the face of her new one.

She was pregnant now, and happy. And she knew what she must do. In all actuality, there'd never been a choice.

COME, COME, her father's Voice had told her so many times. But now it was saying something else…

GO. GO.

And go she would. She would be a sprite in the woods. She

would be the joyous wildwoman, dressed in skins and living on berries and roots. She would give birth to her twins and raise them in the wild…

To start a new race.

Yes! Providence!

GO.

Charity dropped her sundress in the middle of the road. The morning light painted her flesh in a new beauty. Her heart *sang.* And even now, she could feel the precious korms of seed and eggs stirring in her womb.

GO, MY LOVELY DAUGHTER.

Charity walked off the road, stepped gently over some brambles, and disappeared into the woods.

Jack Ketchum
OFF SEASON:
THE UNEXPURGATED EDITION

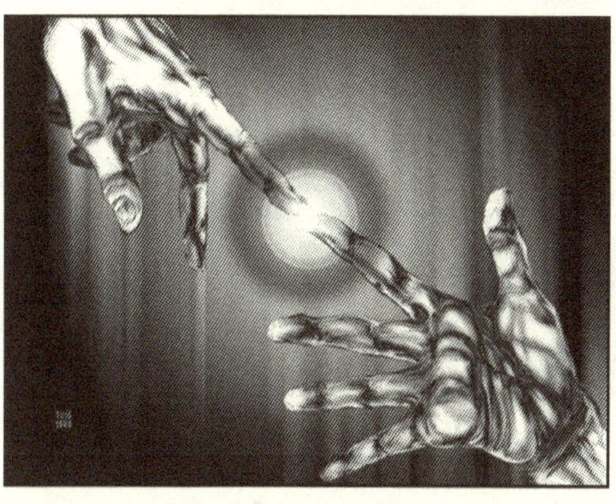

When Off Season was first released in 1980, it took readers by storm and sold over 250,000 copies!

However, the original edition was edited and content was removed from the story at the publisher's request. The whole effect of the book was deemed to intense, in particular the ending—which is completely restored in this edition. The Overlook Connection Press is releasing this edition in it's original unexpurgated state for the first time anywhere. Not only is this the author's original vision, but it is also the first world hard cover release. This book has not been available in the US for almost two decades in any edition.

We have a special introduction by Douglas E. Winter, who has championed this novel for years. Also an Afterword by the author Jack Ketchum. Original cover art by Neal McPheeters (cover artist for The Girl Next Door, Ladies Night, and Right To Life).

- **Introduction by Douglas E. Winter**
- **Afterword by Jack Ketchum**
- **TRADE LIMITED: 1/1000 - Distinctive binding. Original cover art by Neal McPheeters. Signed.**

ISBN 1-892950-10-3 $45.00

Overlook Connection Press

PO BOX 526 WOODSTOCK GA 30188 | 770-926-1762

FAX: 770-516-1469 | E-MAIL: OVERLOOKCN@AOL.COM

WEB: http://www.OverlookConnection.com

www.ingramcontent.com/pod-product-compliance
Lightning Source LLC
LaVergne TN
LVHW050927080826
845145LV00001B/233

* 9 7 8 1 8 9 2 9 5 0 1 3 0 *